NEVER ADMIT TO BEIGE

Jonathan Drapes

NEVER ADMIT TO BEIGE

MACMILLAN NEW WRITING

First published 2006 by Macmillan New Writing,
an imprint of Macmillan Publishers Ltd
Brunel Road, Basingstoke RG21 6XS
Associated companies throughout the world
www.macmillannewwriting.com

ISBN-13: 978–0230–00510–5 hardback
ISBN-10: 0230–00510–1 hardback
ISBN-13: 978–0230–00745–1 paperback
ISBN-10: 0230 00745–7 paperback

10 9 8 7 6 5 4 3 2
14 13 12 11 10 09 08 07 06

A CIP catalogue record for this book is available from the British Library.

Typeset by Heronwood Press
Printed and bound in Great Britain by
Mackays of Chatham plc, Chatham, Kent

For Katherine

Acknowledgements

Thanks to all my family and friends for their input and support, particularly James and Jules for their cover designs, Suzy for her eagle eyes, Cos for the constant advice, Sue Gough for the kick-start, Damian and Miyuki for the rushed Japanese lessons (all mistakes are entirely mine), the team at MNW, and Bill Gates for Microsoft Solitaire.

♣ ♣

1

You can tell a lot about people by the way they get off an aeroplane. Hands twitching over seatbelt clips, legs creeping into the aisle, thighs tense, waiting for the ding as the seatbelt sign goes off. False start? Forget about it. Argy Bargy? Don't be so soft. It's the Galapagos Islands in a big steel test-tube.

Roger hasn't even blinked. He just sits, staring straight ahead with his unnerving, sadistic grin. Not for the first time, I consider abandoning him.

A large woman with a sunburnt neck glowing deep red above her singlet springs to her feet and attacks an overhead locker. She's the first. The chaos begins. The play-by-the-rules Pats-and-Paulas' faces twist. Their eyebrows hop about with disbelief. "Look!" they silently scream to the flight attendants, "these people are standing up before the plane has come to a complete halt. For God's sake, look!" But the flight attendants are well practised in the art of looking without seeing. Tray tables are left down, overhead lockers haphazardly thrown open, small children already sacrificed to the aisle to gain a position or two. In this harsh, cramped world, only the arseholes prosper.

So what about the Englishman with the flaking red skin and the puffy dark flesh where his eyes should be? Well, without question I'm an arsehole. Ask my parents. Ask Kelly. But I'm also tired. Too tired for this race. Watching the scramble does bring a smile to my face, though. It reminds me of home. Trying to hit the M4 on a Friday afternoon for a bank holiday weekend in the Cotswolds. My smile fades. It's a life that's starting to feel like someone else's. Like I read it in a book.

The race runs its course to the exit door. I think a couple of

German backpackers win. It's hard to tell. There's an awful lot of shunting going on.

When only the aircraft socialists and first-time travellers are left, I undo my seatbelt and wrestle my passport and Roger from the pocket under the tray table. "I hope you understand this climate does not go well with my complexion," I say to him.

He keeps smiling.

Even before I step off the plane, the soupy Gold Coast air smothers me in a salty hug. I feel instantly damp. The captain said it was 9.50 p.m. local time, but no one's bothered to tell the steamy February humidity to call it a night. I vow to get back to the indoor life of London and some modicum of sophistication as soon as possible.

Of course the heat only gets worse down on the black tarmac. I guess I could have flown with a better airline, one with a terminal slot that makes it unnecessary to march across the bitumen. But that costs more, and money is not exactly a luxury I possess at this moment. Three weeks ago I could have asked my parents to help me out. But three weeks is a lifetime ago. Instead I lope towards the terminal behind my frugal friends, while the baggage-handlers molest our luggage and we all breathe in short sharp pants to avoid the aviation fumes.

I shouldn't complain really. My parents didn't bring me up that way. It's just that I've had a tough couple of weeks. Well, more like a month actually. I feel like a four-day-old teabag, and sleep is an old friend who doesn't return my calls any more. But at least I'm walking on terra firma again. Given the way things have been going for me recently, I was reasonably certain I'd be just a black scorch mark in a field somewhere by now, in among the melted emergency-procedure cards and charred lifejackets.

But I look at Roger, his incessant grin, and realise that this was never really a prospect. Too easy. Where's the suffering in a quick death?

♣ ♣ ♣

Inside the terminal, the young German couple have been relegated to second position at the luggage carousel by an elderly couple in matching blue tracksuits. That's experience for you.

I take a seat some feet away and wait for a glimpse of pink flowers on a tapestry background. Yes, that's my suitcase. Well, it's my girlfriend's actually, but we split up. Kelly got the cookware, the TV, a truckful of Ikea furniture and the tallboy. I got two months of misery and the suitcase. Not exactly an equitable dividend, but I guess shagging her best friend from uni was a volatile investment.

It's fitting that I should think of Kelly now. She is, after all, the source of my prodigious run of misfortune. Well, she and Roger. They're the reason I'm down to just 300 Fijian dollars and a tenner hidden in my undies. The reason my Christian Fundamentalist parents don't talk to me any more. The reason I'm here. Australia . . . a country I've always wanted to visit, but perhaps not in these circumstances.

The quick appearance of my suitcase does little to lift my mood, since customs is going to be a problem. I accept that. Hell, I wouldn't let a scruffy looking twenty-six-year-old with purple trousers and a pink suitcase into my country. But what choice do they have? Where are they going to send me? I am from the Mother Country, after all.

A bored-looking man in a blue uniform sizes up my tangled appearance. I hand over my passport and landing card and opt for the foppish Englishman approach. If it saw Hugh Grant through the Divine Brown saga, it can see me through Australian customs.

The man shuffles through my things. "This passport been wet?"

"I fell off a boat. It was in my pocket."

He opens my water-wrinkled passport to the photo, holds it beside my tired, peeling face, and squints. "Trigger Harvey. That ya real name?"

"Bit strange isn't it? I was thinking of changing it to Trigger *Johnson*."

The immigration man frowns.

"Ahh yes, it is my real name. Named after my mother's horse actually. People call me Trigg. Some people think it's a reference to trigonometry, but I was never really a maths person—"

"Had a bit of sun, have you, Trigg?"

I nod. "Fiji."

"Business or pleasure?"

"Definitely not pleasure."

He watches me while he swaps my passport for my landing card, like we're the last men standing in a poker game. When he looks down to read the card, only his eyes move. "You've indicated you're here for a holiday. Where are you staying?"

"A hotel?"

"Which one?"

"Err, the big one. Very tall. The Gold Coast . . . International?"

"Well, Mr Harvey, got anything to declare?

"Well. I do declare that these trousers are the grooviest trousers on the Gold Coast ... Mmmha, ha . . . hnnn."

"Very good, Mr Harvey. You see that room over there. If you wait just over there, someone will be with you shortly. Oh, and Mr Harvey? I think we'll be keeping a bit of an eye on you."

Flight AP51 from Nadi to Coolangatta must have been the last flight of the evening. By the time customs let me go, the normal airport buzz has been sucked out of the terminal, leaving just a big empty shell. Everything's closed. I run my hand through my unwashed hair. My fingers come out sticky. It's 11.35 p.m.

On the other side of the automatic doors, I put my suitcase on the ground in front of the empty taxi-stand and sit on it. Silence where there should be commotion. I pick up Roger. Fucking Roger. Why couldn't the customs officers have confiscated him? He is wooden, after all. His head echoes a satisfying thunk-unk-unk around the empty carpark as I drop him on the footpath. I'm wondering what to do and I'm drawing a blank. I don't know if you've ever been to Coolangatta Airport, but like most airports, it's central to absolutely bloody nothing.

♣ ♣ ♣

Despite Australia's less than sterling reputation as a hitchhiking destination, I find myself out on the highway with my thumb stuck up in the air. I can already see the reconstruction of this moment illustrated in those awful colours on the second page of *The Sun*.

The station-wagon is brown, except for one door, which is a sludgy green colour. The steel is bubbly with rust; the tyres lack any tread at all. It slows down with a squeal. At first I can't tell if it's stopping for me or breaking down.

"Where you goin'?" asks the young bloke behind the wheel.

"Ahh, that way," I say, pointing down the road.

He nods. "You're in luck, so am I."

"Luck? Don't get me started."

"Want a spliff?" says my driver as we shoot down the highway, bouncing gracefully through the night on 1960s suspension.

I shake my head.

He manages to roll a joint while weaving in and out of slower drivers who haven't cottoned on to the benefits of driving without functioning brakes. He holds up a small plastic lighter, flicks it with a grubby thumb and drags deeply on his surprisingly neat effort. He holds his breath until his face begins to change colour.

"So what're you doin' on the Gold Coast?" he says in an explosion of smoke that continues long after the question.

"Well, ahh, looking for someone."

"Oh yeah? Like a long-lost brother or somethin'?"

"Not quite. I need to get something sorted out." I take a piece of paper out of my back pocket and unfold it. Written in the witch-doctor's untidy scrawl, above a list of terms and conditions, is a name. "I need to find a guy called Terry Smith."

My driver drags deeply again. "Terry Smith . . . Terrrry . . . Ssssmith." He says it carefully, drawing air in rather than letting it out, not wanting a single molecule of smoke to escape until he's ready. He shakes his head as the sweet clouds pour out of his nose and mouth and are quickly sucked out through the open windows.

"I know a *Doug* Smith. You sure you're not lookin' for Doug?"

"Pretty sure."

"Well, Dougie's a top bloke, so if you wanna talk to him, you know, I can give him a call."

"Oh. Ta."

He nods. Drives. Drags. His eyes are a little glassy.

I turn to my window. The warm, damp air shuffles my clumps of sticky hair. Low-rise concrete shops fly past on one side of the highway, while on the other, an endless array of "budget" motels with sad pools and even sadder Spanish names display their wares like neon prostitutes. Like most first-time visitors to the Gold Coast, I'd thought it was a few miles of tall buildings, white sand and leggy girls in gold bikinis. But we've been driving for about fifteen minutes now and still haven't hit anything like that.

"Difficult," says my driver.

I shuffle back around to face him. "Sorry?"

"Thing about the Gold Coast is, it's like the waves, man. People here are like the waves. They wash up, they disappear, then some more wash up. Transient population. Come for a month, stay for a year. Come for a year, stay for a week. Hard to find people in a place like this. A lot don't wanna be found. That's why they're here."

"Well, I don't have much choice. I can't go home until I find this guy. He's got something of mine."

"Must be important. He got your money or somethin'?"

"Something much more important than money."

The driver flicks the butt out the window. "From England, huh? You must like cricket then?"

"Well, I understand it."

"Next Ashes series you guys don't stand a bloody chance. Not if Warney's on form."

It didn't take much. Just a hint. Just the slightest suggestion to my driver that Shane Warne is not, in fact, the greatest test cricketer to ever don the whites, but a short, fat, overrated tosser in desperate need of a thumping and a half-decent hairdresser. All it took was a nod in that direction and now I'm standing in the middle of nowhere.

I look around me. The shops are all closed and the cheapest budget motel is still $60 a night – and I dare say they're not talking Fijian dollars. Somewhere in the tropics my Barclaycard is buying God knows what for God knows who. I sigh. For the first time I confront the bigger picture: in nine days I might as well jump in front of a train, unless I achieve what I've come here for. In nine days my indemnity runs out.

With this thought it all comes back to me like a flood – mud, silt, floating cows and all. Basically, I'm a cursed man. I'm out of luck. Not unlucky, but actually out of luck. My luck has been, for want of a better term, stolen. Stolen and traded on some illegal international luck market that I had no idea existed. But it's not all doom and gloom; I have a nine day reprieve from this curse, guaranteed in writing.

I guess it all started with the messy break up from Kelly three months ago and her tour of the South Pacific. We were due to go skiing in Chamonix, but when I shagged Camille from Kentish Town, I kind of forfeited my ticket. Kelly cashed it in and went to Fiji instead. Anyway, when she got back to London she sent me an exquisite Polynesian tribal figurine. That's Roger. Five inches of the most vindictive South Pacific hardwood ever known to man. Roger came with a note that read something along the lines of: "I hope it kills you, you sad bastard". That's when I noticed Roger's maniacal little grin.

Of course I laughed. I am a rational person, after all. But then things started to happen: a lost wallet, a sprained ankle, a string of public-transport mishaps. Nothing too bad, I know. Then my parents stopped talking to me. Stopped supporting me. Even stopped praying for me. This wasn't entirely unprovoked. They thought my split with Kelly was a great opportunity to invite me back to the church, so they and their vicar paid me a surprise visit. They found me with Page Three in one hand and, well, something else in the other. Then, not two days after this, a convent in Cork started receiving a magazine entitled *Farm Animal Love* from the UK's second biggest magazine publisher. Unfortunately, this is not an agricultural magazine. More unfortunately still, I was the Subscriptions Manager at the UK's second biggest magazine publisher. Throw in a ton of other little things and, well . . . currently the ledger looks something like this:

Positives	*Negatives*
Still alive	No friends
	No girlfriend
	No job
	No family (to all intents and purposes)
	Unintentional public nudity – twice
	Flat robbed – twice (before eviction)
	Still alive

My morbid stock-take is interrupted by a police car, which slows to a crawl, its lights on full beam. I quickly start lugging my pretty suitcase towards the glow of what must be Surfers Paradise. The police car drives on.

As I walk, I look about at the bizarre spectacle that is the Gold Coast. Somewhere, not too far from here, breathes one Terry Smith, completely unaware that, right now, he is the sole focus of another human being's thoughts. Is he sleeping soundly in one of those ominous high-rises that pollute the northern view? Or perhaps he's sucking down orange whips, trying desperately to "pick up" at some seedy Gold Coast nightclub, with stories of his recent trip to Fiji. Either way, he's here, somewhere. The key to getting my life back. Terry Smith. I *will* find him. I will find him and do whatever it takes to get my luck back. I pull Roger out of my pocket. What do you think of that, you little prick?

His smile seems a little more sincere. Or maybe it's just that he figures I'll be spending the night in a park.

♣ ♣
2

The sound of a young couple shagging fifteen inches from my head is the first thing I am conscious of. I ask God to do something nice for the plasterer whose slapdash work keeps me separated from the eager loins in the next room. God has a significant presence in this building, going by the number of times I heard his name called out during the night.

I lift myself up onto my elbows and look in dismay at the grunge that surrounds me. A glacier of sunlight is moving ever so slowly across a thin green carpet which is covered in the same unidentifiable stains you see on a pavement. It's Thursday morning. Only eight days left now before my curse-indemnity runs out.

As I lie back down, staring at the pasty yellow ceiling and wishing an ego-crushing bout of impotence on the guy next door, the previous night meanders to the forefront of my consciousness.

I had dragged my baggage just far enough along the highway for my forearms to sing, when I found the saviour of many a munchy-riddled student and luckless Englishman: a twenty-four-hour convenience store. The girl behind the counter was young and girlishly attractive in her bright red uniform, swaying unintentionally to Kylie Minogue. She gave me a relieved smile. Relieved because she finally had some human interaction, and relieved because nobody carrying a pink suitcase and looking as lost and sad as I did was about to hold up a convenience store. I took my Slush Puppy to the counter and prayed she would take Fijian dollars.

"How's it going?" she asked.

"Hmm, let's see," I replied. "I've been in your country a little over two hours. The first was spent with men wearing rubber gloves. I then spent a good part of the second hurtling along the highway in a piece of sick on wheels with a stoned chap who showed a rather defensive degree of deference to a fat, chain-smoking dwarf."

She looked up from the magazine she was reading. "You know, most people just say 'good'."

"I'm still coming to grips with the ways of the world down here."

"You know, you remind me of that actor, the posh blow-job one. You should give that a rest. It's like you're trying too hard. What's in the suitcase?"

I looked down at my conspicuous piece of luggage. "My life," I replied.

"It's not very big."

"How big should a suitcase containing one's life be?"

"Well that's a subjective thing, but definitely bigger than that. I'd have one of those huge cargo containers." She held out her arms for emphasis.

"But think of the money you'd have to pay for excess baggage if you ever wanted to go anywhere," I reasoned between Slush Puppy-slurps. "You could never leave the Gold Coast, it would be too expensive."

"That's okay. I don't want to leave the Gold Coast."

I laughed – more *Bridget Jones* Hugh than *Four Weddings* Hugh. "How old are you?"

"Sixteen."

"How do you know you never want to leave?"

"Because I like getting up in the morning. When I wake up, my first emotion – you know, before your conscious self has thought about the day ahead and tried to align your subconscious. You know that point? Well, when I wake up in the morning, at that point, I'm happy. Content."

"And what if one day you wake up and you're not happy? What if one day you wake up and you want to be someplace else?"

"Well, I'd leave."

"Aha! But you can't. You've got that big container."

"I'd just take what I need, put the rest in storage, and go. Now you tell me something." She leaned forward, elbows on the counter, "What if some drug-crazed freak stormed in here right now and shot the place up? Would you be happy dying with only a tacky pink suitcase to show for yourself?"

"Well. I suppose you could . . . ahh . . . see it . . ." Damn! She was much sharper than the bloke at the Tesco Express back home. "This is a good Slush Puppy," I said, hoping to end our repartee. "Very refreshing."

"No, no, no, no, no," she said quickly, shaking her head, her dark hair bouncing. "Is that how you always deal with a tough situation? Avoid it? Is that why you're in Australia, running away from a problem?"

I shook my head vigorously. Finished a slurp. "Actually, I'm running towards a solution. You don't know a Terry Smith, do you? He has my luck." I fished in my back pocket and pulled out the well-creased piece of paper. I handed it over.

1. *The possessor of the good luck cannot knowingly or otherwise tell another soul of his/her dealings with Philip Matango or the good luck will be repossessed.*
2. *The bearer of the anti-luck may take a maximum of nine days (including weekends and public holidays) indemnity from his/her lucklessness, during which time he/she must successfully find the possessor of the good luck and assist them through their crisis.*
3. *All transactions with credit card are subject to a credit check.*
4. *Philip Matango takes no responsibility for the personal suffering or death of luckless persons.*

"It's a photocopy of the conditions of my curse," I said when she'd finished reading. "Philip Matango, he's the little sod bastard witchdoctor who sold my luck to someone else, thanks to my ex-girlfriend. And this little prick," I plonked my travelling companion on the counter, "is the anti-luck – otherwise known as Roger."

For the first time since I had walked into the store, she didn't have an answer. She just edged around slightly so she could measure me up on the exit-door height-lines they use to help identify fleeing thieves. I went on to explain that I got the list of conditions after I managed to track Philip Matango down on some godforsaken island off Fiji. Not an easy task when the gods are against you.

"The thing is, though, this witchdoctor says he can't give me my luck back. It seems he makes two identical figurines each time: one is for *taking* luck, one is for giving *extra* luck."

I explained that the good-luck figurine – Roger's twin – is given to a person who is facing a crisis in their life. It supposedly helps that person through said crisis. I went on to tell the poor girl exactly what the witchdoctor had told me. I explained that the anti-luck figurine – Roger – brings destruction and misery. And the only way the luck can be reverted is if the unfortunate person with the anti-luck figurine – me – finds the owner of the corresponding good-luck figurine – one Terry Smith of the Gold Coast – and helps this person successfully through their crisis. Kind of a karma thing.

The girl brushed away the few strands of hair again, surprisingly warming to the concept. "It's a shame he didn't give you a more specific address," she said.

Karen, as her nametag proclaimed her, turned out to be very understanding and supportive. She fished out a phonebook and we had a look.

My world took on a whole new perspective in the time it took to run a finger down a page. "Terry Smith, Pacific Vista Towers, 2104/466 The Esplanade, Surfers Paradise." For the first time in a month my smile didn't require a word like "wry" or "wistful" in front of it.

"Don't get too carried away," Karen said. "There are still eight T. Smiths. Any one of them could be a Terry as well."

For someone so young and pretty and, well, Australian, Karen was deceptively mature and uncommonly friendly. I'd call her naïve if I wasn't so certain that she was smarter than me. But on this occasion she was off the mark. I had my man. No doubt about it.

Karen managed to talk me out of going to Pacific Vista Towers straight away, by changing my money and giving me the name of a twenty-four-hour motel that would suit my budget: Hairy Palms, a small, unbecoming hovel in the bowels of a place called Broadbeach. I found myself dragging my suitcase noisily along the dirty concrete path, looking for room 6. It was 2.40 a.m., but the hotel hadn't even put on its crusty, semen-stained pyjamas and brushed its teeth yet. More than half the place was lit up, and I could hear assorted noises and lusty cries. The volume didn't diminish when I got into my excuse for a room, either. But once I hit the bed, I didn't hear or see a thing.

Not until now, anyway.

Behind me, the young tigers are finally reaching a climax. I look from the pustular ceiling to the wall. "Oh yeah, oh yeah, oh baby, oh God!"

As the post-coital stench of smouldering tobacco permeates into my room and the sunbeam glacier reaches my knees, I roll off the porridge-like mattress. It's only now that I see the state of the linen I've been immersed in. A wave of disgust rolls up my spine as the once grand green chenille bedspread reveals many adventurous stains, some of them quite recent.

The stench of urine hits me before I even get to the bathroom, getting stronger as I edge towards the shower curtain. Pulling the curtain back I see signs of life where there really shouldn't be any. There is a large blob of slightly hairy black something growing on the floor, and more on the wall. I turn the tap and brown, smelly water explodes from the showerhead, covering my arm and chest before subsiding to a trickle. I turn the tap some more and somewhere in the wall a pipe starts moaning and banging. The trickle slowly dries up. Okay. Good. That was rejuvenating.

As I stride along the footpath, the sun belts my bloodshot eyes, prickles my scalp and turns the smelly water on my arm into a foul second skin. It's not that hard to find the beach at the Gold Coast, you just head towards the overwhelming salty smell of relaxation. Or the slap-slap-slap of day-glo tourists' rubber flip-flops.

I leave my grungy motel towel on the sand and walk quickly towards the water. It feels unnaturally warm as it washes over my bony feet, which are brailed with mosquito bites from Fiji. It's only 7.30 a.m. but already the beach is pulsing. Sandy real-estate is being snapped up – first come, first served; one-day leases only. The Pacific Ocean stretches out until it shakes hands with the arrogant blue sky. It's a glorious day. Thousands of little diamonds dance across the rising waves waiting to be buried in avalanches of foam. The smell is thick and fibrous, occasionally fishy, more often coconutty.

I swim out further, past the first line of breakers, enjoying the temporary restoration of my luck and the touch of revitalising salty water. Growing up in Fulham, the best I got was a weekend trip to Brighton, where the water was cold, the sand a thousand miles away and it was usually raining. Not my idea of fun.

My second skin removed, I continue to wash, possibly to get rid of a month I'd rather forget. A little over four weeks ago I had a good job, I had a girlfriend, I had a social life and social standing. Everything was as it should be: forty-five grand a year, five-a-side on Thursday night, drinks at the Black Boar on Friday night. Kelly and I had even started looking at the Property section.

God, why did she do it?

Why did I do it?

For the past month I have felt so lost. Disoriented. All things solid and dependable have been removed from my life. The only stability I've had has been Roger. It's as if everything I've worked so hard for has been stripped away. And the loneliness! But now I've got a goal. Now I've got direction: Pacific Vista Towers, 2104/466 The Esplanade, Surfers Paradise.

I get out of the water somewhat cleaner, and brimming with excitement. I could be back in London by the end of the week. Plenty of time to reclaim my life.

Slinging my towel over my shoulder, I start walking north, towards the high-rises. The world seems brighter today, the Gold Coast like a jewel. I wonder, does Terry Smith come to the beach often or has he become disillusioned and bored with the endless stream of strangers traipsing about his neighbourhood?

Twenty minutes later I find myself confronted with the grotesque beauty of Cavill Avenue. The whole place throbs with the comings and goings of summer. Japanese honeymooners line up for photos in front of a gaudy steel sculpture that reads: "Surfers Paradise". Overweight young males barely wearing football shorts stare shamelessly at young females barely wearing bikinis. Young men in bad suits harass passers-by with once-in-a-lifetime investment opportunities. An extra long stretch limousine with tinted windows crawls past. Surfers Paradise is possibly the last haven for the lost and classless.

It doesn't take long to track down the Pacific Vista Towers. I march across the foyer of the very nice high-rise apartment complex. Yes, my shorts are still damp and I have no shirt on, but I'm discovering that this is the best camouflage for the Gold Coast.

On the twenty-first floor I stride purposefully down to apartment 2104 with a handful of tourist brochures stuffed into an envelope pilfered from reception. My heart is pounding so hard I can feel blood moving in my fingertips. Just take it easy, Trigg, you're just making contact.

The door opens to reveal a distinguished man with salt-and-pepper hair and a questioning face. Terry Smith.

"Oh, hello," I say in my best I'm-not-strange voice. "Look, I'm staying on the floor below and I was just checking the mail after a swim and well, it seems I got something addressed to you. Just thought I'd do the neighbourly thing and drop it up."

The man takes the envelope and checks the address, written in my best handwriting. I clench my toes to suppress my excitement, waiting to activate the next part of my plan.

He throws the envelope onto a pile of other mail by the door.

"I've been here four months and he still gets more mail than me."

"I beg your pardon?"

"Terry Smith. Used to live here, I suppose. Obviously didn't tell everyone he'd moved. Still, thanks anyway."

"I, ahhh . . . I, gee . . . that's a . . . real shame. Wow. So, ahh, no forwarding address?"

I follow the man's gaze to the pile of envelopes.

"Well, do you know if he's still on the Gold Coast?"

The man shrugs, sweeps his bare foot back and forth over one of the white tiles. "No idea. But I really wouldn't trouble yourself. Very decent of you to bring it up here, but don't feel it's your responsibility to track him down just because it was in your letter-box. I'm sure if it's important, whoever sent it will find him."

"I sincerely hope you're right," I just manage to say.

The door begins to close, but I stop it. The movement is abrupt, but then my brain is too busy ordering my thoughts to bother with motor-control. "You know, I really hate loose ends," I say. "Kinder-garten thing. Incident with . . . plasticine. Came out in therapy. Anyway, I've got to go down the post office later, why don't I just take that mail there and give it to them, you know, return to sender."

The man considers this. He looks at my arm still holding the door open. "I think it will be just fine. Thanks anyway."

I feel the door being pushed against my arm, but my brain won't let it close. Just get the mail, Trigg. "Really, it's no bother," I say, straining a little with the force of the door. Just get the mail.

Suddenly I shove the door and before I know what I'm doing I'm running down the hallway with my towel in one hand and a bundle of mail in the other.

♣ ♣
3

I take in deep lungfuls of hot, stale air and feel mildew spores tickle my nose. My heart is beating madly in my chest, sweat is dripping from my chin onto the pile of envelopes in my lap. With my lack of fitness and the windows and curtains closed, room 6 at Hairy Palms is like an oven that someone's pissed in. Twice. I pick up the top envelope and turn it over and over. The last thing I stole was a postcard of a woman with a Union Jack painted on her boobs. I sent it to my grandpa in Stow-on-the-Wold. My mother yelled two shades of shit out of me, but my grandpa said it was the best thing he'd been sent in years.

A scuttling sound outside my door makes me jump. The envelope is starting to feel slimy where I'm handling it. I rip it open: "Dear Mr Smith. We have a client who is willing to pay top dollar for an apartment in your building . . ."

Eleven of the sixteen letters are from estate agents. Three are from travel agents. One is from a wine club. I take the only non-solicitous letter with me in search of a phone booth. It just might prove helpful.

Inside the booth, I continue to sweat. The receiver smells of cigarettes and I try not to let it touch my skin.

"Hello, Burleigh Waters Bowls Club," says a kindly voice.

"Oh hello, love. I hope you can help me. My name is Bill . . . Ploughman . . . from England and, ahh, I'm trying to get in touch with a friend I met on holiday. Now, I've lost his number, but I remember him telling me he was a member of your fine establishment. His name is Terry Smith."

"Ooh, Terry and Doris haven't been in for some time."

"Bugger. I don't suppose you have a phone number for them?

I'm only here for a week and they made me promise to catch up with . . . in fact, oh they'll love this, do you have their address? Can you imagine the surprise?"

Perfect Preparation Prevents Piss-Poor Performance. The six P's. That's what Mr Langridge taught us in second year rugby and that's what's stuck in my mind right now. I can think of at least eight other memories that I'd rather have rattling around; I can think of three other P's, for that matter. But I can see the merit of this recollection, especially in the panicked afterglow of my efforts at Pacific Vista Towers. I need a plan, a good one, to make the most of the information I have. Terry and Doris Smith, 12 Pleasant Crescent, Burleigh Waters Retirement Village. Unfortunately, planning's not my thing. Back home I had parents to do it, then I had friends, then I had a girlfriend. I had it all worked out, a good wicket. Now the cracks have opened up and swallowed me. I'm not good on my own and it's been a long, lonely month.

A tennis ball rolls against my foot and I realise I'm sitting in a park by the beach.

"You okay?" asks the boy who comes to retrieve it.

"My complexion," I say. "Not suited to the sun."

The boy scuttles back to his friends but chances a look back. I'm sure it's not my complexion that's bothering him. It seems unlikely that an inhabitant of a sun-drenched beach would be given cause for concern by the sight of a dishevelled sunburnt Englishman.

The boy looks back again, into my eyes, and I decide to move on.

Jun's corner store is across the street. The sign on the awning says: "Cigs, Papers, Toys, Drinks, Hot Food". It's that last one that I'm interested in; perhaps silencing the grumbling in my stomach will help me think.

Jun is a little Japanese man of about sixty. He is short and slightly stooped, and if his corner store had been in Los Angeles, he would probably have been cast in a *Karate Kid* sequel by now. He watches me carefully as my eyes adjust to the gloom.

"Sunburn cream is over there," he says, pointing towards a cluttered corner of the store.

"Actually I'm after some food. What do you have?"

"Your face looks like food. Sunburn cream is over there."

Okay. I find a tube of sunburn cream between the Canesten and the lubricant and bring it back to the counter. "If I get this, can I get some food?"

"What is your name?"

"Trigg."

"Your whole name?"

"Trigger Harvey."

"Yes, Tligger Harvey, you may now order food."

Okay. I stand back to look at the blackboard above the strange little storekeeper. The menu is written in a painstakingly neat hand, with a different coloured chalk for each item. At the bottom of the board, bigger than everything else, it says: "Jun's World Famous Chicken-and-Mushroom Rolls".

"World famous?" I say. "That's a big call."

"Absolutely, one chicken-and-mushroom roll coming up for you, Tligger Harvey."

Before I can say anything Jun scurries into the back of his shop and puts some chicken and mushrooms on the hot-plate, leaving me to ponder his hearing, and the fact that he can get his mouth around every word in the English language except my Christian name.

"You are not from here, are you, Tligger Harvey?" Jun calls from over the hot-plate.

"Me? No. From England."

"Ahh, yes. I shot some Englishmen once. In the war."

"I beg your pardon?"

"Ha! Just joking. I have never shot an Englishman."

"That's reassuring."

"Actually, before I come to this country, I never leave Japan."

Jun hums the *Home and Away* theme until he brings out the roll, which he plonks in front of me, grease already soaking into the paper bag.

"It must have been difficult, leaving your old life behind," I say.

"Ahh, Tligger Harvey, my old life was familiar, but we must not confuse familiarity with being happy. It is a crutch for the weaker side of human nature. If we don't let go of the side of the pool, how will we ever know the joy of swimming?"

I chew. Swallow. "Or the horror of drowning?"

Jun smiles. "You know why most people drown, Tligger Harvey? Because they panic. They find themselves out of their depth and in their desperation to get back, they splash and flail about, don't know what is up or down, don't think. "

I nod, although I think he's overlooking alcohol and stupidity as major contributing factors.

"So tell me, Tligger, how you like the world famous chicken-and-mushroom roll?"

I realise that I've eaten all but one bite. I order another and wonder if they are world famous because they come with a philosophy lesson.

As I eat the second roll Jun continues to talk. Thoughts of plans and Terry Smith are replaced with stories of life in Kobe. I wipe a mushroom from my chin and marvel at how relaxed I'm feeling, how the world suddenly seems a more vivid place. "These rolls really are fantastic," I call to Jun, who has disappeared out the back to make up an order for a straggly-haired surfer. "What's your secret?"

Jun sticks his head around the corner. "Ah, very secret indeed, Tligger Harvey. Like Colonel Sanders. Special ingredients."

I grip the counter. The cigarette packs behind the till appear to be dancing, swaying from side to side.

"You'd better slow down" whispers the shaggy-haired surfer beside me. "They're not shitake mushrooms."

We both look at the roll. "Jesus . . . who the hell puts magic mushrooms in their chicken rolls? Is that legal?"

The surfer shrugs. "Unlikely. But Jun doesn't even realise. He buys them cheap from some bloke in Nimbin, down the coast a bit. Thinks it's his cooking that keeps people coming back. I'm not gonna tell him."

The surfer shuts up and reaches into his pocket as Jun returns with a hamburger. His hand comes out empty. "Aww, bugger." Now I don't know whether it's the mushrooms, or whether Jun's philosophies tickled something inside of me that hasn't so much as farted in its sleep since I stopped sponsoring that Oxfam kiddie, but I cover the four dollars for the burger. And it feels good. The guy says thanks and shakes my hand.

I watch the surfer leave with his burger, and then, as if the lords of the cosmos are giving me a big thumbs up, I get my plan. Bam! I rush over to the rack the surfer just walked past and pick up a "Special Agent Action Kit" from among the bags of marbles and dolls. Oh this is good. I just need a few more things. I quickly pay Jun and leave. For the first time in ages my emotional scales seem tipped just ever so slightly towards the positive.

Despite the effects of the mushrooms, I find the store right where the phonebook said it would be. St Vincent De Paul Charity Shop. I can't help but wonder how St Vincent feels about his legacy. St Paul, St Peter, St Mark . . . most saints are memorialised for eternity by great cathedrals and grand churches, not charity shops.

Regardless, St Vincent serves my purpose well and I think he should be proud. It doesn't take long at all to round up what I need from among the racks of camphor-soaked clothes: a bright floral shirt, some Bermuda shorts, a pair of long cream-coloured socks and slip-on loafers, also in cream.

With a head full of somersaults, I change into my charity-shop clothes. They look a little silly, but it's all about context. I jump on a bus heading south towards Burleigh Waters. South towards one Terry Smith of the Gold Coast, Queensland, Australia.

"Hello there," I chime, with a jolly Brit tone and a flash of the floral and Bermuda. "I'm Alan Rintoul, you must be Doris Smith."

The orange-rinsed septuagenarian looks me up and down slowly. "Yes."

"Well Doris, I was hoping to speak to you and Terry, may I come in?"

Doris looks about nervously, then looks me up and down again. There's a glimmer of anxiety in her eyes. "What do you want?"

I smooth my floral shirt and lean down to pull at one of my socks, giving her a good eyeful of my disguise. "Well I've just moved in down the road and I'm getting along and meeting all my new neighbours."

"You're very young to be retired aren't you?"

I'm ready for this one. "Yes, yes, I know. I made a fortune in computer software at twenty, sold out at twenty-five and, well, now here I am. Going to run out the clock with five-cent fruit machines, piano sing-alongs and a little gardening. So anyway, Doris, I just thought I'd come and introduce myself."

Doris looks confused, but she invites me in. "Terry, could you come here? Come here, Terry, and meet our new neighbour," she calls out.

I walk into a pastel war-zone. Every soft colour of the rainbow is assaulting me: the curtains, the walls, the carpet, the sofa. It's like a watered-down LSD trip.

I quickly scan the room, looking for five inches of familiar Fijian timber hiding among the sickly hues. Nothing. Lots of family pictures, knicks and knacks, but no Roger look-alike.

"Please sit down," Doris says, offering me the soft pink modular sofa.

When Terry walks into the room, our eyes meet immediately. His thick white eyebrows shoot up towards his thatch of white hair like a couple of startled, hirsute, albino caterpillars, before settling back down to hood his suspicious eyes. He looks at me as though he instantly knows I'm not here as a new neighbour. I can only imagine the way I'm looking at him.

"Terry, this is Alan – umm, what did you say your surname was, Alan?"

"Rintoul," I say, still captivated by the current owner of my luck, standing right in front of me, “Alan Rintoul.” We shake hands as Doris explains my . . . situation.

“Software, hey?” says Terry. “I try hard to avoid all those modern sorts of things. My son’s right into all that computer jargon, though. Perhaps you could tell me about your software . . . so I could tell him.”

How strange, Terry saying that. Unless he doesn’t consider the satellite dish on his roof, the brand new Porsche Boxter in his driveway, or the Sony Vaio computer to be “modern sorts of things”. I want to ponder this paradox more, but the old man is still regarding me the way a white LA cop might regard a black LA teenager in a red European car. I have to give him an answer. “Soft porn computer-screensavers, Terry. That’s where I made my money.”

Terry doesn’t miss a beat, he just nods. “I thought screensavers were old news, Alan, you know, redundant. And now that they’ve got those plasma monitors, well . . .” Terry is looking deep into my eyes. I think he’s probing for a crack in my story. Why is the old bastard so suspicious? I wish I hadn’t eaten those mushrooms.

A droplet of sweat makes a break for freedom from the captivity of my armpit. Doris is incessantly “tinging” a teaspoon against her teacup and it’s hammering away at my nerve ganglia. I can’t concentrate. Terry is looking at me very hard. I lick my dry lips while the mushrooms gnaw away at my sensibilities. “There’s always a market for porn, Terry.”

What the hell is going on here? These two retirees have taken the upper hand. What are they so suspicious about? Surely Philip Matango wouldn’t have warned them I was coming. Would he? No! Relax. It’s just a little mushroom-paranoia. They’re pensioners, for God’s sake. They’re just worried you’ll batter them and take their change. I have to regain control.

“Ahem . . . yes, it’s a lovely place here, nice and peaceful,” I say, trying to change tack. “Still, must get a trifle boring, you know, same thing, day in, day out. You ever travel? Doris? Terry?”

Terry gives Doris a small sideways glance. Doris stops stirring her Tetleys just for a second, then resumes. They both ignore my question.

"So Alan, which place did you move into? I didn't know there were any going," Terry asks, as he cuts his wife another sideways glance.

I feel like a child in the head teacher's office. I try to sit up higher on the couch. Terry leans further forward in his chair, drawing an answer out of me. "Ahhh . . ." My mouth is very dry. "It's . . . Mrs, umm, Jones's old place."

"Mrs Jones, hey?" says Terry. "And that would be number . . .?"

Doris is up. She's coming around behind me. Terry's trying to hold me still with his eyes, which are bunched up with suspicion. "Number, ahh . . . gee is that tea, Doris? I'd love a cup, if you don't mind. Number ahhh . . ."

I'm standing now. Doris hasn't responded to my request. The situation has just crossed the line. I don't want to do it to a poor old couple, but I have to. Time for stage two.

"Number ahh . . . OKAY, YOU TWO, ON THE FLOOR, NOW!" I pull out my Special Agent Action Kit props. "Agent Greg Hopman, Federal Police." I flash my plastic badge at them, then sweep my shirt aside to give them a look at the handle of my plastic gun, which is tucked into my shorts beside my plastic handcuffs. "Don't talk, don't move, don't even breathe or I'll put a hole in your head the size of South East Asia. Now where's the stuff?"

(Okay, I hate to stop the action here, but things have suddenly become a little weird. I never actually thought I would end up using this part of the plan. I figured I would come in, be the new neighbour, we'd talk herbal tea and high-fibre cereal, and then I'd lead them on to the topic of overseas travel. All going accordingly, I'd look at some recent cruise photos, and if they were my people, I'd generally outsmart them into revealing that Terry did, in fact, purchase a little Polynesian tribal figurine for good luck. If, God forbid, I ever did have to resort to stage two, I thought that at this point in proceedings the poor old couple would be on the floor in absolute mortal fear. I am a little put off, then, when I notice Terry and Doris

Smith are quite calmly lying face down, their hands already on the back of their heads, the looks of mortal fear displaced by looks of resentment and disappointment. I get the distinct impression I am a lot more nervous than they are.)

"Ahh, okay," I say stumbling with my surprise, "we've been tracing a load of narcotics for the last two months, and this is where the trail ends. So where's the stuff? Don't make me bring in the sniffer dogs."

(This is the point where they should start babbling incoherently and pleading ignorance. So I would ask to see their passports, under the pretence of checking if they have been out of the country recently. And if Terry's passport had a stamp from Fiji, I'd have my my man. Again, however, Terry and Doris do not comply.)

"Where's the goddamn stuff?" I yell.

"It's behind the dishwasher," growls Terry.

I beg your pardon? I stand there looking quite stupid and not at all like a federal police officer.

"Detective Hopman, I said it's behind the dishwasher," Terry repeats, getting impatient.

"Right . . . thanks." I walk over to the dishwasher and pull at it. It won't budge.

"You've got to hit that button near the stove," says Doris. "Yes, that's the one."

The whole dishwasher slides out smoothly, revealing a large cavity behind it. It's filled with bags and bags of white powder. "What the—?"

I'm interrupted by Terry arguing with Doris.

". . . Well if you knew he was a policeman why did you let him in in the first place?"

"What was I going to do, Terry? Tell him to go away? Pull a gun on him? You don't think that would have aroused just a little suspicion? Anyway, you're the one who kept rabbiting on about computers and whatnot, making him all nervous like that. Why did you have to push the point so hard?"

"So what if I did? You should still never have let him in, you silly old—"

"Excuse me," I say. At this point I've given up trying to assess things rationally. Logic has thrown its hands in the air and stomped out. It's time to go for broke and get the hell out of this crazy place. "I'm going to have to confiscate your passports . . . Oh, and the place is surrounded, so don't try anything daft," I add for good measure.

Doris gets their passports. I flick quickly through them. Bolivia, Colombia, Japan, Vietnam. No Fiji.

"We tracked these, ahhh, substances from Fiji," I say, hoping to get a reaction.

"Fiji?" they say in unison.

It's not the reaction I'm after. I scratch my head for at least a minute. Then I begin walking, abruptly changing directions, occasionally bumping into old-person clutter. Thank God Terry has a level head on his shoulders, or we could have been here all night.

"Look . . . Greg," he says, getting up slowly and putting his hand cautiously on my shoulder, "I can call you Greg, can't I? Good. What you've got here, Greg, is a bad bust. That means paperwork and explanations for you, and courts and lawyers for Doris and me. Now I can save us all a lot of time and hassle."

And with that Terry walks over to the cavity behind the dishwasher. From among the white powder he pulls out a bag of money, which he pushes into my hand.

"Now Greg, I don't want to be rude, but don't you think you should be leaving?"

Bloody hell! I stare at the pile of cash in my hand. This is all too strange. Logic comes back through the door looking for its car keys, sees the latest turn of events, shakes its head and walks right back out again. I have to keep control. I have to act like a real copper or God knows what these two geriatric delinquents will do to me. Think, you dolt!

"I tell you what Terry, toss in another bag of the paper stuff and you've got a deal."

Terry grabs me another wad of Australian currency and escorts me to the door. I hold up my hand, stopping him from opening it. "Better to be safe," I say.

I open the door just enough to get half my body out and start waving away my imaginary back-up. I look back at Terry and wave the two plastic bags of money in the air. "Wouldn't want the lads to find out," I say, slipping back inside.

The next three minutes are the most agonisingly long minutes of my life. Not a word is spoken, the only sounds come from our stomachs – two very old, one very nervous. Then I nod to them both, open the door, walk down the driveway past the immaculate black sports car . . . and run like hell.

4

Fifty thousand dollars. Fifty *thousand* dollars! Two bags of twenty-five thousand dollars equals fifty thousand dollars!

It's all laid out there before me on the ragged bedspread of number 6, Hairy Palms. Piles of fifty- and hundred-dollar notes. *Fifty thousand dollars!*

The sun has mostly disappeared by now, the sky turning into one nasty big bruise. I look at my watch and realise I have been sitting for two hours. It's dirty money and I know I should turn it in, but I can't go to the police; what if customs gave them my name, said I was suspicious. "Oh hi, here's fifty grand, officers. Pardon? The white residue? Well, cocaine, I suspect." Suspicious enough?

I lie down on the bed with only the dust-mites for moral support and consider my plight. What to do? What to do? My brain has suffered a hell of a pounding, mentally and chemically, and I am still having trouble thinking straight. My mind keeps racing from one thing to the next. My eyes meander around the room, fixing on trivial things here and there. Say, doesn't that mildew stain on the ceiling look like a young Gordon Brown? No, no, it's more like the fat guy from the *Asterix* books. Damn, what was his name?

"COLLIN!" comes a shrill female screech from outside my room somewhere.

No, I'm pretty sure it wasn't Collin; all the names ended in ix . . .

"COLLIN!" she yells again.

"Obelix!" I reply.

"Obelix?"

I pad over to the window and edge the mouldy curtain aside. The woman outside looks positively batty, hair all over the shop, large kitchen knife in hand.

"Collin, get out here now, you bastard! I know you're here somewhere, you filthy fucking pig . . . And bring that little slut with you."

After some more swearing and banging and knife-brandishing the woman finally leaves, albeit without Collin. She has helped me decide what my next move will be.

It takes me just two minutes to pack. The fifty grand and Terry Smith can wait – right now, I'm getting the hell out of this crazy place.

I count more than 250 cars before a taxi finally stops for me. I guess that's understandable – I probably should have changed first. In fact, when you're standing on the Gold Coast highway dressed like an extra from an early *Love Boat* episode, with a pink floral suitcase and $50,000 in drug money, you're probably lucky the police don't stop first. Or worse, a carful of drunken antipodeans.

I lug my stuff into the taxi and collapse on the back seat.

"Where you headin', pal?" mumbles the driver.

Now there's a good question. "Umm . . . take me to . . . take me to the 7-Eleven at Mermaid Beach." God, why didn't I think of Karen earlier? She'll know what to do.

"Nice clothes. You lose a bet or something?" she says as I straggle through the automatic doors.

"Correct. I bet you *wouldn't* be more of a smart-arse this time than you were last time."

"Touché." She looks at my suitcase. "I see you still haven't added to your life, though."

I look around, pick up the nearest sizeable object to hand. "I'll buy this, then."

"A boogie board?"

"That's right. I think I'll take up surfing."

"That," she says, looking at the $19 piece of mesh-covered foam, "is not surfing."

"Who are you to judge? Look at it." I turn it over in my hands. "'The Bandit' – it's got a scary-looking shark on the front, and a leash thingy . . . the shark's wearing a bandanna. Seems like a great addition to my life."

"Okay, Trigg, and how are you going to pay for that? More Fijian dollars?"

"Well," I say as I tuck the Bandit under my arm, "let me ask *you* a question; I find a $50 note on the street, and I saw the person who dropped it. Do I keep it?"

Karen thinks for a while. Brushes some hair away. "Let me ask you a question, Trigg. If the person you hate most in the world told you the funniest joke in the world, would you laugh?"

"I don't know. I guess it depends."

I turn the Bandit over in my hands.

"Depends on what?"

"On the situation, on what kind of mood I was in, on how funny the joke was. I guess the funniest joke in the world would be pretty funny . . . I honestly don't know."

"Exactly," she says. "Hypotheticals, Trigg. Whether we like it or not, life is not black and white. There's no right or wrong, only debates about right or wrong. What if it was a struggling young mother who dropped the money, is it okay to keep it then? What if it was a corrupt businessman? What if you were down to your last cent? What if you'd just won millions of dollars in the lotto? I guess the point is, Trigg, I can't say yes or no to whether you should keep the money. No one can. Not even you, not until it happens right there in front of you. And then, if you decide to keep it, it is the right thing to do, because at the end of the day it's only right or wrong in your head, in your perception of reality."

"Okaaaaay . . . what if it was fifty *thousand* dollars, which hotel would you stay in?"

"Oh that's easy. The Marriott."

I proceed to spill the beans to Karen: Terry and Doris, the drugs, the $50,000, everything. I have to tell someone, it's too much for a weak spine to bear. Once again she is very sporting.

"Boy, that's a tricky one," she says when I'm done. Then she looks at me with her big blue eyes. "Tell me Trigg, do you trust me?"

"No. I don't even know you."

"But you just told me you pilfered $50,000 from a couple of drug dealers and you've decided to keep it."

"Hmm, okay, I guess I do. Why?"

"Well, I've got a . . . friend . . . who might know what to do about the money. You know, whether it's safe to keep it or not. He's had some experience with this sort of thing. I could call him, I swear he's a good guy, he won't ask any questions – well, any more than he has to."

I think hard about this. For some reason I *do* trust Karen. She took me under her wing before any of this drug money stuff even came up. "Okay," I say.

Karen nods. She gets me to keep an eye on the store while she goes out back and makes the call. She returns about five minutes later.

"Alrighty! If you're going to hang on to the money, the first thing you've got to do is launder it."

"Launder it? How the hell am I going to do that?"

"Easy. Look at the Yakuza."

I stare at her blankly.

"The *Yakuza*, Trigg. You know – tattoos, little fingers missing. The Japanese mafia. They launder money here all the time."

"What? Here?" I wave my arm around the store, looking anxiously at the Japanese customer who is grabbing some milk from the fridge.

"No, you dickhead, here on the Gold Coast. They bring the money in and invest it in legitimate businesses, or—"

"So what, I've got to buy a golf-course or something?"

"—Or they take the cash to the casino and clean it there."

I give her a sly, knowing look and nod slowly. I have absolutely no idea what she is talking about.

Over the next half hour, an exasperated Karen explains what she knows of the Yakuza and their money-laundering at the casino. "But they've got connections," she says, "so they can clean huge amounts of cash. You, on the other hand, are going to have to do it slowly, you know, a bit each night. That way, no one will get suspicious."

I nod, but I am still no closer to comprehension.

"I tell you what," she says, sensing my despair, "what if I help you?"

I let out a relieved breath. "That would be wonderful. Thank you. When should we start?"

"Well, I'm free later tonight," she replies, her eyes holding mine for just a moment too long as she bites her lip. "I finish at eleven. So why don't you check in at the Marriott, and then I'll drive up and meet you there about half past."

Jesus in a jumpsuit! What the hell was that? I swear she just hit on me. No, it's just your imagination. Remember that time you "could have sworn" Silvia Furst was hitting on you at that wedding? Remember confronting her near the bathroom, declaring that you felt the same way, telling her how gorgeous she looked? And then she got all upset and cried, and her mascara ran and ruined the wedding dress. It's just your imagination, your ego.

"Is that okay . . . Trigg?"

"Oh . . . yes. That sounds perfect. Half eleven. I'll see you then." I pick up my suitcase and drop the boogie board. I pick up the boogie board and drop my suitcase.

"Okay, seeya."

And with that she just turns around, no hint of anything untoward. I should be exhaling with relief right now. I should – but my first emotion is a sharp stab of disappointment. This could get dangerous.

"Where ya going, mate?" the overweight taxi-driver drawls as he pulls away from the footpath. I don't hear him. I can't get my mind off Karen. I'm trying not to think about her . . . but that look in her eye. If she'd held me with it a second longer I'd have melted – or turned to stone. Guaranteed. Stop it Trigg, the girl's only sixteen. Yeah, but she's the most mature sixteen-year-old I've ever met; hell, she's the most mature *person* I've ever met. That's not the point, Trigg, and you know it.

"Where ya going?" the driver says more forcefully.

"Oh," I reply, surprised to find someone else in the cab with me. "Ahh, to the Marriott, thanks."

With one look, a chewed lip and a slight twist to her voice, Karen has gone from being just an attractive, albeit fascinating, check-out operator, to an obsession. A very unhealthy one at that. Beauty that's so natural it can't be beaten down by a cheap uniform; the edge of a blue bra-strap poking out like a welder's flame. A blue bra with a red uniform! Jesus, what am I supposed to think? Fiery blue eyes that could barbecue any male between the ages of twelve and a hundred. And lips, oh my God, lips that just beg to be kissed, lips that are moistened and bitten and frequently turned upwards in a considering pout . . . Trigger Harvey, you shut up right now! I'm trying, I'm trying. And stop reading those bloody romance novels.

"What is age all about anyway?" I ask the cabby as we shuttle along the Gold Coast Highway. "I mean, it's just a number. What does it matter how many times you've been around the sun? You can have two people of the same *chronological* age – say, two sixteen-year-old girls – but one can be much older than the other.

The cabby fixes me with a droopy-eyed look in the rear-view mirror.

Christ, I've got to get my mind off this. "Could you turn on the air-conditioning, please?" I ask, noticing the dampness forming under my arms.

The same droopy-eyed look.

What the hell is it with this guy? "Hey, I've got $50,000 in illegal drug money in my suitcase," I state.

Is that a flicker of interest? No.

"You know, my sister's a hermaphrodite, all female bits and male bits. She's quite messed up, but it's worst on Sunday afternoons because the football is on TV the same time as *What Not to Wear*. Drives her nuts. She flicks around during the ad breaks, sends her hormones all out of whack . . ." Nothing. Not even a glimmer in his eyes, not even a tightening across his slumped shoulders. The man is a rock of ambivalence.

"Here you go," he says finally, "the Marriott. That'll be nine-fifty"

I give him ten and lug my suitcase and the Bandit out of the cab.

"Tape 'em," mumbles the cabby.

"I beg your pardon?"

He turns to me slowly. "Tape 'em. Why doesn't your sister tape 'em? Then she could watch 'em one at a time."

Sly old bastard, I think to myself. Whether he meant to or not, he's managed to keep my mind off Karen. For a little while at least.

I am still grinning as I drag my belongings through the grand doors of the Marriott Resort. A blast of icy air hits me, instantly turning the perspiration on my body into exhilarating little electric charges. I think I'm going to like it here. Giant cane fans swing slowly back and forth from the ceiling, circulating the exclusive air. Well-groomed staff are busy attending to guests; cleaners are busy polishing the slate-tiled floor; lounges are busy being plush.

I pay cash for one night, with the option of staying on indefinitely. I have to use money borrowed from Karen – well, from the 7-Eleven till, if we're being honest – in lieu of laundered drug-money. Only yesterday, the price would have caused my heart to jolt, like it had just discovered that my lungs were intending to bill it for oxygen. But now – pah!

"Hi, I'm Shawn, the assistant concierge here at the Marriott, if I can help you in any way at all, Mr Harvey, please make sure you let me know. May I take your bags?"

The concierge's polite manner seems in contrast to his look. He is only about eighteen, with that sun-bleached type hair that sees more salt water than fresh. He leads me up to the twenty-first floor and opens the door to my new room. Walking towards the glass-doored balcony, I'm glad that I chose the ocean view. I step out of the room and the Gold Coast lies before me like a Christmas-decoration factory that's been hit by lightning. And then it just stops, cut off by the inky black of the Pacific. It looks like the edge of the earth. And a very bawdy earth at that.

After Shawn puts my life down near the door and leaves, I quickly find the room-safe, and deposit the $50,000. Then I try to relax.

For the next hour-and-a-bit, I languish on one of the two queen-sized beds, in my temperature-controlled room, flicking around the myriad of in-house TV channels and picking at the wood-fired pizza from room service. Despite the array of hyphenated luxuries, though, I am not at ease. Every time I think of Karen I begin to panic. I try to squeeze her out with other, less volatile thoughts: the white towelling robe I'm wearing (Karen in a white towelling robe); the white clothes I had to wear for cricket in school (Karen in cricket whites – wet ones); my first Ian Botham cricket bat; Ian Botham's 5-for-11 against Australia at Edgbaston; great cricket games of the eighties; songs of the eighties; movies of the eighties; *Breakfast Club*; Molly Ringwald . . .

After some quality time spent watching monster-truck racing, I finally think it safe to peek into my subconscious again. Karen is gone, but her replacement is more dismaying. Terry Smith! All the money in the world and a whole room full of foxy naked convenience-store teenagers isn't going to help me if I don't find the right Terry Smith. I can only presume that it's like Karen said: one of the T. Smiths in the phonebook must be a Terry. Surely.

But then, I'd been sure about the Terry I visited today.

The weather forecaster inside my head is pointing to a large negativity front that's threatening to drive away the pleasant optimism we've been experiencing for the better part of the day. And wouldn't you know it, just in time for the weekend. Tomorrow's Friday, which means I only have seven full days left, and the last two have felt like a couple of hours. Bollocks!

I'm panicking all over again and when I try to get back on the train of thought, the conductor tells me my travel card has expired.

It chugs away without me, leaving me stranded at Terrysmithville.

I have to do something. I look at Roger, who is lying on the second bed, his wooden nub of a penis pointing to the ceiling. "Talk to me, you stupid little sod."

He just keeps staring straight ahead, and for the first time I glimpse the possibility of not getting my luck back. I don't like it at all. I throw a beer bottle at Roger and reach over to the little cupboard under the phone.

There they are. Eight T. Smiths, in smudgy black and white. The clock radio by the bed says 10.50 p.m. The first six numbers prove fruitless, and abusive. However, the seventh number, T. Smith of Mermaid Beach, gets my heart pumping again.

"Hello," comes a weary male voice.

"Good evening, is Terry there, please?"

"Who is this?"

"Ahh . . . I'm from the . . . credit card company. We think Terry's credit card may have been stolen."

"Really? Well sorry, mate, Terr's still at work. You could try her there."

I scribble a number on my Marriott stationery and hang up. Nothing, for a few seconds. Then I scream loonily into the pillow, kicking my legs and upsetting the muck around me. "Terry Smith, Terry Smith, Terry Smith," I sing, to the tune of "Here we go, here we go, here we go": "Terry Smith, Te-rry Smith."

A knock at the door stops my celebration. I jump off the mattress, further upsetting the pile of muck, which I quickly sweep onto the floor and under the bed. The clock radio blinks 11.25 with its irritating red eyes.

"Someone's happy," Karen says, still in her red uniform.

"I just found another Terry Smith . . . *Terry Smith, Terry Smith, Terry Smith* . . ."

Karen heads for the bathroom with a bag of clothes and I head back towards the phone. Grabbing my list of T. Smiths, I dial the last number. It's Tyrone Smith. He's been asleep. He doesn't care if his credit card has been stolen or sealed in gold leaf, I can still shove it up my arse. The way I'm feeling right now, that wouldn't particularly bother me.

I snatch up the Marriott notepad where I jotted the number. Who the hell is still at work at 11.30 p.m. on a Thursday night? Pressing each number with the utmost care, I dial.

"Hello, Hot Shots," screams a strained female voice above a din of music and people.

"Yes, hello, is Terry Smith there please?" I yell back.

"Hang on."

The phone is put down with a thump. I wait for about a minute, listening to the music. I swear I can smell the cigarette smoke. I write the name Hot Shots on the Marriott notepad, then trace over it again and again, until the pen goes through the page. The faces of various bar-tenders, DJs and bouncers I've encountered over the years come rushing through my consciousness.

The phone is picked up. "Hello?"

"Hello. I'm after Terry Smith."

"Yeah, that's me."

In a daze I pull the phone slowly away from my ear.

"Hello? You still there? Who is this?" The voice sounds distant and tinny now, but no less unexpected.

I hang up slowly, as Karen walks out of the bathroom. "What's going on?" she asks, noting my lost expression. "Trigg?"

I sit down on the bed, still staring at the phone.

"Trigg, what is it? Who were you calling?"

♣ ♣

5

"What do you mean Terry is a Terry?" asks Karen, sitting down beside me.

"No, I said Terry is a *Terri*. Terry number two is a woman."

We look at each other for a while. I start to say something, but stop. Karen rolls her eyes and speaks instead. "You know the boy in the movie *Boys Don't Cry*? Well . . . I hate to be the one to break it to you, but that was a woman, too. And the girl in *The Crying Game* . . . that was a man. It's a mixed up, crazy world we live in. It must be very tormenting for a poor, innocent Londoner."

"There really should be an age limit on sarcasm."

"Oh come on, Trigg. What's the big deal?"

I jump up from the bed, face contorted, my body one big shrug in lieu of an adequate explanation. "I don't know. It's just . . . it's like . . . when you've spent almost every moment of the last week giving a person you don't know an identity, and then it turns out to be totally and utterly wrong. It's just thrown me. Besides, I'm not good with women. I mean, I can natter, but when it comes to deceiving them, I go to pieces. Most men do. You watch *Judge Judy* sometime."

"Hot Shots isn't a courtroom, Trigg, it's a nightclub. Just pretend she's any other girl you're trying to pick up."

"Are you joking? That's the hardest deception of all."

Karen lets me pace for a bit. But just a bit. "Well, you're going to have to get over it, because laundering this money is a priority. I've got to replace the cash in the till before morning. Get ten grand from the safe and let's go! Maybe we can go to Hot Shots when we're done."

I nod unconvincingly, then stop. "But you have to be eighteen to get into a nightclub."

She smiles. "Have to be eighteen to get into the casino, too. By the way, you've had your driver's licence for a while, haven't you? I'm still on my learners, so I'm only supposed to drive with experienced drivers."

For the first time since she arrived, I notice what a bit of makeup and a somewhat skimpy dress can do. Oh dear.

By the time we pull into the casino carpark in Karen's flaking maroon VW Beetle, she's managed to talk some sense into me. I'm now intrigued by this pattern of cross-dressers in movies with "cry" in the title. And yet in *Cry Baby*, Divine – the consummate drag queen – plays a man. It *is* a mixed-up crazy world.

A metallic grinding of brake-drum on wheel cylinder signals we have found a place to rest the Bug. I try to open my door, but it won't budge. Karen laughs. "Hasn't opened since I bought it." She gets out and makes her way around the distinctive bonnet to the passenger's side. She looks illegally gorgeous. Out of the shop, her dark schoolgirl hair is allowed to flow down over her neck to just below her shoulders. Her tanned body shines in the harsh light from the fluorescent tubes, contrasting perfectly with her matt-silver slip-dress. Come on, Trigg, remember: sixteen. But she looks at least twenty-five. Sorry, buddy, no go.

I feel very conspicuous walking through the casino carpark with this beautiful young woman and $10,000 in cash stuffed into the pockets of the grooviest trousers on the Gold Coast. Conspicuous in a good way.

"We'll have to be careful once we get in," Karen says. "So don't go acting like you know me. We'll split up for ten minutes, then follow me to whichever table I go to."

What is this girl doing to me? Just when I'm floating along like a horny schoolboy she becomes completely business-like, then when I'm almost in control again she gives me a look or touches my arm and sends me back into orbit. If I didn't know better, I'd swear she was conducting some sort of sadistic experiment. It's never going to happen, Trigg, she's still in high school. Just keep thinking: it's never going to happen.

We walk up the stairs and round the corner. As casually as I can, I give Karen a bundle of fifty $100 notes. I want to feel like a rich boyfriend, instead I feel like a sugar-daddy. Karen grasps my hand as I give her the money, and nods. "Now, remember everything I told you."

Actually, I feel like a sugar-little-brother.

Walking into the casino is like walking onto the set of *Top of the Pops*, but with carpet and old people. I chance an anxious look to the other side of the wide entrance where a neckless security guard is giving Karen back a plastic card. As she walks over the threshold, she looks at me and mouths the words: "I want you bad". Actually, she may have mouthed the words: "Fake ID". It's difficult to tell.

Karen heads left and I head right. I am on my own. And as a twenty-six-year-old male from the world's most cosmopolitan city, I'm a little disconcerted that the absence of my teenage chaperone should make me feel so vulnerable. At least I won't be alone for long.

I wander around the garish world for a while, get myself a drink, and take it all in. It's crowded and mad. It strikes me that an Australian named George Lazenby was once cast as James Bond. I think I understand now why it didn't work out. Still, what would I know? The sum total of my gambling experience involves Brighton Pier and pennies.

The allotted ten minutes goes by quickly in a Las Vegan haze and I find Karen at a roulette table just like she said. Choosing a seat at the opposite end, I sit down awkwardly and wait for the ball to stop. When it finishes its plastic gymnastics, I take out ten illicit $100 notes and throw them on the table.

"One thousand dollars," yells the croupier as she flicks my cash around. Someone in a ridiculous uniform looks over her shoulder and nods. "Markers, hundreds, fifties or twenty-fives?" she asks.

"Ahh, there's $1,000 there."

"Yes, sir" – patronising pause – "but which chips would you like?"

"Oh. Twenty-fives, please." Excellent Trigg, really tip-top.

We place our bets. It's a simple plan, really: I bet on the opposite of whatever Karen does. If she bets black, I bet red, if she goes odds, I go evens, if she bets on the top dozen, I bet on the middle and bottom dozen – you get the picture. Despite its simplicity, it does seem a damn sight more complicated than just lobbing the ill-gained money onto a table, getting fifty grand in chips, and then changing it back again at the cashier. Karen assures me that casinos are onto this sort of thing. That's why she's imposed a limit on us of $10,000 per night; any more might arouse suspicion. She also stressed that we shouldn't interact in the slightest. "You might think you're anonymous in a casino, Trigg, but they're watching." I thought this was a little melodramatic, but then she knows more about these things than I do.

It takes us two hours to clean the $10,000, and in that whole time she doesn't acknowledge my existence once. It's a relief to get outside and discover that she's still talking to me.

"How did you go?" she asks.

"Good. I felt like we could have cleaned much more."

"Come on, Trigg, you know what I said."

"Yeah but—"

"Don't even think about it. You don't want to see my nasty side."

Right now I'd pay a million quid to see her nasty side. I feel like a teenage boy with a major crush.

She starts walking down the stairs. "Maybe we could leave Hot Shots for tomorrow night, huh? Between this, and work, and school, I'm stuffed."

And yet, at the same time, she makes me feel like the old man with the busted fly in that "special" section of the newsagents. I catch up to the source of my schizophrenia and we exchange tales as we search for her car.

There is an unpredictable electricity hissing and fizzing about as we drive back to the Marriott. Karen tells me stories about her other under-age exploits, occasionally letting her eyes linger a little longer on me than on the road. I'm a mess. All the right feelings . . . wrong girl. It's somewhat of a relief, then, to finally pull up at the hotel. At least my turmoil will be over for the night. I try to open the door, but of course it won't budge. Karen comes running around to let me out.

"Thank you," I say as I hop out of the car. We both turn to close the door at the same time and bump into each other. To stop myself stumbling, I put out a hand which inadvertently wraps around Karen's back. We end up with our faces a few inches apart. Karen takes a shaky, shallow breath, and it suddenly all makes sense. I can see it in her eyes. She's going through a similar torment to me. We stare for ages, until, finally, she wraps her arms around my neck. Still we maintain a deep eye-contact. I can see the thousand-and-one thoughts going through her mind and I'm sure she can see mine. We shouldn't, it's not right, I think. "It's silly to fight it," she says, before leaning in and kissing me.

Game over. I kiss her back, amazed at the sensuality. Her lips, her tongue, so silky-smooth and wet, and her hands pulling me closer, forcing passion into the kiss. My hand slides down her back, brushing the curve of her bum lightly. Two perfect scoops of ice-cream draped in silk, not yet ravaged by fast-food binges or work-place bitch'n'eat sessions. Two perfect scoops of ice-cream, usually draped in a schoool uniform. I break away.

"Shit. I should go," says Karen.

"I think so."

She smiles. "You are terrible at deception."

♣♣ 6

The clock radio says 06.47. I've had one of those nights where you could swear you didn't sleep a wink, yet you can remember dreams and the moment of waking up. I slump my way to the balcony and throw open the thick curtains; Hello, Mr Su—WHAM! Instant blindness. I stumble around the room with my hands balled up and pushed into my eye sockets. Whack! I go sprawling across one of the queen-sized beds. Now I only have one hand to press into my burning eyes, the other is grabbing my stubbed big toe, waiting that split second between whacking it and the inevitable pain that follo— "Owwww." I let out a howl Mick Jagger would be proud of, before petering off into a string of muttered profanities worthy of a nod from Keith. Welcome to Friday: day three and counting.

"What's wrong?" asks Karen sleepily.

She still hasn't opened her eyes. She looks so natural and beautiful. My God! And I thought I knew frustration before! "Nothing, nothing at all, just a broken toe." Karen half smiles and her youth shows through.

I get up off the bed and walk around some more. It has been one of the strangest nights of my life, romantically speaking. Sure enough, Karen didn't go home. We kissed next to her car until a waiting limo shooed us out of the driveway, at which point we put her car in the basement and ran to the lift.

Like a couple of horny kids – well I guess she still is – we pawed clumsily at each other in the ascending lift. When I walked into my room, the view of the coast was the last thing on my mind. I dragged the curtains closed and turned to where Karen was sitting on the edge of one of the beds. And I couldn't do it. She's sixteen!

It's legal, it's legal, my dark side kept yelling.

Don't wear her out, stud, she's got *school* tomorrow, my conscience kept countering.

We looked at each other. With a sympathetic smile she slid the thin shoulder straps of her dress back into place. I did up the buttons of my shirt. Talk about your awkward moments. "Ermmmm-mmmmm."

That didn't quite do the trick.

"Don't, Trigg," said Karen. "I don't want to rush you, if you're not ready."

Not ready? Who the hell does she think she . . . actually, she's right. I guess that's it. I'm not ready. My loins disagree – vehemently – but I'm just not sure how comfortable I feel about shagging a schoolgirl. Oh Christ, listen to me! The guys at work would crucify me. But Mum and Dad would be proud. Maybe even the vicar. That's if I still had a job, or any of those people were talking to me. It's quite incredible how much your life can change in just a few weeks. From comfortable to chaos. I'd never even had a pigeon shit on me until I met Roger.

Karen and I spent the night side by side, but in different beds. I drank mini-bar vodka, Karen opted for Jack Daniels. And when that ran out, she pulled a joint from her purse and lit it up.

In the black-hole darkness, strangely illuminated whenever she inhaled, we couldn't see each other, but we talked for hours. Karen told me how she had lived with her brother since her parents died in a car wreck four years ago. I told her about Kelly and tried to make my fading life in London sound interesting. She's so different to the photocopied girls back home. Different to any girl I've ever met. We talked about all sorts of rubbish. Daft, trivial things that I wouldn't dare bring up back in London. I tried to convince Karen to travel, telling her how much she'd love it. Unconvinced, she told me again that she was happy right here. The last thing I remember talking about before she finally succumbed to sleep was finding Terri Smith. It's so nice not to be alone.

♣ ♣ ♣

"What time is it?" Karen slurs, disrupting my pained hobble down memory lane.

I watch her trying to get her bearings, and smile. "Five past seven, time to get up, it's a school day."

"Jesus, Trigg, you sound like my father."

I attempt to hide my discomfort by looking everywhere in the room except at her.

"I'm sorry," she says. "I forget that just because I'm comfortable with their deaths, doesn't mean other people are."

Good Lord, how can this girl possibly feel it's her position to apologise to me? I want to just hug her. Turn into marshmallow and smother her and not let go. I want to take her back to London and show all the Soho princesses swimming in the shallow end what it takes to get to the deep end. If only she were a few years older. Or I were a few years younger.

"Anyway, I'm not going to school today," she says. "I'm going to help you find Terri."

I start to protest, but then consider who I'm talking to. "Only if you're sure that's all right."

"Yeah. I'll just go home, get some clothes, put the money back in the till and meet you back here in, say, two hours."

"I've got a better idea . . ." I go on to explain how I've been planning to hire a car. Easier to get around the coast. Something small and inconspicuous. Besides, it helps remind me that I am the adult. Karen is strangely reluctant to be picked up, but I manage to persuade her – whining is a very underrated negotiation tool. She gives me her address and directions, and a meeting time of 9.00 a.m.

I sit for a while after she leaves, thinking about the previous night. She is perfect. Gorgeous, smart, no-nonsense . . . not out of puberty yet. Argggh! I try to recapture the narcotic moments when we were kissing and pawing, but they sit despairingly out of sight in the periphery. It all seems so unreal. Eventually I get frustrated, so I put my injured toe back to work and locate my sunglasses. Time to have another go at the curtains.

In a majestic gesture I throw them open. I still have to squint, such is the nature of the day outside, but I quickly forget about the flood of light bursting through my irises and the dull pain in my big toe. It is, once again, a glorious day.

The Gold Coast never ceases to amaze me. The landscape now has structure. No longer is it just the pretty lights and then the thick, black nothing I'd seen last night. Now it is buildings of all shapes, sizes and colours, scattered pine-trees, and a thin strip of unbroken white followed by a vast, deep blue ocean. The coast has taken on yet another persona. It even sounds different, this high up. Crisp and light. Like a celery stick snapping. And as the view recedes in perfect perspective to the south, I can just make out the massive headlands that interrupt the arc of beach. They seem to float among the salt haze, like mountains emerging from the clouds. My luck is out there somewhere.

Roger and I roll slowly up Karen's street in my fire-engine-red 1965 Mustang, top down, Oasis on the stereo. I'm searching for numbers on letterboxes when I hear a vague voice trying to pierce the cocoon of pistons and Liam Gallagher. Karen is already waiting on the steps of her place. She jogs towards me, laughing at my choice in cars. Oh God, there it is again, that pang of passion and lust. I struggle to put a ceiling on my goofy smile. She greets me by placing both elbows on the passenger door and leaning in, her tanned breasts pushing out from beneath her bikini top. Her sixteen-year-old, tanned breasts, Trigg. Shut up, just let me look.

"Small and inconspicuous?" Karen teases.

I drag my eyes away. "Well, something around here should be. Anyway, you're lucky; the assistant concierge at the hotel had to talk me down from a Ferrari." I'm not joking either. This is a dangerous place for a young gent with a pocketful of drug money.

With Karen sitting at my side and out of my direct view I am able to concentrate on other things. Which is a bit of a waste because we have no particular plan in mind, other than to cruise past Terri's place and take it from there. I have the page from the phonebook torn out and Shawn from the Marriot has lent me a street directory. We don't need it though, Karen knows the street. Francis Street. It's one of those strips of bitumen that link the highway and the esplanade, the ones that make the Gold Coast look like a giant ladder from the air.

Terri lives in a small, dark house that has been converted into a duplex by slapping some plasterboard up the middle and putting in another toilet. At least that's what it looks like from the outside. I park the Mustang about fifty yards down the road. "What do you think?" I ask Karen.

"Well, you could drive this sucker right through her lounge room, a ram-raid type of thing."

"You know, that really doesn't help."

We put our heads together, and decide it's Karen who should go. She'll pretend she's from the Fijian Tourism Bureau and ask Terri to do a "recent visitor" survey. If Terri looks completely flummoxed then Karen will pretend she has the wrong address and I'm back to square one. Any other reaction will be tantamount to her admitting she's the one I'm looking for. We will then reconsider Karen's ram-raid idea.

I fidget with the radio while Karen trudges off towards Terri's place. Pending failure keeps me facing straight ahead, busy at the dials, but after a couple of minutes curiosity taps me on the shoulder one too many times.

Karen is already walking back towards me. That was quick. Can't be a good sign. I try to read Karen's face as she gets closer. I think I see traces of disappointment. "Well?"

She shakes her head and my heart sinks.

"She's not there. The place is all locked up."

Not there? Not there! That's okay. That's good. It means we're still in business.

Karen can't understand my excitement at what she considers a failed effort. I leave her to ponder the complexities of it and jog off to have a look around myself. I might see Roger's double through a window or something.

While the dusty, weatherboard duplex looks okay, the yard is another matter. The gate is only just hanging on to its rusted hinges, so I straddle over it and onto the cracked concrete path on the other side. Tall clumps of grass are growing out of the little walkway. The lawn is a battlefield, where turf and several types of weeds are in a very slow fight for supremacy. Gardening obviously isn't Terri's strong suit.

The front window yields nothing promising, so I make my way around to the right. Thick bougainvillaea runs wild all the way up the side of the house. I force my way into the tangled, scratchy shrubbery and find a tired, flaking white fence that has long ago been consumed by the plants. I climb over it and further into the depths, until I find another window behind a thicket of branches. Working my head through the sticks and twigs, I discover only that the blinds are drawn. There has to be another window around the back. A twig goes up my nose in search of my brain. I sneeze sloppily into my muffling hands and struggle on.

Eventually I reach the back yard. Bingo. And as I crane my neck out from the semi-jungle, I can make out what looks like a window. I emerge from the confusion onto the scraggly patches of green that constitute the lawn. Now I can clearly make out a pair of French doors. Even better than a window!

I have a quick look around for neighbours – quite unnecessarily, given the overgrown foliage. Satisfied, I move around further. The doors are filthy, but I can make out a small sunroom, complete with coffee table and couch. In contrast to the exterior, the inside of the house actually looks quite neat. I walk a little closer to the wooden steps that lead up to the doors. Beyond the grubby glass, a polished wooden floor and a large set of bookshelves reveal themselves. The shelves are filled with various framed photos, books (obviously) and . . . and . . . Oh Lord! Is that what I think it is?

I can make out a small wooden figurine, but the years of grime won't allow me any more detail. I move closer still, walking hesitantly up the four or five steps. My shirt is actually moving to the rhythm of my machinegun heartbeat. I try one of the tarnished door-handles. Slowly. The lock clicks loudly and the pressure on the door gives way. I have come too far now to let a couple of words like *Break* and *Enter* stop me. Slowly, I pull the door open, my eyes straining to see through the narrow gap. Just a bit further—

RUFF, RUFF, RUFF, RUFF, RUFF!

Sweet Jesus! I slam the door shut, the glass wobbling with the force. Stumbling backwards off the patio, I catch sight of the meanest-looking dog I've seen in a long while. It's the sort of Alsatian you'd expect Fred West to have called his best friend. Frothy saliva is now smeared all over the glass and paw-marks stretch up to where my chest would have been. Am I imagining it or is the dog trying to pull the door handle down?

I bolt through the foliage, like a bad actor in a cheap horror movie. When I emerge on the other side, I'm scratched and bleeding – probably worse than if I'd stayed with the dog – but at least I'm saved the indignity of screaming. I try valiantly to regain my composure, but I am shaking like the proverbial leaf.

"What happened?" asks Karen when I find my way back to the car. Judging by the concern in her eyes, I must look rather traumatised.

"D-d-d-dog . . . big . . . big dog."

"You don't like dogs?"

I shake my head.

"Okay, hop in. I'm driving."

"Where are we going?"

"A place I go to chill out."

We drive south for about twenty minutes, the Mustang aching to get out of the busy stop-start traffic. Finally Karen turns out of the congestion, but only to pull into a carpark. We climb out of the car and I follow her up a path which wraps itself around a steep headland that juts out into the surf. I don't recognise the headland, but it must be one of those I saw floating in the salt haze this morning.

"Where are we?" I ask.

"Greenmount Hill."

The headland forms a long rocky point, which winds back to a protected, sandy cove. The cove then opens out into a long, sweeping white beach. "It's a lot prettier than Broadbeach."

As we continue around the path, Karen points out various landforms and the names of famous Gold Coast surfers that have been carved into the massive rock-faces – Mark Occhilupo, Rabbit Bartholomew, Ian Berrisford.

About a hundred yards on, we round the outermost edge of the point and she stops talking. I follow her gaze and I am silent too. I slump, somewhat involuntarily, on the conveniently-placed metal bench. It's not a spiritual moment, nor do I find God, but the view is overwhelming all the same, especially in my heightened state of agitation. From where we sit, I can look directly down the coast and see the huge arc of land that is the Gold Coast. The high-rises of Surfers Paradise look even more sinister as they appear to rise out of oblivion due to the sea haze masking their bases. Somewhere among them stands the Marriott Resort.

Karen taps me on the shoulder. Points. A young surfer – can't be more than fifteen – has just taken off on a large, translucent green lump of Pacific Ocean. Perched on the side of the hill, jutting out into the break, we are sitting side-on to the action. The strange perspective gives me a whole new outlook on the sport. We are close enough to see the boy's facial expressions. I can look down the wave, almost from his point of view, and watch it go from a fat green lump to a vertical wall of water. He tears along it with exhilarating speed, just outgunning the tumbling wave. The water looks so inviting, so green and cool and clear. Perhaps I should come here with the Bandit.

"This is fantastic," I say to Karen.

"Why?"

"What do you mean 'why'?"

"You see out there, Trigg, the way the swells line up like corduroy as they roll into the beach, all equally spaced and equally sized. Really rhythmic. Like something out of the physics class I should be in. You see that one just going under that boat? See it? Keep your eye on that one. That guy on the boat, he didn't even notice it . . . hardly even felt it, it was so small. Just another bump. But look at how it's getting bigger, growing out of nowhere. And faster, look how much faster it's going now. See? Look at the way the colours change. Thick bluey-green, and now it's getting lighter – from jade to emerald. Lighter and faster and bigger. Look at it now, it's getting really translucent, sucking up all that water, the sun is shining through it. And now it's started to trip. Stumbling over the rocks. Watch how it wraps around the point and breaks. Some parts give up easily and collapse, other parts resist, standing until you're sure they can't stand any more. And then they collapse too. It's inevitable, Trigg, they will collapse. Hundreds of miles across the ocean, just for this."

We sit and watch. My mind wanders. Back to London, back to Kelly, back to my old job, back to a time when luck was something I only ever thought about when I entered a lottery. It all seems a little pathetic now. My God, the things I used to get stressed about. The things I used to aspire to. What a self-obsessed, narrow-minded little tosser I was. I can't recall a single day in England when I didn't take everything for granted, when I was even aware of the cocoon I was living in. And then came Roger. And just about everything that has happened since has been profoundly bad, but at least I feel like I've been living, not merely existing. I feel like I'm aware. My actions have consequences; each moment has been alive with purpose. Through turmoil, I've found a bizarre contentedness.

Putting an arm around my neck, Karen leans over and kisses me on the cheek.

♣♣

7

It's a Friday and Karen has to work from 3.30 p.m. until some ungodly hour. We agree to meet in my room at the Marriott in the morning, where we'll have breakfast and sort out a new plan of attack for Ms Smith. What I don't tell Karen is that I have no intention of waiting until tomorrow. I'm more determined than ever to lift the curse. I just have to wait until I'm sure Terri is at work.

Back at the hotel, I use some clean money to pay for another night and check up on my much-needed laundry. In his Gold Coast drawl, Shawn tells me it isn't ready, but assures me it will only be another hour or so. The sun hasn't even gone down, Hot Shots hasn't even put on its make-up, and I'm ensconced back in my room. Bored. I flick on the TV. Nothing. I read some tourist brochures, but the bikini-clad girls just remind me of Karen. I pummel Roger with a pillow but he won't fight back. Then, suddenly, I feel guilty. And excited. And I know why.

I open the safe and take out the dirty money, which I place on the desk beside what's left of the clean money. The difference between the two piles is massive. I take $10,000 from the dirty pile and place it temporarily on the clean pile. It looks much better.

With Roger guarding the Mustang, I make my way up the increasingly familiar stairs of the casino. This world doesn't recognise time; it has a constant crowd of people, sequestered away, day and night. This suits me fine. If I'm going solo, the more people for me to hide among the better.

I do a quick trip around the floor, checking out the croupiers and cashiers. Not too many familiar faces. Still, it's going to be quite a risk playing both red and black, and odds and evens, by myself.

I locate the busiest, rowdiest roulette table. There isn't room to sit down. Excellent. I change $1,000 for chips by leaning over a large Greek kid with far too much gold jewellery. When the time is right, I put $100 on red. Now I just wait for the right time to bet on black. And wait. And wait. The ball is spinning and I'm still waiting. The ball lands on black . . . and I'm still waiting. This could be harder than I thought.

"Good evening, sir, nice to see you here again. Would you like a drink?"

I turn around and my heart constricts in my chest when I realise the waitress is talking to me. "Again?"

"Well, last night, tonight . . . Would you like a complimentary drink? The casino likes to look after its regular guests."

I snatch a bourbon and coke from the tray and knock it back in one. I snatch another. "Fanks," I say through a mouthful of ice. The girl leaves and I down the second drink. Maybe this isn't such a good idea. "You might think you're anonymous, but they're watching." Isn't that what Karen said?

Well so what? So what if they know I've come two nights in a row? Doesn't mean they're on to me, does it? I reach into my pocket and play with the roll of fifty- and hundred-dollar notes. They form quite a wad. In my other pocket, my chips chankle away against each other. I wish I knew what to do. Everyone is looking at me, at least it feels that way. I move away from the table. I check my watch . . . I pretend I'm looking for someone . . . but these guises can only be used so much. It's time to bite the bullet, get back on the horse.

Right after the seafood buffet. I sit in the casino restaurant and wrestle with my bravado. But I just can't do it. I can't risk getting caught and blowing my cover – do I have a cover? Cover or not, I'll just have to wait for Karen. Good God, that's tragic.

It's just after 9.00 p.m. when I leave the casino in a blaze of disappointment, $9,900 in cash and chips burning a shameful hole in the pocket of my trousers (which now sport several unfortunate cocktail sauce stains). Finally it's time to go after Terri Smith. And this plan is the very *epitome* of spontaneity and bravado. I just have to check Terri's house first. And then go back to the hotel to pick up some clean money in case I needed to bribe anyone. And change my trousers. But after that, practicalities be damned!

Orchid Avenue is like a miniature version of Ibiza: bright lights, thudding music, lots of skin and lashings of fake tan. One brochure boasts that it has the highest snog-per-square-metre ratio in Australia. It is also home to Hot Shots nightclub – quite possibly the answer to my prayers.

I slowly walk past the entrance, my hands thrust deep into my pockets. Most people are wearing very little. Some are in jeans, some in shorts. Certainly, I'm the only one sporting a crisp pair of tight beige slacks. They're not mine, let's get that straight. They were all Shawn from the Marriot could find in the lost-and-found when he told me that my washing was not only unwashed, but now missing.

I walk by the entrance again. The signs are all good. When I drove past Terri's house earlier all the lights were out. It's a Friday night so I'm reasonably sure she will be working. There's a girl at a cash register chatting to a gorilla-like bouncer. That could be her, that could be Terri Smith. Simple as that. Time to turn it on, Trigg, just talk to these people in their own language and keep it cool.

I walk up to the door. The girl and the bouncer stare at my trousers. "Alright?" I say.

"Can I 'elp you?" says the bouncer, in a way that implies it's more of a warning that a question.

"Hey, you're from England. Wicked. I'm from Fulham, man. 'Sabout yourself?"

"Brixton."

"Oh, right . . . well I'm from the rough part of Fulham."

"Can I 'elp you?"

"Ahh, yeah, I want to go in." I gesture past them, up the stairs. They look at each other with raised eyebrows.

"Sorry, pal, private gig."

"Yeah, yeah that's right, wicked, and I think you'll find I'm on the list."

They shake their heads slightly as they looked at each other. "What's your name, then?"

"It's . . . ahhh, it's . . . Marcus."

"You gotta last name, Marcus?"

"No, no. It's like the Madonna thing, you know. Sometimes I spell it with a K."

"I see. Well, Mar-Kus, I'm sorry, but I specifically need a surname".

"Okay, it's . . . Sharp. Marcus Sharp."

"Marcus Sharp, hey? Alright, let's have a look here." He picks up a clipboard. "Rogers, Samuels, Sharp. Marcus Sharp. Here you are, sir."

"Really?"

"No! Now piss off before I shove your head down your neck!"

"Aww, come on. Give us a break for back home, hey? One for the Queen?"

"I'll break your fucking arm if you don't sod off."

I reach deep down into my slacks and pull out a wad of currency. "Well give us a break for—" I try to remember the names of the Australian historical figures represented on the bank notes. I can't. "Give us a break for this lot, then, hey?"

"Go on then, sir, 'ave a good evening."

The girl at the cash register is suddenly all bleach-blond hair and polished white teeth as she stamps my wrist. "Thanks, Terri," I say. She looks confused, so I make my way upstairs.

Tracing the source of the booming beat, I turn right at the top of the stairs and come to a frosted glass door. On the other side, I can make out a mash of silhouettes writhing about. Casually, I push at the door, but it proves too stiff. I put some weight behind it and it relents, shooting me out on the other side, into the throng of people. Lots of people stop what they're doing to look at me. And then it strikes me: everyone is in lingerie and underwear. I smile. It's a private party, a *lingerie* party, and I'm wearing slacks and a shirt. I stand out. I will have to strip down to my underwear so I can be inconspicuous – Oh Lord! Right there, that's where my smile abruptly disappears.

I walk out of the gents with my slacks and shirt in hand and the cash forming a bulge in my smalls. Except they're not *my* smalls. They're an old pair of Kelly's that must have got mixed up with my things. And they shouldn't really be called "smalls" – more like "bigs", as in: "big pants for those days when she was feeling fat and frumpy." It had seemed like a reasonable idea at the time. They were comfy, supportive – and my only option until my missing washing turned up. Fortunately they're big enough to accommodate all the cash I have on me.

A few people point and laugh.

Doubled over, I shuffle quickly to the bar, where I find a vacant stool.

"Love your jocks," says the trashy woman behind the bar.

I look up at her in semi-shock. I had completely forgotten about Terri, and now I begin to wonder if this is her . . . this saggy, plastic, fake-tanned, collagen-implanted Barbie doll. "Thanks, they were a present." I order a drink.

She returns and splashes my vodka, lime and tonic on the damp bar-mat. "Can I start a tab?" I ask hopefully.

"It's all paid for honey," she says, "thanks to Peaches Models and Escorts." She looks at me expectantly.

"Yes," I reply, picking up the drink, "cheers to Peaches."

She keeps looking at me and attempting to pout. She's making me very uncomfortable. Then she speaks. "You're obviously not a model, so are you, like, a manager or a photographer or something?" As she asks, she thrusts her plastic boobs at me. I rock back in the stool. I'll have to play this one carefully. I look around and see three other girls behind the bar – one in four chance that this is Terri Smith. Please, Lord, no. "Yeah, not a model, that's right," I say. "I'm a new-talent manager. I'm responsible for finding new models."

"Really?" She thrusts again. Harder. It's like having two footballs going for my head. This time I overbalance on the stool and have to grab the bar to save myself. I regain my composure quickly, but I have vodka, lime and tonic all over my chest. The woman licks her swollen lips. "You know, I can help you clean that off."

It's time to act. If she is Terri, I'll have to take control quickly. If she's not, I have to get away even quicker – Oh God, is she playing with her nipples? I take a desperate stab. "Yeah, I'm actually hoping to speak to Terri Smith, I've heard some good things about her."

"Oh." Her body slumps. I breathe a massive sigh of relief. "That'd be right," she continues, "it's always Terri. *Terri's so hot, Terri's so awesome* . . . stupid little slut." She walks away without telling me which of the other girls is Terri, but that's okay, her glare leaves a trail of daggers heading straight for an intense-looking blond girl at the other bar.

Holding my clothes over my enormous knickers, I inch towards the other bar. Sitting down quickly, I turn my attention to the girl I hope is Terri. Do your stuff, Trigg, be confident, be confident, get in the zone.

"A bottle of Veuve thanks, love," I say.

"We've got beer, vodka or bourbon. Which one do you want?"

"Surprise me."

She gives me a tired look and fixes me a drink. I give her a look back – confidence, charm, a little bit of mischief.

"We're not allowed to serve overly-intoxicated people."

I blink twice. "No, no, no. I'm not drunk. It's . . . it's an eye problem. Usually I wear contacts, but . . . ahhh . . . they took them. The bloody chambermaids at my hotel. I tell you, anything that's not nailed down."

The Terri Smith-prospect gives me my drink, but I can see she's far from convinced. I take a long slurp . . . bourbon and coke. It's time to salvage the moment. Stay cool, Trigg, stay cool. I casually swing around on the stool and face out towards the crowd, my back to the girl. "You know, I'm a photographer," I say, like it's no big deal to me but should be to her. I take another sip of my drink.

"Yep, all the big shoots, Jodie, Heidi, Giselle, Kate before it all went downhill, you name 'em, I've shot 'em. 'Course, I'm always looking for fresh new talent." Another sip. "And let me just say, I'm looking at you, and I'm seeing a—"

"Excuse me." It's the man on the stool beside me. "There's no one there."

I swing around. Sure enough, the girl has gone to the other end of the bar and is chatting with a dark-haired co-worker. I finish my drink. Fast. This is not going well.

Clunking my glass down with calculated carelessness, I slide off the stool, heading for the dance floor. I manage to work my way through the pulsating mass and manipulate myself so that I emerge with my back to the Terri-prospect and her friend. "Come on, love," I yell into the blob of wriggling people, "if I dance with you, I have to dance with all the others." I back into a stool, right in front of my quarry.

"Models," I say, with a shrug of the shoulders and a shake of the head. The girl I hope is Terri Smith and her friend look at each other, then both give me that sisterhood cluck that says: "Typical male". I'm making this very difficult for myself. I manage to pull a twenty out of my knickers without anyone seeing, and put it on top of my shirt and slacks, which I place on the bar. "Is there a cloakroom or somewhere where you can put these things?" I ask the dark-haired girl.

She snaps up the note and complies, leaving me alone with the girl I really want to speak to. "Is there a phone around here?" I ask quickly, before she can escape with her friend.

"Payphone near the stairs."

"Listen," I say, conspiratorially. "It's a really important call. Surely you've got a phone back there in the office."

"Yes, we do."

And she walks away.

I run around a few people and cut her off. "I mean, it's *really, really* important."

She rolls her eyes. "Shit. Follow me."

She walks abruptly through a door behind the bar, and I have to skip a little to keep up. My mind is working overtime. The plan has been to get this girl alone, I haven't bothered to think beyond that.

"There it is," she says, already turning to walk back.

Shit, Trigg, do something. What? Anything, for God's sake. "Uhh, Terri?"

The girl spins around, her eyes suddenly alive. "How do you know my name?"

Well, that's my first question answered, I think, as I splutter on. "Look, Terri, I don't really have to make a call, I just had to get you alone to—"

"How do you know my name, you creep?"

"That's really not important. Now, can you please listen to me? Could we just go somewhere quiet for a while? I have a room at the Marriott, or . . . or maybe back to your place . . . I have money, I'll give you $300 . . ."

I put both hands in my big lacy pants, trying to find some cash. The look on her face says it all. Perhaps I could have handled this whole thing a little better.

"Fuck off!" She rushes back out the door, leaving me to reconsider my circumstances. It doesn't take me long to realise I have to go after her.

I take two determined steps towards the door . . . and then a whole lot of little scared ones in the opposite direction. The hinges are still shaking from where the two huge bouncers have pushed their way through, Terri in tow.

"That's him," she yells over the two sets of impressive shoulders. "Prick."

I bolt.

"Oi, come back 'ere you little shit."

Yeah right, I think, as I barrel over a table towards another door. I shoot through it without looking back and sprint down a hallway. I have a lead, but I can tell from the commotion behind me that they are right on my tail.

I bash open one of the three doors lining the narrow corridor. Bollocks. A storeroom. I reverse and, as I shoot back out, I see two large men dressed in black. They are close. And none too happy. I try another door, on the other side of the hallway, which leads into another corridor. I have now completely lost all sense of direction. I throw open another door. There are people everywhere. In their underwear. I'm back in the main room. I bolt for the frosted glass doors. Finally I know where I'm going. But before I get to them, the English bouncer from downstairs pushes his way through. I stop on the spot. The bouncer is scanning the crowd – looking for me, I am certain. Shit, shit, shit. I have nowhere to go. I bolt back onto the dance floor, into the throng of people oblivious to my plight. It proves to be good camouflage: I can see out but the bouncers can't see in. But it can't last forever. I watch the thugs closely as they stand on stools, craning their necks to survey the room. Waiting, waiting. Waiting, waiting. Now! Suddenly I spring out of the crowd and surge for the unguarded door.

And just as suddenly I stop. My legs are still going, but not the rest of me. The massive hands clasp me like a rollercoaster safety-bar.

"You stupid little fucker."

I land at the bottom of the stairs with a potato-sack thump. My ears are ringing and my stomach aches like buggery from the pounding, but nothing seems to be broken. "Have a nice night," says the girl by the cash register as I roll past.

Shawn and the other staff at the Marriott watch open-mouthed as I limp through the grand foyer in my big pants, my face bruised.

"It's alright, I'm from London."

I sit for ages that night in my anonymous room. Utterly depressed, with a wad of sweaty, smelly money sharing the darkness beside me. This whole thing isn't going to plan. I've blown it with Terri, no matter what Karen comes up with tomorrow. I press the button on my cheap digital watch. A dim yellow light struggles from somewhere under the glass face. 3.00 a.m., Saturday, February the 13th. Only six days left.

♣♣

8

I spend the night physically comfortable in my lush queen-sized bed, but unable to sleep. Six days! It took me longer than that to find my car keys once. I'm grateful, then, when the gremlins in the clock radio finally tear down the bright red number 5 and put up the 6. That means: "Trigg you can get up now and you won't be considered a freak, an insomniac, or one of those weird, obsessive men who pride themselves on beating the dawn every morning". And the beauty of this is, once I actually consider getting up, I start to feel drowsy. And so I finally sleep.

By 8.29 the gremlins have set up a little garage band in the clock radio. And at 8.30 precisely they fire up, doing a tinny cover of a Powderfinger song. I'm happy to get out of bed now, because in half an hour Karen will be here, and she'll make me feel better.

Half an hour ticks by. I go and track down my missing washing. I have a shower. I try to read the paper, but as distractions they all prove as futile as trying to read gardening magazines.

Three-quarters-of-an-hour ticks by.

An hour.

An hour-and-a-half.

Karen is running almost two hours late. It's just as well I have the mirrored wardrobe doors open, that way I don't have to watch myself pace about and rant and rave. I don't have her phone number, so I can't call her. I don't even know her last name, to look it up in the phonebook. All I have is her address. Day four of nine is slowly ticking away and I'm sitting around scratching my balls.

I play the "five more minutes" game for another half hour – you know the one: five more minutes, then I'll . . . Finally, at eleven o'clock, I put on some clothes, grab some cash, grab my wallet . . .

oh no . . . my driver's licence! It's still in my slacks. At the nightclub! Shit, shit, shit. It's too much to think about. I rip off a page of Marriott stationery and take a pen: "Find Karen; Get driver's licence back; Talk to Terri Smith". Hmm, okay, I guess when you look at it on paper it's not that much, but it's the impossible complexity of each of these tasks that worries me. I stuff the piece of paper into one pocket and in the other I shove Roger. "Don't complain, you got me into this."

I cruise slowly up to Karen's driveway in the Mustang. What I see hits me for six. Right in the middle of the patchy front lawn stands a "For Lease" sign.

I pull up to the footpath and climb out. The house doesn't look any different from yesterday; mind you, it's a pretty nondescript house. Karen's car is missing too, another bad sign. But then, I don't remember seeing it there yesterday.

I knock on the door but there's no answer. Looking in through the windows I can make out only stray pieces of furniture, nothing to suggest any serious habitation. For lease? What the bloody hell . . . ?

Eviction! They *must* have been evicted. It makes sense; a young brother and sister, hard times, can't afford the rent. They must have been evicted. Those bastard estate agents. And what about Karen? Here I am sitting on a small fortune, which she is helping me legitimise, and she doesn't even ask for any. She doesn't even call to ask for help moving. Maybe she was hoping I'd offer her some of the loot. Maybe that's why she was helping. Oh you daft prat, Trigg. Why didn't you offer her a cut of the cash?

I have to find her. I have to help her. It's the very least I can do.

I make my way over to the neighbour's house and try the doorbell. No answer. Don't tell me they've evicted the whole street! In order to build one of those resorts maybe, the kind with its own postcode. I try the other neighbour and am relieved to hear movement on the other side of the door.

"Hi," I say when the door is opened. "I'm wondering if you know where the people next door have gone?"

"What?" replies a short red-headed man in his early thirties.

"I think they've been evicted. A girl called Karen and her brother?"

"Karen? Dunno what your talking about, mate. No Karen ever lived there," he says as he scratches his testicles through his nylon rugby-league shorts.

"But . . . but I was here with her yesterday. Right here."

"You must be mixed up, pal. No one's been living in that place for weeks."

"No *you* must be mixed up. You should open your eyes more."

"Look, mate, there's no fucking Karen ever lived there. All right?"

"But—"

"Are you fucking deaf? Fuck off!"

He stands in the doorway brooding and scratching his bollocks as I jump back into the Mustang. I'm furious. I want to go back and hammer his scrunched-up little red head. But I settle on giving him the two fingers. On the maturity scale it scores a solid two-and-a-half. On the bravery scale it probably rates a four. It would have rated higher if I hadn't waited until he'd gone back inside. Still, I feel better.

Better, but not at all happy. They don't know what's happened to Karen when I ask at convenience store either. All they can tell me is that she worked her full shift last night. I hurtle back to the Marriott in a total muddle. Despite the confusion that has settled in my head like low-lying cloud, I know the best thing to do is to wait. Wait for what, you idiot? I don't know, wait for Karen, I suppose. And then what? How should I know, it's her show now – she's been playing Caribbean stud poker, when I thought we were playing snap.

When I get to the Marriott, Shawn is busting to tell me something. "Trigg, your sister came just after you left. I let her into your room. I hope you don't mind."

"My sister?" I haven't spoken to my sister in four weeks, since I backed over her dog. Is this national "Make Trigg Go Crazy" day?

Shawn senses something is wrong and automatically goes on the defensive. "Yeah, your sister, Karen. She told me you were expecting her." The low-lying cloud in my head gets denser. "Is everything all right?" Shawn asks.

"Yes Shawn, everything's fine."

I slide the card quietly into the electronic lock of room twenty-one-oh-three. Karen must have realised she'd missed our rendezvous, probably after she was done moving her stuff. So she turned up here, late. She must have felt so bad about being late that she couldn't just call, and now she wants to surprise me. Well, I'll show her a surprise.

Slowly, I twist the door handle . . . then I burst in, yelling in mock seriousness, "What do you think you're doing . . . you . . . little—" There is no one there. Empty. I check the bathroom, the balcony – nothing. I look around for a note or something. No. Maybe she went down to breakfast looking for me. I pick up the phone to call the restaurant, but I never get to dial. I just stand, looking at my reflection in the mirrored wardrobe doors. I don't remember closing those.

I put the phone back on its cradle.

Slowly I slide the doors open, watching my image disappear.

Bitch.

Bitch.

BITCH, BITCH, BITCH, BITCH, BITCH!

I slide the mirrored door closed again. The image that appears is vastly different from the one that was there seconds before.

Idiot.

IDIOT, IDIOT, IDIOT!

The safe is empty. Completely empty.

I'm not sure which hurts more, the money being stolen, the humiliation or the betrayal. The number of times I was all goofy and silly in front of her. The number of times she must have thought "What a fucking cakewalk!" Well, you know what they say about a fool and his money. Bloody hell, I spilled my heart out to her. I thought she spilled hers out to me. She must have seen me coming a mile off. I walk over to the wardrobe again and pull out my sneakers. Still, it could have been worse. I pull the $8,000 of clean money out of the Adidas.

I can't tell you why I split the money up. Too many John Le Carré novels, maybe. I don't know, but I'm glad I did. I walk over to my discarded trousers – still the grooviest, but now the dirtiest, too. I reach into the pocket and remove the $9,900 in cash and chips I'd meant to clean last night. At least she'll get a hell of a surprise when she realises she only has $30,000.

9

It's 3.30 p.m. on a tourist-brochure Saturday afternoon when I eventually haul the Mustang back onto the highway. The roads are relatively quiet, but I hold the big V8 back – I'm still feeling tired, betrayed and completely drained. I stop at a red light. The Gold Coast Highway. What a paradox. It's basically nothing but speed limits and traffic lights. But I'm too exhausted to get agitated. All I really want to do is recover my licence, then get back to my room and have a long bath. I would have stayed in my room all day but I have to get to Hot Shots before it opens. Otherwise all my friends from last night will be there – and I just don't think I'm up to seeing them again. I'd rather take a punt on a cleaner or duty manager or someone.

When I get to the front door of the nightclub it's all closed up. "That'd be right," I mumble. I give the door a shove and it glides open. "That'd be right," I mumble.

It's eerie to be back inside the club again. The pulsing, artificial light of the previous night has been replaced with a charcoal-sketch grey. The frosted glass door is now merely a door, not a chalky window onto the debauchery beyond. I hesitate before pushing it open, not knowing who or what is on the other side. Like last night, it is stubborn, and again I shoot out the other side, startling the plump girl who is restocking booze behind one of the bars. Thankfully I don't recognise her, and I can tell by the puzzled look on her face that she doesn't know me. So far, so good.

"Sorry," I say. "I'm looking for some stuff I left here last night, some clothes."

"Oh, right." She puts down a bottle of bourbon. "Where'd you leave them?"

Here's the tricky part. Let's just hope Terri's friend put them away and forgot about them. "Ahh, I gave them to one of the girls working here, I think she put them out the back."

"Okay, I'll go and have a look. What exactly is there?"

There is nothing in her eyes to suggest she's thinking: "Just wait and I'll go and call the bouncers who want to dance on your face some more", so I tell her. "Let me see, there's a shirt and some . . . browny-coloured trousers." One must never admit to beige, under any circumstances.

The girl returns a couple of minutes later empty-handed. "Sorry, couldn't find them."

I curse silently. "Normally I wouldn't bother, but my driver's licence is in the pocket. Is there anywhere else they could be?"

"Umm, I could go and ask Mr Kawabata, he's the owner. He's just out on the veranda."

"That'd be terrific, if you don't mind."

I follow the girl down one of the labyrinthine corridors, then another and another. We emerge on a sunny wooden deck at the back of the block. The girl begins to cross over to where a group of people are enjoying a few drinks on this clichéd Gold Coast afternoon. It's just as well I didn't find myself cornered out here last night or I would have been in really deep tro—Oh no!

I bound silently over to the girl, trying to intercept her. "Ahh, never mind," I whisper. "I just remembered, I took them home after all."

"Really, are you sure because—"

"Well, my word! Look who it is, Doris. It's Detective Hopman," says Terry Smith. "I didn't think we'd have the pleasure again. And so soon. Please, sit down, have a drink."

"Ahh . . . yes, I'd love to, but I'm on duty, you know."

Terry Smith laughs. "That's hardly behaviour befitting an Australian federal police officer. Come on, sit down. We were just talking about you."

"You were?"

"Why yes. I was just telling Mr Kawabata here" – Terry indicates the serious Japanese man in the dark suit beside him – "how you've been snooping around and how you blackmailed me into giving you $50,000 of *his* money. And Mr Kawabata was just trying to decide whether to take you out to sea and feed you to the sharks, or just pack you up in a box and pop you in the foundations of one of his new high-rises. So, what are you drinking?"

I'm gone.

With fewer obstacles to negotiate, and more lucidity, I manage to make it out of the club without any assistance. Scrabbling back out into the daylight, I almost trip over Terry and Doris's black Porsche, right out front. I must have walked straight past it on the way in.

I bolt blindly off to the right and around the corner, looking for a surveillance point. For the first (and probably last) time, I am grateful for the abundance of tacky souvenir shops in the area. I dart into one, pull on a pale blue terry-towelling hat embroidered with dolphins, and hide behind a rack of postcards.

A massive Japanese lump spills out first, then Terry and Doris and Mr Kawabata, followed by the plump barmaid. I try to pull the hat down a little more, but a balaclava it is not. I move closer to the postcard rack instead. The plump barmaid quickly walks back inside, but the Smiths begin harassing passers-by about my whereabouts. Thankfully, no fingers point in my direction, and after a few short investigative walks, they appear to capitulate. But they don't go back in, they just loiter around the entrance. Then I realise what they are waiting for. I cuff the postcard rack when I see the girl return with my clothes. Terry snatches them from her and removes my driver's licence. Damn! From where I'm standing I can see Terry's face. He's not going to be buying Trigger Harvey a pint at the Burleigh Waters Bowls Club any time soon.

I wait until the lynch mob is well back inside before I break my cover. I have to buy the hat, a Surfers Paradise tea towel and eight postcards featuring an assortment topless women, before the shop owner lets me leave.

The Mustang's steering wheel is shaking a little more than the smooth bitumen warrants as I drive back along the highway. My nerves are becoming more and more ragged as this odyssey rambles along. Every Panama hat and thatch of white hair is making me jump, which is frightfully inconvenient on the Gold Coast. It's definitely time for a long bath. Right after I've stopped off at Jun's and grabbed some chicken-and-mushroom rolls. Seven ought to do it.

Although I won't admit it to myself, I am hoping like hell that there will be a message from Karen waiting for me when I get back to the hotel. An explanation. But there isn't. By the time I've paid for another night, Jun's rolls are cold. I eat them anyway. They do the job. I lie back on the thick bedspread, wait for air traffic control to give the bed clearance, and enjoy the flight.

10

The sun moves a millimetre more in its sluggish journey to the horizon. Just enough to catch the mirror and reflect straight into my eyes. I shake my head vigorously, roll to a sitting position and look for my girly suitcase. I had an idea while I was doing somersaults in the ether. I'm going to break into Terri Smith's place. Tonight.

My suitcase contains only a few black articles of clothing. I pull out a pair of black, fleecy tracksuit pants and a pair of green socks. My old trainers aren't quite black, but they're quiet, and will be handy if I have to run for my life. As for covering up my top half, my Chelsea jersey will have to do. I have my doubts about the wisdom of a plan hatched during a mushroom-riddled sleep, but I am still in a semi-euphoric, still-a-bit-stoned, just-woken-up state, and I probably won't realise just how stupid I'm being until it's too late. I take the $16,500 out of my sneakers and put it back in the safe. This time I make a point of ensuring that no sixteen-year-olds are watching as I change the combination. I slide back the wardrobe door and look at my outfit. It's with a pang of disappointment that I realise I look more like a football hooligan than a cat burglar. And my blond hair is a dead giveaway. I'll have to fix that.

My instructions to Shawn are explicit: "If my *sister*, Karen, comes back, let her into my room . . . and then don't let her out. No matter what! I don't care what you have to do, Shawn, just don't let her out. Entertain her, tell her lies, nail the bloody door shut. I don't care. I could be a while, and I might be in a bit of a rush when I get back, but that's not your problem, okay? Your problem is Karen. Understand?"

"That's a really gay rugby-league jersey."

♣ ♣ ♣

I could go to any convenience store for my supplies, and Karen's is actually quite inconvenient, but I am giving self-delusion a go. I want to walk through the CCTV-monitored doors, past the newspapers and plastic-wrapped skin-mags, and there she'll be, choc-full of perfectly reasonable excuses. I pull up abruptly outside the distinctive green and red store. My heart is a little helicopter inside my chest. I don't want to look, but I know I have to. Come on, Trigg, you can do it. I swallow hard and jerk my head towards the window.

Well, you didn't really think she'd be there, did you?

No.

Maybe.

The automatic doors open and I step into the frosty, sterile store. All I can do is half nod at the teenage boy reading *Playboy* behind the register. I walk straight to the refrigerated section. But then I turn around. "I'm looking for Karen, she's supposed to be working here now," I say.

"Yeah, tell me about it," the teenager replies over the top of Miss January. "I'm working a double shift because she didn't show up. Believe me, mate, you're not the only one looking for her."

No matter how much you expect something, no matter how many times you tell yourself not to get your hopes up, it still stings when the truth becomes unignorable. I try to push the whole saga to the back of my mind and resume my shopping. Pork sausages and bacon. Beef Doggy Treats – *Your Dog'll Love 'em*. Rubber gloves (washing-up gloves – they were all they had). And lastly . . .

"Excuse me, do you have any black baseball-caps?" I ask the assistant.

"Black caps? No, sorry, mate . . . Oh, hang on, we've got some dark blue ones. That do?"

"I suppose. Where are they?"

He returns with a blue cap so dark that nine out of ten American housewives would probably call it black. Except for the light brown foam breasts protruding over the peak. I turn it over in my hands, reading the caption: "Random Breast-Tester".

"Is this all you have?"

The guy shrugs. "It's not a clothes shop."

I exhale heavily. Nothing can ever go smoothly, can it? "I'll take it."

I throw my assorted meat-products onto the passenger seat, on top of Roger. "I hope you're a vegetarian, you little tosser." He just stares at me, as inanimate objects do.

I make a detour on my way to Terri's place, cutting the Mustang's headlights as I coast into Karen's supposed street. The "For Lease" sign is still wedged in the front lawn, and there are no lights on. I cut the engine. It would be a shame to waste such good surveillance clothes.

I sit for about fifteen minutes, with nothing to look at but darkened houses and the baseball cap. They both reminded me of Karen. I try to force her from my consciousness and concentrate on surveillance, but she just lingers like an awkward silence. Turning the cap boobs-down, I notice that there's a light in the neighbour's house.

Fifteen minutes later I become aware that I am fondling the foam boobs. I put the cap down, and go back to watching. Goddamn thieving little minx, with her long hair and nice skin. I pick the cap up again. And put it down again. "I don't want to rush you if you're not ready," she'd said. If *I'm* not ready! I pick the cap up again. And put it down. I pick the cap up and rip at the foam boobs. "Slag, slag, slag, slag."

Finally I throw the cap down in frustration. I just can't get Karen out of my mind. What's her sodding story? There's no way a sixteen-year-old could be that calculating and cold. I saw her eyes, she was sincere. When we were sitting at Greenmount, watching the waves, talking about her parents, she was sincere. She opened up. Impossible that a cold hearted, thieving bitch would leave herself that vulnerable.

I sit for another fifteen minutes. Slowly I slip out of the frustrating real world and into my own head. Into a world where conspiracies run rampant and sixteen-year-old girls with massive foam tits are burned at the stake. And then a scurrying cat or something yanks my attention back to the house. The only solid conclusion I can arrive at is that Karen ripped me off and therefore is not about to come back to this place. So maybe it's time to get a little proactive.

Quietly, I undo my seatbelt, careful to keep the metal clasps from clinking together. I reach for the door handle, but stop myself just in time. On a night as still as this, a car door opening would echo down the whole street. Besides, this is a convertible. I sit up high in the seat and work my legs out from under the steering wheel. With a half twist, I get one leg up near the top of the door. Then, with the grace and precision of a Romanian gymnast, I swing my other leg silently over so that I am poised to jump out. And then, with the grace and precision of a British gymnast, I topple back onto the steering wheel.

BAAAAAAAAAAAAAAAAAAR!

My arse is pressed against the horn. I try to lift it off, but I can't get any leverage. I'm like a turtle on its back, arms and legs flailing.

BAAAAAR!

Finally I manage to roll off and back onto the seat. Everything is silent again. Then I hear front doors opening. Shit.

I fumble the key at the ignition. The Mustang kicks over and revs into the red until I take my knee off the accelerator. Then, in the sort of move I was trying for in the first place, I wind up in a driving position. I slam the gear-stick into first, and drop the clutch, but there is still plenty of time for my eyes to widen at what they encounter. The neighbour I had the run-in with earlier is standing at his door, but it's not him that causes me to bounce the red convertible off the gutter, it's the other man looking over his shoulder. A tall man in his mid-twenties, with dark hair and a familiar looking face; familiar, in the sense that if he put on some lipstick and eye shadow, he would look an awful lot like Karen.

After an erratic drive, I wind up in a deserted carpark by the beach. I decide to stay there and think about things. It's a perfect place for procrastination. Just take an hour or so and mull things over. If that was Karen's brother, what was he doing at the neighbour's house? The neighbour who didn't know Karen? And what's he got to do with my money and Karen's disappearance? And where is the little thief herself? I let out a sigh. There's no moon, just a suggestion of it behind a thickening mass of clouds. I have to act now. Roger has worked his head out from under the assorted meat products and is grinning stupidly at me, practically daring me to act. I sigh again as I turn the key.

I don't realise just how dark it is until I try to negotiate the jungle that runs up the side of Terri's place. It is almost pitch black. There is a single dim light on inside the neglected duplex. It threw me at first, the light. I thought she must have been home – Terri, or the mystery man who answered her phone that first time – but after fifteen minutes of keen observation, I am reasonably certain the coast is clear. In my dark outfit I am almost invisible among the tropical shrubbery, except for the odd chunk of skin-coloured foam still sticking to the cap. I figure half a foam boob stands out less than my blond hair.

Eventually I wrestle my way to the edge of the vegetation, where I hang for a beat to survey the scene and check my meat products. Outwardly, I have been as quiet as a comatose church mouse, but inside my chest, my heart has been banging away furiously. I move on anyway, out into the back yard.

Scuttling up the wooden steps, I arrive at the French doors. Please let them still be unlocked. I hold my breath as I wrap my yellow, washing-up-gloved fingers around the metal handle. The theme music from *Mission Impossible* is belting through my head to the quickening rhythm of my pulse. I ease the handle down until the tension indicates it has engaged the locking mechanism. I allow the air out of my lungs before taking some more in.

Forcefully but smoothly, I pull the handle down. It creaks, and then with a click that, to me, sounds like a gunshot, the tension in the door disappears. I breathe again and pull the door open a crack with my right hand, while my left hand fishes around in my pocket. Washing-up gloves don't allow much dexterity, and there are a few anxious seconds as I fail to grasp anything. Finally, my fingers wrap determinedly around a Doggy Treat. I pull it out and slide it a couple of inches through the crack, taking my next breath as I click the door shut again.

It's too late to turn back now – there is evidence – so I gently tap on the glass. Nothing happens. I tap a bit harder – wake up, you stupid dog! Then I hear the telltale scratching on the wooden floorboards, followed by an inquisitive growl. I can hear the dog walking, but I can't see him. Then he barks. Loudly. And again. He steps around the corner and trots curiously towards the door, growling with compulsion and bearing his impressive fangs. Come on, come on, don't be such a drama queen. And then he *does* come on: he springs towards the door with saliva trailing behind him. *Kawhump!*

The impact of the glass doesn't seem to bother him; he just keeps on barking and lunging. Jesus, shut up already. "Doggy Treat, Doggy Treat," I say in a hushed, singsong voice, as I point to the ground. "Yummy, yummy Doggy Treat."

He keeps barking.

"Are you fucking stupid? Look, Doggy Treat, yum."

Finally the dog gets the message. He does a double take and then snaps up the snack. Quickly, I empty the rest of my doggy banquet from my pockets. I shove a handful of bacon, sausages and Doggy Treats up to the glass. "Mmmm, yummo. You want some of this? Hey, Spot? Yeah, yummo."

The Alsatian's tail wags wildly, his green eyes are alive with greed. With my yellow rubber palm facing up, I reach for the door handle, showing as little fear as possible. The dog couldn't care less, he just hangs his tongue out and keeps his eyes on the prize.

In one swift but crucial movement, I whip open the door with one hand, and throw the food out into the yard with the other, careful to keep the door between myself and the pooch. The dog bolts straight out into the yard, and I slip into the house, pulling the door shut behind me. The dog looks up and lets out a half yip, but then he goes back to his food. Part One accomplished.

I tiptoe straight over to the bookshelf where I saw the figurine yesterday, but even before I get there, I know it's not Roger's lookalike. I falter at the initial disappointment, but keep pressing on, like an action movie hero who just took a bullet to the shoulder. Passport! Where would she keep her passport? As quietly as I can, I slink over the polished boards and look into each room.

A desk sits against the far wall of a spare bedroom, with a computer, scraps of paper, and several manila folders competing for space on the desk. I yank open the top drawer, too quickly and too loudly. A rummage through reveals only old photo-processing envelopes and other odds and ends. Next drawer. More manila folders. Third drawer. Still nothing, just a bunch of computer discs and computer manuals. The bedroom, try the bedroom, Trigg.

The dim tendrils of light reveal several taped-up boxes stacked haphazardly in the corner, and assorted pairs of frilly underpants scattered across the wooden floor. She obviously isn't the tidiest girl in the world. I follow the trail of thongs to Terri's underwear drawer, which is already half open. Invasion of privacy is the last thing I'm concerned about now, so I grab handfuls of the cotton pants, digging for the bottom of the drawer, where I hope Terri keeps her valuable documents. That's when it all starts to happen.

The first sensation is a chill that runs up my spine, like an ice-water epidural. Then comes the surreal awareness of voices, and footsteps – even before I consciously hear them. My brain sort of freezes up. It assesses the situation and declares its independence from my body quicker than a Cuban baseball player can defect to the United States. I am left to run on autopilot, just a bunch of reflexes left to deal with this terrifying turn of events. I begin to focus on trivial things, like the fraying shoelace on the battered Nikes beside the bed; the wet smell of dog; the intricate curves of the pewter photo-frame on the dresser. Then the sound of a key slotting into the front door snaps me back to reality, giving me the impetus I need to run.

I am only a few steps away from the French doors when – *clunk* – I hear the lock on the front door surrender its grip. And that's when Spot decides he's a guard dog again. His ears prick up and he runs to the glass doors, barking his frothy head off. I come to a cartoon-like stop, and reverse direction. The front door is opening, people are laughing just a couple of sheets of plasterboard away. This is a complete disaster.

"Hey, who the fuck are you?" comes the masculine challenge, a mishmash of fear, aggression and primal curiosity.

Oh shit, oh shit, oh shit.

"I said who the fuck are—?"

"Hey wait, you're the prick from the club the other night."

Oh shit, oh shit, oh shit.

"What are you doing with my underwear, you fucking pervert?"

Oh shit, oh shit, oh shit.

I drop some underwear and run from side to side, just ten feet from the blur of growing aggression. Then I grab the only thing I can see, the television remote control. "Don't move, any of you," I scream, as I jab the remote control at the four or five figures. The funny thing is, it actually throws them. They stand there looking half shocked, half bemused.

"What the . . . it's a remote control, you moron."

"Yes . . . yes . . . that's right. How do you think it changes channels? Radiation . . . yes . . . same as mobile phones. Don't move or I'll give you all cancer." I thrust the remote control at them threateningly. They stare at me like I am absolutely, certifiably insane. If it keeps them at bay, I'll take it.

But then Terri breaks the deadlock. "You fucking, fucking, pricking, fucking . . ." She lunges at me. I press the remote control, setting the little red light off, but it doesn't stop her, doesn't even slow her down. Then the two blokes approach.

"Stay back, I'm a football hooliga—"

It's too late. A bunch of fists and feet bulldoze me to the ground. Trivial things, I focus on them again – a sort of coping mechanism, I suppose: I can smell Terri's perfume, it's pretty damn sexy; the foam boob remnant finally rips free, taking half the cap with it. And then, among all the voices and screeches, I hear a familiar voice.

"Hey, what's going on?" Someone is pulling at people, grabbing ballistic fists. "Come on guys, what's going on?"

Slowly a modicum of calm takes over. My attackers stop, and a familiar face (to match the familiar voice) looms over me. He looks down at me strangely. "I know you," he says, sounding as surprised as anyone else. "How do I know you?"

I want to help him out, believe me, but I have temporarily lost the ability to utter anything more meaningful than "Awaaar amaaar app app". Then he saves me the trouble. The clouds over his face clear and he beams; he actually smiles. That's got to be a good sign.

"You're from Jun's. You're the one who lent me the money for the burger."

"Four dollars," I say, hesitantly.

"Yeah, yeah, that's right. Terri, hey Terr', this is the guy I was telling you about, the one who restored my faith in humanity." He grins broadly and looks around for Terri. The two slack-jawed guys look at him, and then back at me. Confusion reigns.

I smile broadly back, nodding enthusiastically to all of them. "I restored his faith in humanity . . . me . . . I did."

Terri steps forward and drags her venomous eyes off me to level the guy with a ghastly look. "No, Ian," she spits, "this is the guy I was telling *you* about. The little pervert who thought I was a prostitute."

"No," Ian says. "Nahh – can't be."

Just when I think Terri's contemptuous glower can't get any nastier, it does. I don't know who she wants to hit more, me or Ian. Please let it be Ian. "Then what the fuck is he doing with my underpants?" She leaves the statement hanging in the air, with that mouth-open, go-on-top-that look mothers pass down to their daughters.

Ian's grin leaves his face. "Oh man! What are you doing with my girlfriend's underwear?"

I pick my watch up off the floor. It's 10.30 p.m. I let out a long, rhythmic sigh. "Are any of you in a particular hurry?"

• 11 •

"Ow, Sod it!"

Day five of nine begins.

I rub my head. My body aches terribly, too, but not because of the beating from the angry mob last night. On the contrary, it's because of the hospitality and sympathy of the angry mob. I feel like I've just been used for tackling-practice by the British Lions.

When the grin slid off Ian's face last night, I knew I had to spill the beans. Only the absolute truth had a chance of absolving me. And even then it was only a slim chance.

I was given my "Breast Tester" cap back, what was left of it, and ordered to sit on the cheap futon couch, while everyone positioned themselves around me in the cramped living room. The atmosphere was aggressive, but I was being allowed the chance to defend myself – probably because they didn't know what else to do with me. I sat on the far side of the couch; Terri and Ian sat hand in hand beside me, while the two other blokes looked on eagerly. Meanwhile, Spot, whose name is actually Barton, was allowed back into the house, where upon he trotted up to me, barked once, and started nuzzling my pockets. I peeled off my washing-up gloves and gave him my last Doggy Treat as I began to describe the last month to my attentive audience.

I can be pathetic. And I don't have to try very hard. Before I even got to the Fiji section I could see the empathy in everyone's eyes. Except maybe Terri's. With each pained sigh and anguished "tut" that greeted my cursed experiences, the ice melted some more. And by the time I got to my arrival on the Gold Coast, we were slugging rum and there was nothing left of their aggression but puddles (although I got the impression that Terri was still far from convinced). I went on to tell them all about Hairy Palms and Terry and Doris and Karen. And I told them about the night at Hot Shots. Basically I told them everything – except about the $50,000. I'm not completely stupid.

By the time my little monologue was finished, I was exhausted and completely sloshed, so after some cajoling from Ian, Terri let me sleep on the futon for the night.

Now my watch proclaims coldly that it is only 5.13 a.m. I try to go back to sleep, but my sludgy brain won't allow it. I try to stretch, but my aching body won't allow it. So I lie back down in an awkward little ball to face the thought I have been trying to ignore: I have no Terry Smith – male, female or otherwise. Terri confirmed it last night. The most disabling wave of depression sweeps over me. I am stuffed. The fact that I still have five days left is irrelevant. I have completely, totally and utterly exhausted all my leads.

For half an hour I stare at a crack in the wall, caught up in that dangerous state of solace where you take comfort in defeat – failure is still closure, after all. Eventually I decide to take my thoughts for a walk.

The beach is mostly deserted at such an early hour. The water moves about moodily, cold and menacing without its friend the sun. An older couple, plucked straight out of a cheesy bank commercial, have braved the dawn for a power-walk. "Good morning," they say in their hold-hands-we're-so-happy way.

"Sure is," I reply, "if you're not doomed to a life of misery and failure for no reason other than that you chose to go out with a cold-hearted bitch." I half mumble it, half yell it. It doesn't matter, Mr and Mrs Pension Scheme aren't waiting for a response. I sit down on the cold grey sand while the pre-dawn wind plays flirtatiously with my hair.

It's with this thought that I stumble across a most interesting revelation. At first I'm not sure if it's good or bad, so I kind of edge cautiously up to it, the same way you'd investigate a funny noise in the garage; it's not the impending doom of a life without luck that's depressing me, it's the fact that my adventure is over. Suddenly the solution seems simple and I get quite excited. Just keep searching for Terry Smith. But the reality of the situation is another story. I have absolutely no idea where else I can look or what else I can do to find my target. In the end I decide not to push it, and settle for cautious optimism.

With this straggly bit of quasi-closure, I let my mind drift. My body lets go of its knots and niggles and I am suddenly aware of the beach again. The sun is slowly rising over the horizon (actually the sun isn't going anywhere, it's staying right where it's been for the last however-many gazillion years). Either way, the clouds of the previous evening have gone to gloom-up some other city, and another magnificent Gold Coast day is taking shape. Out beyond the foam, a lone surfer takes off on a sudsy wave. I have to squint as the sun is getting stronger (actually, the sun is getting weaker, but we won't keep harping on about this). The surfer is just a silhouette, but what a graceful silhouette. I watch with bleary-eyed admiration as he rides the wave all the way to the beach, putting in turns and bounces and throwing up huge rooster-tails of spray. He looks so in-control, like he can counter whatever the unpredictable wave throws at him. It's not until he is walking up the beach that I realise it's Ian.

He alters his dripping course up the sand when he sees me. I tense up. I have no idea what to say to him after last night. I mean it's not every day you find a stranger rifling though your girlfriend's knickers. I shift my weight in the sand. It's one of those scenarios where you can make eye-contact long before you can start a conversation. Normally I'd look everywhere but at the person, but strangely, I don't feel compelled to with Ian. His eyes are so unassuming and friendly. Salt-stung green, set in a deeply tanned face.

"Morning, Trigg, how'd you sleep?"

"Very well, thanks."

"Really? That futon's awful. God knows I've spent my fair share of nights on it." His eyes drift slightly and I can almost see the arguments with Terri. "So, do you surf?" he asks, his eyes sauntering back to the here and now.

"Sure." I am a little concerned that the first two things I've said to Ian have been complete lies. I don't know why I said yes. Maybe to impress him.

"Well why don't we grab some breakfast, then we'll go out and catch a few."

"Absolutely." I am already thinking of ways to get out of this, and yet at the same time rejoicing in the way Ian has put things at ease.

Terri is still in bed when we get back, so Ian and I quietly eat our cornflakes and discuss my situation. I feel comfortable with this guy, like I can relax around him. That's a pretty big thing for me. But it doesn't mean that I actually do relax.

"I don't know, Trigg, if it was me . . ." Ian pauses to shovel in another spoonful of cereal from his third bowl ". . . if it was me, I'd be a little worried."

No shit, I think to myself, fully aware that Ian seems like the kind of guy who wouldn't be worried if he suddenly found himself sitting in the middle of a pack of frenzied tiger sharks with a meat-flavoured wet suit and a sign saying "Eat Me" stuck on his back.

"Still," he continues, through another mouthful of cornflakes, "it's not like we won't sort it out."

Yes. That's the spirit. That's what we want to hear.

"Unless you've got no more leads, Trigg. That could make it tough." No, not what we want to hear. "That'd make it really tough."

As Ian's summation starts to sink in, Terri emerges from the bedroom. She walks straight to Ian and gives him a long kiss on the mouth. "Morning, babe." Then her mood stiffens a little. "Morning, Trigg. How are you going?"

"Excellent, thanks." Three for three in the lying department.

"No he's not," says Ian, "he's screwed."

Terri shoots him a look that confirms his incorrigibility. "What star sign are you, Trigg?"

"Virgo."

"Virgo." She considers this for a moment. "Hmmm."

Hmmm? Is that good or bad?

♣ ♣ ♣

I never get to find out. Terri isn't really in the mood to shoot the breeze. Each attempt to start conversation is quickly dealt with and discarded. I can't really blame her, what with the whole prostitute/ breaking-in/underwear thing.

Ian walks me outside. "Don't worry about her, mate. She's still a bit pissed off. Got a lot going on at uni." Turns out Terri works part-time at Hot Shots to pay her way through university, where she's studying law. "I think she actually likes you, though."

A laugh pushes its way out my nose and I nod.

He looks over his shoulder and pushes a piece of paper into my hand. "Look, Trigg, if you need any help or whatever . . ."

I unfold the sheet of notepaper. It's a phone number. "Thanks."

"Hey. You restored my faith in humanity. It's the least I can do."

"Ian, I think you may have too much faith in humanity."

When I put the key in the ignition of the Mustang, I'm actually feeling pretty good. Twenty minutes later, however, as I pull into the Marriott driveway, it's another story. My positive perspective is slipping away, and Roger just keeps smiling at me the way an adult smiles at an over-optimistic child. It's as if my arrival back at the hotel signals the start of the game's second half. It's time to get back on the field and face the opposition: striker – a thieving teenage tease with an excellent sidestep; defenders – two very tough, very experienced veterans, each with a bag of dirty tricks and a never-say-die attitude; wing – a deceptive and frustratingly elusive Terry Smith. And as I run out of the tunnel and take the field, I look over my shoulder for my team and I see . . . no one, just a half-interested supporter in the back of the grandstand, and his girlfriend, who'd rather be out dancing.

And a water-boy. Don't forget the water-boy. Shawn motions me over with a frantic wave. "Are you going up to your room, Trigg?"

"No, Shawn, I thought I'd try someone else's room this time."

No response.

"That's a joke, Shawn."

"Oh, right . . . ha ha."

"Why do you ask?" My thoughts jump straight to Karen, but I don't want to get my hopes up.

"Oh no reason, just wondering."

We are standing under one of the giant fans in the otherwise empty foyer, staring at each other. An intellectual standoff . . . of sorts. Shawn is looking a bit too proud of himself.

"Cut the shit, Shawn, is it Karen?"

"Sorry Trigg, don't know what you're talking about."

I stare at Shawn. He stares at me. I give him my most sincere you'd-better-level-with-me-now-or-else look. He continues to smirk. "Fine," I huff, and stalk towards the lift. If that scheming little bitch is in my room I shouldn't be standing around having staring competitions anyway.

Shawn follows me into the lift and we travel up in silence. I stare impatiently at the numbers, trying to brood up enough of a storm to counter Karen's disarming looks. To be honest, I'm kind of enjoying the drama. Some of the adventure is back.

We are almost at the twenty-first floor and I am mentally rehearsing my opening line:

Karen, what are you doing here? – too boring.

What the fuck are you doing here? – too crass.

You've got a lot of explaining to do! – too much like a bad American TV drama.

Oh . . . hi there . . . uhh, Kerri isn't it? – perfect!

"Last chance, Shawn, what's going on?"

"Sorry, Trigg, it's a surprise."

As we approach my room, I whip the key-card out of my pocket with a flourish, to show him my annoyance. "Come on, Shawn, at least tell me when she got here."

"*They*, Trigg, when *they* got here."

Have you ever seen the way James Bond – or any consummate action-hero, for that matter – handles a disarming revelation? Poise, grace, like they were expecting it all along. Well, at this moment, any resemblance I bear to those characters is purely accidental. I don't stop, don't even hesitate, I just keep walking, straight past my door, straight down the corridor, and into the little room with the ice machine. *They?* I am a little thrown, to say the least. There is only one conclusion I can conjure at such short notice: "You mean she's got her brother with her?"

"Who?"

"Karen."

"What?"

"What?"

I take one last exasperated look at my door before motioning a confused-looking Shawn deeper into the ice-machine room. "Exactly who did you let into my room?"

"Your grandparents."

"My what?"

"Your grandparents."

"Shawn . . . I'm from England. A long way away. Muchos miles. It's unlikely my grandparents are going to just drop in."

Shawn gives me one of those disappointed looks a dog gives you when you're not overjoyed with your shredded, saliva-soaked newspaper. "They wanted to drop off your driver's licence."

"My driver's licence? Bloody hell, Shawn, it's Terry and Doris! Oh, this is not good. I'm buggered. How did they find me? Shit, really not good." This time there is no accidental poise or grace, I merely stand there, whimpering. Sure, an elderly couple probably aren't the scariest underworld figures around, but they're the scariest underworld figures I know. "What the hell are we going to do, Shawn?"

The assistant concierge raises his eyebrows. "We?" He turns quickly for the door. I grab him.

"Come on, you let them up here. Into my bloody room! You can't leave me here alone."

"Trigg, get a grip. They're pensioners."

"Yeah, it's like a double whammy. First they bore you with stories about their bowels, then they kill you."

"Trigg, what the hell is going on?"

"Look, just tell me this, is the woman in my room about seventy, with an orange rinse? And the guy's about the same age and looks like his eyebrows lost a fight with a Van de Graaff generator?"

Shawn nods.

"Okay, they're not my grandparents, Shawn, they're drug dealers. And I did something to really piss them off, which is why they're looking for me."

Shawn smiles, nods, waits for the punch-line.

"Look, Shawn, you're just going to have to trust me on this one. I'll give you the full explanation later, but right now you've got to get them out of there without them seeing me."

Shawn frowns, like he was just about to sneeze but couldn't.

"Okay, here's what we'll do. You'll need to borrow an outfit from the kitchen, something white and sterile-looking . . . and a hairnet . . . and then we'll get you some stuff from the nurse's room – a face mask, a stethoscope, you know. You put it all on, they won't recognise you. Then you come up here and knock on the door. When they answer it, you explain that you're a doctor from the Gold Coast Hospital and that you specialise in infectious diseases – you'll have to make your voice deeper. Then you tell them that what's happened is you've traced a particularly nasty case of . . . botulism . . . to my room. We'll get you some technological-looking things, too . . . pH testers from the pool . . . and you can wave them around and look concerned. Then you ask them if they've been feeling okay, and no matter what they say you look shocked and say that that's the first sign of serious infection. Then you tell them they have to get to the Gold Coast Hospital immediately. That's when you accompany them down to the foyer and put them in a cab. Okay?"

Now he looks like he was just about to sneeze, but farted instead.

"Well, have you got any better ideas?" I say.

"I could tell them you called the hotel from Byron Bay to say you'll be away for a few days."

"Yes . . . well I suppose we could try that."

♣ ♣ ♣

Shawn knocks on the door of room 2103 and I push a little further back into the ice-machine room. It's a long time before the door opens and Terry sticks his head out. I strain to hear what's going on, but I can't make out anything over the buzz of the refrigerator behind me. Terry looks frustrated, though, and Shawn is doing a lot of head shaking and ignorant gesticulating. When Doris appears at the door a moment later, she places a controlling hand on Terry's shoulder. They all talk for a couple of minutes, then Terry closes the door, leaving Shawn standing alone. He gives me a quick wink.

"What?" I mouth, using a big questioning hand-gesture. He winks again, nods and looks back towards the door.

I try to get his attention. "Pssst."

Nothing.

"Psssssssst."

Still nothing.

"Pssssssssssssssssssssssssssst."

Shawn finally turns in my direction, looking very annoyed. "What's going on?" I whisper, using the big questioning hand-gesture again.

He is still looking at me as if to say "Shut up and get back in your hole", when the door opens again. Doris looks at the assistant concierge and immediately follows his line of sight. I jump blindly back into the ice room and trip over the ice buckets. My landing is not pretty, nor is it quiet. I end up on the ground, wanting desperately to whimper for the sake of my aching back-side, but wanting even more desperately to stay quiet, on the off-chance that Doris didn't see me.

And that's how Shawn finds me, five minutes later, still clutching my arse, with a frightened, pained expression on my face. "What happened?" I ask him. The question squeaks out about two octaves higher than expected.

Shawn offers to help me up, but I decline. He tells me how smoothly everything went. At first Terry and Doris were a little dubious. But in the end they left, on the proviso that Shawn call them as soon as I return. And that he keep their visit a surprise. The strange noises coming from the little room down the corridor didn't help, but some fast talking from Shawn sorted that out – something about the ice machine being on the fritz. He then accompanied the two pensioners downstairs and into their car.

Shawn obviously wants a more detailed explanation of my predicament, or a tip, because he's looking at me in a very expectant way. But I need to think about my next move. After many promises to give him all the details later, Shawn leaves me alone in my room. And I leave him with strict instructions to keep an eye out for Terry and Doris, just in case they don't buy his story.

I push aside a pile of folded clothes on my bed and lie down. There are more clothes stacked on the chair and the desk. What the hell is all this about? I didn't leave them there. I haven't folded clothes since I was fourteen. And then it happens again, that sinking, blood-heading-south feeling. Christ, the money!

I swing my head around. The mirrored wardrobe door is wide open. The safe is closed, but looks far too vulnerable for my liking. The code? What's the code? My mind has seized up. For a minute I don't have the slightest clue what the four precious numbers are. Assorted telephone numbers, birthdays and PIN numbers all make good cases. My finger is poised over the keypad like a flaccid penis.

Oh of course! 1966, the last time sport made the front page for a good reason.

With a big swallow and shaking hands I punch in the code. There is a pause as the safe thinks about it. Then the light goes from red to green. Like taking off a plaster . . . I slowly ease it open, bit by bit (I'm not particularly brave when it comes to pain). I peek inside . . .

The relief is overwhelming.

I quickly pick up the folded clothes – one of the benefits of being ransacked by the elderly, I suppose – and put them in my suitcase. I have to leave the Marriott. I have to leave now. At this moment, it's the only thing in my life I am sure about. Loneliness once again strides confidently over the dance floor of my psyche, taps adventure on the shoulder, and asks if it can cut in. It doesn't matter where I go, I've still got no leads. And now I've got the Bingo Mafia after me, too. If they can track me down here, who knows where else they can find me.

Downstairs, I give Shawn the closest thing I can to a full explanation. I tell him about the curse and looking for Terry Smith. I also give him a whopping tip. He asks me where I'm going, so I tell him I'm staying with friends in Brisbane, just in case Terry and Doris come back to pull out his fingernails.

So here I am, a bruised, sunburned pom with $10,000 in dirty money, a ladies' suitcase, a dodgy body-board, and a sinister little bastard called Roger, smiling incessantly at me. It isn't long before I realise I have to call Ian.

We meet at a health food place, in a booth at the back. Ian chews silently on his veggie-burger as I tell him about Terry and Doris and the money. When he's finished, he wipes his mouth and shrugs. "Come and stay at my place."

Simple as that. To be honest, as soon as he'd reassured me that he didn't live with Terri, I was kind of hoping he would say that. In fact, I couldn't have laid down more hints with a cement mixer.

As I follow Ian's rundown brown Kingswood along the highway, I try not to think about the sort of home a surfer might occupy. I'm sure it sits more on the Hairy Palms side of the disinfectant bottle than the Marriott side. And what if the two guys from the other night live there? They didn't exactly take a shine to me. Imaginary fleas are already crawling over my body as I see the Kingswood's brake-lights glow. I am expecting Ian to turn right, but he turns left.

"Bloody hell," I mutter, as I follow the Kingswood into the driveway. A large timber house squats lazily in front us, the only thing between us and the beach. A few bushy bougainvillaea with bright red flowers block out the concrete monstrosities on either side. This can't possibly be Ian's house.

He manoeuvres the Kingswood into the garage, then comes over to give me a hand with my stuff.

"How many banks did you rob?" I ask, as we pull my suitcase from the back seat. Ian chuckles politely. He thinks I'm joking.

The house is a defiant protestor against the Gold Coast's obsession with themed architecture and concrete. From the driveway it doesn't look Italian, it doesn't look Greek. It's not Spanish and it's not Balinese. It's just a beach house: dark timber, decent yard, lots of glass. I shake my head slowly in disbelief and go through a list of possible explanations: filthy rich parents, lotto, life insurance scam, organised crime. I'm dying to know the answer, but I'm silenced by something unfamiliar – tact.

Inside, Ian gives me the dossers' tour. Downstairs is split in two, one side for the garage, one for the laundry, pool table, gym, wetsuits and surfboards, which are scattered over the floor. A big sliding glass door leads out onto a neat little patch of grass before a few straggly bits of dune grass herald the start of the beach. "I spend most of my time upstairs," Ian says. When we get there I can see why.

He waves his hand around the big open-plan room. "This is . . . umm, I don't know . . . the living room?"

It's hard to tell which is out of place, the beautiful old dining table built from recycled wood, or the big plasma TV. They both look like they belong . . . just not with each other. It's the setup of someone who doesn't care about aesthetics – or someone who cares a lot.

Ian quickly shows me the two bedrooms, the bathroom and the kitchen, all of which are remarkably tidy and symmetrical. But the pièce de résistance of the whole house is beyond the four walls. Two big glass doors open to a massive timber deck, the beach at your doorstep, literally. I've never seen anything like it in the UK – or the Costa del Sol, for that matter. I feel I could jump from the balcony railing and land on the sand. And on top of this, there is a big deckchair and a hammock. It's just about the perfect beach set up, better than the Marriott, and it makes Hairy Palms look like . . . well, Hairy Palms.

I sit Roger in the hammock, hoping the view might cheer him up and stop him being such a vindictive little wanker, while Ian dumps my stuff in the second bedroom. It brings back memories of the expensive holidays Kelly and I used to go on, and the anticipation of standing at the hotel door, fiddling with the key, waiting to see just how good the room was going to be. And once it had surpassed all expectations, the simple delight of knowing we had the next few days to just loll about in it. Contentedness is not something that has been in abundance for me lately, but right now I'm swimming in it. And it feels good. Except for one thing. That question, stinging me like sea-lice: How the hell does a bummed-out surfer come to live in a place like this?

Oh well, tact be damned. "So, I suppose you don't work on a Sunday?" I say.

"Oh, I dunno," Ian replies, "depends on how you look at it. I guess I work every day."

He doesn't offer anything else. Hmm, fifteen-love to Ian.

I don't get any more information out of him, but I do get some food and a couple of beers. A nice runner-up prize. We spend several hours just sitting out on the deck. Terri has gone to the university to work on an assignment, so it's just Ian and me. We talk – not so much a conversation punctuated by silences, rather the other way around. Neither of us say much, neither of us feel we need to. It can take married couples years to reach this stage.

♣ ♣
12

"The point is, Ian," I slur, "not just that Benny Hill was a genius, but that the little old man he often patted on the head, he was a genius, too. They were geni-eye. That the plural of genius?"

One of the two Ians in front of me laughs. "I guess there's a fine line between genius and pervert."

I attempt to sit up in the deckchair. "Geniuses? Maybe it's geniuses. Ian?"

Ian is saved the ignominy of replying by the phone ringing.

"That was Terri," he says on his return. "I was supposed to be going out to dinner with her, but she's going to stay back at uni for a while. We should grab something to eat. What do you feel like?"

The casino greets us with open arms, the ones it wraps around you while it feels for your wallet. Ian and I eat at the café, and in between mouthfuls of pasta and more beer, I quietly explain Karen's money-laundering system.

Ian is probably a little apprehensive; I'm so hammered I honestly can't tell. He doesn't seem like the kind of guy to flirt with the law, but then Karen didn't seem like the kind to steal $30,000. I plough on, and with a little perseverance I finally recruit the lanky surfer as my partner in crime.

The first time it happens, I take no notice. Nor the second. But when two excitable young girls approach, their breasts thrust out, it becomes a little hard to ignore.

"You're Ian Berrisford, aren't you?" says one.

Ian looks at his feet, shrugs, nods.

The other girl flicks her hair. "It's really nice to meet you, Ian."

"I'm Trigger Harvey," I say to the girls' breasts.

"Look, Trigg, why don't I meet you at the table we agreed on, okay?" says Ian awkwardly.

I leave him with the two girls and concentrate on finding the roulette table. Very strange, all these people who seem to know Ian.

I sit for ages at the roulette table, watching while Ian is slapped on the back by person after person. Drugs, I think to myself, he has to be selling drugs. Explains everything really. Or maybe he's on *Neighbours*.

"Sorry about that, Trigg," Ian says as he finally takes a seat.

I bury my fuzzy head in my fuzzy hands.

"Oh . . . bugger . . . sorry," he says.

Now he remembers that we aren't supposed to know each other. I look up at the croupier, a woman about my age with a pointy face, tanned skin and too much red in her lipstick. She doesn't appear to know Ian, but she can't stop looking at him. An excited glint dances about her eyes as she struggles to maintain the lithium demeanour her job requires. She can't stop the smile that Etch-a-Sketches its way across her face. I pick up my chips and move to another table. Definitely a drug dealer. I'm living with a drug dealer.

I slurp drunkenly on a gin and tonic at another roulette table as Ian fights his way over. Yet again, the croupier can't help but take quick glances at the shaggy-haired surfer. This time it's a guy, about thirty, with deep lines splaying out from the corners of his eyes into his tanned, square face. "Do you know that guy?" I ask the croupier.

"Yeah, that's Ian Berrisford."

I pick up my chips and drink and walk to another table.

I am fast running out of tables, but this time I'm in luck. The croupier is a middle-aged Asian man who shows no interest in Ian whatsoever. And to Ian's credit, he manages to take his seat without so much as a peek in my direction. Now if only the room will stop spinning, we'll be in business. I take another sip of my gin.

"Twenty-four . . . red," calls the croupier. He collects up my chips, which are sitting on black, counts them up, and places them beside Ian's chips, which are sitting on red. For half an hour it's easy-peasy. But when you're living outside of the cocoon, in pursuit of your luck, nothing stays that way for long.

Karen!

My glass, and what's left of my drink, tumble to the floor. The table shakes as I jump to my feet and grab my chips. The croupier yells after me as I take off but I'm too drunk to take much notice, especially since the commotion has caught Karen's attention. Even through the layers of clingfilm that seem to have been placed over my eyes, I see her eyes as clear as day. Just for a fraction of a second, before she turns and hurries through the crowd.

I take up the chase, and the casino tilts to the left, causing me to stumble to the floor. Somewhere behind me there's one hell of a ruckus, but it sounds too distant to worry about. I haul myself to my feet again and get back to basics: one foot in front of the other. I lose count of the number of people I run into. I bob and weave and lurch and dodge, and every now and then I am rewarded with a glimpse of a hazy thatch of long dark hair in the distance. She's making for the exit.

And then I'm on the floor.

A large security guard leans into my shaky view as I lie flat on my back. I can only assume that he was responsible for knocking me down. With an appalling lack of foreplay, he hauls me to my feet by my trousers and locks my right arm behind my back, bending it like a paperclip. But he doesn't have my left arm.

I launch what must be over $500 in chips into the air. Acting on impulse, I slur at the top of my lungs: "Scaaaab graaaab!" People come from everywhere, and the space around me becomes a veritable frenzy. I end up on the ground again, but so does the security guard, and I'm back on my feet in a flash. Well, maybe not quite a flash, considering the alcohol I have in my system, but quicker than the security guard at any rate. I trundle towards the exit and in the commotion I manage to get out of the casino and into the foyer.

But there's no Karen.

I sprint down the stairs towards the carpark.

I tumble down the stairs towards the carpark.

I lurch into the carpark.

But there's no Karen.

There is, however, a flaking maroon VW, just pulling out of the carpark. I muster all my functioning neurones and run. Over the gutter, along the footpath, through the garden. I emerge at full sprint, just behind the reluctant piece of German engineering. It buzzes along, gathering speed and sending plumes of blue exhaust smoke my way. But I smell nothing. I feel nothing. I am numb-drunk.

Suddenly a red glow invades my vision. The brake lights! I run full speed into the back of the Volkswagen.

I smell nothing. I feel nothing . . . I am unconscious.

♣ ♣

13

"Oh my God, Trigg . . . I'm so sorry."

"About braking, or about taking the money?"

"About everything."

♣ ♣
14

I can't move my head. Even the slightest, fraction-of-a-millimetre shift sends little swords of excruciating pain through my brain. I don't know if it's a hangover or the aftermath of my collision with the Beetle last night. It has to be both. And I think someone must have kicked me in the back of the head for good measure. Maybe it was Karen.

In those rare moments when I open my eyes, I can make out the spare bedroom in Ian's house. How I got back here is anyone's guess. The last thing I remember is running after Karen's car . . . no, wait . . . I woke up, that's right, and she was there. She apologised, I think. Actually, it hurts to think.

I get out of bed about half an hour later. I don't want to, but it's that or throw up on the floorboards.

With the remaining toxins from the previous night now flowing through the Gold Coast sewer system, I feel a little better. Well enough to throw back a couple of aspirin, anyway. I take a long, cool shower to wash away more toxins, then I take my sorry head and burning throat out into the living room, picking up a note that Ian has written.

Ian's house is even more outstanding in the morning. The sun streams in through the open glass doors, like a movie star entering a party. And the kitchen window plays picture-frame to the natural beachy beauty beyond. Ian's note says he's gone surfing. I squint at my watch – 8.25 a.m. Keen bean, I think to myself. I'm glad he's out, though. My ambition to be a model houseguest is far from being realised.

I help myself to some cornflakes and the deckchair. More bits and pieces of the previous night make themselves known to me. By far the most vivid and enticing of them revolves around Karen's feet. I hadn't seen them before – well, of course I'd *seen* them, I would have noticed if she hadn't had any feet, but I'd never really paid them much attention.

Gingerly, I send some cornflakes down to see how my stomach is going. They don't report back, so I send down some more.

Nice feet, they were. Not small and dainty, but not like flippers either. Probably a pleasant odour as feet go. The feet of a doer, a girl who'll give anything a go. Feet that scream of adventure and fun from within their beaten sandals. Oh if only those sandals could talk. If only they had tongues. Tongues! You've got to admire a pun in the face of adversity; it's what separates the action heroes from the extras.

"Hey, morning, Trigg. You sleep okay?"

I crane my neck slowly so that I can see over the railing. Ian is standing on the grass. He's either trying to shake water out of his ear or he's developed a chiropractor's dream tic. "Is being unconscious the same as sleeping?"

"I think so."

"Then I slept very well."

"Good."

I wait until Ian has got all the water out and jogged up the stairs before I launch into my heartfelt apology. To say I feel awful about my behaviour yesterday is an understatement. Ian has taken me in, been a chum without even knowing me, and I repay him by getting sloshed, bombarding him with Benny Hill trivia and manipulating him into coming to the casino where I do my best to get us arrested.

But Ian responds as only Ian can: a sheepish look, a "Don't be silly".

"I'm a big boy, Trigg. I can make decisions for myself. Besides, it was kinda fun . . . I was thinking we could go back this arvo."

"Are you kidding? That's the . . ." I hold off on telling Mr Neon Sign that I can't possibly go to the casino with him again. ". . . Sure, maybe this afternoon. Good surf?"

"Yeah, it's a little sloppy . . . nor'easter – you know how it is."

"Absolutely." I have no idea what a nor'easter is.

Ian proceeds to rummage about in the kitchen and emerges with a massive pasta bowl of cornflakes, which he refills a few minutes later.

"So what exactly was last night all about?"

"Ahh yes. Well, I'll tell you my bit, and then if you can fill in the gaps, we should have something resembling an account."

Ian nods.

"Okay. First I got so drunk I thought I was Boris Yeltsin . . . then I saw Karen. That's why I took off. I was trying to stop her, but people kept jumping out in front of me, trying to stop me—"

"Like that elderly Chinese woman you knocked down?"

"Exactly, the Chinese woman. And tables and chairs. And eventually some security guard, who knocked me on my arse. I guess he thought I was trying to steal chips or something. Anyway, this security guard was huge, well-hard – must have been on the juice" – I make the hypodermic-needle-injecting-into-arm action – "and he hauls me up and tries to secure me. But I was driven, Ian; on a mission. We had a bit of a scuffle, the guard and me. I think he took a few swings, but I was too quick, and as I ducked under a right cross, I came up and landed one plumb on his jaw and knocked him into—"

"You threw your chips in the air and yelled 'scab grab'. It was an eighteen stone Samoan woman who knocked the guard down, trying to get to your chips. Knocked you both down, actually. Now *she* was driven."

"Really? I could have sworn . . . anyway, I managed to get away – *one way or the other* – and bolted down to the carpark. That's where I saw Karen's car, just driving away. So I took off after it. I made it out onto the road and then . . . then I think she ran me down."

"The way I heard it you ran into the back of the car."

"What?"

"Well, the car had to slow down for a speed bump, you kept running—"

"No, no, I mean you *spoke* to her, you spoke to Karen?"

"Uhh, young girl. Very pretty?"

"With nice feet."

"I suppose, I didn't really look at her feet."

"I can't believe you spoke to Karen. Sweet Jesus, you had her. If only you'd known it was her."

"Yeah, that's a bit of a trip isn't it? I would never have guessed though. This girl seemed really upset about hurting you, really genuine – not the cold piece of work you described."

"Yes, well don't let her fool you. She's a cold-hearted, thieving little bitch . . . with nice feet."

"And a cute smile."

"She does have a cute— No! She's a little terrorist, a modern-day Bonnie and her brother or neighbour or whoever that guy at the house is, that's her Clyde."

"Well anyway," Ian continues, "I found this cold-hearted Bonnie stroking your face and crying. But that's not the weird thing, what's funny is that when I turned up, she seemed to know that I was with you. Straight away she told me what happened, handed you over to me and then left."

"Well, *everyone* seemed to know you, Ian. What's all that about?"

"What do you mean?"

"At the casino. Every second person stopped to say hello to you."

"Oh well, you know how it is."

"No."

"Just friendly, I s'pose."

"Come on, Ian, not even Barney the Dinosaur has that many friends."

"Well . . ."

"Are you dealing drugs, Ian?"

"Come again?"

"Nothing. Sorry, never mind." It's time to shut up while I still have a friend. And a host. Besides, the look on Ian's face tells me that slinging crack is not his thing. Mind you, I've already been sucked in by Karen's apparent sincerity. I mumble something to Ian about my head still being a bit messed up and he finishes the story. Apparently I came to for a while in the taxi, blubbering something about the difference between paedophilia and indecent assault. That sounds about right.

"Listen Trigg, just a warning," Ian says. "Terri's not overly impressed with your effort last night."

"What? How did she find out?"

"Ahh . . . I told her."

"You told her?"

"Well, I thought it was funny."

"Oh bollocks."

"Yeah. Look, she might be on the warpath. But don't worry, just keep your head down."

Ian stands to leave, but I stop him with a hungover hand. "Ian, why are you doing this for me?"

"I told you Trigg, you helped me out, you restored my faith in humanity."

I shake my head. "Seriously, why?"

"That is serious, Trigg. And now you're down on your luck, so I'm helping you out. It's karma."

"Jesus, you're not going to sell me a smiley face sticker are you?"

"No, I'm talking about real life karma. Nothing mystical. Just doing for other people what you'd hope they'd do for you if the situation was reversed. Besides, Trigg, I just . . . I just get on well with you. It just happens that way with some people. And I like the fact that you have no idea who I am . . ." He stops.

"What do you mean?"

He thinks for a second, shakes his head. "Never mind."

I nod. Cryptic bastard. "Hey," I call out, as he walks inside, "I feel the same way."

Ian smiles awkwardly.

My host has to go out for a few hours, something to do with photographs, which he seems a little coy about. It gives me the rest of the morning to try and put my life in some sort of order – when

I'm not thinking about Karen. I get the phonebook out to double-check for T. Smiths, hoping desperately that I've missed one. I haven't. I call directory enquiries and ask for T. Smiths from the Gold Coast. They give me even fewer than are in the phonebook. Things are not looking good. I rack my brain trying to think of another way to find my man.

The only other thing I can think of is to get my hands on an electoral roll. And I have no idea how to do that. Do I break into the council chambers? Kidnap a politician? I resolve to ask Terri later. She's studying law, after all, so she might have some ideas. If she doesn't rip my head off first.

I throw my suitcase on the bed and make four piles: dirty clothes, clean clothes, dirty money, clean money. Unfortunately the two dirty piles are far larger than the two clean piles. I can't do much about the money without someone to help me, so I cram the cash into one of my shoes and hide it in the wardrobe. The clothing dilemma, however, can be solved.

The laundry looks as if it hasn't seen much in the way of apparel-cleansing action. There's no scungy build-up of detergent, the washing machine still has the plastic film over the control buttons, and the inside of the drier is like a mirror. But then again, board-shorts and T-shirts don't demand much washing.

I empty my clothes into the sparkling tub of the washing machine and start searching for detergent. When I open the third cupboard along, it starts an avalanche . . . and very quickly, clean clothes no longer seem like a priority.

Magazines and news-clippings cover the laundry floor. And every one features Ian. He's on the cover of more surfing magazines than I could poke my boogie-board at. And the news clippings have headlines such as: "AUSSIE CLEANS UP IN HAWAII".

"Bugger me!" I mumble. This guy's a surfing god. I mean, I thought he was good, but this is ridiculous. There are even ads for board-shorts and wetsuits and stuff, all featuring Ian. He's got sponsors!

As I flick through the clippings, I began to realise how a young surfer might afford a house like this. There are photos of Ian holding up big novelty cheques with lots of zeros on them. His entire body seems to be leased by shoe-, clothing- and sunglasses-companies. I am living with surfing royalty and I didn't even recognise him. I don't deserve to own the Bandit. I shuffle through some more clippings, and just when I think I'll get away without the help of a facial surgeon, my jaw drops even further.

Berrisford Wins World Title

In perfect twelve-foot waves at the Banzai Pipeline on the North Shore of Oahu, Australian surfer Ian Berrisford clinched his first world title. Berrisford needed only to make the final to secure the crown for 2002, but the Aussie went one better and won the Pipe Masters event with a consummate display of tube-riding.

Sweet Jesus! That explains the casino. All those young, tanned people slapping him on the back, giving him admiring looks.

I jump a mile when I hear Ian's car pull into the driveway. My gut reaction is to simultaneously begin cramming magazines back into the cupboard and rehearsing excuses. I get the cupboard sorted just in time, but not the excuses. And now I'm breathing heavily and sweating.

In my panic, I jump onto one of the pieces of gym equipment.

"Jeez, that bugs me, Trigg," Ian says as he saunters in. "They set up a time, then they change it at the last minute. Happens so often . . . what are you doing?"

"Just thought I'd get a bit of a workout in."

"Cool." Pause. "You know, it works better if you stack some weights on it."

"Oh. Okay."

"And face the right way."

". . . I'm pretty much done anyway."

Ian nods, then his face brightens "Great, we can go for that surf."

"Yes . . . Oh no . . . I really blasted my shoulders on the weights.

It's probably best if I give them a bit of a break."

"Oh right. Yeah, that's probably best. Do you mind if I go out? I'm trying to get in at least two surfs a day."

"Sure, sure. We all have to work."

Ian brightens again. "Hey, we can go tomorrow morning. Down to Kirra. There's supposed to be a new swell coming through."

"Really? Ahh . . . big swell?"

"Oh, you know, six foot or so."

Six foot? I look at Ian. He looks about six foot. That's not so bad. "Sounds good, mate. What time do you think?"

"Oh, around five-ish."

"Five-ish? Great, great."

"Cool." And with that, Ian takes off his T-shirt, ties the drawstring on his board-shorts, and picks up a surfboard from the pile that lie scattered on the floor. "Oh, are you going to be around in a bit?" he asks.

"Sure."

"Good. Terri's coming around. You can give me a hand."

"Sure. With what?"

"Terri's stuff. She's moving in here this arvo."

My mouth remains a gaping chasm as he disappears over the neat little strip of lawn.

I am so dead.

I quickly tidy up the magazine cupboard and run back upstairs. Grabbing all my stuff, I throw it into my suitcase. I'm not planning on doing a runner, but I want to be able to disappear quickly if the need arises.

A kind of tense nausea overcomes me as I walk around the house, with no particular destination in mind. I flick on the TV and flick it off again. I pick up a pair of binoculars and wander out onto the deck. There's a topless sunbather . . . and another one. But not even these saucy beach fungi can distract me. I look out to sea. There's a large pack of teenage surfers. Strange thing about the Gold Coast – at any time, be it the middle of a school day or the middle of the night, there will always be a pack of surly teenage surfers within a stoned throw of you.

Suddenly the pack seems to part, as a wave comes through. And there is Ian, right in the middle of them. He takes off on the wave and what he does on it blows me away. He zooms along one way, then suddenly throws his surfboard up into the breaking lip and comes zooming back down the other way. And he makes it all look so effortless.

"Is it the Ian Berrisford show again?"

I forget to keep my head down as I turn, but it doesn't matter. Terri isn't even looking at me. There's no anger in her eyes, just pride. She smiles. "You know, he loves it, really. All the kids and stuff. He tries to make out that it's no big deal, but if they weren't there, I think he'd be pretty disappointed."

I smile too, for my own reasons, as Barton scrapes across the deck and nuzzles my hand. "So how's the world of law going?" I ask.

"It's going. There are enough lawyers to make sure it never stops."

"Hey that reminds me of a joke . . . I guess it reminds everyone of a joke. Do lawyer jokes piss you off?"

"Only when lawyers tell them. Honestly, if I had a dollar for the number of lecturers who start the class with a lawyer joke, I'd probably have enough to sue them for misrepresentation."

Terri sits in the hammock. She has to move Roger, who's been there all night and is probably well pissed off by now. I don't care in the slightest. With any luck the damp sea air will have penetrated him and he'll already be rotting from the inside.

"Look, Terri, about your moving in here; I had no idea—"

Terri silences me with a taloned hand. "I know what Ian's like. I'm sure he didn't say anything to you until it was too late. And anyway, it's his house, he can do what he wants. I'm just glad to be out of my little shit-box."

Terri and I watch Ian in relatively companionable silence. Barton collapses in a shady corner with his tongue lolling on the dark wood. Then Terri speaks. "So what are you going to do now?"

I consider this for a good minute before responding. "Honestly, I don't really know. It's bizarre, but not once have I questioned this whole situation. I mean, all I've got is some strange little Fijian fella telling me to find a Terry Smith on the Gold Coast with a wooden figurine like mine and – hey presto – my problems will all be over. For all I know, Philip Matango could be some village fisherman who's sucked down too much kava and caught too much sun. What's to say this Terry Smith's even here? Hell, what's to suggest that he even exists? I mean, this could all just be a wild-goose chase . . ."

"You're hardly one to talk about sucking down too much kava."

"Oh. Yes. Last night. Look, I had a few drinks, and if you must know, I actually pulled off some pretty clever stuff."

"You ran into the back of a parked car."

"It was not parked! It was slowing down . . ."

Terri lets out a disturbingly unfeminine hack of laughter. "What are you? A dog?"

"Actually, I was chasing after Karen."

This shuts her up.

For about three seconds.

"You're kidding!" she says, suddenly wide-eyed and curious. "I thought she'd done a runner."

I throw my hands up in the air. "Apparently not."

"Hey, maybe she's a bunny-boiler," Terri continues with an excitement I haven't seen in her before. "Maybe she's pissed that you wouldn't sleep with her and she's stalking you. Yeah, she's got your money and now she wants your . . . your . . . your little Trigger Junior. Did she have scissors?"

"She's not stalking me to cut off my penis."

Ian chooses that moment to plonk his exhausted self into the deckchair. He looks quite relieved that Terri and I are talking. "Who's cutting off whose penis?"

"No one," I snap. "No one is losing any pieces of their anatomy in the near future. Now, since you're both here, I need to ask the two of you a question."

They ignore me.

"He still likes her you know," Ian says to Terri.

"Who, the bunny-boiler?"

"She is not a bunny— a stalker . . . she's only sixteen!" I interject.

"Yeah," Ian continues, seemingly unaware of my presence, "I can understand it, though, she is a cute one."

Terri nods. "It's always the cute ones." She follows this with the knife-stabbing motion from *Psycho*.

"Jesus, give her a break will you! She's just a kid," I retaliate.

"See?" Ian says to Terri. "I told you he still likes her."

"Do you, Trigg? Do you still like her?"

"I . . . for God's sake . . . I . . . well, she does have nice feet."

In its own way, it's a beautiful scene. We're sitting out on the deck, bantering away like three friends from way back. For a moment it's easy to imagine another life. A life where I live on the coast and the three of us are old chums. But where is Karen? What about my luck?

Like I said, it's just a moment.

I blink hard. "Look, enough about Karen. I really need your help with something."

"Hmm?" says Terri. "It's not illegal is it?"

"No, no, it's nothing illegal – I don't think. Actually maybe it is. I don't know. That's what I want you to tell me. I need to get my hands on an electoral roll. Any ideas?"

"Have you considered just calling the state electoral commission?"

"Well of course . . . but . . . no."

"Just call the electoral commission."

I get the phonebook and look up the number for the electoral commission. I finally find it in the "Government" section and pick up the phone.

"How did you go?" Ian asks when I return to the deck.

I shake my head. "What a game! The woman wouldn't tell me anything at first, so I had to tell her I was registering a website under my name – www.terrysmith.goldcoast.com – and that I wanted to check with any other Terry Smiths to make sure they were okay with it. Pretty good, right? Yes, well, still no-go. So I gave her Terri's old address, and drug-dealer Terry's address, and told her that I'd already checked with these two, but I just wanted to know if there were any more. She said she couldn't give out addresses to the public. So I said I didn't want addresses, I just want to know if there are any more Terry Smiths on the Gold Coast.

"And?"

I sigh, shake my head again. "She says the electoral commission does not give out that sort of information to the public."

"Ouch. You're really screwed."

"Ta."

"Don't top yourself just yet, Trigg," says Terri, "I can go check at the uni. Heaps of students come from interstate. And what about the internet? You'd be surprised what you can find."

Actually, after some of the email attachments I've been sent in my time, I don't think anything on the internet would surprise me. It's well worth a shot.

"You can use my laptop," says Ian.

"Or," Terri interrupts him, "you can use my computer."

"But it's not set up yet . . . oh, I get it. Come on, Trigg, can you give us a hand with Terr's stuff?"

My plans are temporarily put on hold while Terri heads back to the university and Ian and I unpack a carload of her stuff. It gives me a chance to talk to Ian about his surfing. He's a little unresponsive until I confess my discovery of the magazine cupboard. He starts off slowly, modestly, but warms up.

"It was a real mixed blessing," he says, as he scratches his head with a stray curling-wand. "World title made me a lot of money, but totally changed my life. Suddenly it's all about interviews and appearances. I had hundreds of new 'friends'. I'd just started seeing Terri but I didn't have time for her. You can imagine how that went down. The next year I came seventh. Just couldn't hack the pressure."

"And then?"

"Well, my sponsors and new friends began to lose interest. I sort of realised that it's a pretty fickle world, no matter what you do. I guess that's when I figured out that I'm in control, you know, the good and the bad. No point blaming someone else, or hoping they'll get you out of a fix. Next year I won the world title again. Then I quit. I'm still sponsored, and every now and then I'll go and do a video or something, but I don't do the tour. It's much better now."

We finish unpacking Terri's little bubble Mazda and set to work on the computer. Ian's words are still fresh in my mind: no point blaming someone else, or hoping they'll get you out of a fix. My old close-my-eyes-and-hope-it-goes-away attitude just won't do anymore.

Having set the computer up, we try ten different search engines with a hundred permutations. Nothing. The Gold Coast City Council site? Nothing. It looks hopeless until we get to the Australian Bureau of Statistics site. I wipe forty minutes of computer radiation from my eyes and stare with growing trepidation at the screen. We've taken a turn-off from the information superhighway, driven down through an information super-town, and somehow wound up in this promising information super-alleyway. The site offers no addresses or phone numbers, but it does offer listings of residents based on 2004 census results. And they are divided by electoral zones. It's basically the information that the woman refused to give me earlier.

I stretch my neck from side to side and swallow. A long, dry swallow. This is a rather big moment.

I click my way to the Gold Coast zone, then I click on "Sm-So". With my nervous, damp fingers I scroll the cursor down the page until I find the Smiths. There are hundreds of them, heaps more than in the phonebook. I click on until I reach the Ts.

I scroll down further.

There is a "Terri".

And a "Terry".

And that's it.

A breeze kicks up in the little spare room that is to be Terri's study. I am numb. Never has the hopelessness of my situation been delivered to me so succinctly or in a way that is so conducive to just sitting and dwelling. Ian puts a hand on my shoulder. It does nothing. As a double whammy, Terri returns home and delivers the news that there are no Terry Smith's registered at the university. This is a lot different to coming seventh in the World Surfing Championships.

"Are you sure you didn't miss any?" Terri asks.

Well, Terri, maybe I did, because, you know, I tend to take the single most important thing in my life pretty haphazardly . . . "Yes, I'm sure."

"Did you check for Terrance Smith?"

"Yes . . . well . . . *bugger*! Look, I'm sure there weren't any, I would have seen them."

"Well then, it's been nice knowing you."

My emotions are starting to win the arm-wrestle with my common sense. "What the fuck am I supposed to do now?"

"Hey, come on, mate, it's not all that bad," Ian soothes, "don't forget we're going for that surf in the morning."

"Yes. Terrific."

"Look, I know it seems impossible now," he says, "but you've got . . . how many days have you got left?"

"Three."

"You've got half a week left, man. You're just over halfway and look how much you've done already – on your own. Now you've got two assistants. We'll start asking around at Kirra tomorrow, those guys know everything that's happening within a mile of the sand. Jesus, Trigg, we'll comb the whole Gold Coast. Terry Smith – *your* Terry Smith – is here somewhere, and we'll find him. It's no big deal. I mean, sure, if you had one day left or something, then you'd have every right to be getting a little panicky, but three days, three-and-a-half really . . . that's ages."

I raise an eyebrow at Ian's questionable maths, but let it pass in favour of a more depressing statistic. "There are no more Terry Smiths here, remember?"

"Are you kidding me? Only about half the people who live on the Gold Coast are actually registered here. People come and go all the time. That's the way it is. I guarantee there's at least one more Terry Smith on the Gold Coast."

"I've heard that before."

"Well, it's true. You've barely scratched the surface."

I look at Terri. She shrugs in agreement.

"So," Ian continues, "here's what we're going to do. We're going to find that girl of yours."

"Sorry?"

Terri and I both look at Ian with big question marks for eyes.

"Well, if you've only got three more days to track down Terry Smith, you need to give it one hundred percent. You've got to take control. And I don't reckon you can do that until you sort out this thing with Karen."

I laugh nastily. I don't mean to, it just spills out. "And just how do you propose we do that?" "Did she ever tell you which school she goes to?"

I shake my head.

"But she lives – or lived – in Miami?"

I nod my head.

"Well, it's just gone 3.30, so if we rush we might just catch her walking out of Miami High School."

Ian and I take different cars, so that we can cover both exits. I only hope things are going better where he is. All I can see are girls who can't be a day over fourteen, traipsing out the school gate in their grey, sack-like dresses, dragging their bags and doing all the awkward things that girls that age do. Maybe Karen has already left. I'm trying to be positive, trying to *take contro*l, but my heart's just not in it.

I drum my fingers on the white steering wheel of the Mustang. The trail of young girls is thinning out. I'll give it ten more minutes.

"Good afternoon, sir."

I stop drumming with a start and look up into the reflective sunglasses of a young policeman. "Jesus, you scared the hell out of me."

The cop nods, but he doesn't say anything. He just looks at me with his mouth set slightly askew. I look back. What the hell does he want? Oh no, it must be the drug money. Say something, Trigg, say something. "I was just lost in my own little world, didn't see you."

The cop simply nods again, leaning on the doorframe. I nod back.

"Having car problems, sir?" he finally forces from his tight little lips.

"No, no. Car's fine. These old Mustangs, they just go and go."

"So what are you doing here, sir?"

"Nothing? Just looking for a girl."

The cop's tight little lips twitch, and then they begin to shake. "You make me SICK!"

"I beg your pard—?"

"You think that just because you don't touch makes it alright, huh? Well, how would you feel if it was your daughter?"

"I . . . no . . . I . . . it's . . . Jesus." I wipe the cop's spittle from my face and try to protest, but I can't talk and he's not listening.

"Driver's licence."

"I . . . I don't have it."

"Where is it?"

"I . . . I left it with my trousers, at a nightclub. I can tell you which one if—"

"I don't want to hear what you get up to with your pervy mates. Just get out of the car, you're coming down to the station."

The desk sergeant sniffs. It's the eighth time in two minutes. He looks down at the computer screen and then back at me. "Looks like you're a live-one Mr Harvey. A heads-up from the boys in customs." He sniffs. "Sus-pish-us." He says the word like it holds a particular fascination for him, like a movie star might utter "Oscar". "Also says you came to Australia via Thailand."

"It was a stopover."

"Just enough time to nip down to Koh Pi Pi and get sunburned with your sicko mates, hey?"

"I spent the night in a hotel near the airport."

"Well, different strokes for different folks, hey?"

Thank God for "call connect". By the time I track down Ian's house and talk to Terri, I can't decide whether I'd rather be in the cell with the drunk freak who keeps informing me that he has the skills to kill me in less than four seconds, maybe three . . . or outside with the boys in blue who are seeing red at the prospect of having a paedophile in their midst.

Terri arrives not a moment too soon and manages to get me off the hook. Luckily she has a friend who has a daughter at Miami High and she tells the police I'd gone to pick her up. Phone calls are made, stories vouched for. Then she throws a fury of legal mumbo-jumbo at the rookie constable and his sergeant. She's going to make a hell of a lawyer some day. She even has the police apologise to me.

She doesn't say much in the car, though. Not until I ask if we can go via Jun's for a few chicken rolls.

"Jesus, Trigg, get a fucking grip. I don't see how getting stoned is going to help you. It's just going to make you even more daft." She thunks my forehead with two of her fingers.

"Can we at least go past Karen's place? You heard Ian, I have to get her out of my mind so that I can concentrate one hundred per-cent on finding the right Terry Smith. And my car's impounded until tomorrow . . ."

"If I take you there will you shut up?"

♣ ♣

15

"Kill the engine," I whisper to Terri as she turns her Mazda into Karen's dark street.

"Don't be a wanker."

We amble down the street, first past Karen's place and then the neighbour's. Karen's house is in darkness, the "For Lease" sign still on the front lawn. Even ice-cool Terri is taken aback, though, when we see that the neighbour's place is the same: not a single light on, and a "For Lease" sign outside.

"That's weird," she finally says.

"Too weird. First Karen and now the neighbour."

"Do you think it's tied in with all this Terry Smith business?"

"I don't see how. All I can think is that it has something to do with the drug money Karen stole."

Terri smirks. "Maybe they're frightened of you."

I'm working on a particularly acerbic retort when I notice something. "How long has that car been there?"

Terri looks behind at the maroon sedan parked down the street. It's a dark night, hard to make out much detail, but there are two men sitting inside. Occasionally a cigarette glows. "I don't know. It looks vaguely familiar, though. Might have been behind us on the highway."

"Let's go for a drive-past."

Terri turns the Mazda around and slowly approaches the sedan. The men are huddled down in conversation. They pay no attention to us as we drive slowly past. "Probably a domestic," she says.

"Well if I was having a domestic in a dark street, I'd certainly notice a car driving slowly past me."

Behind us, the car suddenly roars to life, and with a squeal takes off down the road. Terri and I look at each other.

"You've got to follow it," I blurt.

"But I'm not a very good driver."

"Pretend you're in a John Grisham book."

Terri flings the car around and guns down the street. The maroon car is driving without it's lights on, but I glimpse it turning around the corner. "Left," I shout, as I grab onto the dashboard.

We are seriously outpowered, but in the little backstreets of the coast, manoeuvrability is king, especially when the driver considers front lawns part of the road. As we graze yet another letterbox, the maroon car drives under a streetlight up ahead, but I can't quite make out the two men. By the time we reach the highway, they are still in sight. This quickly changes, though, on the open straight road.

"Can you see them?" I ask Terri.

She shakes her head.

I cuff the dashboard.

It's going on 9.30 p.m. when we get back to Ian's, going on 11.00 p.m. when he and Terri go to bed, and it's just after 11.30 p.m. when I get out of the taxi at the casino.

I probably should have gone to bed, too, but I still have a lot of cash to clean. Tossing and turning in bed wasn't going to help. It's time for another crack at going solo. And this time I'm not going to chicken out. It's time I made my own luck, like Ian said. And, well, okay, there was always the chance of seeing Karen again.

After last night's disaster I'm aware that I have to keep a low profile. From the second I walk into the foyer, though, I feel like I'm being obvious. Quick, go to the tables or it will look like you're up to something fishy. But not too quick, or it will look like you're too familiar with the place. Finally I settle myself at a roulette table with the now customary free drink. The trick is going to be timing; put my first bet on, say, black, as soon as the betting opens, then wait until the croupier is just about to wave her all-powerful arm over the green baize, then throw down another twenty-five on red. Do this every third or fourth spin, then, after four bets, move on to another table and do it all again.

Without an accomplice, Karen's system is much harder on the nerves, but it does seem to be working. The problem is, it's slow. After a noisy, smoky hour, I have only 800 clean dollars to show. Combine that with last night when, thanks to Mr Celebrity Surfer, I only managed to clean two grand (500 of which went up in the air when I was trying to escape), and it leaves me in a bit of a hole. I still have $7,000 to get through and I am fast running out of tables. I'd be better off trying to *earn* the money on a street corner in Surfers Paradise. At that moment I catch my still-peeling, still-bruised, still-British reflection in a mirrored wall – the street corner isn't an option. It's time to up the ante.

I start laying down $50 bets, then 100, then 200. Luckily there are enough Japanese businessmen here for me to hide among. And after just one more hour I've cleaned $2,600. God, why did I waste so much time with pissy little bets?

Karen is quickly receding from my mind. There's been no sign of her, and right now that doesn't really bother me. I attempt a couple of $300 bets. No problem. This is a breeze.

Do you ever get the feeling that things are going *too* well? That, any minute now, it's all going to come crashing down around you? Well I don't, so I almost wet myself when a forceful hand is placed on my shoulder with the words, "Excuse me sir, may I have a word with you?"

Sweet Jesus! The man looks like a tree wearing a suit, and not a small tree either – the sort of tree that can take five generations of lovers' initials and still not look vandalised. "This isn't like it seems," I protest. "Oh God, you probably hear that all the time."

"Sir, we've noticed you've been quite a regular visitor to the casino of late."

"Right. Yes. Well here's the thing. Yes, my behaviour has been a little odd . . . but there's a perfectly good explanation, which . . . is . . . ahh."

"Sir, I've been asked on behalf of the management here at the casino to give you this."

What? A punch? A wedgie? A . . . a *key ring*? I'm speechless. It's like he's given me verbal Imodium. "What's this?" I finally ask, letting the cheap trinket dangle from my fingers.

"Sir, that's a High Rollers key ring. Despite last night's incident, your regular visits and the increase in your betting amounts suggest you might be more comfortable playing in the High Rollers room."

I stare alternately at him and the key ring. "You mean I can keep gambling?"

"Of course, sir."

"In the High Rollers room?"

"Yes, sir."

"Which is . . .?"

"Over there, sir."

I nod and begin walking towards the surprisingly unostentatious entrance.

"Ahh, sir." The tree follows me, wraps one of its heavy boughs around my shoulder. "Sir, you – how do I put this? – need to be appropriately attired to enter the High Rollers room."

"Appropriately attired? These trousers have been declared the grooviest trousers on the Gold Coast. Do you know what that means? There are no trousers on the entire coast groovier than these trousers."

"Yes, sir, they are very snazzy, but you need to be wearing a jacket and tie."

"Well then why did you give me this key ring?"

"For your future visits, sir."

"Well, we'll just see about future visits. You know, you're not the only casino in town."

"Actually, sir, we are."

"I see . . . good."

Our dialogue grinds to a halt and the tree leaves me. Tree! . . . Leaves! . . . It's probably a good time to quit for the evening.

I land in the back seat of the taxi, up $3,000 and a key ring. Not a bad night's work.

Back at Ian's, the bed feels a little more comfortable than usual. Abusive policemen and disappearing tenants recede in my mind. I'm exhausted; I fall asleep in my friendly new home and dream not of luckless scenarios and faceless Terry Smiths, but of the waves I'll be tackling on the Bandit tomorrow morning. Fantastic waves, like those I saw with Karen . . .

♣ ♣ 16

"Sweet Jesus," I whimper, "I'm not going out there."

The sun is poking over the horizon, just enough to make the waves wrapping around Kirra Point look positively menacing. Just enough to make the beachfront carpark seem like the safest place on earth. "You've got to be bloody kidding me," I say to Ian.

"Come on, Trigg, they're perfect."

"You said they would be around six foot."

"Well, yeah, but the swell's still building, they might reach six foot yet."

"What? They look about twelve foot."

"Ooh, I'd say more like four."

This is just terrific. As if the trauma of being woken up when it was still dark wasn't bad enough, I then have to tell Ian about ten times that I'm not joking about the Bandit before he believes me. And then we pull up at the carpark and here are waves bigger than houses rumbling in. "I'm not going out there," I repeat.

"Okay, Trigg, that's cool. I don't want to push you. I can ask about Terry Smith myself."

"Alright, I'll come out. It's only water. What's the worst that can happen?"

"I guess you could drown."

"Yes. Thank you. That was rhetorical."

"Listen, Trigg, if you are going to come out, I . . . I really can't let you take that thing." He points to the Bandit.

"What? Why not? Are you embarrassed?"

"No, Trigg, it's not that I'm embarrassed – well I am, but that's beside the point – it's more about the fact that you *will* drown if you take that out there. That piece of crap will get water logged in no time, and you've got no flippers, and you yourself said you're not a very good swimmer, and—"

"Piece of crap? This cost me $20! Look at the shark, he's got tattoos . . . he's wearing a bandanna!"

"Graphics aside, Trigg, you'll be safer on a proper board. You're just going to have to trust me on this one. There's a spare in my board-bag if you want."

"Fine."

I look out at the massive surf again. I really don't want to go out anymore, but this is no longer about just going for a surf. I have to do it. If there's one thing I'm learning, it's that risk equals life. Adventure equals life.

Ian pulls out one of his spare boards and hands it over. I've never actually held a surfboard before. It's surprisingly light, but also surprisingly hard – *painfully* hard, potentially.

"So how much have you surfed before?" Ian asks as we make our way down to my inevitable doom.

"Oh, less than you'd think."

"Right, well just stick with me on the way out. We'll go out through the rip."

"Through the rip. But they drag you out to sea."

Ian hesitates ". . . Yeah, that's the point."

"Oh."

"We should probably stretch beforehand, especially after your shoulder workout yesterday. Oh, and Trigg, that's a leg rope – it goes around your leg."

This is just what I need, some more time to stare at the waves. Admittedly, the sun is up higher and the ocean looks a little bluer and less menacing, but on the other hand, the waves look even bigger.

"Let's do it," Ian says as he steps into the water.

The water is surprisingly warm as it rushes around my skinny shins, but I am shaking like a cheap vibrating bed all the same. I follow Ian's lead and jump over several broken waves that come up to my chest. The surfboard makes hollow "thunt" noises as it takes the impact of the water. Meanwhile, during those precious moments of contact, my toes scrunch into the sand to stop me from being taken by the drag of the tide. Then a break comes and I can see all the way out to where the other surfers are. Ian immediately jumps on his board and starts paddling smoothly. I try to lie on my board, but slip straight off the front and end up under the water. When I do finally manage to get on the board, Ian is waiting for me.

My arms are burning after only thirty yards – surely not a good sign, since we have at least another sixty to go. And then it happens. I see a lump of water starting to swell up. I look over at Ian. He must have missed it, because he's pushing his arms through the water just as smoothly as ever.

The lump is getting bigger. It's as big as a block of flats, and only about thirty-five yards away. Shit! Why didn't I stay on the beach? I swear I'll be satisfied with a mundane predictable life if I can just get through this. Oh Christ, the wave is even bigger now. It's blocking out the sun. I try to paddle harder but my arms simply refuse to cooperate. It's far too late to turn back, but I'm not going to make it over the swell, either. The bastard's going to break right in front of us.

"Ian, watch out, there's a wave coming," I holler.

He looks at me with a puzzled expression.

I point frantically. "The wave, bloody tidal wave. What do we do?"

"Duck dive."

Duck dive? What the fuck is that all about? "What do you mean duck—?"

BOOOOOOOMMMM!

Have you ever been hit with a bag of cement? Well neither have I, but I don't imagine it's very pleasant. And if you were then thrown into the cement mixer with that bag of cement, and the cement mixer was turned up to full speed it would be even less pleasant. Well, that's what it feels like. Water is forcefully replacing the air in my nose. I have no idea which way is up, except that it's never the direction I'm going. My leg is being pulled away from my body by the leg rope, like a chicken drumstick at an Alabama family reunion. My lungs are in full-blown panic mode. I can quite honestly say, without any hyperbole, that I am about to die. And then I pop up.

Thank God.

And then I see the next wave.

When I finally make it out past the break I'm certain I am the happiest person there. I can't breathe properly, and my arms feel like pieces of burning string, and I'm still shaking violently – but by God I feel good.

I struggle awkwardly to a sitting position, like the other surfers. And, to my credit, I stay on for a good eight seconds. If it had been a raging steer, rather than a surfboard, this would have been considered quite an achievement. But it's not a steer. And I slide unceremoniously off the back of the board, flinging it high into the air.

I have no idea where it went, but I can easily tell where it lands. The closest thing I've seen to a link between man and pit-bull is paddling towards me with little fires where his eyes should be. I start swimming away as fast as my burning pieces of string will carry me, but he gets hold of my trailing surfboard and slowly reels me in by the leg-rope.

"Give him a break, man, he's just learning."

"Fuck off, pal, or I'll . . . hey, Ian . . . how ya going?"

"Good, Dazza, good."

"Haven't see you for a while. How's life off the circuit treating ya?"

"Yeah, pretty good, mate. More time for . . . hey Trigg, you can stop swimming now. Dazza won't hurt you."

I stop my frantic flailing. And sink. Luckily the pit-bull hasn't let go of my leg-rope, so it's easy for Ian to find me, about four feet below the surface.

When it becomes clear that I am with Ian, I'm given special treatment. Which is to say I am allowed to sit there and exist without being hassled. This is fine with me. Ian, meanwhile, uses his network of friends to ask about Terry Smith.

Out behind the waves, I have a totally new perspective. From the front, the swells looked like great mountains of water, capable of breaking surfboards, backs and anything else that crossed their paths; but from behind they look quite small and powerless. And it's different watching the surfers from behind, too. They disappear over the front, as if on a super-fast liquid escalator, only to reappear amidst a spray of water a second later. Naturally, if I'd had the Bandit out here things would be different. I do my best to ensure that everyone understands this.

After about twenty minutes, my mind wanders from surfing and Terry Smith. I'm not sure if I've been subconsciously avoiding the topic or if I'm merely stupid, but either way it gives me a hell of a fright: how do I get back to land again? Despite my worsening sunburn, I go quite pale. I put the question to Ian, as casually as I can, the next time he paddles over to report on his findings, or lack thereof.

"Just catch a wave, Trigg . . . Just paddle, I guess. I'll come in with you."

"Don't you want to keep surfing?"

"Well, yeah, but I'll come back out again."

"Don't be silly. I'll be fine." I've lost enough face today without having to be accompanied back to the beach.

"Are you sure? It's not a problem."

"No way. I insist you stay out here."

"Well, if you're sure." Then he thinks for a moment. "Hey, I've got an idea." And he cups his hands and yells to all the other surfers, "Are any of you guys going back in? If you are, could you take Trigg with you?"

Well, I thought I'd lost enough face today, but this rips the rest of it from my mortified skull. A freckled kid who looks about twelve volunteers his services.

I accept quickly, thinking it better to just get the hell out of here. I must be one of the few people who can claim to have heard a collective giggle from a pack of surly surfers.

The sun and shame play an evil tag-team game, combining to burn my face a crispy red as we sit out at sea, waiting for a lull. Wave after wave goes through, and the prospect of drowning myself becomes more and more inviting. But eventually the lull comes. I put all my humiliation-fuelled energy into covering the 200-or-so yards between me and the sand.

After about forty frantic yards, I notice Junior is keeping up with relative ease. This bothers me. But not nearly as much as the wave I notice brewing up behind us.

"What do I do?" I ask in a panic.

The kid shrugs. "I dunno. I'm taking it in."

I look over my shoulder. My right eye starts twitching. The wave is getting closer. It's not that big, but it's getting steeper and steeper, waiting to break right on top of me. Logic suggests I should keep paddling towards the beach. I do this. Unfortunately that's the same direction the wave is heading, and it's faster than me. Before I realise what's happening, it picks me up and I'm staring down a vertical wall of water as high as my old second-storey flat. But I don't stay there for long. In a split second I'm screaming down the face of the wave, involuntarily leaning back to stop the nose of the surfboard from digging in to the water. And then I shoot out in front of the wave, skimming across the surface of the undisturbed water, until the bumper-car white-water catches up again and gives me an almighty shove. I bounce around in the turbulence all the way to the beach. I let out a crazed holler. It is absolutely the best fun I've ever had in the water – and that includes the time I kissed Mia O'Kane in her parents' pool.

"Did you see that?" I scream at the kid, who stands up a few feet away. "Did you see me ride that thing?" I don't wait for his response. I'm hooked.

By the time we pull into Ian's driveway, the wave has grown to eight feet high and I'd cut ruthlessly across the face of it, dominating it all the way to the sand. Ian seems to take my word for it. Sure, we didn't get a single lead on Terry Smith, but boy do I have a good story.

Ian is still grinning as he walks through the front door. Maybe that's why he misses the brown envelope sitting on the doormat.

"Do you know what this is, Terr'?" he calls out after I pick it up and hand it to him.

Terri is sitting out on the deck, eating a grapefruit or rockmelon or some sort of exotic fruit. She takes the envelope from Ian. It has no writing on it – it's just a blank brown envelope. "I didn't hear a thing. It's probably one of the local surf companies, want you to do an appearance or something. You should think about getting a new manager."

Ian shakes the envelope, then rips it open. His crisp blue eyes move back and forth like little typewriters. "Jeez, this is alright."

Terri snatches the piece of paper from him. It looks like a photocopy of a newspaper article. "Holy shit!" she exclaims. Her eyes positively shine as she hands the page to me.

It's a newspaper article, dated September the 4th, 1997.

Allegations Don't Stick to Slick Japanese Businessman

An arrest warrant based on allegations of money laundering and corruption against Japanese businessman Tetsuya Suzuki has been dismissed due to lack of evidence. A representative of the mysterious Suzuki, who also operates under the name Terry Smith, claimed that he is relieved, but still outraged that the allegations were made in the first place. However, had the warrant for Suzuki's arrest been issued, it is thought unlikely that it would have resulted in a hearing, as the reclusive businessman has yet to be positively identified. Suzuki operates through a complicated network of companies and representatives, although it has been alleged that he resides on the Gold Coast for up to six months of the year.

I sit down heavily in the deckchair, holding the page carefully. Barton wanders over and nudges my leg.

"Jesus, Trigg," says Ian. "I think this is it."

The sky has never looked bluer, the sand never whiter and the water never more immaculate that it does at this moment. The sun is shining through the page, emphasising the imperfections that the photocopier has imparted to the surface. Such a bland little gathering of innocuous words, from years ago; I'm sure the journalist never thought his prose would move someone so much. It is truly a gift from the gods; even, dare I say, a stroke of luck.

"So who do you think put it there?" Ian asks.

I shrug. "I have absolutely no idea. And I don't really care." (I do care, and I do have an idea, but the endorphins have temporarily flooded the part of my brain that fosters curiosity.)

"More importantly," says Terri, "what are we going to do about it?"

I shrug. "I have absolutely no idea. And I don't really care."

Terri and Ian look at me strangely.

"Just give me a minute," I say.

It doesn't take long for the adrenaline molecules to sidle up to the endorphins and ask them to kindly move along. "I need the phonebook," I proclaim as I carefully read the rest of the article.

Alas, there is nothing particularly useful among the remaining paragraphs: Tetsuya Suzuki, 44 years of age; from Kobe, Japan; alleged links with the Yakuza; on the board of several prominent Japanese companies with holdings on the Gold Coast; alleged financial interests in restaurants, golf shops, tour operations and nightclubs; alleged involvement in illegal casino operation in Surfers Paradise.

The phonebook proves fruitless too. There is no T. Suzuki. I don't bother with the Yellow Pages; it's unlikely that the head of organised crime on the Gold Coast would advertise. The internet provides a lot of information, but it must have been the journalist's primary reference resource as well, because most of what I find is covered in the article. I'm not discouraged, though; in fact, I'm probably the most encouraged I've been in months.

And it isn't just me. Ian begins ringing around his friends; Terri puts a dissertation on hold and drives out to the university to see what she can dig up. I grab a lift with her to the police impound, where I pick up the Mustang. I'm off to check out the only Japanese contact I have on the Gold Coast.

♣ ♣ ♣

"Ahh, Tligger Harvey, long time no see." Jun offers me a chicken-and-mushroom roll but I decline. We catch up for a bit and I tell him, within reason, what I've been up to. When I tell him about the amazing coincidence that I am living with Ian, he is very philosophical. "That is no coincidence, Tligg, that is fate. You are with Ian because you have something to share with each other, something to give each other. You just have to work out what that is."

"Wow, Jun, is that a Shinto thing?"

"Oh no, I am reading *The Celestine Prophecy*. Hey, maybe you are there to tame the dragon lady." He unleashes his high-pitch laugh. He's obviously met Terri. "Don't you dare tell her I say that," he adds, more seriously.

We chat some more about arbitrary things, before I move the conversation in the appropriate direction. "You must get a lot of customers, Jun, know a lot of people here on the coast. Have you ever come across Tetsuya Suzuki?"

Jun's joviality vanishes. "No," he says curtly and turns away.

"Are you sure?" I ask. "Tetsuya Suzuki? He's also known as Terry Smith?"

"No! No Terrys. No Tetsuyas." He starts to busy himself with gratuitous stock-rearranging.

"Come on, Jun, a guy in your position must know a lot of Japanese people. You're positive you don't know this Tetsuya Suzuki?"

His exasperated hands work even faster. "What do you mean by that?"

"Nothing, just that—"

Jun doesn't wait for a reply. "Why do you want to know about this person anyway? I think you should go."

"Please, Jun, it's really important."

"No! No Tetsuya. Go now. Get out. You not welcome here anymore, Tligger Harvey. Not welcome. Go."

Jun physically ejects me from the store. His state is somewhere between panic and fury, and his English goes to pieces. I'm completely dumbstruck. Not a single word manages to make it from my brain to my lips.

"No Tetsuya. I not know," Jun keeps repeating in ever-thickening Japanese.

I stand on the footpath outside the store, literally at a loss for words. I can see Jun peering at me over the sanitary pads. He looks scared. Scared of what? This is getting strange . . . strang*er*.

With confused steps, I make my way back to the Mustang. There's no point trying to talk to Jun again. Not today, anyway. But I'm certainly not finished with him.

Ian's deck welcomes me back; I take up position in the hammock, with Barton plonked down in my shadow, murmuring happily to himself. I feel like a Jamaican psychiatric patient, as I swing slowly back and forth and fill Dr Berrisford in on my fracas with Jun.

"Jeez, Trigg, that's pretty weird," he says, stating the obvious, as usual. "Maybe I could have a chat to him after I've finished ringing around. I know him pretty well."

"No, no. It's something I should sort out with him. I'll just give it a few days."

A few days! It's amazing, a few days used to mean so little to me. It was nothing. But in this new context a few days is everything.

"So what are you going to do for the rest of the day?" Ian asks.

And there's the irony. So much to do and yet nothing to do. God, how I'd love to be able to answer with a comfortable: "Hmm I don't know. I might go down to the beach for a while, have a bite to eat, catch a movie". The funny thing is, though, if a life of aimless leisure were on the menu, I'd probably reject it in favour of some sort of drama. In the end I answer the question with a shrug.

"What about credit cards?" Ian says. "Check out whether any credit cards belonging to Tetsuya Suzuki have been used on the coast."

"Yes," I begin slowly, "but how do I get that information? And even if I can, how's that going to help me find the guy?"

"Come on, Trigg, it's worth a try. You might get the name of a shop – that's a good starting point."

"I suppose you're right. But where the hell do I start?"

"Ring up Visa."

"And say what?"

We sit in silence.

After such an immaculate morning, thick clouds now move slowly across the sky, like a procession of stooped old men in grey dressing-gowns, shuffling across the nursing home lino on their way to the toilet. Out to sea, the water from the sky and the water from the ocean meld into each other, replacing the usual crisp horizon with a bleak stroke from a thick wet brush. And the strong wind has turned the surf into a Shakespearean drama. The hammock doesn't seem quite as comfortable as I remember it.

"Mick!" Ian suddenly blurts, sitting up straight and breaking the quiet. "Why didn't I think of him earlier?"

"Who's Mick? Does he work for Visa?"

"Better. He runs a surf school."

Within the hour Mick is sitting in the deckchair, while Terri, Ian and I look on and the rain tumbles all around us. I immediately recognise his scruffy black hair and bent nose from my night of terror at Terri's old place.

"Well, whaddaya reckon?" Ian asks Mick.

"Well, I s'pose I do get a few Jap businessmen in me surf classes."

"Exactly," Ian replies. "So you can just ask them if they know of this Mitsubishi guy."

"Suzuki," Terri and I correct.

"So whaddaya reckon?" Ian asks Mick again.

Mick hesitates, pulls at the neck of his faded red muscle-shirt. "Gee I dunno mate. I mean, shit, he tried to give me cancer with a remote control."

"Come on, man, give him a break. He said he's sorry."

"Oh jeez, Ian, I dunno."

"Please," says Terri entering the equation, as she winds her blond hair around her finger. "Do it for me."

"Awww okay, Tezza." Mick blushes.

"Pathetic," I mumble.

Terri shoots me a look that could melt an iceberg. "Trigg, why don't you go and get a pen and some paper so we can write down the details for Mick."

I go inside and return with a biro and scribble-pad.

"Okay," she says in her lawyer voice. "Mick's had an absolute crackerjack of an idea, haven't you Mick?" Mick gives an "aww, shucks" shrug. "He'll still ask his punters, but he reckons he'll have more luck talking to his other contacts, the ones that run the tours for Japanese tourists and businessmen. I'm sure you'll remember that the article talked about Tetsuya's supposed links with the tour business here on the coast."

I nod.

"Okay, great. Well, Mick, when do you think you can get around to calling these people?"

"Tomorrow, maybe."

"You don't think you can do it any sooner?"

"Well . . ."

"Pleeeeeease."

"Awww."

Within two hours Mick is before us again.

"Well?" I demand, a little overanxious.

Mick glares at me. "If you're gonna be like that, mate . . ."

"Trigg, could you get us something to drink," suggests Terri.

I skulk inside again. As if you can get cancer from a remote control. Moron.

When I get back out to the deck with a bottle of Coke and some glasses, Mick is soaking up the attention.

Terri gives me a quick update. "Basically, Trigg, most of Mick's contacts were very reluctant to talk about Tetsuya, even though they'd all heard of him – it seems he has more than just a *link* to the tour business. But one guy did mention an illegal casino that Tetsuya runs. Apparently it operates from an apartment in Surfers – big spenders only, some come from Japan and the others he recruits from the High Rollers room at the casino. It's all kept very—"

I spit my drink all over the floorboards. Fumbling about in my pocket, I produce the keys to the Mustang, which I hold aloft like a playing card at the end of a magic trick. "The High Rollers room," I say, shaking the key ring.

"Where on earth did you get that?" asks Ian.

"I have my ways." I swirl my coke and knock back a slug, like James Bond with a Martini. Except that he probably wouldn't spill it down his chin. And he'd be wearing a suit, not a grey T-shirt with sweat stains under the arms. And he would have got his prize through stealth and intelligence, not dumb luck. But other than that – very James Bond.

Mick leaves us to take his class. He says he'll ask around some more, but I think I have what I need. The High Rollers room, that's my way in. I'll get myself invited to Tetsuya's private casino. Not for the first time that day, Karen crosses my mind, but this time it isn't in a Page Three way. If she was around, she'd know just what to do. She'd make sure I got invited to play with the big boys. She'd know just how much to bet and which games to play. It feels like so much longer than just last week that she was, for a day or two, my best friend in the world. This whole thing has been such a dizzying whirl.

Tetsuya Suzuki. I say the name over and over to myself until it sounds like no more than an awkward clash of syllables. Tetsuya Suzuki. Otherwise known as Terry Smith. Hopefully known as the guy who travelled to Fiji and put his faith in a five-inch piece of Pacific Island hardwood. It's time to find out. God I feel nervous. God I feel alive. The adventure is back, and with it comes that feeling of exquisite trepidation. I wouldn't trade this bowel-loosening anxiety for all the after-work drinks and five-a-side in the world.

The consensus among the think-tank assembled on the deck is that I should go to the High Rollers room and throw around as much cash as possible.

"And what if I do get invited to Tetsuya's casino?" I put forward.

"You go," answers Ian.

"Yes, and then what?"

Blank stares are exchanged. Some bloody think-tank!

"Look," Terri begins, "let's worry about getting you there first. After that, all your actions will be very situation-dependent."

We nod. The think-tank is satisfied.

It's three o'clock in the afternoon and I've made a checklist of what I will need for the casino: Cash? $10,000 should do it; suit and tie? Ian said I could borrow his; High Rollers key ring? Got it; Cunning and nerve? Still looking – under the bed perhaps.

I retrieve the cash from my footwear, taking out all $12,000 – dirty and laundered – just in case.

Then Ian brings in his suit.

"Are you bloody joking?" I blurt.

It is probably meant to be grey, but it's so shiny it looks silver.

"There are medieval knights still looking for that thing."

Ian looks confused.

"Look how shiny it is," I say.

Now he looks a little hurt.

I try to enlighten him a little more softly. "Look, when did you buy that?"

"I didn't. One of my uncles gave it to Mum in, ahh, 1984."

"And when's the last time you wore it?"

"Ahh, graduation, 1998."

"And people laughed at you, right?"

"No."

"Are you sure?"

"Yes."

"Well they damn well should have! It's terrible, Ian. I'm sorry, but you should burn it – or melt it. I can't wear it. I'll have to buy one."

"There's not enough time, Trigg," says Terri. "Just wear the suit. It's not that bad."

"Okay, okay. Have you got a tie, Ian? – Oh for Christ's sake." The fashion-challenged surfer is holding up a black strip of vinyl that looks more like a belt than a tie.

I change into the clothes. I look at myself in the mirror. I shake my head and sigh.

Driving into the casino carpark this time I don't feel suspicious. I don't feel like everyone is watching me. I just feel like an idiot. True, an idiot with $12,000 and a bright red Mustang, but an idiot all the same. And if people are staring as I enter the casino, I don't notice. I just keep my head down and walk towards the High Rollers entrance. The important thing is not my wardrobe; it's to look calm and experienced, like I've been around big bucks and bigger suits all my life. And when my nerves jangle a bit too much, I'll just have to remind myself that all I have to do is find out if Tetsuya Suzuki has been to Fiji recently. Simple.

"Good evening, sir, aren't we looking spiffy this afternoon. Welcome to the High Rollers room, may I see your key ring please?"

I produce the trinket for the skinny doorman.

"Thank you, sir, have a wonderful evening and good luck."

Allowing myself to raise my head a little, I make my way down the hallway. What greets me is completely different to the mad scene outside. Sedate jazz mingles with the smoke of cheap cigarettes and expensive cigars. The tables are well spaced-out and the atmosphere is nothing like the cattle-shed feel of the casino proper. While it is still tacky, it is a classier kind of tacky – if that makes sense.

A waiter quickly appears at my side to take my drink order. I ask for a scotch and water. It seems appropriate. When he returns, I take a healthy mouthful, stand back, swallow and check out the scene. I can't see much, though, with my eyes watering the way they are. I double over, my throat raw and burning.

"I didn't know you drank scotch."

The voice is familiar, but the feet are a dead giveaway.

Karen shushes my questioning mouth with a finger to her painted red lips. She has a black cocktail dress splashed across her amazing body and her hair twisted into tight braids which flow down over her bronze shoulders. Once again she looks absolutely stunning. For a sixteen-year-old, Trigg, don't forget – a *thieving* sixteen-year-old, at that.

"Let's have a seat," she says, indicating the scuffed burgundy leather couches.

Karen orders a vodka and cranberry juice and we wait in silence until it arrives. She takes a sip and speaks. "A few things, Trigg: firstly, I'm sorry for the way I disappeared; secondly, I did not steal your money like a common thief; thirdly, I'm sorry you ran into the back of my car – and fourthly, stop looking at me like I just ran over your puppy."

It's obviously my turn to talk, but what do you say? I have a million and one questions for her, none of which I can get out. "You have nice feet."

Karen is perplexed. She looks from me to her feet and back again. "Umm, thank you."

I nod boyishly, aware that my wits are finally starting to regroup. "I have so much to ask you. Can we get a drink outside?"

Karen shakes her head. "Not now, Trigg. I assume you're here to get invited to Tetsuya Suzuki's private casino, and we don't have time to waste."

Well, make that a million and *two* questions.

"Okay, here's the deal, Trigg. We do *not* talk about the past, not a word, not now anyway. I will explain it to you, but not now. And you have to trust me. Okay?"

"You said that when I told you about the money."

Her business-like demeanour cracks momentarily as she remembers. "That's right. You trusted me then."

"And you stole $30,000 from me!"

"It wasn't yours, Trigg. It was drug money."

"That didn't bother you when it was paying for the mini bar."

She smirks, almost proudly. "Touché. Come on, let's get this over with and I'll explain everything to you when we're done." She reaches over and pats my shiny right thigh. She knows the buttons to push, the little minx. I agree to her conditions. What choice do I have?

With Karen prodding me in the back for moral support, I take a seat at a roulette table. Exactly how much money does one change into chips in the High Rollers room? There really ought to be some sort of a booklet with the key ring: *So You've Finally Hit the Big Time: The Ins and Outs of Being a High Roller.*

I watch the gruff-looking, overweight smoke-machine beside me for a hint. He pulls out a wad of hundred-dollar notes and throws them disdainfully across the baize. One, two, three, four, five, six . . . forty-eight, forty-nine, *fifty*. Wow, $5,000!

The croupier banks the cash and counts out the chips. One, two, three, four, five. Five! Bloody hell, that's $1,000 a bet. I do some quick calculations and figure that I don't have the capital to make a big impression . . . unless I take a different approach and go for the quick impression!

From beneath the glare of my jacket, I withdraw the $12,000 – clean and illicit – and throw it at the croupier with enough detachment to match my neighbour.

"What would you like to value your markers at, sir?" asks the smug croupier, checking out my Saville Row nightmare.

"Thousand," I reply without a trace of a squeak.

"Very good, sir." He counts out the twelve chips and slides them in front of me.

I let the first three spins of the wheel go by, pretending to study the numbers. Each time a bet is placed, Karen gives my hand a little urging squeeze, but I smile calmly at her.

Then it's time to get myself noticed.

Beside me, the lung-transplant-in-waiting has been playing dozens with thousand dollar bets. This is what I have to trump. I take four chips and put them on 5, another four chips on 15. My birthday and my mother's birthday. Then I put two chips on red, and two on the top dozen. Total outlay: $12,000. Money left: not a brass razoo.

My heart is pumping fast, my palms are wet, and my feet are screaming at me to tap them, fidget them, anything. It's an all-or-nothing, one-off chance to get noticed. The walrus beside me coughs, and the croupier looks a little less pretentious. I just hope to God that the right people are watching. I'm only going to get one shot at this.

"Jesus Christ, son, what'd you do? Sell a kidney?" wheezes my playing-partner.

In response to this glowing advertisement, more eyes look our way, and a few bystanders became onlookers. This is good . . . more, more!

After a bit longer than usual, the wheel is spun. The ball rolls around the rim for an eternity before slowly making its way towards the centre like a cyclist in a velodrome. And then, as if someone has put speed bumps on the velodrome, the ball hits the wheel and jumps and stumbles. And jumps and stumbles. And stumbles and crashes. On number 15!

Well I'll be completely, totally and utterly buggered. Everyone lets out wild hoots and jealous "Oh my God!"s. People pat me on the back, Karen for once seems speechless, and the walrus finally coughs up a lung. But I just sit there, the personification of cool, calm and collected, and let some noxious gas escape my tortured bowels.

The total winnings: $140,000. Clean.

With a sudden crowd looking on, I play three more spins, outlaying $50,000 and losing $28,000 of it. When Karen finally nudges me in the back, I address the croupier and the spectators: "If you'll excuse me, my *wife* will kill me if I lose any more." I shoot Karen a grin and a wink. The sort of polite chuckle that only money can buy ripples through the crowd.

The cashier's facial expression, hiding under her over-dyed red hair, suggests she is impressed but has seen better. I arrange for cash in preference to a bank cheque. It will be delivered in a small briefcase. That's when my façade begins to crack. *A briefcase full of money!* I want to run around the room yelling and screaming. I order Karen and myself another drink and we take a seat on a couch off to the side. I don't even feel the scotch as it slides down this time.

"Your wife?" says Karen.

I put a finger to my lips, enjoying the reversal.

"I think that's illegal," she says.

It's a nice moment, an interlude where I can pretend we have just met, or at the very least don't have a history of deception and burglary.

But then she slips quickly back into her old persona. "Now let's just pretend we're having a good old casual conversation," she says.

I nod and begin chuckling. Why oh why am I putting my faith in this girl again?

Karen chuckles back, her seductive blue eyes glowing and her little nose scrunching.

Oh, that's right.

The minutes creep painfully by and our ruse becomes laboured. "What are we doing here?" I ask, amid fake chortles.

"Just keep doing it," Karen replies.

After another minute or so we are approached by a rather smarmy, lank croupier. Karen's plan starts to make sense.

"Excuse me, miss, sir, we have a special suite available for the use of our VIP guests. If you plan to play some more later on, you might be more comfortable waiting upstairs."

"Thank you, that sounds wonderful," Karen replies.

The croupier looks around before escorting us over to pick up my briefcase full of currency. It's smaller than I'd hoped.

It's all I can do to keep the excited little giggle locked up inside my throat. The suite before us completes my James Bond fantasy. It makes my room at the Marriott look dowdy. My, what chintzy opulence! Where does one start? With the sunken spa next to the floor-to-ceiling window overlooking the Gold Coast? Or the king-size bed with the quadraphonic sound-system? And how should I break it to Karen that we have to make love? We have no choice, you see, the Bondesqueness of the situation demands it.

I have to sit down. Perhaps the leather lounge in front of the gratuitously large television?

"I hope the room is to your liking," smirks the croupier. "If you need anything, just call reception. Otherwise, relax."

As soon as the door closes, I pounce. "What on God's good earth is your story?"

"Where do you want me to start?" says Karen

"Gee, I don't know, how about the beginning?"

"Tut tut, sarcasm doesn't become you."

"Just tell me this, did you have me pegged as a sucker from way back, or only after we got to know each other a little better?"

"Trigg, I never . . . everything I said, everything I did, was sincere."

"Including ripping me off."

"I didn't rip you off!"

"Well it was a pretty bloody good imitation. Say, would you like to take the briefcase now, or would you rather wait until I'm out searching for you again?"

"Look, Trigg, I'm not going to lie to you . . . so I'm not going to say anything at all."

"I beg your pardon? What about the mystery house suddenly coming up for rent – yours and your neighbours?"

Karen looks pleadingly at me, her striking blue eyes beginning to moisten. "I can't say anything, Trigg. I . . . I just can't. Don't you understand this is killing me? On the one hand I'm hurting you, but if I tell you anything, I'll be hurting someone else."

"Well at least tell me how you knew about Tetsuya Suzuki . . . and how you knew where to leave that envelope."

And with that she slumps down in the couch and buries her beautiful face in her hands.

How can you negotiate with that?

I slump down beside her and she nestles up against me. This ride isn't going to get any easier. I think about what to say. It probably isn't a good time to tell her that we have to make love because the situation demands it. So instead I say nothing at all. This is the Karen from Greenmount, the one telling me about her parents. She seems so vulnerable beside me . . . like a mixed up schoolgirl.

All that changes with a knock at the door.

"Good evening," the tall, pointy Japanese man at the door says. "My name is Mr Kensu, how are you enjoying the casino?"

"Fine thank you, Mr Kensu," says a streaky-faced but impeccably-composed Karen.

"Yes, it's wonderful, thank you, Mr Kensu," I add. "Do we have you to thank for this room?"

"In a manner of speaking . . . however, it is more the hospitality of my employer that you are currently enjoying."

"And who might that be?"

"Indeed, you may meet him later this evening if you so choose, Mr . . .?"

"Bond . . . ini. Mr Bondini."

"Indeed, Mr Bondini."

"And this is my wife . . . Mrs Bondini. What exactly can we do for you, Mr Kensu?"

"On the contrary, Mr Bondini. It is what I can do for you. It appears you enjoy your gambling, and it appears you enjoy doing so when the stakes are a little more . . . interesting. Am I correct?"

"Obviously."

"Well I would like, on behalf of my employer, to extend to you an invitation to, ahh, play with other likeminded people in an atmosphere that may be a little more to your liking."

"I'm listening."

"My employer runs a private establishment where persons such as yourself can enjoy themselves without the pressures of being somewhat of a tourist attraction."

"And?"

Annoyance flickers across his pleasant demeanour. "Would you like to gamble at my employer's private casino?"

"I think, Mr Kensu, that I would like that very much."

"Excellent."

♣ ♣

17

A big, black movie-star limousine is waiting downstairs to whisk the three of us off to the private casino. I grab Karen's hand so hard that she lets out a little yelp. This is all so exciting. Too exciting to let fear get in the way. This is a movie, and I'm the star. The suave, resourceful, women-fall-in-my-wake star.

We get into the back of the limousine and there is another Japanese man already in there. He is massive. And mean-looking. And when he pulls out two blindfolds, I begin to question my role in the movie.

The blackness, punctuated by harsh Japanese words, is unnerving. The phrase "it was a good idea at the time" prods my grey matter. Karen's hand is a great comfort: while mine exudes sweat and anxiety, hers oozes calm and control.

Eventually, after God knows how long, the limousine doors are opened and we are gently manhandled into a lift. My guess is that we go up about twenty-five floors, after which we are led for some distance, until finally a door is opened and our blindfolds removed.

"My sincere apologies, Mr and Mrs Bondini, for the barbaric inconvenience, but it is to protect yourselves as much as us," says Mr Kensu. "Now, can I get you both a drink?"

It's lucky that Karen answers, because I am rendered speechless. I thought the High Rollers room was lavish, but this is something else. The suits are more expensive, the cigars fatter, the smoke thicker. The scene is, well, heavier. There are about forty well-dressed people playing at an assortment of gaming tables, or lounging and quaffing the free alcohol. Again I feel the twinge of embarrassment at my ridiculous suit.

A wisp of a Japanese girl, wearing a tight blue dress, returns with our drinks. Karen seems to be soaking up the adventure. She smiles broadly, raises her eyebrows and takes off into the smog.

"Your wife is very confident, Mr Bondini," says Mr Kensu.

"Yes, she is quite a sort."

"Indeed. Quite unlike the women in Japan. Very, ahh, sexy."

"Sexy and spoken for, Mr Kensu."

"My sincere apologies, Mr Bondini. I mean no disrespect."

I ask him which of the men in the room is his boss, so that I can thank him for the invitation. He tells me that his employer prefers to remain anonymous. Before I can press him further, he is called away to attend to something – or someone – and I set off into the acrid tobacco-cloud to find Karen.

My gorgeous new wife is watching a game of blackjack, offering advice to a fat American in a too-tight suit (but at least you can't check your teeth in his). The porky redneck is lapping up the attention, smiling lasciviously at Karen and patting her arse. And she is letting him!

I take Karen's wrist, perhaps with a little too much force. "Hello, *dear*. You didn't take long to settle in. Enjoying yourself?"

She shakes her arm free. "Yes thank you, *darling*. I'm just chatting to Darryl here."

"Howdy," pipes up the walking, talking American cliché, seemingly oblivious to the fact that his lechery is a touch out of order. "What do you think, honey, should I stay or should I hit?"

"Gee, Darryl, I just don't know. I wouldn't want you to lose because of me," replies Karen, all fluttering eyelashes and big blue eyes.

"Aww, shit, honey, it don't matter, it's just a couple of grand, a bit of a warm up."

"Oh Darryl . . ." Giggle, giggle.

Okay, okay, take it easy, Trigg, take it easy.

I take Karen aside. "What are you doing?"

"What am *I* doing? What are *you* doing?"

"Hey buddy, you wanna give me back my good-luck charm?"

hollers the fat American, his red chins wobbling like hams.

"I'll be there in a jiff, Darryl," Karen calls back.

I turn and stalk towards the door.

Karen catches me. "What's with you, Trigg?"

"What's with me? Well not you, that's for sure. You're too busy being a daft tart. These Japanese hookers have got more class than you."

"Fuck you, Trigg! I'm trying to help you."

"Well, unless you think I'm after a threesome with tubby over there, I'll be damned if I can see how you're helping me."

Karen is on the verge of tears again, angry tears. "Jesus, Trigg, who the hell do you think you are? Our objective here tonight is to find out as much as possible about Tetsuya Suzuki. All I did was pick the easiest target in the room. But, you know what, if you don't want my help then that's fine. Just say the word and I am *so* out of here."

Hmm, reasonable explanation. Suggests a reasonable response. Something along the lines of: "I'm sorry, but I didn't realise" or "Please don't go, now that you've explained the situation, I'm more drawn to you than ever". Or how about . . .

"Fine, Karen, why don't you go back over there and keep *helping* me? Who knows, you might make a couple of hundred bucks if you play your cards right."

Yes, Karen didn't think it was very reasonable either.

Now it's her turn to break for the door. I catch her in the hallway, just outside the room. But no sooner have I spun her tear-soaked face around, than Mr Kensu is beside us.

"Leaving so soon, Mr Bondini?"

I look at Karen with pitiful desperation; she has the answer to that one. She looks at me intensely for a few seconds, sniffs and shakes her head. "No, Mr Kensu, the smoke is becoming a bit too much for my eyes. I came out here to get some fresher air."

"I see. Perhaps you would be more comfortable out on the balcony."

We are shown out onto a balcony enclosed in tinted glass, with exhaust fans working overtime.

"I am so sorry," I blubber, once Mr Kensu has left. "It's just all been too much, you turning up out of the blue and being so mysterious. And I know it's not like we're really married, but I just couldn't help fantasising. And well, if the truth be known, I haven't been able to stop thinking about you since that night in my room, but you're just a schoolgirl . . . with nice feet . . . and I just . . ."

Karen puts her finger to my lips. She smiles through the tears and I can't help myself. It's narcotic. My knees buckle, my stomach breaks a world pole-vault record and my brain explodes with pleasure. I cup her gorgeous face, her blue eyes more striking than ever thanks to the tears, and I kiss her. To the outsider it's a conservative kiss, a you-may-kiss-the-bride kiss, but I force more passion into that kiss than any other in my life.

"I'm sorry about before, I just had no idea what you were trying to do," I say, when we break away.

Karen smiles again. "I should have explained what I was doing. I guess if the situation were reversed, I'd be pretty pissed off."

I consider this for a moment. "So would Darryl."

Karen laughs. Then it's her turn to cup my face. She gives me a quick, tender kiss and walks back into the gaming room. She's right, we have work to do – Tetsuya Suzuki work. Firstly, I have to find out if he's even here tonight, which isn't going to be easy – there are about twenty men who look Japanese enough, and important enough, to be him.

I saunter over to a roulette table and take in the scene. Three Japanese men are playing, as well as another man who looks vaguely familiar, in a weren't-you-the-sidekick-in-a-movie-once? kind of way. Around them are an assortment of exquisite Japanese girls who, under their makeup, look about the same age as the Miami High School girls from yesterday. Cigars are being smoked, scotch is being imbibed, breasts are being touched and hors d'oeuvres are being nibbled. The chips are being cashed at a thousand dollars a piece. I pat my fat pockets. In for a penny, in for a pound, as some poor bastard once said.

I throw $20,000 on the table and receive cursory glances from my playing-partners, but not much else. This isn't going to be easy. I can only hope that Karen is having more luck.

I watch the white ball do a few laps, biding my time and trying to think of a plan. I can't just ask anyone straight out where Tetsuya is, that would be far too suspicious. And given the obvious paranoia about security, far too dangerous. I have to gain trust. Whose trust, I'm not quite sure. Maybe there's just a big collective trust. Either way, the best start is to gamble, make like any other everyday punter laying out thousand-dollar bets in an illegal Gold Coast casino.

I play for about half an hour; nothing too risky. I win a bit, I lose a bit. I guess I stay about even. But it's getting me nowhere. There is precious little interaction at the table and definitely no chances to inquire about Tetsuya.

I find Karen back at the table I dragged her from earlier. Uncle Sam's obnoxious nephew has his podgy arm around her narrow waist. I swallow resiliently and stride forth.

"Well howdy there, look who's here, honey. What'd you say your name was?"

"I didn't."

Karen looks at me. It's not a nice look.

"Trigger Bondini," I say with a wink to Karen. I hope she takes it as a wink. I'm not a very good winker.

"Say, Trigger, why'nt you pull up a seat and we'll get down to some serious gamblin'"

"Actually, I was hoping you'd take your hand off my wife's arse long enough for me to have a word with her. You think you can handle that, Tex?"

Karen leads me by the arm to the other side of the room. "I'm sorry, I'm sorry," I say. "I just can't help it. When I see him with his buttery arm around your waist . . . I mean, you're just a schoolgirl, after all."

"Very chivalrous," Karen replies. "I don't think he's much more use to us anyway. From what I can gather, no one really knows who Tetsuya is. He's very protective of his identity. If he is here, he could be any of these Japanese guys." She looks around, doing the head-check I did earlier.

"So what do we do?" I ask.

"I don't know, why don't we go and play some blackjack?"

"Ahh, two problems. One, I don't want to go anywhere near our American friend again. And two, I can't play blackjack."

"Okay, well, *one*, we'll use the table in the next room, and *two*, it's easy; just get as close as possible to twenty-one without going over."

"I didn't say I don't know *how* to play, I said I *can't* play. There are tactics and moves and little things."

"Oh Jesus, Trigg, pull your finger out. It's easy."

I take a seat among four rapacious Japanese men. They nod courteously at Karen, ignoring me. So I twirl a chip professionally around my fingers just to let everyone know I'm no amateur. Of course I drop it. It rolls three feet and comes to rest under one of my more serious-looking counterparts. Now sure, if it was 20p, I'd let it go, a quid even – better that than crawl around with my grey-suited arse in the air like a mirror ball – but this is a thousand dollars.

I slide smoothly off my seat but wind up wedged between the table and the chair. My legs are useless and my arms are good only for flapping helplessly. Karen doesn't quite know what to do.

"Can I help you, sir?" asks the croupier.

Now I have everyone's attention. Terrific. I look at the surly Japanese man above my chip. "Could you reach that chip under your seat for me, please?"

He looks at me deadpan. The croupier mutters something to him in Japanese. The man pats the carpet under his seat. I nod encouragement – as much as I can. He finds the chip and hands it to me, like a child giving a peanut to an elephant.

"Thank you."

He looks at me seriously. Then bursts into laughter. And his friends all laugh. Their booming, resonant Japanese laughs.

I clamber back to my seat and try to stand up, but Karen's firm hands on my shoulders insist otherwise. I look up behind me. Using just her eyebrows, she reminds me that we are here for a reason. I suck up my pride and turn back to the table. The other men are wiping their eyes and regaining their composure.

I place my adventurous chip and one of its more docile friends in a little rectangle marked off on the felt. The dealer sweeps around the first time and flicks me a ten of hearts. He deals himself a six, which seems to please my playing partners. He then gives me another ten on the second round. Ten and ten, that's twenty – pretty damned close to twenty-one if you ask me.

"Would you like to split?" asks the dealer

"Are you kidding me? I've got twenty! I'm not going anywhere."

Karen whispers in my ear.

"Oh, right . . . yes, I'll split."

I split my tens and win both hands when the dealer busts. It seems Trigg's wallet just keeps getting fatter.

Or maybe not. I manage to lose the next four hands straight. What's more, I don't think I've gained anyone's trust. In fact, I think the only thing I've gained is disdain. I've done nothing but constantly change my mind, dispute rules, ask if I can have cards that have been dealt to other players, and consult Karen on tactics. Things are not looking overly optimistic and I'm certainly not endearing myself as a confidant. Still, you never know. I decide to check the water.

"So, what sort of car do you drive?" I ask the man to my right.

. . . Okay, well unless there's a new Honda called the "grunt" I don't think I'm about to be privy to any information this group has. Mind you, that's not a bad name for a car.

I give Karen a beseeching shrug of the shoulders. She gives me an apologetic one right back. What to do? What to do? I notice all my gambling buddies are smoking cigars, maybe that's a way in. Before the dealer can do his thing again, I ask him where I might find a cigar. He motions to someone behind me.

"Would you care for a cigar?" A fat Monte Christo materialises over my shoulder, accompanying the fat Japanese accent.

"Thank you." This should be interesting, my first cigar. I know from movies that you have to bite off the tip. I've never seen anyone rip off half the cigar before, though. Tobacco spills all over the baize, much to the annoyance of my gambling chums.

"That's an outstanding suit you're wearing." It's the same voice that offered me the cigar.

I turn around to see a man who, well, who needs more than a sentence to describe. He's a Japanese man in his late thirties. He is wearing an off-white suit with a pale blue T-shirt underneath. He has the sleeves pulled up and a three-day beard, as well as dark sunglasses and short, thick blow-waved hair. He is a Japanese version of Don Johnson in *Miami Vice*.

I am taken aback. The man stands checking out Ian's suit, while the remainder of the cigar hangs impotently from my lip, a bit of dried saliva the only thing still debating with gravity. Fantastic, now I have to spend the rest of the night discussing tailors with Don Johnson.

"Do you mind if I take a seat?" asks Don.

I take what remains of the cigar from my mouth. It takes a little bit of my lip with it. I indicate the empty seat beside me. "Of course, Mr."

"Somatsu," says the pathetic and yet still quite menacing-looking man. He sits down. "So where did you get your suit, Mr . . .?"

"My friends call me Trigg." Anyone prepared to speak to me tonight receives instant friend status. "As for the suit, my wife bought it for me." I address Karen. "Karen, this is Mr Somatsu."

"A pleasure to meet you, Mr Somatsu," Karen says with a twisted expression which is probably a reaction to what he's wearing.

Somatsu spreads the charm like Marmite. "No, no Karen, the pleasure is all mine." He takes her hand and kisses it. "Especially if it is true that you are responsible for your husband's clothes."

"Well . . . ahh . . . thank you. That's a pretty swanky get-up you've got there yourself."

Somatsu's eyes light up underneath his superfluous sunglasses.

He gives himself a satisfied once-over. "Thank you very much."

An awkward silence follows. Mr Somatsu taps a chunky gold ring. Having exhausted "regrettable fashions of the mid-eighties", we have no other subject to move on to. Mr Somatsu takes the opportunity to throw a huge wad of cash at the dealer – who doesn't seem too surprised. It seems our eighties throwback is a regular, and a loaded one at that. Quite possibly a good person to know in the search for Tetsuya. And he is willing to talk to me, which is one up on everyone else in the room.

We settle back into playing blackjack and things bump along quite happily for a while, until I get into another, let's say, *dialogue* with the dealer:

"Yes, I realise you just gave it to me, but surely it's my prerogative to give it back if I don't want it," I say.

"What are you talking about, you can't give a card back," stammers the dealer.

"Why not?"

"You asked for that card."

"No I didn't, I asked for an ace."

"Well you can't just give something back if you don't like it."

"Sure I can. I'm a child of the nineties – the 'me' generation. I can give anything back."

Mr Somatsu, who's been watching like a tennis spectator, opens his gullet and roars with laughter. "Haw haw haw! I find your style very amusing, Trigg."

Yes? Well I find your fashion sense fucking diabolical, but you don't hear me laughing about it.

We play some more, but it's hard to concentrate. Mr Somatsu guffaws at just about everything I do. And Karen can't help but join in. Finally, the whole table is in stitches. Except me. I'm busy assessing Mr Somatsu's potential use to me. Finally I can take it no longer. I merely pick up my chips and skulk away.

Karen follows me out onto the balcony. As does Mr Somatsu.

"Good idea, Trigg, let us take a break," says my new best friend from beneath his dark glasses. Karen hides a smirk.

"Mr Somatsu, I think you've been taking a break since 1987," I say.

"Haw, haw, haw!" He holds his sides, unable to decide whether to nod or shake his head.

I look to Karen for help. She can do nothing but laugh along.

"You are very funny, Trigg. Verrreee funny." He pulls out three cigars. One he puts in his mouth, the other two he gives to Karen and me.

Cigar etiquette not being my forte, I am desperate for a lead to follow. I'm not overly surprised when it's Karen's. She expertly rips the top off the cigar with her teeth before clenching it firmly in her mouth. That'd bring a new spin to getting busted smoking at school.

"Can I offer you a light?" Mr Somatsu asks her. He produced a gold Zippo lighter, which he ignites by flicking several times against his cream trousers.

Karen leans towards the flame and puffs away like a banker, or a movie star.

I manage to negotiate the tip of my cigar a little more successfully this time and I grasp it between my molars. Mr Somatsu holds the dancing flame in front of my face – three flames if you count the reflections in his sunglasses. I aim for the middle one, but then I see something that renders the muscles controlling my jaw powerless.

The cigar falls to the floor, seemingly in slow motion. The flame hovers inches from my face, illuminating Mr Somatsu's hand. On his right hand, the one without the gold ring, half his little finger is missing. "The Yakuza – tattoos, little fingers missing," Karen had said. How did I miss it before? Is it possible that I am staring at the answer to my quest?

Things snap back to normal speed and I pick up the cigar from the floor, dust it off and pop it back into my mouth. Directing it towards the flame, I suck back – never once taking my eyes off the Japanese man's pinky stub. I cough sharply. This could be the man,

Mr Somatsu, Terry Smith, Tetsuya Suzuki. I want to just blurt it all out to him; the possibility of instant confirmation is painfully enticing.

But it can't happen that way. Even if he is the one, the curse dictates that he can't admit it, lest his extra luck be voided, in which case neither of us get it. But still, the chance that my search could be resolved in a few minutes . . . Oh God, this is worse than the time I found out Janelle Gough was a lesbian and I wasn't supposed to say anything. And I cracked. I told Vicky. And look where that got me. My left testicle still hangs strangely. Strength, Trigg, you're going to have to do this the hard way.

"Say, Mr Somatsu . . ." *cough, hack* ". . . how long have you been . . ." *hack, wheeze* ". . . coming here . . .?" *cough, cough . . .*

"Oh, for a while, Trigg."

"Right. What? A month? A year? Couple of years?"

"Yes, something like that."

I can't work out whether he's dodging the questions or just struggling with English. I press on. "And tell me, Mr Somatsu, did they pick you up at the casino, too?"

"You know something, Trigg? You are very funny, but you ask a lot of questions. I'm sure we will catch up later on."

And with that he leaves.

Bugger!

"That was all very interesting," says Karen.

"My God, Karen, you've no idea just how interesting."

I explain my theory of Somatsu's missing little finger.

Karen and I talk on the balcony for twenty minutes or so, discussing the possibilities. Miss Pragmatic 2006 strongly doubts that Mr Somatsu is Tetsuya Suzuki, but she does concede that he's the closest thing we have to a lead, and, as such, shouldn't be wasted. I, on the other hand, am high. Even if Mr Somatsu isn't Tetsuya Suzuki, it's a pretty safe bet that unless he lacks rudimentary nail-clipping skills he has ties with the Yakuza. So then it's just a short jump to assume that he knows the man who goes by the alias Terry Smith.

"Well, what should I do?" I ask Karen.

She thinks for a second. "Why don't you just find him, do up your seatbelt and go along for the ride?"

It's not hard to find Mr Somatsu, he's standing at the bar listening to the Tom Jones tune that is wafting out from some unseen speakers. He's sort of jiggling around and taking in the scene while he taps at his gold ring. He certainly doesn't look like the head of a Japanese criminal organisation. But then again, maybe he does. I make a mental checklist of potentially useful information – which, in an ideal world, I would obtain thusly: "Excuse me, Mr Somatsu but could you please arrange the following statements in order, from most true to least true: (a) I am Tetsuya Suzuki, aka Terry Smith, who recently bought a good luck charm from a Fijian witchdoctor named Philip Matango; (b) I go by the alias Terry Smith, but I have not been to Fiji recently; (c) I am not Terry Smith, but I am the head of the Yakuza here on the Gold Coast; (d) I am a member of the Yakuza on the Gold Coast."

Since it's not an ideal world, I jiggle my way up to the dancing Japanese man and say: "You're drinking scotch?"

Somatsu stops tapping his ring. He stops jiggling. "Trigg, I am drinking the blood of the last person who asked me too many questions." He lowers his glasses and for the first time reveals his eyes. They are scary-looking little slits of fire. And then he opens his mouth wide, sucks in all the immediate air and pushes it back out again as roaring laughter. He resumes his tapping and jiggling and I begin to doubt my assumptions. "I am drinking twenty-year-old scotch, Trigg. Would you like some?"

"Thank you."

Mr Somatsu gestures to the bartender. It's a small gesture, a gesture that smacks of familiarity. And authority.

We drink our scotch in silence as we watch the curious circus around us.

"So what brings you here, Trigg?" asks Somatsu, sounding philosophical for the first time.

"Well, you were sitting here."

"No, not the bar. What brings you to the casino, what brings you to the Gold Coast?"

"The scotch."

"Trigg, I do not mean the bar."

"Neither do I."

I have no idea where I'm heading with this, I just hope it sounds intellectual, a little philosophical even. I follow up with a knowing nod.

Somatsu leans back and nods slowly as he considers my answer. "I see. That is very interesting."

"Interesting indeed."

"Very."

"Yes."

We both nod slowly.

"What about you, Mr Somatsu, what brings you here?" I am reluctant to let my breath go. Surely this is where he says: "Well, Trigg, someone has to head up the Yakuza here on the Gold Coast".

But instead he simply says, "Business."

Business . . .? That's not too bad. Not quite what I was hoping for, but not what I was fearing either. Yes. Business. Good. Time to push on now.

"What sort of business are you in, Mr Somatsu?"

"Well, business, you know."

"No, not really. I mean blow-up rubber dolls? Real estate? Prawn farming?"

He doesn't respond. First points to Somatsu. I put my head down and dive in for another go. "So, do you get to travel much in your line of work, Mr Somatsu?"

"A little."

"Wow, that must be interesting."

"Yes."

"Mostly to Australia?"

"Mostly."

"Have you been to many other countries?"

"A few."

"Really? What's your favourite country?"

"Australia."

"Any other favourites?"

"Japan."

I retreat to my corner, like a boxer unable to get past his opponent's defences. That's okay Trigg, you're doing good out there. Don't ease up now. He's getting tired, I can tell. I was watching – his left hand is starting to droop. Go for the left side, Trigg. Set him up with a few jabs and then go in for the kill.

"Another scotch, Mr Somatsu?"

"Thank you."

I order two more glasses of the smoky liquid. "I've been doing some travelling lately," I venture.

"Really?"

"Yes. Some amazing places. I think my favourite place must have been . . ." Wait for it, wait for it – okay, now! "Fiji."

"Really?"

Nothing. No flinching, no grimacing, no shaking. I, on the other hand, am reeling. His defence is too strong. Somewhere in the distance I can hear my coach yelling out instructions: "Keep going, Trigg, keep going. Don't give up now. The left, Trigg, the left". I fumble about on the ropes, mustering up the energy for one more swing. "Tell me, Mr Somatsu, have you ever been to Fiji?"

I connect. Mr Somatsu stumbles backwards – metaphorically.

He hesitates. His nonchalant, girl-gazing expression hardens ever so slightly.

"Ahh . . . no, not to Fiji."

Sure he shakes it off, he is a professional, but I've stung him. I swill some more scotch for want of anything better to do. It is slowly lowering the shades in my head, making everything a little fuzzy and taking off the harsh edges. Probably not the best time to get drunk. "Mr Somatsu, will you excuse me for just a second?"

"Certainly, Trigg. Need to think up some more questions, do you?" He cocks a cynical eyebrow.

I locate Karen and drag her back out onto the balcony.

"It's him! It's him, Karen!"

"Oh my God! Are you sure?"

"Absolutely."

"So he admitted he has the figurine?"

"No"

"But he admitted he's Tetsuya?"

"No."

"So . . . how come you're so sure?"

"Look, you're just going to have to go with me on this one. I just know."

"Okay, okay. So now what?"

"I'm not sure."

"Okay . . . so you're sure it's him . . ."

"Pretty sure."

"What? You said absolutely."

"Yeah, but I've had some time to think about it."

"What? Thirty seconds?"

"Well I tend to jump to conclusions. I mean, I'm fairly sure – but you know, unless he actually admits it, or I see the figurine, I can't be *absolutely* sure, can I?"

She sighs. And if one were more sensitive to the subtleties of women, one might take that sigh as an indication that she is getting a little frustrated with me, and one might act accordingly. I am not overly sensitive to the subtleties of women (or schoolgirls) so I press on . . .

"Here's the way I see it. He's not about to confess to being the head of the Yakuza, or to returning from Fiji with a wooden stowaway, so we have to trick him into admitting either of these things, or find some conclusive evidence that confirms them. The question now is how do we do this?"

"What about asking him about travelling."

"I tried that. He's very cagey. It's going to take a lot more work than that."

"Well at least he likes you."

"Not if I ask too many more questions."

♣ ♣ ♣

We come up with a plan. Okay, not really a plan, more of an angle. Alright, not even an angle, let's call it a desperate stab in the dark. With a butter knife. The bottom line: I track down Mr Somatsu again, engage him in conversation and hope I find a window of opportunity.

"Ahh, back so soon," says Mr Somatsu, over the top of the Genesis song *Invisible Touch*. "I don't understand it, Trigg. With a wife such as yours, if you are not gambling, then why are you still here? If you know what I mean."

"Weeeeeell . . . Karen finds the whole thing a bit of a turn-on, you know, all the money and power. She really has a thing for men with a lot of power. Yep, money and power . . . and snappy clothes."

I watch intently for a response, a blush, a sideways glance from behind the sunglasses, a "Well, that's funny, Trigg, because, as the head of the Japanese mafia here on the Gold Coast, I embrace all of those qualities". All I get is a snort and a nod.

"Yes," Somatsu continues as he goes back to work on the chunk of gold on his left hand, "that is the difference between men and women. While men will also go for money and power, they will settle for poverty and the brains of a ten-year-old if the girl is pretty enough. And they say that women are fickle creatures."

"Ooh, I don't think men are fickle, Mr Somatsu, just shallow."

For half an hour or so, Somatsu and I discuss the problems inherent in falling on the male side of the species. It's interesting, but unproductive. I am making absolutely no headway. Karen must be bored beyond humour, so the next time she ambles casually into sight, I subtly motion for her to join us. Perhaps she can salvage something.

"Are you enjoying yourself, Karen?" Mr Somatsu asks.

"Ooh yes, Mr Somatsu. There's something about power and money that I find so . . . so intoxicating."

Somatsu looks at Karen and then raises an eyebrow my way, as if to say: "I see what you mean."

I in turn raise my eyebrows to Karen, to say: "Please, like I haven't already tried that tactic – give me some credit."

Marvellous things, eyebrows.

But Karen isn't so easily shaken. She goes straight onto her next offensive. She yawns and looks at her watch. "But even as impressive as this is, I have a big day tomorrow, so we should probably get going soon. What about you, Mr Somatsu, do you have a lot on tomorrow?"

"I'm not sure about a lot, but I do have an early day. I have a golf game at 7.30."

"Really? Trigg loves golf, don't you, darling?"

I am mid-sip on my fourth scotch. My one and only golfing experience involved a girl named Di Webster, a putter and eighteen novelty obstacles, including a stamping fibreglass elephant.

"Ahem . . . yes, that's right. Love the game, can't get enough."

Somatsu perks up visibly. "That is excellent, Trigg. What is your handicap?"

Other than my complete lack of co-ordination? "Five," I reply, plucking a number from the ether.

Somatsu is impressed.

Bugger, wrong number.

"Five! Well then, I insist you play with me tomorrow. You can give my some pointers. I am only off fifteen."

"Well, marvellous, Mr Somatsu, I'd love to but—"

"He'd love to, Mr Somatsu," Karen interjects.

I give her a what-are-you-doing? smile, but she gives me a you-know-exactly-what-I'm-doing smile right back. And I do know what she's doing. And she's right. It's time to cut our losses for the night and line up another meeting – something she's achieved with outstanding tact.

But golf? Bloody hell!

It seems Mr Somatsu is meeting one of his business associates at Sanctuary Cove. He would be most honoured if I would join them. A time is set: 7.20 a.m., sharp.

Karen and I make our exit soon afterwards. To be honest, I

couldn't wait to get out of there – the monotony of inoffensive music from decades past was giving me a headache, the smoke was pushing little pins into my eyes, and there are only so many golfing anecdotes you can blag. We are blindfolded again, taken down to the basement and put back into the limousine. In contrast to our first trip, I feel completely at ease and not the least bit intimidated.

Our blindfolds are taken off when we get back to the public casino. A plastic key-card is shoved into my hand and, in very rough English, the monster who was with us on our first excursion explains that we can use the suite at the casino for the evening. I suddenly find myself anxious again, but for a different reason. Do it, Trigg, she's a babe. *Don't* do it, Trigg, she's a *babe*.

Standing in front of the automatic doors, I shift awkwardly, not quite able to look Karen in the eye. I notice she is doing a similar dance. This is where she's supposed to take control of the situation. I don't choose confident women for nothing. No! I've got to take control, make my own luck.

"It is a very nice room, Trigg," Karen says.

"Yes," I reply, "very nice. It would be a shame to waste it."

"An awful shame."

"And you know how the Japanese are with offers of courtesy – very easily offended if you refuse."

"That's true . . . shall we, Mr Bondini?"

"Absolutely, Mrs Bondini."

"*Ms Logan*, please. I don't believe in such an archaic practice as taking a man's name."

"Yes dear."

For the second time this week, I hurry through an expensive hotel lobby with Karen on my arm and a body full of hormones. It's just like I'm sixteen again. Except for the hotel. And the girl on my arm. But the hormones are uncanny. The room is just as intoxicating as earlier, maybe more so, because my mind is lighter. I have the whole night to explore every nook and cranny of this opulent playground. And Karen. I vaguely consider the golf game the following morning (with no clubs, no transport and a shiny grey suit as my only attire), but file it in the "later" basket, along with my moral obligations to Karen.

I follow her onto the plush leather couch. It's been quite a day. Actually no, if I'd had a minor car accident, or caught up with a friend I hadn't seen in years – that would be quite a day. But I've won $140,000, been manhandled by a Yakuza thug, overcome a marriage crisis, and made friends with the potential answer to all my problems. I'd say it's been an absolutely amazing, slap-me-in-the-face-with-a-dead-fish, day. When I think of it like this, I can't help but be overwhelmed. And just as if all the day's scotches and cigars have been concentrated into my next breath, my head starts swimming. Sweet Jesus, what a day.

♣ ♣

18

"Trigg. Hey, Trigg," the samurai whispers as he wields his lethal . . . golf club over my head. "Hey, Trigg, wake up," he whispers again, in his sensual, velvety voice. "Aren't you forgetting something?" And then the graphite-shafted club comes down with a sickening . . . beep.

Beep?

BEEP . . . BEEP . . . BEEP . . . BEEP . . . BEEP . . .

I sit straight up, taking in huge gulps of air while the obnoxious alarm bleats away. But I can't see.

Desperately, and probably more asleep than awake, I scratch at my eyes – only to come away with a piece of paper that has been sticky-taped to my forehead. Slowly my heart-rate begins to slow. I am on a couch in an amazing room with the Gold Coast stretched out before me. Reality snaps back. But instead of ceasing, my gulps become more panicked; I fell asleep! Where's Karen?

Tentatively, I examine the piece of casino stationery.

Good morning, Casanova.

I'm sorry I couldn't stay.

It's just easier, and safer, this way. Besides, I've got school today.

I know you're dying for an explanation, and it will come, but you're just going to have to keep trusting me.

It's about 6.45 a.m., if I set the alarm right, which means you've got a golf game in three-quarters-of-an-hour. There's a car waiting for you downstairs. I checked with the casino and the golf pro at Sanctuary Cove is expecting you – his name is Scott. If you leave now you should have time to buy some clothes and some clubs.

Good Luck, Trigg. You will never be far from my thoughts.

Love, Karen

My first thought is the briefcase, or more specifically, the hundred-odd grand *in* the briefcase. I find the case sitting on the bed in the main bedroom. I don't remember putting it there. Actually, I can't remember putting it anywhere, so maybe I did put it there – the details of last night are a little hazy.

As I reach for it, I can feel my heart just waiting to tear itself in two. Surely not again. Surely. I unclasp the latches and my heart does a little somersault of joy. The money is there! She didn't take it! If only she was still here, too.

I quickly turn off the clock radio and note that it is indeed just after 6.45. I have to ring Ian and Terri and give them an update, but it's far too early. I'm so hungry that my stomach is starting to eat itself, but breakfast isn't an option, either. I have a game of golf to play.

I have the window of the car down, my aching head angled to get maximum breeze. The briefcase is stashed at the casino, minus enough cash to buy some clubs and clothes. With Ian's shiny suit and the money, along with my bleary eyes and lack of showering, I could pass for a seventies rock star. Except we're not in the seventies, so I guess I just pass as a rather well-off, unhygienic sap.

The front desk informed me that Karen left at around 2.15 a.m. I briefly thought about going after her, but the bigger picture beckoned. Maybe I'll go to her school after golf . . . hmm, maybe not. But there are still so many questions, so much I want to know.

When I arrive at the picture-perfect Sanctuary Cove, Scott is indeed expecting me. It's about ten minutes past seven so there's no time for chitchat. I give the pro an abridged version of my predicament, which he takes in with a disarming lack of surprise. Rubbing his freshly-shaved chin, he looks at me through his sun-squinted golf-pro eyes and nods. "No worries."

In no time, I have a set of graphite-shafted King Cobra golf clubs by my side for a mere $2,400. Unfortunately there is a problem in the clothing department. While the pro shop has an abundance of shirts, it has only tartan plus fours in the trouser department. It seems that we all have one area in life where bad luck seems to haunt us. Mine just happens to be clothes. I shudder to think what will happen if I don't sort myself out before my indemnity expires.

My options lie depressingly before me: Ian's shiny silver suit-trousers; underpants; or LSD-inspired plus fours. Or . . . or maybe . . . "Say, Scott, they're some nice strides you've got there."

He's a tenacious little bastard – seems he isn't so keen on wearing the plus fours either. But a thousand dollars tends to change a person's mind.

I nip into the dressing room and whip on the pro's white slacks. Well, I whip them halfway on. When I called him a tenacious little bastard, I didn't mean it figuratively. I work the slacks over my thighs like condoms over a couple of watermelons and emerge from the dressing room looking like a well-dressed cyclist. Thankfully, there are no other golfers in the shop and Scott is too absorbed with his own sartorial dilemma to see the humour. And I'm in too much of a rush to really care anyway. I have ten minutes to learn how to play golf.

Scott, now wearing the plus fours, does his best to teach me what has taken far more coordinated men decades to become *almost* proficient at. He shows me a grip, tells me to keep my head down, and insists that the harder I try to hit the ball, the less distance it will travel.

I have a practice hit into the net outside the shop. And you know what? Compared to Crazy Golf, it isn't too bad. Nice and smooth, not trying to hit the ball too hard. Scott even seems to forget about his trousers for a while as he adjusts my stance slightly.

Then I have another go. I try to smack the absolute bollocks out of the ball.

I miss.

Scott frowns.

I swear.

A thirty second lecture on biomechanics and I'm ready for another go. But before I can even think about my back swing, a glint from the carpark catches my eye. I feel a few more million nerves fire up and my stomach does a convincing impression of a hooked trout as I watch the limousine pull up. But when the doors open, my nerves shut down completely and the trout makes a dive straight for my bowel. I watch in utter disbelief as Mr Somatsu's playing-partner steps onto the carpark bitumen. This can't be happening. My body is numb. My brain is operating on its emergency generator. All it can utter is "run".

I walk as fast as my tight trousers will allow me, back into the pro shop, and hide behind a rack of putters. Pushing my face against the silver shafts, I peer into the carpark. I'd recognise those big white eyebrows anywhere. Scott follows me in to see if I'm okay. I tell him that I have to hide, that I can't let the elderly gentleman wrestling his clubs out of the boot of the limousine see me – under any circumstances. Unperturbed, he rubs his chin and shrugs, as if I were telling him that I thought it was going to rain. "No worries."

I hop anxiously from one foot to the other as Mr Somatsu and Terry Smith make their way up the concrete path. My mind is racing around like a hyperactive child with a blindfold on, bumping into possible plans of action and tripping over elaborate excuses. Scott just keeps rubbing his chin and squinting.

They are about to walk around the last corner, past the last hedge of protection.

"Why don't you jump in the dressing room?" Scott suggests.

I bolt. Straight into the dressing room.

"Good morning, Scott," Somatsu's voice rings out. "How are you this morning?"

"Oh, you know," the pro replies, calm as you like. Boy I bet he's good with the pressure putts.

"Excellent. Scott, this is a business partner of mine, Mr Smith."

"Morning," Terry grunts.

"Say, Mr Smith, I wonder where our third is?" Somatsu queries.

"Oh, he's in the dressing room," says Scott.

What? Bastard! I take back what I said about the pressure putts.

"And how are you, Trigg?" Somatsu bellows over the door.

"Oh—" I try again, in a disguised, deeper voice: "Oh, just fabulous, thank you."

"That's excellent. I see Scott here is working his salesmanship on you."

"Ahh . . . yes. I'm thinking of getting some of those plus fours."

"Indeed. I have several pairs myself."

"I just bet you do, Mr Somatsu."

There is an awkward silence for about a minute. I imagine Mr Somatsu tapping impatiently on his garish gold ring. I can actually hear feet shuffling on the thin carpet and feel eyes burning holes into the changing room door. Finally Mr Somatsu breaks the silence. "I can assure you, Trigg, they are fine trousers. I'm sure they will look very good on you – they look just super on Scott – but we have to tee off."

"Why don't you go on, I'm just not sure if they make me look a little big in the hips. I'll meet you out there."

"Oh, come now, Trigg, don't be silly. Come out and give us all a look."

"I'd really rather not."

"I insist. We're not budging until you do."

Oh for the love of God! It's been about five minutes now and it's dawned on me: this is an inescapable situation. There is absolutely no way I'm getting out of this; I'm going to have to face Terry Smith. Will he shoot me? Surely that would be a breach of club rules – at least a one stroke penalty. I bet that's why Tiger Woods never kills anyone.

Three times I reach for the door, but pull back at the last second. I can hear the impatient sighs. Okay, okay, on three: one . . . two . . .

I push open the door and stride defiantly out. I'm looking straight into Terry's eyes when he registers just who I am, and somewhere deep, deep inside I take a macabre pleasure in watching as he tries unsuccessfully to make all the pieces fit. He just stands there while Somatsu looks me up and down.

"Hmm, those are not the trousers I thought you were talking about. If anything, those trousers take all the shape out of your buttocks. What do you think, Scott?"

Scott is watching the proceedings much as a university student might watch *Jerry Springer*; waiting for the boyfriend to reveal to his unsuspecting girlfriend that he is a two-timing, transsexual, homophobic, racist vegetarian. "A little," he says.

Terry is still staring, saucer-eyed. I've no idea how Somatsu explained my late inclusion in the game, but whatever he said, it isn't synching in Terry's head.

Somatsu turns to solicit support from his elderly playing-partner. He pauses for a beat. "And obviously Mr Smith here agrees."

Hearing his name, Terry seems to snap out of his hypnosis.

"Oh, My apologies," Somatsu proclaims. "How rude of me. Mr Terry Smith this is Mr Trigger Bondini."

"Bondini, now, is it?" Terry mumbles. He makes his way over and shakes my hand. "You're fucking dead," he whispers into my ear.

Now, like most people, I've heard that a few times – ex-girlfriends, doubles partners, you know; but this is the first time I've actually believed it. And I'm a little shaken.

Then Terry continues. "Do you have any idea who this is?" he asks Mr Somatsu, with an accusing growl, just dying to spill the beans.

Mr Somatsu responds by lowering his glasses and looking me over. My heart gasps. I find I've wrapped my hand around one of the putters.

"Yes," says Somatsu. "This is Trigger Bondini, wearer of fine apparel and my new friend." There is a possessiveness in his voice that seems to herald a warning to all and sundry.

I hold my breath as I wait to see if Terry will cut me down, then and there. But he's a cagey old bastard, he knows how to play games. He simply nods and withdraws to his position behind Somatsu.

Well this should be a very interesting game of golf. There's nothing like the imminent threat of physical violence to lift one's game.

"Well, the sun isn't waiting for us," Somatsu ventures, "and luckily for you, Trigg, neither are the fashion police!" He bursts into deep retching guffaws at his own joke.

At this precise point in time, I'm prepared to say that the Sanctuary Cove Pro Shop is the strangest place on earth.

I look about me. Somatsu is still laughing, Terry is still glaring and Scott is still . . . doing whatever it is that Scott does. It's enough to mess with my head. But if there's one thing the last week-and-a-bit has taught me, it's how to function in situations that would once have left me a gibbering mess.

"We'd better get going then, hadn't we?" I say.

Outside, Somatsu takes a coin from his pocket. It's not Australian currency. In fact it appears quite antique. Japanese, presumably. Its worn surfaces look very authentic, cradled in Somatsu's hand. Again I am drawn to the stub of his smallest digit and the story it must be bursting to tell.

"Shall we flip for honours?" Somatsu asks, not waiting for a reply. "Heads and it is Trigg, tails and it is Terry."

He flicks the coin high into the air before snatching it prematurely out of its arc. He turns it over on his wrist. "Tails – Terry."

The old man nods.

"What about you?" I ask Somatsu.

"I always go last, Trigg. I like to know what I have to beat. Good luck, Mr Smith." He shakes Terry's hand, then he takes mine, his gold ring digging into my knuckles. "Good luck, Mr Bondini." He doesn't let go until I'm looking directly into his sunglasses. A long pause follows. Just as I'm starting to squirm, Mr Somatsu looks from me to Terry and back again. "Gentlemen, it is customary to wish each other good luck. Sometimes luck is more important than talent."

Finally, I offer my hand to the old bastard, and Terry envelops it in his sun-bitten mitt. He either has a naturally firm grip or he's trying to crush my hand with his deteriorating muscles. Whichever, I give as good as I get. And we stand, eye to eye, trying to squeeze submission out of the other.

"Good," says Mr Somatsu. "Let us pursue a little white ball for a few kilometres . . . where is Scott?" He turns to look for the pro.

Terry relinquishes his grip, but only to point an arthritic finger at me. "I know what you're up to," he whispers. "You're dead."

Scott arrives with a pair of golf buggies, towing one behind the other. Hmm, I think to myself, three into two does not go.

"You have the honour, Terry," says Somatsu. "You take the first buggy. Trigg and I will take the second one."

My breath spells out "relief" in the crisp morning air. But the very next breath spells out "despair". I have a big problem on my hands – or in my hands, to be more precise. Hell, I don't even know which club to use.

I sit beside Mr Somatsu as we buzz along behind Terry, down the little white concrete path through the trees. I've never actually been on a proper golf course before, and it's an interesting spectacle up close, as if someone has gone over the whole place and aligned every blade of grass. My fascination with the botanical perfection, however, quickly gives way to the task ahead. What on earth am I going to do?

"Urrghhh," I moan. "Ooohwarggg."

"Is anything the matter, Trigg? You do not sound so well."

"Arghhh, it's just a bit of a stomach thing. But it's quite bad."

"Oh dear, that is unfortunate. But you know, in Japan we have a particularly effective remedy."

Well that's just super isn't it! "Really? What would that be, Mr Somatsu?"

"Golf, Trigg." He lowers his reflective glasses. It's enough to remind me that I am here to play golf with him so that he can benefit from my "superior game", and nothing is going to change that.

"Hey, I feel better already."

We stop at the first tee. The aggressive morning sun is in the process of taking back any moisture the earth may have stolen during the night; there's a wafty, summery aroma – the kind of smell that takes you back to a world of flapping about in cricket pads while bored parents read the paper.

The fairway looks gorgeous but uninviting; so pretty, but so narrow and long. A tiny red flag lies limp against a white pole about three hundred yards in the distance; the sand in the surrounding bunkers is so white it almost shines.

Terry and Mr Somatsu pull out what I assume are "woods". I go to my own bag. There are three woods, so I grab the one I had the practice swing with earlier.

My playing partners are now swinging their arms around, bending their backs and going through all sorts of contorted golf swings. I follow suit. But my club sails through the air, about twenty feet, ending up over near the buggies. I receive an assortment of questioning looks.

"Gotta let your clubs know who's boss," I say.

Somatsu immediately hurls his club down the fairway and looks to me for approval. I give him a reassuring nod. Terry shakes his head in disbelief.

It was probably the sweat that caused my club to slip. It's now seeping lazily out of every pore – and not necessarily because of the thieving sun. It runs acridly into my eyes as I follow Terry's gaze down towards the flag. Jesus that's a long way.

Terry unzips one of the pockets in his golf bag and removes a ball. Then from another pocket he takes a little plastic bag and squeezes out a fluorescent pink plastic tee. I watch uncomfortably as he whacks the ball down the fairway.

"Lovely shot," Mr Somatsu says, applauding.

"Indeed," I add, trying to sound as unimpressed as a player with a handicap of five would sound. "A *Hot Shot*," I call as a witty afterthought. Well, it seemed witty at the time.

"Thank you, gentlemen," Terry replies in a smarmy, top-that voice. "I believe you're up, Detective Greg—I mean, Trigg."

I amble casually over to my bag, unzip one of the pockets, and declare (in as disappointed a voice as I can muster): "Oh no, I don't have any balls. I can't believe this. I'll have to go back to the pro shop and buy some. Won't be a sec, don't wait for me, I'll catch up."

I'm almost in the buggy when Mr Somatsu stops me. "Nonsense, Trigg, I have plenty. You can use one of mine. Come on now, we're behind time as it is."

"Oh, thank you, Mr Somatsu."

He hands me a ball in its own little box, and a tee with T.S. emblazoned on it. T.S! If my heart could speed up any more it would. T.S. – *Terry Smith*! Surely this is proof. The endorphins have the front door open and are on their way to the park in my brain, when their mother calls them back. T.S. *could* stand for Terry Smith . . . or it could stand for Tetsuya Suzuki . . . or Tom, Tim, Tony or Tyrone Somatsu. Or maybe just "Tough Shit". Anyway, back to my original problem.

I push the tee into the ground near where Terry placed his. At least, I almost do: the seam on Scott's white slacks gives out before the tee ever touches the grass. A three-inch gape now reveals my blue-and-white-striped underpants. "Hello," they're saying. "Hello, Mr Japanese Man, hello Mr Old Person, I'm Trigg's underpants. It's a pleasure to meet you." There are a couple of high-pitched titters from behind me and a heavily-accented proclamation that I should have gone for the plus fours. It's amazing how slapstick humour can cross cultural boundaries and negate $50,000 grudges. Maybe Benny Hill really was a genius.

I wait a few seconds for my audience to settle down before continuing. I press the tee lightly into the soft ground; the higher it is, the more chance I have of hitting something – maybe even the ball. I balance the ball on the tee and admire my handiwork. There is no getting out of this one.

I stand for a bit, staring down towards the green. On the outside, I'm calm, but inside my head, the walls are closing in. My mind searches frantically through the fog for some sort of plan. Anything.

I step up to the ball. I place my feet the way Scott showed me. I lock my little finger and index finger together around the soft rubber grip. I look at the flag. I look at the ball. I look at the flag. I look at the ball. I draw back the club. I swing my shoulders smoothly. I hit the ball.

Sort of. It skips about forty yards along the ground, in a direction that only slightly resembles the one in which it was supposed to go. I turn and look squarely at Terry. And I say, "What the hell did you do that for?"

"What? Do what?" asks a confused Terry Smith.

"You coughed, just as I was about to hit the ball. I can't believe this. Such disgraceful manners. You heard him, didn't you, Mr Somatsu?"

Terry splutters his innocence, quite exasperated.

"Honestly, Terry," I continue. "I don't really know you, but you seem like a decent chap. I just can't believe you'd do something like that." I stomp over to my bag and throw my club back in.

Mr Somatsu turns to Terry. He lowers his sunglasses and slowly shakes his head. Terry is rightly beside himself with injustice, but this just seems to disappoint Somatsu even further. I have just bought myself forty yards of grace. Unfortunately, those forty yards will be crossed by buggy, so they don't equate to much time. But like they say, you've got to play golf one shot at a time.

"My sincere apologies for Mr Smith," Somatsu offers.

Terry is purple with silent rage. A heart attack is most certainly not out of the question. I have never seen anyone so angry. And I've witnessed a lot of anger.

"If you would be so kind, Terry, as to keep your coughing to yourself while *I* tee off."

Somatsu's swing is very precise and determined, just as I expected. Neither Terry nor I utter a sound. Somatsu clouts the ball a good 150 yards, straight towards the flag. "You take the first buggy, Trigg, I'll go ahead with Terry. No doubt a player of your capabilities will catch us up."

I dance a little jig on the inside, as Terry and Mr Somatsu zoom off in their buggy. The obvious thing to do is to make a break for it, as fast and as far as the little electric motor will take me. But that would leave me with a lot of unanswered questions. So, against all my survival instincts, I drive down to where my ball lies. I have to take this risk.

The grass is scruffy and scraggly. Obviously this part of the course doesn't receive many visitors. In the distance Mr Somatsu and Terry are motoring along, so I jump out and pocket my ball. They are about to witness the longest second shot in history.

"What happened? We did not see you play your second shot," Somatsu remarks when I finally catch them up.

"Oh, that's a shame. It was an absolute cracker."

Terry glares at me. "You know that's very dangerous, playing your second when the people in front aren't watching. Some may even say it's rude. Young bloody whippersnappers these days, always too impatient. Bet it wasn't that way when you were a kid, hey Mr Somatsu?"

"Ahh, impatience and enthusiasm are two sides of the same coin, Mr Smith. Besides, a player of Trigg's ability isn't about to hit the ball anywhere near us. Where did you lay up, Trigg?"

"Ooooh, about fifty yards up ahead."

"Outstanding, I do believe that's the longest fairway drive I have ever seen."

"Indeed, but it was off a bit and went into the trees on the left."

"Good, good, we all need a challenge."

Terry has given up trying. He mutters profanities to himself as he yanks out a club and walks to his ball. He stands and looks towards the flag, still muttering and clodding up the grass with his spiked shoes. He takes a few angry practice-swings.

"So what do you think of Mr Smith's action, Trigg? Do you have any pointers?" Somatsu looks at me with innocent curiosity while Terry freezes, mid-swing, daring me to comment.

"Not at all. He has an exceptional swing." Terry relaxes. "For an older gentleman."

Terry turns and takes an angry breath, about retort, but he

swallows his words before the first one spills out. Resuming his stance, he takes out his frustration on the ball, which only compounds his anger by shooting off into the trees.

"Fuck it!" he shouts, thumping the ground with his club. "Fuck it . . . fuck it . . . fuck it."

"Now Mr Smith, there is a time and a place, is there not?" Somatsu scolds – just the sort of thing you need to hear when you are so enraged that you can actually picture the nearest object to hand being entered as "Exhibit A" when you're charged with murder.

Terry's hands are shaking badly as he jams his club back into his golf bag. Somatsu continues unabashed, "Well now, it looks like you two amateurs are over in the trees together, let us see if I can't do better than that."

We drive up to where Somatsu's ball lies, about thirty yards up the fairway. Again he clips it with the utmost precision and it continues its uneventful journey towards the green. "Well, well, look at that, will you? Now, where did you two lay up? Oh that's right. Ha ha ha!"

I feel I should be offended, the only thing worse than a bad loser is a bad winner. But then again, I've just played the longest second shot in history, so why should I get upset?

I do start to panic, though, when logic suggests that Terry and I should now share one buggy, while Mr Somatsu takes the other. Fortunately, Somatsu has little respect for logic. He feels like walking, and insists that Terry and I take a buggy each. Fine by me.

Reluctant to interact with Terry outside Somatsu's protective shadow, I shuffle over to the buggy and zoom off. This will also give me time to plant my ball. An excellent plan indeed . . .

"What's your rush?" Terry calls out as he pushes his buggy to catch up. "I thought we could have a little chat."

"Sorry, what was that?" I yell, pressing a cupped hand to my ear and the accelerator to its limit.

The little electric motor whines like a kid in a supermarket. But the effort is doing me no good. Terry is catching up. I turn off the fairway, but Terry follows me as I steer around the tall gum-trees, getting closer by the second. "Come on, son, I just want to tell you a little story. It's about an undercover cop."

"Sounds interesting," I call back. "Maybe later, gotta get into the zone right now, you know, focus on my next shot."

"It's just a quick story, Trigg. It doesn't have a very happy ending, but I really think you should hear it anyway."

I manoeuvre back out onto the fairway, yelling over the moan of the buggies, "If it's the one where the senile drug-dealer tries to expose the clever undercover cop, and no one believes him – I've already heard it."

Terry has caught up by now and we are side by side, both buggies at their limit – which isn't much, really. "Oh no, this one's much better," Terry continues, little flecks of spit flying. "You see, in this one, the smartarse undercover cop gives back the $50,000 he took from the Sean Connery-like older gentleman, because if he hadn't, the Sean Connery-like older gentleman would have killed him."

"Sean Connery? Yeah, I can see it . . . if he was just a bit older, fatter and dumber."

"You little fucker . . ."

I squeal like a Bond girl as Terry pulls out his putter and takes a swing at my head. Luckily, he hits the metal bar supporting the canopy. I take the opportunity to turn back into the trees. The golf buggy Grand Prix is on.

I weave in and out of the trees at breakneck speed (for a golf buggy), but I can't shake Terry. With his extra speed he's beside me again in no time. He takes another swing and again hits the canopy.

"Why don't you use the laser in your watch, Sean?" I yell as we negotiate a series of scraggly bushes. I don't know why I do this, provoke people who really shouldn't be provoked. I just can't help myself. Sure, if I knew karate or something then it would be acceptable. But I don't. It's definitely a problem. I could try and explain this to Terry, a fireside chat between unlikely confidants. Then we could walk back to Mr Somatsu, slapping backs and smiling conspiratorially at our own private joke—

"Ooowww!" What the . . .? "Ooowww! Bloody hell!"

Terry is throwing golf balls at me. Really hard. Impulsively, I yank the wheel and ram into the side of his buggy. It takes the old man completely by surprise. His furry eyebrows hit the brim of his Panama hat and send it flying. I have to strike again. No mercy! No mercy!

I ram the old man again, before he has a chance to gather himself, this time knocking his golf bag off the back off the buggy. Terry is weaponless. He is vulnerable. It's time for the kill. But just as I start to jag the wheel, Terry rams me.

I bang my head hard against one of the bars holding up the canopy. I see a few stars, but not as many as that old bastard's about to.

Reaching over my shoulder for one of my clubs, I swerve around yet another tree. I don't know which club I pull out, but it feels damn menacing in my hand. But I'll wager it doesn't feel nearly as menacing as the gun Terry is now holding. The blood drains straight from my head, leaving me dizzy. This has suddenly become very serious. Game over. All I can think to do is hit the brakes; the buggy skids to a greasy stop on the slick grass. Terry watches me over his shoulder. That's probably why he doesn't see the tree.

He couldn't have hit it harder if he was trying. The side of his head slams against the steering wheel and the gun goes sailing away onto the ground. He's out cold.

As soon as my body starts accepting messages from my brain again, I clamber out of the buggy and run over to Terry. He's slumped heavily against the steering wheel, a thin line of blood running down his cheek.

Oh shit. He's dead.

Then I notice his chest rising and falling. I'm forced to toss up between relief and panic. I make a few hesitant attempts to resuscitate him, but have no idea what to do. The last person I saw unconscious was a cute winger I collided with at mixed five-a-side. But on that occasion, one of the other players was a med student – and the cute winger hadn't been toting a gun. Bugger, the gun!

The pistol is lying innocently in the wet grass, the sun glinting off its barrel. I pick it up hypnotically. It's cold. Really cold. A gaggle of goose bumps shuffle their way up my arm and down my spine. The gun won't fit in any of the pockets of my split trousers, so I shove it in my golf bag. I look back down at Terry, who is still unconscious. For some reason all I can think to do is get him his Panama hat back.

When I return, Terry is still away with the fairies, so I place the hat over his mussed-up white hair and give it a pat. I feel a little better.

"Oh my, what has happened here?"

I whip around and find myself staring at Mr Somatsu.

"Ahh . . . ahh . . . horrible thing, he just . . . I didn't really see what happened, he was behind me. I guess he lost control. All I heard was a dull thud. He's unconscious," I add as an afterthought.

Somatsu toys with his gold ring. "Yes, I see that. Well we had better get him to a hospital."

"Yes, yes," I agree, finally seeing a way out of my predicament.

Somatsu uses his mobile phone to call Scott. About five minutes later, Scott reports back that an ambulance is on its way. All is going well; Terry is still in Disneyland and, as such, unable to tell his side of the story.

The next few minutes pass unbearably slowly. Smalltalk about the weather somehow doesn't seem appropriate. Nor does deep conversation. I now realise that this man with whom I have been feeling such a strong bond is actually a complete stranger. So we stand beneath the shady gum-trees in a silence that threatens my very sanity. One minute, I'm sure Mr Somatsu knows exactly what happened and is waiting for me to own up; the next, I'm positive he's oblivious to anything but the inside of his mirrored sunglasses. Not that he utters a sound or bats an eyelid. He doesn't have to, such is the power of his presence. He'd make a captivating thriller movie – just him, on his own, staring at the camera for an hour-and-a-half.

After an eternity – or twenty minutes, depending on your relationship to the situation – an ambulance ambles its way over the perfect grass. It receives only cursory glances from the other golfers; I guess with so many retirees taking up golf in their twilight years, this is not an uncommon sight.

The first man to emerge is young and wiry with a small head, the second is overweight and sweating dreadfully despite the shade. They introduce themselves and make a few perfunctory inquiries. When asked what happened, I merely nod towards Terry's unconscious body slumped in the banged-up buggy, and spout something about elderly drivers.

Satisfied, the older, sweatier one kneels down beside the elderly drug-pusher and slaps him lightly on the face.

"Terry . . . hey, Terry . . . come on, mate, wake up."

Terry stirs. "Hmmph wzzzit nggghrrr."

"There ya go, mate, you're okay, aren't ya? Just a little bump, hey?"

The ambulance man is treating him like a geriatric idiot. I like him immediately. He begins to ease Terry out of the buggy. "Okay, mate, I'm just going to put you in the back of the ambulance here. Nice and easy. And then we're going to go to hospital for a bit, nothing scary or anything, just a check-up."

The younger man comes over and together they lead Terry towards the ambulance. Terry stares at them wide-eyed. "Hey, look at you, had a bit of a fright, have ya?" says the older man.

"What are you doing, you moron?" Terry blurts.

"Come on, Terry, you've had a bit of an accident, you're probably in a little bit of shock."

"Accident? Accident my arse! That little cretin ran me into a tree. Now get your hands off me! I'm going to smash his bloody head in!"

Terry tries to get away, but the younger man restrains him. "Hey! Terry!" he says. "Take it easy, mate. You're coming for a check-up and that's that."

Realising he's pinned, Terry turns his vitriol on me. "I'm gonna get you for this, you little fucker! I know what you're up to. And I've told other people. You're fucked, you are."

I nod sympathetically. "Poor old fella, he's a bit muddled up."

This sends Terry off his rocker, but the ambulance men manage to keep him under control and get him into the back of the vehicle. I can still hear him spewing threats as they drive away down the fairway.

And with that, he's gone, leaving a strange calm hovering over the clipped fairways and lush roughs. I turn around hesitantly. Mr Somatsu is sitting in one of the buggies, sidesaddle style, turning his putter over and over in his hands. The glint off the shaft is matched by the reflection from nine meticulously-manicured fingernails and one gold ring. His sunglasses are levelled right at me and I can only speculate as to what his eyes are doing.

"I . . . he . . . umm . . . we . . ." I give up.

Then Somatsu speaks. "I guess that means I win."

"I beg your pardon?"

"Unless, of course, you'd like to keep playing."

"What?"

"Well, after two shots, I was closest to the hole. So I win . . . unless you would like to keep playing."

Wow, that's cold. I mean, I'm not queuing up for the Terry Smith fan-club, but come on.

My incredulity must have been showing. "You are probably right, Trigg, we should stop. Besides, it is starting to cloud over."

And the spell breaks. I look around me. Indeed the sun has disappeared, hidden behind thick, grubby cotton-wool clouds. And other golfers are just going about their lives. Two men in their forties whirr past in a buggy just like the one Terry ploughed into the gum tree. They smile and wave, completely oblivious to the mayhem and deception so nearby. They are completely unaware of my life; the curse, the quest, the whole lot.

It's a very humbling moment, realising that my "big issues" mean nothing to all but a few people. The huge majority of the world couldn't care less if I wind up a loony, talking tersely to a five inch Fijian figurine as I wander the streets searching for a place to sleep. They've got their own lives to worry about.

At that precise moment I understand, I mean *really* understand, just what Ian was talking about. My future is entirely up to me. My responsibility, no one else's. Fate? Pah. There's no such thing as fate. That's just religion for atheists. No, in this world we make our own beds. You can't win the lottery if you don't enter.

I am staring vacantly over the plush green golf course when Mr Somatsu speaks.

"Hello, anybody there, Trigg? What do you think we should do for the rest of the morning?"

I stare at the mirrored glasses for a few seconds, still a bit vacant. "I'm not sure," I say slowly. "I guess I don't have any plans, I thought we'd be here all morning." I think about it some more. "I am a little hungry."

"Some food, perhaps?"

"Yes," I reply, warming to the idea. And then I see my opportunity, an opportunity in a world where fate does not exist, a world where you make your own luck. "But do you know what I could really do with first, Mr Somatsu?" I look up at the sun, wipe a hand across my forehead. "I could really do with a swim. You don't have a pool, do you?"

♣ ♣

19

We are in the back of Mr Somatsu's limousine, back on the Gold Coast highway, chatting amicably. Somatsu asks simple enough questions, I make up outrageously fabricated answers. This is going to be another long afternoon. Eventually we wind our way off the highway and into the canal estates, a complex of glittering waterways, cul-de-sacs and waterfront homes. Some canals cater to the working-class; some cater to the affluent small boat crowd; others cater to the wealthy. We're not cruising any of these. We are driving among the canals for the offensively rich.

All the houses are gargantuan, but that's where the similarities end. There are garish mansions that look like oversize Barbie Dream Homes. There are architectural self-indulgences that are more about art than comfort. And there is everything in between. Several times I see homes that scream: "Crime boss lives here!" And maybe one does; just not my crime boss.

After some time, the limousine finds its mark. While I can't see much in the way of Shinto spirituality, it does seem a terribly appropriate abode. It's two stories of quintessential eighties.

Casa Somatsu is an amalgamation of immaculate white-rendered concrete and dark reflective glass, wrapped around a broad angular frame. The house is disproportionately low, considering its width, but rather than appearing stunted or squat, it looks sleek, like a car that's been lowered until its chassis almost scrapes the ground. And the whole thing is surrounded by a tall, cream-coloured wall. "Subtle" was obviously not in the architect's dictionary.

The limo enters the gates and slides down the driveway to the big steel door of a basement garage. The garage itself confirms the status of the owner. Only someone with too much money would keep a garage this clean.

Mr Somatsu's sinewy young bodyguard materialises and opens the limousine door. He is introduced to me as Morris. Mr Somatsu explains that Japanese men often take local names if they are living in a western country.

My host is sliding out of the car, but I put a hand on his arm, perhaps a little eagerly. "Have you ever taken a western name, Mr Somatsu?"

He lowers his glasses and looks at my hand, grasping his arm. "Yes, Trigg, I have. In my line of business, I have had to take many names."

I quickly let go.

Once out of the limousine, I have to squint against the combination of brilliant white tiles and fluorescent light. I'm not in a garage, I'm in an operating theatre. The very thought chills me.

We enter a large lift and ascend to the second floor. The white theme continues and I'm forced to follow Somatsu through a half squint. His perpetually-present sunglasses make a lot more sense now.

We take off our golf spikes and he leads me through a vast living-area, which opens out onto a huge curved balcony. "You see this roof, Trigg?" Somatsu asks when we get outside. He is pointing to the sky.

"No."

"Exactly," he crows. "There is no roof, but if I want one, I just press this button and it will be there in less than five minutes."

"Amazing." It's all I can think to say.

Somatsu is unperturbed by my lack of enthusiasm. "Please, take a seat, my friend. A drink perhaps, before we take our swim?"

Morris stands to attention, waiting to take orders.

"Orange juice, please," I say.

"No, no. No orange juice," Somatsu interjects. "We will have two pina coladas, thank you, Morris." Somatsu explains that he has a fulltime chef who is also a renowned cocktail maker, not to mention martial arts expert.

"And now if you will excuse me for a moment, Trigg, I have to make a quick phone-call. Morris, would you call the hospital and get Mr Smith's room?"

"No!" I blurt. "I mean, I'm sure he's fine or they would have called us, you know, for more information."

"I'm sure he's fine, too. That's not what I need to talk to him about."

"Oh. What is it then?"

"Ahh, the questions again. It is a business matter, Trigg, if you must know, and it simply cannot wait."

I can feel sweat returning to my forehead.

Morris returns with a cordless phone, which he hands to his boss.

"Ahh, good afternoon, Mr Smith, how is the bump?" says Mr Somatsu as he walks back inside and slides the reflective glass door behind him.

I wander over to the door. In the reflection I can see beads of sweat queuing up at my eyebrows. And . . . and if I listen really hard, I can hear Mr Somatsu on the other side. I press my ear up to the glass.

"I am pleased to hear that," Mr Somatsu says. "Now, will you definitely have that information for me by tomorrow night?"

Pause.

"I'm sure I don't have to remind you of the magnitude and importance of this meeting."

Pause.

"Splendid, splendid. I will see you then."

Pause.

"Yes, very good. Goodbye Mr Smith."

Pause.

"Yes, yes, he is still here with me, I won't forget."

Somatsu puts the phone down and I spring back to my seat. He re-emerges from beyond the mirrored glass and stares at me. For too long. There's no telling what Terry has told him about me. Somatsu's face gives nothing away. Finally he clears his throat. "Mr Smith had some interesting things to say."

I cough nervously and try to straighten up in the chair.

"He said to tell you . . . you're fucking dead. Poor old Mr Smith," continues Somatsu with a chuckle. "He never was a particularly good sport when it came to golf. Now, perhaps we should enjoy our drinks down by the pool. I'll tell Morris."

I allow myself to breathe again as I follow Mr Somatsu, nodding enthusiastically.

"Look, Trigg," my host says as we walk back inside. I turn and look at the balcony door. "One-way glass! People cannot see in, but I can see out. Marvellous ingenuity. What will they think of next?"

My fraying nerves beg for a reprieve. Mr Somatsu hums happily to himself, a roving thumb rolling his gold ring around his finger as the lift descends. I have absolutely no idea what he knows and what he doesn't. Maybe this whole thing is one elaborate sting. Maybe he's friends with the Japanese men that were having drinks with Terry at Hot Shots. Maybe he thinks I'm an undercover agent. Oh Jesus.

We get out of the lift on the ground floor. An entertainment area opens out onto a large patio, which leads down to the pool. "You must come to a party here sometime, Trigg. I have magnificent parties. Hundreds of people. You may even know some of them. The Gold Coast is a small place."

I laugh nervously.

"Or a video night. I have video nights also. Well, they are DVDs, but 'DVD night' just does not have the same ring, does it? I have all the classics: *Top Gun*, *Flash Dance*, *Police Academy* (only One and Two, though – Three through Seven just lack something for me), *Wall Street*, *Girls Just Want to have Fun*, *Cocktail* . . ."

Our drinks arrive, cold and creamy and the perfect accompaniment to a morning by the pool. Rather than sip my pina colada slowly as I watch the sun shatter the water into glinting shards of glass, I gulp it down like Stella at a Chelsea game.

The alcohol washes over my neurones and drowns my paranoia. It's just the false sense of security I need to get back to the bigger picture. Something Mr Somatsu said during his conversation with Terry Smith has me thinking about Philip Matango's list of conditions. They state that whoever holds the good-luck figurine will be facing some sort of crisis.

"Tell me, Mr Somatsu, what are you doing tomorrow night? Karen enjoyed your company so much, she insisted I invite you to dinner. She'll be very disappointed if you can't make it."

Somatsu stops tormenting his ring for a second and stares. "I have a meeting, Trigg."

"Really? Surely you can postpone it. It's the only free night Karen and I have for some time."

"Not this meeting, Trigg."

"Must be important."

"All meetings are important."

"Yes, but what could be so important that you can't spend an evening with your two new friends?"

"I would hate to have been around you as child, Trigg. Nag, nag, nag. Question, question, question." Mr Somatsu animates his comment with little hand-gestures. Which is fine, until he goes from the "quacking chatterbox" gesture to the "crushing a person's throat" gesture.

I feel it best not to pursue this line of questioning.

Mr Somatsu then peels off his golf shirt to take in the sun. He reveals a moderately fit body . . . covered in tattoos. Intricate patterns, cherry blossoms and Japanese insignia in a tangle of reds, greens, blues and yellows adorn his torso and shoulders. On his back he sports a magnificent golden dragon.

"You have some very interesting tattoos, Mr Somatsu."

Mr Somatsu gives his body a once-over and nods.

"I used to collect temporary tattoos when I was a kid," I say.

Mr Somatsu stares at me. I order another drink.

My drink arrives and I suck it down much like the first. A third is definitely in order, but I hold back. Although blissful inebriation is still on the agenda, other concerns take priority. I have to find Roger's look-alike. And the sooner the better.

"So, do we have time to take look around your house before

lunch?" I ask, prodding a straw among the ice, for any alcohol I may have overlooked.

A small crease forms above my host's sunglasses.

"I'm sorry for being so eager, Mr Somatsu, it's just that it's such an impressive house, and so stylish."

"It is, Trigg, but I think we should wait. I am very hungry. Do you like chicken fajitas?"

"Ahh, sure. Although right now I could really go a chicken-and-mushroom roll from Jun's."

"What?" barks Mr Somatsu.

"Don't get me wrong, I'm a big fan of Mexican. It's just that—"

"No. What did you say just before?"

"I'm a big fan of Mexican?"

"No, no. Before that."

"Ahh, I could really go a chicken-and-mushroom roll from Jun's?"

He lowers his sunglasses. "You mean Jun who runs the corner store?"

"Yes, do you know him?"

"No. Well . . . yes. I met him once or twice. I think."

He stares at me, almost challenging me to contradict him. I stare back with a blank, confused gaze. He stares for a while longer and then simply slides his glasses back into place. Cool as a cucumber, he says, "I think a tour is an excellent idea."

He stands and walks happily back up the patio, leaving me to wonder what just happened. It was certainly very strange. But then "strange" is becoming the norm. What has me excited, though, is that the only reaction I've witnessed recently akin to Mr Somatsu's belonged to Jun. And that was when I mentioned Tetsuya Suzuki. It's just another bit of support for an ever-strengthening theory.

I push myself up and follow Mr Somatsu into the house, matching his smile tooth for tooth.

Padding barefoot over the spotless white tiles, Mr Somatsu walks me into his lounge. Two plush white couches flank a massive stereo system.

"You like music?" I ask.

"I like good, hard rock 'n' roll, Trigg. And until the day Bon Jovi's 'Living on a Prayer' falls from the charts, I will know I am not alone."

In the kitchen we pass a fiery little Japanese man, red and sweating above boiling pots, whom I take to be the chef. The furniture in the house suggests that if this is the decade of Ikea, then the eighties probably belonged to moulded plastic.

It's all very impressive in a "Lifestyles of the Rich and Infamous" way, but the house lacks personality. Where are the little knick-knacks and bits-and-pieces that make a house a home? Knick-knacks and bits-and-pieces that might include a Polynesian Tribal figurine?

The sterility continues down the hallway. Overpowering white. The few paintings that hang on the walls are pointless pastel prints of generic beach scenes. I follow my host down the stairs at the end of the hallway. "You have some interesting art, Mr Somatsu. Do you collect?"

"Not particularly. Bits and pieces."

"What about sculpture? Collect any statuettes? Figurines?"

Mr Somatsu stops midway down the staircase. He turns slowly, pushes a hand through his hair and frowns. "So many questions, Mr Bondini. Questions, questions, questions. Is it normal to be this curious?"

"Well . . . I . . ."

"Perhaps it is. Perhaps it is me that is rude, not asking you enough questions."

"I . . . no . . ."

"I have an idea, Mr Bondini. I will ask you one question. Just one. But you must answer me with the truth. You have honour, yes, Mr Bondini?"

I nod.

"Excellent." Mr Somatsu takes a step back up towards me. I retreat. "So, what would I like to know about Trigger Bondini?" he muses. "I could ask you what your real name is." Somatsu laughs, but it's not one of his good-natured guffaws. He takes another step towards me. "Tell me, Trigg . . . what is your mother's maiden name?"

"Ward."

He nods and a big smile stretches across his face. "Excellent. Well then, we must eat." With that he brushes past me back up the stairs and wanders back down the hallway. "Come now, please, Trigg. There is nothing to see down there anyway."

We never go for the swim. Out on the front balcony we are served Sol beer and chicken fajitas to rival the finest Mexican cuisine. Actually, "finest", "Mexican" and "cuisine" are three words that don't often share the same sentence, so I guess the bar is set pretty low to begin with.

Mr Somatsu lets little bits of fajita fly as he wrestles with his voracious laugh.

Here we are, two old buddies again. It's like nothing happened. But I still have the damp underarms to remind me that it did. I have to stay on guard. And at some point I have to explore the house – alone.

"That is absolutely the finest Mexican food I have ever had," I tell him. "I'd say that chef of yours is a keeper, Mr Somatsu."

"Indeed, Trigg, he is a master with the skillet. I will be sure to pass on your regards."

"Mr Somatsu, I have to make a phone call. Do you mind?"

"Oh?"

"I'm sure you understand that some phone calls just can't wait."

"The little woman?"

"Ahh . . . yes."

"Certainly, Trigg. I will have Morris bring out the phone."

Morris appears as if by subliminal command and I take the cordless phone from him. After the little "incident" at Karen's school, I have memorised Ian's number.

"*Hello. You've reached Ian and Terri. Please leave a message after* . . ."

"Hi Karen. It's me."

"*. . . the beep and we'll get back to . . .*"

"Fine, darling, just fine. How are you going?"

"*. . . you as soon as . . .*"

"That's good. Listen I'm still with Mr Somatsu, just having some lunch."

"*. . . possible . . . Beeeeeeep!*"

"Yes, yes, golf was fine, Mr Somatsu is quite handy with a driver . . . What's that? . . . Oh really? . . . Oh really? . . . Oh no . . ."

I put my hand over the mouthpiece. "I'm just gonna go inside," I whisper to Mr Somatsu. He regards me through his reflective sunglasses, but I don't wait for a response.

Once inside, past the chef and his boiling pots, I put on my hushed, urgent voice. I quickly tell the answering-machine what's happened since I left the beach house for the casino about nineteen hours ago. With any luck, it will pass the message onto Ian and Terri. I press "end" on the phone, but I don't put it down. I know where I have to look: downstairs. I don't know where Morris is, but it's a risk I'll have to take.

The steps lead down, then take a U-turn. I quietly slink down the first flight, then edge my way around the blind corner, half expecting Morris to be waiting for me. He isn't. But neither is much else. The "hospital ward" theme continues.

Immediately at the bottom of the stairwell are five doors. I shimmy up closer to them. Only the first is open. I snake my head around, but immediately wrench it back. About six feet from where I'm standing, on the other side of the plasterboard, Morris is sitting at a desk reading some papers. My gut reaction is to bolt back upstairs and pretend I never started this little expedition. I can't, though. Something even more powerful than my gut is telling me to keep going. It's telling me that seven days ago I landed on the Gold Coast with a quest. It's telling me that I've been through so much and I'm now so close. It's telling me that I only have a day and a half left. If I'm going to keep going, I have to move now. It doesn't take all afternoon to reassure an insecure wife.

With no plan of attack I jump softly across the open doorway to the first closed door. The knob turns and thankfully releases its grip – quietly. I slip inside and close it softly. Turning around, I find myself staring straight into the chilling green eyes of a . . . chinchilla cat. I silently scold the animal for scaring me, and take in the room. It's obviously a guest bedroom and a bloody big one at that. What's more, we finally have some decoration. There are paintings on the walls, bits and pieces on the desk, and a massive bookshelf dominated by a set of encyclopaedias wedged between two ornate elephant bookends. Carvings adorn various other shelves, but no matter how hard I squint, none of them look like Roger. I open the drawers in the desk then check out the bathroom, but, as I expected, I find nothing even slightly South Pacific. I am disappointed, but buoyed by the fact that there must be ornaments in other rooms too. I have to act fast, though. I have already been missing for about five minutes and Somatsu is sure to get suspicious soon.

A connecting door allows me to get to the next room without braving the hallway. It's another guest bedroom. Like the first, it is extensively decorated and . . . oh my God! I am immediately drawn to a small wooden carving sitting on a bookshelf. My adrenal gland jumps into overdrive. For a second or two I am sure I've found Roger's twin. But it's not to be. The carving is definitely South Pacific, maybe even Fijian, but other than its size and colour it is nothing like Roger. Still, I take heart in its presence; I mean, who goes to the South Pacific and only brings back one thing?

I quickly search the rest of the room, to no avail. Disappointment starts taking some serious ground from optimism. And there are no more connecting doors.

I return to the hallway. Morris is still at his desk, writing something. He seems to be concentrating very hard. I creep across the hallway and try the door opposite. Thankfully it opens. I'm having a very good run, creating my own luck. I close the door behind me. It doesn't take a genius to realise I'm in a bathroom, probably the last place you'd keep a Polynesian figurine. I sit down on the toilet and scratch my head. To make it to the final door will require a dash down the hall in full view of Morris. If I only had a distraction.

I lurch over to the vanity and open the cupboards. Nothing presents itself as a possible distraction. I open the drawers. Top one. Middle one. When I try the bottom one, it won't open. I keep tugging at the handle, which moves in and out, but the drawer itself won't budge. I'm not sure at exactly what point I notice the movement behind me.

I stumble back as the white-tiled wall beside the toilet splits apart to reveal an entire hidden room. Jesus, what's all this about?

Stepping quietly inside, I take in what is obviously a large study-cum-library; like the rest of the house it's a disturbing clash of decades. Bright, angular furniture and brighter, oversized decorations surround sleek, state-of-the-art equipment: computers, fax, scanner – the works. Piles of folders and charts and open books are scattered across a large desk. The library itself consists of two huge bookshelves, each stretching from floor to ceiling and nine feet long at least. In keeping with the desk, they are a mess. Books and magazines slump awkwardly among the other miscellaneous clutter that bookshelves attract – audio cassettes, playing cards, vases and the like. The room has a very lived-in feel to it. This is definitely not a guest bedroom, it's—

"Exactly how much privacy do you require, Trigg?"

I feel Mr Somatsu's hand on my shoulder but I don't even flinch. The phone bounces on the carpet. All I can do is stare at the bookshelf, at Roger's twin. I am speechless. I have so many emotions running through my system, that I am literally speechless. I must have looked right past it at least twice. And even now that I do notice it, I don't get too excited – I've been mistaken too many times already. But there it is. No denying it. God knows I've spent enough time staring at Roger to recognise his double. My arms feel impossibly heavy, my legs are barely holding me up. I have to admit, a big part of me never thought this moment would come. Three inches high, same chocolaty-brown wood, same maniacal grin. Right there in front of me. I've known relief before – I've found missing socks, sunglasses, wallets, I even found a missing Polaroid of me and Kelly that I lost at my parents' place – but this is different. This takes the relief I've known and turns it into one of those mind-bending statistics, like "stretching to the moon and back forty-two times". In fact "relief" does a pathetic job of summing it up. It must be like the moment the baby pops out, or maybe even greater than that.

"Trigg?" says Somatsu. "What are you doing in here?"

I pick up the figurine from the shelf. Turn it over in my hands. "This is an interesting little figurine."

"Yes, it is very nice."

"Where is it from? It looks South Pacific."

"It is Fijian."

My breath catches near my throat. Absolute confirmation.

"Yes, my boss brought it back from there a month or so ago."

"Your . . . what?"

"My *boss*, Trigg," Somatsu replies carefully, as though it might be his English that's upsetting me, "these are all his belongings."

"What . . . What are they all doing in your house?" The room starts to spin.

"My house? Oh no, this is not my house. This is the house of my boss. I just live here while he is away. He is away often."

Oh Christ, oh Christ, oh Christ. My tongue is stuck determinedly to the roof of my dry mouth.

"This would be your boss Tetsuya Suzuki, otherwise known as Terry Smith?"

"Why would you ask a question like that?"

I ignore his question and plough on, fearing that I may not stay in control much longer. "When is Mr Suzuki due back?"

Somatsu eyes me very warily. "You still have not told me what you are doing in this room."

"WHEN'S HE DUE BACK?!"

Somatsu lowers his dark glasses. His eyes are concerned and furious at the same time. "Not in the immediate future."

My body goes limp and my skin turns ice cold, starting at my face and sliding down, rendering my muscles useless.

♣ ♣

20

It's a bit off-putting, waking up with a "Morris" in your face, flicking water at you. For a second my brain is on the fritz, confusion reigns. I have no idea where I am, how I got here – anything. And then it all comes back to me, like a head-on collision. If only I could have stayed in my daze.

"Trigg, you are alright, yes?" asks Mr Somatsu – second-in-command, *not* the owner of the figurine, *not* Tetsuya Suzuki-aka-Terry Smith.

I shake my head, which triggers an intense pain above my right ear. Reaching up, I feel my hair stuck together. My fingertips have blood on them. I shake my head again, despite the pain.

"You passed out and hit your head on the edge of the desk as you fell," says Somatsu. "How do you feel now?"

I feel terrible. Not from any head-knocks or brain-pain. Fatigue, depression and defeat are a big wet blanket, wrapped tightly around my whole body.

"I'm okay," I lie. "I needed the bathroom . . . the fajitas . . . my stomach . . . the wall, it just opened."

Morris must have carried me back out to the balcony.

"How long was I out for?"

"Thirty minutes or so. This has been quite a day. First Mr Smith and now you. I had better be careful."

I try to laugh, but just can't bring myself to do it. I feel so heavy. The prospect of walking seems as unimaginable as flying. I just sit there, taking in laboured gulps of air.

"Would you like me to call a doctor, Trigg?"

"No thanks, I'll be fine. I should probably go, though, you know, have an early night."

I want to get out of here so badly, away from the freaky Japanese man, his freaky bodyguard, the house, the whole episode. And find Karen. Find Karen and hug her. Cling to her while I tell her the whole story, while she strokes my hair and I breathe in her smell. But that's not about to happen, is it? I blink hard, forcing the exhausted tears back down. "Do you think Morris could drive me home?"

"Of course, but I insist I come along."

"Sure." Whatever.

We pull into Ian's driveway just as the sun is setting, turning the clouds over the ocean an electric pink. It takes all my energy to bid an almost enthusiastic farewell. Mr Somatsu takes Ian's number and tells me he will call in the morning to see how I am. While I'm fairly certain he is genuinely concerned, I am absolutely certain he is genuinely suspicious.

I watch the limousine reverse out of the driveway and accelerate down the street, then I lope up the steps to the front door with my golf bag. I press the doorbell. Ian opens the door. He is immediately concerned. It almost makes me feel better. I even manage a smile, before I pass out again.

♣ ♣

21

I feel hands stroking my face. They are soft and warm. "Karen?"

"Sorry, Trigg, just me."

I open my eyes and Terri slowly comes into focus. She smiles. Ian suggested she had a tender side, but until now I just thought he was under the thumb. He's there, too, sporting a kind of goofy, relieved grin. Terri stops stroking my face. "You bastard. We were worried. What happened?"

It takes me at least an hour to relay the details, from arriving at the casino yesterday to being dropped here. Unfortunately, reliving the experience at Tetsuya Suzuki's house makes it all too real again and I slump back into a depression that no one can pull me out of.

"Come on, Trigg, it'll be alright," says Ian.

"Pull your head in," says Terri.

They try hard, but I'm up against something they obviously can't fathom. It's all too easy to remember the misfortune I endured before leaving London. "It's over," I reply. "The indemnity runs out at midnight tomorrow. Even if I knew where Tetsuya Suzuki was, there's no way I could get close to him, find out what his 'crisis' is, *and* help him, all within thirty hours. No way."

Ian puts his hand on my shoulder and gives it a squeeze. It will be hard to leave them (yes, even Terri). Unfortunately, that's exactly what I have to do. It's not fair to drag them into the hell I am due to enter come midnight on Thursday.

"So what do you want to do now?" Terri asks, when it's obvious I'm not about to snap out of my mood.

"I don't know, go to a pub?"

"Okay. Let's all go to the pub. Great answer. I hope we're all up for a big one. Especially you, Trigg. If it's true that from midnight tomorrow you will be without luck and you're going to be miserable for the rest of your life, then let's make sure you enjoy tonight."

"Terr'!" scolds Ian, with a small shake of the head.

Terri is about to reply, but I get in before her. "It's okay. Terri's right."

"So . . . you're feeling better then?" Ian asks.

"I'm just saying Terri's right." The optimism slides from Ian's face. "Well I guess I do feel a little better." I muster all my energy and try to smile over the top of the waves of negativity. It feels more like an impotent sneer.

Terri starts laughing. "I'm sorry," she says, "but that's the look you kept giving me that night at Hot Shots. I think you were trying to look seductive." She keeps laughing, despite her efforts not to.

"Terri, stop it," says Ian, but he's laughing too. Both of them, my so-called friends, giggling away like village loonies. Insensitive pricks.

I try desperately to maintain my melancholy, but finally I can't hold on any more. I begin laughing too. I have no choice but to let it go. And it's such a relief. The sooner we get to the pub the better.

The Miami Tavern is a good example of how London pub-culture never quite stumbled across the seas to Queensland. It's all so bright and open and tragically functional. The only thing dark and smoky about the place is a couple of overly-tanned backpackers struggling to get their heads around Queensland's tough smoking laws.

We take a seat in the beer garden, under the potted palms and the bright yellow "XXXX" umbrellas. In the thick, salt-soup dusk, a flickering red neon sign proclaims the establishment to be the "AMI TAVERN". I conclude that either the "MI" isn't working, or the place is run by a friendly French person. Either way, it's a long, long way from the watering holes of The Fulham Road.

It's a while before anyone musters the energy to move. In the end, it's Ian who makes his way through the tables to get the first round.

The younger faces in the crowd come alive with recognition as they track his path towards the bar. Outside, the breeze causes citronella flames on bamboo poles to flicker, making patterns dance across the whole scene. It's perfect. No one could feel uptight in this place. It is simply impossible. Of the thirty-odd other patrons, some are talking, some are laughing, some are just sitting in silence – but none are stressing.

After an hour or so, we settle into a nice pace. I am feeling much better, busy relaying anything I overlooked in my earlier, rushed account of the day. With four or five lagers in me, the world is becoming gloriously fuzzy again. I am beginning to slur, and every time I see a girl who looks even remotely like Karen, that old lager-lust wells up. It's either going to be a very good night or a particularly bad one.

My bladder is also aware of my increasing alcohol consumption and my trips to the men's room become more frequent. This is a good thing, though, because I have come to enjoy my jaunts to the inner sanctum of the Miami Tavern. The old regulars either sit hunched at the bar mumbling to each other, or feeding the hungry fruit-machines. The rest of the crowd (young men with long hair and tattoos, and a few drinks under their belts) would normally intimidate the hell out of me. But tonight I feel that they respect me. It's probably my groovy trousers . . . or the fact that I'm here with Ian Berrisford.

I bang open the men's room door yet again. And yet again I'm greeted by that stench known to males the world over and a handful of adventurous females. Normally I might have gagged, but the same wonderful fuzz that has taken the sharpness off the pain has dulled my other senses too. I find I can actually breathe in the stink and think about my predicament without retching or wanting to top myself.

Okay, so I'm not going to find Terry Smith before Friday. So what? I undo my fly and fish around for what I need.

"So what?" I say to the guy standing beside me. "So bloody what?"

Despite being mid-stream, he manages to edge away from me. He finishes quickly and leaves, but is immediately replaced by another.

"Bring it on, I say. Give me back my sodding curse," I continue to my new audience. "I actually want it back. Fuck tomorrow night. Bugger the imden . . . indemnity. Now! I want it now!"

Again I fail to receive the encouraging backslaps I would like. I push on. "I mean, I can still find Terry after the two weeks. It's not like that's all the time I've got, is it?"

The guy shrugs nervously, splattering his shoes in the process.

I have well and truly finished emptying my bladder and the urinal ledge is now just a soap box for me to greet newcomers like a destitute preacher. "You didn't count on that, did you, Kelly?" I shout. "Did she?" I ask a young surfer guy who can't be more than seventeen. He shakes his head, then nods, confused by the double negative. "Didn't count on friends like those people outside. God bless 'em."

I ramble on.

"I'd die for them you know," I tell the next poor soul who enters. "I'd die for them and I'd kill for them. And then there's Karen. Can you imagine a better bird than Karen?"

"She certainly is special."

I squint through the blur to see who has spoken. At the far end of the urinal is a man with dark hair and one of those annoyingly-chiselled faces.

"Hey," I call, "I know you. You're . . . you're . . . oh Jesus!" I almost fall over. "You're Karen's brother! Bloody hell. Don't take what I said the wrong way."

"I don't know what you're talking about, Trigg."

Through the swirling haze I see him look anxiously towards the door as it opens. Then he looks alarmed and darts into one of the stalls.

Slowly, carefully, I turn to see who the latest arrival is. I find myself looking at a large Japanese man in a dark suit. "Hey, geezer," I slur. "That was Karen's brother. She stole my money, but I love her."

The Japanese man stands just inside the door, staring at me blank-faced. Something is happening. My alcohol-soaked neurones try valiantly to kick-start the cognition process. The door opens again and we are joined by another dark-suited Japanese man, an even bigger one. This one holds the door shut while the first guy approaches.

"Hey buddy," I dribble, "you look just like afrenamine . . . Morris. Yeah, Mozza – you know him? Like you, but not as fat – OOOOOOF!" I've just been hit in the stomach harder than ever in my life.

"You forking dead, cop." I can barely understand him, so thick is his Japanese accent. I'm turning blue and the "breathing thing" has deserted me. For the third time that day, I lose consciousness.

When I come to, I am in the back of yet another limousine, with gaffer tape around my hands and mouth. I instantly panic when I can't get any air in, then I remember my nose, and the most treasured inhalation of my life fills my lungs. I can vaguely remember, like it was a dream, being picked up off the cold, tiled floor of the men's room and passed through the small window over the urinal. Then I must have been dragged over the ground out the back of the tavern, taped up, and packed into the back of this limo.

I start thrashing about, panicking terribly. My stomach aches like hell and the bump over my right ear is throbbing. It's awfully dark and a fog of cigarette smoke has replaced the air near the roof.

The two oversized Japanese men sit opposite me, uninterested in my struggles. It's their coolness, their calculating manner, that scares the pants off me. It's like they've done this so many times they are a little bored. I start to feel gut-emptyingly nauseous. Oh Christ no, not with my mouth taped up. I snuffle air into my body at a disturbing rate, trying to stem the nausea, but there is more cigarette smoke than oxygen in my frantic breaths. My head is still fuzzy with alcohol and it isn't so enjoyable now. I'm on the verge of losing it. And then the door opens. And in bounces Ian.

His hands and mouth are taped too. He looks at me, not with

confused panic, but with eyes that say: "Gee, this is a bit weird".

This has an instant calming effect on me. The nausea passes quickly. I look at Ian and shrug. He looks back at me and shrugs. "Cop" – that's what the muscle called me before I blacked out. Cop? I've had some strange moments over the last few weeks and this is right up there with the best of them. But perhaps the strangest thing of all – so strange, that I'm hesitant to even admit it to myself – is that in some perverse way I'm enjoying this. I'm back in the game. I'm alive again. And, as mortified as I am, it's exhilarating to know that the adventure isn't over just yet.

Why do they think I'm a cop? This has to involve Mr Somatsu. It simply has to. And Terry Smith. Of course. He's the one who thinks I'm a cop. But what about Karen's brother? What's he doing with them? Assuming he *is* with them. I've sobered up considerably, but still not enough to get much cooperation from my brain. Where are they going to take us? Why aren't they blindfolding us? Suddenly, one of the Japanese men produces a syringe.

They can take the gaffer tape off my mouth right here and now, because I'm not going to speak. I can't. Even Ian's eyes have bugged out. My heart is hammering away like a rabbit's, forcing my gulps back up my throat. This is it, I think to myself. This is fucking it. I'm going to die right here. Murdered in the back of a limo, out the back of some functional Gold Coast pub.

I manage to find my tongue again and I try to speak through the gaffer tape, try to tell the Japanese men they can have the money back. But my efforts produce only muffled garbling.

I shut up, though – albeit momentarily – when the glass screen that separates the driver's compartment slides down, inch by inch, to reveal a face I have seen before. A Japanese face. I can't place it in my inebriated state . . . until the man pulls out my driver's licence. It's the man who was having drinks with Terry and Doris: Mr Kawabata. The owner of Hot Shots.

He looks carefully at my licence, then back at me. He grins and gives a single nod. It's an icy grin; a single silver tooth picks up the orange glint from the interior light. The screen slides up again as the larger of our two captors grabs my arm and rolls up my sleeve.

I repeat my pleas, but to no avail. The second man, the one who punched me, holds up the syringe, points it towards the sunroof and pushes out the air. I have no idea what Ian is doing at this point: my attention is focussed solely on what's happening to me. In fact, I suddenly find myself quite calm. I recall a story I read once about drowning and how, when you give in to your fate, it's actually quite pleasant. Maybe that's what is happening to me. I just hope it's one of those drugs that makes you go to sleep, rather than the sort that cuts off your air supply and makes you foam at the mouth.

I barely feel the prick as the needle goes in, but I feel the drug the instant it hits my bloodstream, racing up my arteries to my brain. And then I'm in a wonderful, dreamy place. The next thing I know is sleepiness beyond description. So sleepy. My eyelids are like a couple of concrete blocks. I panic again at one point, just for a second, as I try to fight my fate, but then I give up and let the pleasant feeling roll over me.

♣ ♣
22

The primal blackness is pierced by swirling trails of red and purple. I am completely relaxed and content. A light beckons me and I follow it as its intensity increases. I can feel the grip my eyelids have over my eyes loosening. Open your eyes, Trigg. The reds become harsher, like pinpricks. Suddenly everything is flooded with an amazing white light that makes me scrunch my eyes up tight.

"Aww, damn it!" a voice calls out.

Who said that? God? I open my eyes again, but once more the light blinds me.

"You little bugger," says the voice.

What is this, some purgatorial fight between good and evil for my soul? I blink hard, trying to squeeze vision back into my eyes. Gradually a figure comes into view. It's . . . Ian. And he's playing a Sony PlayStation. Well of course he is, it makes perfect sense doesn't it?

"Shit," he barks as he jerks the keypad.

I try to speak, but my tongue is as useful as a bar of lead.

"Hey, Trigg, you're awake. Cool."

"Where . . . Wha . . . What the hell is going on?" I manage.

Ian shrugs. "Dunno. I was hoping you knew."

"Where are we?"

"In a room."

"A room where?"

"Ahh, I'm really not sure. But it has a PlayStation."

"Yes, I can see that. How long have you been awake?"

"About an hour."

"And what have you worked out?"

"Umm, about what?"

"About this." I wave my cement-like arms around the room.

"Ahh, nothing really."

"Is there a way out? A door or something?"

"There's a door, but it's locked."

I gingerly get to my feet and take a few cautious steps. I sit down, then get shakily up again. Ian hesitates before reluctantly putting down the control.

We are in a large room, with a distinct oriental feel. It has two doors but no windows. Every comfort has been taken care of: a plush couch, ornate Japanese cushions, board games, a TV, a DVD player, and the PlayStation. Everything, except a way out. Of the two doors, one leads to a bathroom and the other is indeed locked. The light is artificial; so is the air – pumped in through a vent in the bathroom. One thing is for sure, they haven't brought us to Terry and Doris's place.

"What are we going to do?" I ask Ian.

"Well, they've got Colin McRae Rally on PlayStation."

"I see. Maybe not now, but you know, if they don't torture and kill us, definitely later."

Ian nods. Something tells me he missed the sarcasm.

"We've got to get out of here, Ian. What do you remember about last? . . . Jesus, they've taken my watch. It could have been days ago . . . or hours."

"Yeah, they took my watch, too. All a bit of a blur. I was just sitting with Terr', and one of the old fellas came and told us that you were losing it in the toilet, so I went looking for you. When I got around the corner near the ciggy machine this big Japanese guy pulled a gun on me and marched me out a back door. Called me a 'fucking pig', then taped me up and threw me in the back with you. They jabbed me straight after they did you."

"They think we're police, Ian. I think it has something to do with Terry and Doris, and maybe Karen's brother. We really have to get out of here."

"Okay, how?"

"I don't suppose you know how to pick locks, do you?"

Ian shakes his head.

I look carefully around the room. My eyes settle on the collection of DVDs. "*Die Hard*!"

Ian considers this for a second, then nods. "Okay."

"No, no, no, we're not going to watch it. The ventilation ducts. That's how Bruce Willis gets about in the movie. There's a big vent in the bathroom. That's how we're going to get out."

Using a washer from one of the taps, Ian undoes the screws holding the ceiling-grill in place. Carefully he lets it hang on its hinges . . . to reveal a hole just bigger than a basketball.

I can see that he's wrapping a mental tape-measure around me. I puff out my chest and try to make my shoulders look bigger, but it's no good.

"I get claustrophobic," I say, but we both know I'm going to be the test pilot on this flight. I size up the hole again. This is not going to be pleasant.

In a burst of innovative thought, I take a bottle of moisturiser from the medicine cabinet over the basin. Stripped to my underpants, I cover myself in the slippery, pleasant smelling cream. If nothing else, it's good for my sunburn and I'll make a lovely corpse.

I pull myself up into the black hole, using the toilet for leverage. Jesus, it's a tight fit. Ian takes my feet and pushes me further.

I'm fighting claustrophobia now. My arms are pinned by my ears and I can't move my head. All over my body I feel an ominous cold pressure and the blackness is so thick it's hard to breathe. The only saving grace is being able to wiggle my legs. Ian then gives me another shove and I lose that privilege too.

"Hey look," Ian says. "I don't even have to hold you anymore."

He gives me one more shove and I'm able to feel the cold aluminium with my feet. I'm all the way in. And I can't move an inch. If I stay in here for even a second longer I'm going to go completely insane.

"Get me out of here . . . GET ME OUT OF HERE! GET ME OUT OF HERE!"

I feel Ian scrabbling for my feet and then I feel my lubricated body sliding back down the chute. I emerge from the vent and fall onto the floor, naked and gooey.

"Congratulations, Mr Harvey, you're a boy," says Ian.

He laughs. We both do. It's that or cry.

Back in the main room, Ian looks at me very seriously for a few seconds. Then he stands up determinedly. "Okay," he says. He begins walking around the room, deep in thought. "What if we just talk to them, explain that it's all a mistake?"

"But it's not *all* a mistake. I took $50,000 from them."

"How can you be so sure this is about Terry and Doris? How can Karen's brother be involved with them?"

I think for a second. "It's a good question, but either way, we're beyond talking our way out of this. We need to escape."

"Okay." He resumes his thinking and looking.

After a couple of minutes he stops in his tracks. That broad Aussie smile of his moves across his face like a domino trick. Ian is taking charge. This should be interesting.

The former world champion surfer jogs over to the bathroom and returns with two screws from the vent. He pulls the cushions off the couch and, using the sharp end of one of the screws, begins ripping at the lining underneath. Blindly, I follow suit, and we have the couch's wooden frame exposed in under a minute.

A series of parallel leather straps run from the back of the couch to the front. Ian begins breaking them with a series of kicks. When he's done, there is nothing but a single piece of wood dividing the couch frame into two separate hollows. Satisfied, he returns to the bathroom, but rather than use the screws to put the grill back in place, he throws them on the tiled floor and lets the grill hang. Back in the main room, he proceeds to throw all the mess from the couch into one of the hollows. And then he hops in.

"Okay," I say, "now I'm going to need an explanation. What good is hiding going to do?"

But Ian is being strangely businesslike. He has a look of intense focus that I saw out in the surf, like he's taking control, making his own luck. "Don't worry, just hop in," he says.

I do as I'm told and we hunker down into impossibly cramped positions, pulling the cushions into place on top of us.

And we wait.

And we wait.

It must be at least an hour before we hear footsteps on the tiles outside the door. The sound of three locks being released is followed by the door being opened. I suddenly forget the cramps racking my body as it fills with that addictive mixture of terror and excitement. We hear a single set of feet walk into the room and stop abruptly. Then they rush over to the bathroom and the door is flung open. There is a loud crash of something being dropped, followed by swearing in Japanese; then the feet sprint from the bathroom and out the door.

Suddenly Ian's plan becomes clear. We throw off our cushions and stumble towards our escape. Ian grabs me. Shaking his head vigorously, he manoeuvres me so we are standing behind the open door.

"What are you—?"

He holds a finger to his lips as the sound of footsteps approaches. Although we can't see anything from behind the door, we can hear three sets of feet run past us into the room. Then, as they file into the bathroom, we can see they belong to the two men from the limo and another man. They are speaking in frantic Japanese and inspecting the open vent. Ian taps me on the shoulder and we slip quietly around the door, which Ian then closes as silently as possible. There is one key-operated lock and two manual deadbolts. Ian clicks the bolts into place, and our captors are trapped

"Wow," I whisper, "that's the most brilliant thing ever. Now what?"

"I don't know, this is all I thought of."

Suddenly someone begins rattling the door on the other side and we both jump an impressive distance. We spring into action – it's completely lacking direction, but at least it's action.

At the top of a long set of stairs, we spill out into a very modern, very chic living-area – like Somatsu's would have been if he had any taste. Hey . . . that's unusual; if Somatsu's house actually belongs to Tetsuya Suzuki, why is it decorated in Somatsu's style? And why does he employ the chef?

A sharp crack of wood exploding below prompts Ian and me to sprint across the large entertaining area. Sunlight bursts in through a glass door – which tells us two things: firstly, it's daytime; secondly, we have a way out. Ian reaches the escape-portal first, but it won't open.

The hairs on the back of my neck are on full alert as he fiddles with the lock. I'm certain we'll be sprung at any second. There is another crack of splintering wood from below.

Finally, Ian opens the door and we tumble out onto a paved area surrounding a massive swimming-pool. We look around frantically. Beyond the pool lies the canal. Behind us looms a gigantic, oriental timber mansion. It makes Tetsuya Suzuki's house look like a fibro beach-shack. I realise now that we were in the pool house. Ian breaks off towards the left, heading for a large timber fence. I follow. Unfortunately, a bloody great Rottweiler decides it looks like fun, and follows too. He makes Barton look like a poodle. Maybe that's why I reach the wall before Ian. I'm not good with dogs.

The wall is nine feet high if it's an inch, but I don't even slow down. I just jump straight at it and somehow scrabble my way to the top. As I get my head over, an ear-piercing alarm shatters everything – the sort of noise that makes you try to retract your head into your shoulders. The result is pandemonium. I exchange a quick glance with Ian, a "this'll make a good story one day" moment, and we jump onto the thick grass on the other side. My heart sinks a little as I realise we are back in the canals, back among the maze of streets, waterways and luxury homes. Ian takes off down the road at a sprint. He doesn't seem to know where he's going, but since his plans have worked so far, I follow him.

We run flat out for ten minutes, but it does us no good. For every corner we turn, we're faced with another three. We are getting more and more lost. I stop Ian and relieve myself of this theory. He agrees. We have to get out of the area, or at least out of sight. Ian runs his hand through his thick mop of sun-bleached hair. He's turning around in circles. Then I have an idea.

I jog up the street and find what I'm looking for. With Ian in tow, I run up the driveway of a house, jumping over a skateboard on the way, straight to the front door. The doorbell is one of those annoying ones that plays an electronic tune.

My foot sends a gobbledygook of Morse Code through the welcome mat as we wait. Not a second too soon, a middle-aged and heavily-made-up woman answers the door. "Yes?"

"Hi there, I'm Rockin' Robby Rayfield from Sea FM, is your son home?"

"What's this all about?" She shows no sign of releasing the door.

"Well ma'am, let me introduce you to Ian Berrisford, the world surfing champion." I drag Ian out from behind me. He waves and smiles shyly. "Ma'am, your son Andrew—"

"Paul."

"Of course, *Paul* – has won a free surfing lesson with Ian here."

"I see." She edges the door closed a little more.

I step forward a couple of inches. "So is, ahh, Paul in at the moment?"

"I'm sorry, I don't understand this. If Paul won a competition, why didn't he tell me?"

"Well it's a surprise. He doesn't know he's won yet. Is it possible that we could meet him?"

Her eyes crinkle. "Well, you don't look like you're from the radio."

"How do you know? It's radio."

Just as we're about to get a door in the face, a voice rings out from behind her. "Oh my God, Ian Berrisford!" bawls the young teenager.

For a moment it all hangs in the balance. The woman is far from convinced, but her son has just confirmed my story – well, part of it. She turns to her boy: "Paul did you enter a radio competition to win a surfing lesson with this man?"

I hold my breath, poised to run if I have to.

"Ahhhh . . ." Paul weighs up the situation, looks at Ian. "Yeah."

The woman looks from her son to Ian and back to me. "Okay," she says sourly, "so what happens now?"

"Well, let's go."

"What? Now?"

"Absolutely. Ma'am, Ian here is a professional sportsperson. His time is in constant demand. Quite frankly, we're damn lucky to have him."

She looks up and down the street. "Where's your car?"

"Oooh, that's a good one. Umm . . . well, we had the big Sea FM beach-cruiser right here, we were going to do a live cross. We had the music, the scantily-clad beach-girl driver, the works, but . . . ahh . . . one of those high-rises in Surfers Paradise fell over, so they had to drop us off and go and cover that."

"Oh my Lord! What happened?"

"Uhh well this building was . . . standing up . . . and then it . . . fell over. So can we go? You're driving."

"Oh yes, yes of course. Just a moment."

Luckily the prospect of massive casualties has shaken her up enough to play along. She goes to fetch the car keys.

"Nice work," I say to the kid, "keep playing your cards right and you can hang out with Ian all afternoon."

"Cool."

Paul jogs off to get changed, and Ian pulls me aside. "Hey, Trigg, I know desperate times call for desperate measures, but I don't know, this is all pretty deceitful."

"Sweet Jesus, Ian. You'll never be the next James Bond with that sort of attitude."

Paul and his mum return and we all load into the Range Rover. The woman is still asking questions about the high-rise disaster, which I obviously don't have answers to. And she wants to know more about the competition. And then she asks why Ian and I are hunkering down in the back seat of the four-wheel drive. Questions, questions. God, I almost wish we'd never made it over the wall.

Ian directs the woman back to his place without any of the goons spotting us. I wait with Paul and his mother while Ian runs upstairs to get changed and tell Terri that he's alright. We cross on the stairs as he returns and he gives me a wink.

Now, is that the "everything's fine with Terri" wink? Or is it the "good luck, you'll need it" wink? I can hear the former-world-surfing-champion/escape-plan-genius laughing with Paul and his mum as they head towards the beach. Normally I would take this as a sign that everything went well upstairs, but Ian's the sort of guy who could walk out of his own bankruptcy hearing with a smile on his face.

I get to the top of the stairs and start shaking. So much so that I can't grip the doorknob. It's strange, almost like my body is a step ahead of my mind, because a second or so later, a wave of light-headed awe comes over me. Ian and I came *very* close to some *very* serious shit back there. This isn't make-believe. I know I've been through some pretty heavy stuff since I landed on this strip of sand and concrete, but nothing comes close to the coldness in those men's eyes last night. They were more than capable of killing us without a second thought, I have no doubt about that. So why didn't they? It's hard to say, when I don't even know why they took us in the first place.

Eventually, I manage to get a grip – on the doorknob, if not my mind. I push open the door and Terri is standing there waiting for me.

"Jesus Christ, Trigg, where the hell have you been?" She shoves me hard, right in the chest.

"I—"

"And now you've gone and dragged Ian into this shit." She shoves me again.

"We—"

"I've been worried sick." She's on the verge of tears, but manages to give me another hard shove. "And look what I found under the door when I got home." She holds aloft another brown envelope.

Finally she stops and just stares at me with her red-rimmed eyes. I think I preferred it when she was hitting me.

"Well, what did Ian say?" I venture cautiously.

"Nothing! Just that it was a 'pretty weird trip', and that he has to go and give some kid a surfing lesson. He said you'd explain everything."

I stand in front of the trainee lawyer and try to construct my defence. "Well, it's a long story."

Terry shakes her head and glowers. Obviously I've chosen the wrong opening statement.

"Look, will you just back the fuck off?" I say. "I've been kidnapped, drugged, held captive in some strange bloody house, and, well, almost killed. I'm sorry if I worried you, but I did not choose to get knocked unconscious and kidnapped, I did not choose to have anything to do with this fucking mess. Cut me a little slack!"

My last word hangs in the air like a drop-shot at Wimbledon.

"I'm sorry," I say, regaining my composure.

Terri stares at me like a cat about to pounce. Miss Marple's not happy. But then she winds in her claws. "I'm sorry, too. It was just a God-awful night – one minute you're both there, the next you're gone. The police weren't interested . . . I didn't know what to do. And then this was under the door when I got home." She holds up the envelope again. It's the same as the first one we received, so there are no prizes for guessing who it's from.

I remove what looks like a piece of paper torn out of a school exercise book (just to make me feel guilty again). There is a single line of writing: "Trigg, stay away from Somatsu – it's bigger than either of us thought. You don't know what you're getting involved in. K."

There's something unnerving about a person who knows your every move and can drop in and out of your life whenever they please. Especially when you're in love with that person.

"What's it all about, Trigg?"

That is a very good question. "Let's sit down, have a drink and I'll tell you exactly what happened."

We sit out on the deck with a bottle of white wine. Further down the beach, Ian is busy with Paul, under the watchful eye of his mother – and twenty or so fans. Ian Berrisford, King of the Kids.

I explain, in as much detail as I can remember, the events following my fateful visit to the men's room (although I may have left out a few of the earlier details!).

"Boy, it seems like just yesterday I was sitting out here explaining my loss of consciousness", I joke at one stage. I receive a polite laugh. Since I've barged in on Ian and Terri's lives, they're world has taken a turn. I just wonder if it's a turn they can tolerate. Everyone wants a bit of action in their life – up to a point.

Again, the thought of disappearing in the middle of the night and giving these people their old lives back pokes my conscience. Part of me still thinks it's a good idea. Unfortunately, a growing part of me is a lonely coward.

By the end of my debriefing, Miss Marple is back on board. She agrees that last night sounds beyond Terry and Doris, that they are pawns in this whole thing and it's probably more to do with Mr Somatsu or Tetsuya Suzuki. Especially after Karen's note. Terri is of the opinion that I must have said or done the wrong thing during my day with Mr Somatsu yesterday.

"I hate to sound like a broken record," Terri says, "but what now?"

Luckily, I'm saved from having to answer that. We watch quietly as Ian traipses up from the beach, casual as you like, stands briefly under the outdoor shower and saunters up the stairs onto the deck. Terri throws herself at him and showers him with kisses. Just quietly, I think she's turned on by the way Ian engineered our escape.

With the love-athon over, we settle back down again while Ian voices his recollections of the escape. While the verbs he uses match mine, his adverbs are much more humble. Humility is like an afro wig: anyone can try it on, but only a few wear it well. Ian is one of those select few.

When Mr Modesty finishes talking, we sit in silence, contemplating the situation. The think-tank has stalled. It's Terri who eventually breaks the silence.

"You can't sit back, Trigg," she says certainly. "I've studied a few cases involving the Mafia in the States. These people don't quit. They don't just forget or give up. If you get on their bad side, they'll find you. I'm sure the Yakuza are no different. They can't afford to be. So the way I see it, you have two options. One, you can get as far away from the Gold Coast as possible and keep trying to hide. Or two, you can confront the situation."

"Can't I just give them their $50,000 back? I have money to burn after the casino."

Terri frowns. "Trigg, this is not about money anymore. If that's all it was, they'd either have it back or you'd be dead by now. This thing goes way beyond money." She breathes out hard, making her nostrils flair. "I think it's safe to assume that their believing you're a police officer is inextricably linked to this whole thing. So, if you can prove that you are *not* a police officer, then, theoretically, you're off the hook."

"Theoretically?" I say. "That's what worries me. I'm sure that, save for a few dodgy coppers, the Yakuza aren't the police force's biggest fans, but by the same token, I'm sure they don't just go around kidnapping police for the hell of it. Which means it's something else that they are interested in. The problem being that, whatever this 'something' is, it might be an issue even if I'm not a policeman."

"I think you're both right," says Ian. "True, you might be in deep shit whether you are or aren't a cop. But Terri's right, you can't hide, you've got to tackle them head-on, try and sort something out, convince them that they have no business with you. I think what we have to do is pay Mr Somatsu a visit."

"Are you kidding? That's like narrowly escaping a lion attack and then going back to see if you can pull its tail."

"On the contrary, Trigg," Terri responds, expanding on her original theory, "it's the safest thing to do. The Yakuza are like any organised-crime group, the last thing they want is attention, especially the people near the top. There's no way Somatsu will do anything to you personally, in his own place. He can't afford to get directly involved. In fact, he may be the one person who can call this whole thing off. It's the perfect plan."

"He did say he was going to call this morning. Why don't we just wait?"

Terri and Ian shake their heads.

♣ ♣
23

I pull the Mustang up a few houses down from Tetsuya Suzuki's mansion. Finding it after just one visit was difficult. What I have to do now, though, I fear will be impossible.

It's a race against my cowardly-pragmatic side as I walk to the front gate. For a while I don't even notice that Terri is alongside me. When I protest, she insists that since Ian's now involved she should be too. My continued objections are met by the very good point that a lawyer could come in handy.

So the plan is set. Terri and I will go inside, while Ian sits in the car outside, ready for the unexpected. We have a time limit of twenty minutes before we have to make contact with him. Otherwise he calls the police. It's not a lot of time, so I have to make sure I don't let Somatsu throw me with his chit-chat. We have to get in, get to the point, and then let Ian know we're okay.

Terry Smith's pistol weighs unnaturally in my pocket, pulling one side of my shorts down lower than shorts should go, as we tip-toe to the white concrete fence. It's no higher than the one I scrambled over earlier in the morning, but without the whole life/death thing to motivate me, it's going to be difficult. I step back and run at the obstruction. I make it three-quarters of the way up. I pick myself up off the grass and take another run up.

I touch the top this time, I'm sure. I felt the top edge of the wall, just before the rest of my body collided with the concrete. I shake my head and stand up again. A few quick stretches, a bit of a jog on the spot, and I'm ready for another go.

"Trigg, the gate's open."

"Right . . . what about cameras? Any cameras?"

"I can't see any, but it doesn't mean they're not there."

"Well, we can't go through the gate then. The element of surprise and all that."

"I think we've already lost the element of surprise."

"Right . . . well, let's go then."

The gate slides open easily, but this is immediately followed by an ear-bleeding . . . silence. Nothing, no alarm, not even a beep. Morris doesn't seem like the sharpest knife in the drawer. It's quite possible he just gaffed up and left the gate open.

We edge our way around the house, careful to duck under the ground-floor windows. From what I remember of the layout, the best approach is through the doors near the pool. We creep slowly along between the house and the tennis court, the thick lawn swallowing up our footsteps. The pool and the canal beyond it come into view as we slink around the far corner of the house to the large patio. The main door is locked, but there's another one off to the side.

With Terri peering over my shoulder, I look into the room through a gap between the drawn curtains. It affords a good eyeful of what is obviously a bedroom, but not enough of a view to be absolutely sure that it's empty. I push the door but it won't budge. Bastard! Terri points to her watch, like I need reminding just how up against it we are.

Moving her aside, I take four steps backs, then drop my shoulder hard against the door . . . and bounce back into Terri with a clatter.

"It's a sliding door, you dickhead," whispers Terri as she pulls it open and marches inside. Well, perhaps I loosened it up.

The room is empty, of people at least. We stand and stare for a moment, mouths open. It has to be Mr Somatsu's bedroom, and he's obviously made himself very much at home in Tetsuya Suzuki's house. It offers an amazing insight into his well-guarded life. A leopard-skin duvet lies haphazardly over black satin sheets, a television is built into the wall, right beside a six-foot Swatch Watch. And beside the watch, a huge poster of Wham . . . framed! . . . signed! It's tempting to stay and explore, but Miss Marple points to her watch again, then to the bedroom door. She pads over to it and begins to pull it open. Quickly, but quietly, I push it closed again. Morris's little room is at the end of the hall. This is going to be difficult.

I take the handle with all the courage of a chicken on its way to the chopping block. Terri slaps at my hand and takes the handle again. I slap at her hand. She slaps my forehead with the base of her palm, so I back off. When she whips the door open, Morris isn't there. The element of surprise is now ours. We quickly scuttle to the stairs and around the first bend. I reach into my shorts and take out the pistol. It's time to get some answers.

Terri smacks me on the back of the head. Pointing at the gun, she shakes her head indignantly. "What are you doing?" she mouths.

I point behind her and when she turns to look, I continue up the stairs . . .

. . . and stop dead. The pistol falls to the floor. A body is slumped against the wall in the hallway, a neat little red dot just to the right of the middle of its forehead, a not-so-neat red mush on the wall behind. Terri gasps and grabs my arm. I grab hers harder.

"What's going on, Trigg?"

I shake my head, dumbfounded. "It's Somatsu's chef. This is bloody serious, Terri."

"Gee, you think?"

"We should get out of here."

Terri shakes her head. "No. You're caught up in this, and so is Ian. We've got to try and figure out what happened."

"Are you crazy?" I hiss. "A man is dead here. Shot in the fucking head. Let's get out of here. How do we know they're not still here? Or coming back?"

Terri nods and steps over the chef-cum-martial-arts-expert-cum-corpse. Up ahead I hear her moan. Morris is lying awkwardly on the floor of the deck, a claret-like pool around his head. The walls are closing in again. This is too heavy. Far, far too heavy.

Terri checks the rest of the upper level. She finds a half-finished bowl of nachos on the balcony, still warm; a glass smashed on the ground, maybe from a struggle. I stand motionless except for the slow shaking of my head from side to side.

"Come on, Trigg," Terri says, "he's not here. Let's go."

"Wait a minute." I trudge past her and pick up the pistol, which I reluctantly put back in my pocket. I make my way downstairs and check the secret room. No one is there, alive or otherwise. A violent shiver runs down my spine as I exit the front door of Tetsuya Suzuki's house – the kind of shiver you get when you narrowly avoid a car accident. I wish to God I could leave all this behind me, locked inside the house. But I just know this isn't the end. I jog quickly across the driveway, hoping to outrun my panic.

"What happened? Are you guys okay?" says Ian when we get back to the car.

"Did you call the police?" I ask, more out of breath than my short run justifies.

"No, I was just about . . . no."

"Good, then let's get the hell out of here."

"Where are we going?"

I jump into the back seat and fumble my seatbelt on. My hands are shaking terribly. "There's only one place left. One person who might be able to shed some light on this . . . this disaster." I rub at the stubble on my cheek. "Anyone fancy a chicken-and-mushroom roll?"

We have to handle things with Jun very carefully, he's the lone thread our scanty web is hanging by. Who knows, if I can get Jun to talk, perhaps I can find Mr Somatsu. And if I can find Mr Somatsu, perhaps I can locate Tetsuya Suzuki. And if I can do that, perhaps I can assist him and get my luck back before midnight.

Terri and I sit in the park while Ian enters the store. There's a strong cool breeze coming off the beach, which contrasts nicely with the afternoon sun. The result is an overwhelming listlessness. Our sprawled bodies straighten, though, about fifteen minutes later, when Ian emerges. He jogs across the street in front of a passing car, his arms laden with groceries. We eyeball him expectantly.

Ian dumps the groceries at our feet and we are momentarily distracted by the contents: Coke, pasta, two boxes of tampons, ice cubes, toilet paper, tennis balls, baked beans, bread, and a cap-gun. With a bemused shake of the head, I look at Ian. I noticed Terri is too.

"What?" he says.

"What happened?" Terri replies.

"Oh right. Yeah. Well I went in there and Jun was talking away to another customer. Then he saw me and his face sort of hardened."

Ian contorts his face to demonstrate.

"So I said g'day, and he gave me this weird forced smile, like he was suspicious or something."

Again we get a re-enactment.

"Then he went back to talking to the customer, but I still felt like he was looking at me, so I just wandered around looking at stuff."

We even get a demonstration of Ian's wandering around looking at stuff.

"Then the customer left, so it's just me and Jun. I tried talking to him, like I normally would – you know, surfing, Ricky Ponting, that sort of thing. Anyway, he was still really guarded and I felt like a bit of an idiot just wandering around, so I started putting stuff into a basket – to buy some more time – and I kept talking. And after a while Jun started to warm up, cracking one-liners, that sort of thing. Meanwhile, I've got all this crap in my basket, so I have to buy it because I don't know what else to do."

"Well, then what happened?" I ask.

"Well, then things were kind of back to normal, so I thought I'd test the water properly. I asked him if he'd seen you around this morning."

Ian is going to make us ask again. It's Terri's turn. "And?"

"Well, then he looked scared. Like he was doing a hundred maths problems at once and none of them were working out. But he didn't lose it. He just said he hadn't seen Trigg for a while. Then he said he had to go and do some stuff out the back, so I left."

"What do you think?" Terri asks, posing the question to anyone who cares to answer.

"He sounds a bit calmer, but he's still upset," I reply. "I think it's best if I don't go in there. I think you probably should, Terri."

Terri sets off across the street with a determined stride.

Then she returns just as quickly. "He's closed the shop!"

We stare blankly at each other. Ian's eyes widen. "Shit! Around the back."

We abandon the groceries and run across the street behind Ian. He bolts down a set of basement steps and flings open a graffitied blue door, and we stumble into a big underground carpark. We stand completely still in the overwhelming silence, breathing heavily as our eyes get used to the gloom. A huge sense of anticipation hangs in the air, but nothing is happening. And then a door clunks open and we all jump. Terri lets out a little gasp. Actually I think it was me. Luckily Jun is preoccupied with his own thoughts and doesn't hear it. His sandals slap-slap against his feet as he makes his way over to his old yellow Toyota Corolla station-wagon. That's where we ambush him.

"Hi, Jun, sorry to bother you, but we just want to talk to you," Terri says in her sickliest little-girl voice.

Jun looks up with a start, then he stares at us, like he's struggling to find words that will do justice to exactly how pissed off he is at this invasion of his privacy. Then he just turns and runs.

"Wait, Jun. Please, I really need your help," I plead as I take up the chase.

He heads back towards where he came from, his sandals really clipping along. He's a fast little bugger for an older man.

"Come on, Jun. I really need your help." I'm catching him.

"You do not want to do this," Jun yells back as he suddenly veers left, behind a shiny red Honda.

I follow his path. "Do what?" As I turn, I realise I'm the only one giving chase, and for a second guilt overwhelms me. Is this really, really low? Chasing a little old Japanese man around a carpark?

But the guilt subsides when I realise I'm really gaining on him.

Jun has run in a circle, pretty much straight past Ian and Terri, who seem too dazed to try and stop him. I give them a pleading look as I brush past them, but they just look at me with the same bewilderment you might see on the face of an intellectual trying to make sense of a Benny Hill chase-sequence.

We do another lap and I'm getting puffed. Jun is worse, though, I can hear him wheezing. "Tligger, do not do this," he keeps repeating in between gasps for air.

"Please, Jun, I just need to know a few things."

Finally Jun takes a wrong turn and I corner him between a dank concrete wall and a black BMW. I approach slowly, feeling like a trapper descending on a frightened fox. Again I feel guilty as I see the fear in his eyes. Whatever he knows about my Yakuza friends, he doesn't want to confront it.

"Jun, my life is in danger and I think you might be able to help. Can I just ask you a few questions?"

Jun looks despairingly to his left and right. Then he looks me straight in the eye. I continue to approach.

"I told you not to do this, Tligger," he says with resignation. Suddenly, with dazzling control, and speed that belies his years, he steps forward and catches me square in the bollocks with his left foot, before chopping his right hand into my throat. Before I can say "uuurrrgghhh", I'm lying on the cold, shiny cement, not knowing whether to be more concerned about the sickening pain growing in my testicles or the fact that I can't breathe. In the end I don't have to worry about either. I pass out. Just for something a little different.

When I come to, I'm slumped against the door of the BMW with Ian holding my shoulders so my limp body doesn't topple. My nuts ache terribly, so much so that I lean over and throw up. I'm dazed and very confused.

As I gingerly sit up straight, all eyes are on me, including Jun's. He looks quite upset. "I'm sorry, Tligger, so sorry." His eyes are heavy with regret. "I have not raised a fist in violence for twenty years. And now . . ." He sighs heavily, as heavily as I've seen a man sigh. He looks like an alcoholic waking up with his first hangover after falling off the wagon. "I thought this nightmare was over, but what I realise now is that it will follow me forever. I cannot escape it. It pains me more than you can imagine to see what I see when I close my eyes. Still," he brightens just a little, "I think it will be a relief to get it off my chest."

♣ ♣
24

After struggling valiantly with the hammock, Jun opts to stand. The think-tank is once again assembled on Ian's deck, the unofficial headquarters for Trigger Aid 2006. On the walk back from the store, Jun was stoical. We are anxious to hear what he has to say, but his first words are a question.

"So why do you wish to know about a man called Tetsuya Suzuki?" he asks. He has just passed a point of no return.

I tell Jun the story so far. I talk uninterrupted for twenty minutes and not once does Jun's concentration break. He takes in everything I say with great consideration, but gives nothing away. When I finish, he stares intently out to sea for about five minutes, battling all sorts of demons. Then suddenly he snaps back to us. "Alright," he says. "I can help you." What follows is the most amazing tale I have ever heard.

Jun takes a long, preparatory sip of water. "You are indeed dealing with the Yakuza. Older than the Sicilian Mafia, more powerful than the Chinese Triads. As you have no doubt guessed, I have a history with Mr Somatsu and Tetsuya Suzuki, but before I go into that, it is imperative that you understand the workings of the Yakuza."

We are hanging on Jun's every utterance. He takes another frustratingly long sip of water.

"The name Yakuza comes from a Japanese card game called *hanafuda*. It is a little like blackjack. Players are dealt three cards, if the numbers add up to twenty, this gives you a score of zero; the worst possible score. One combination that will give you twenty is eight, nine and three, or, in Japanese, *Ya*, *Ku* and *Sa*. It is a worthless score. You see, the Yakuza is made up of those considered worthless by society.

"Most members are from broken homes; they are attracted by the loyalty of the Yakuza. The Yakuza becomes their family. This is why the oyabuns, the leaders, wield such power; honour and family. They are like the Dons or the Godfathers in the American Mafia. There is no tolerance of disloyalty. When you see a Yakuza with a little finger cut off, it means he has failed his oyabun. It seems barbaric, but you must understand that this was derived from the days of the long sword, where cutting off a finger would weaken a man's grip. Many westerners think that a missing little finger is a sign of honour within the Yakuza; they couldn't be more wrong. Tattoos, on the other hand, are a sign of honour. This comes from when criminals were tattooed with a black ring around each arm for every offence they committed. Of course tattoos became synonymous with toughness and strength."

Jun pauses and looks out to sea, leaving us hanging on the edge of our seats. "So where do you fit into all this?" asks Terri.

Jun takes another sip of water. "For centuries, there have been battles among different Yakuza gangs for territory. In the 1960s, several gangs were powerful, none more so than the Yamaguchi-gumi. It was to this gang that I belonged, as did a young man named Tetsuya Suzuki."

Terri speaks for all of us when she prompts Jun to continue.

He takes a long, shaky breath. "Some years after I became a member, the oyabun of the Yamaguchi-gumi died of a heart-attack. The battle to become the new leader was fierce. In the end a man named Takenaka was chosen over his close rival Hiroshi. To say Hiroshi was upset would be an understatement. He took 13,000 of the Yamaguchi-gumi members with him and formed a rival gang, the Ichiwa-kai. I was one of those 13,000.

"The split enabled many men to rise quickly through the ranks of both the Yamaguchi-gumi and the Ichiwa-kai. Indeed, while I was rising in the eyes of my new oyabun, Tetsuya Suzuki was rising up the ranks in the Yamaguchi-gumi. Then, in 1985, Takenaka was assassinated. This resulted in the bloodiest battle yet. War was declared on the Ichiwa-kai. With this, civilian blood began to spill and the Japanese authorities could no longer turn a blind eye to the Yakuza. In 1992 they passed the Boryokudan Countermeasures law. It forced the Yakuza to expand their operations overseas, into the United States and mainland Asia. These ventures were hugely successful and, ironically, the Yakuza became even wealthier and more powerful. Of course they branched out further, overtaking the islands of Hawaii and reaching into Australia, especially here on the Gold Coast. In fact, the Yamaguchi-gumi felt the foothold they had here was so important, they stationed their third-in-command here, one Tetsuya Suzuki."

Jun looks down, almost mournfully. His tale is obviously finished, but there are simply too many gaps.

"That's an incredible story, Jun," I begin cautiously. "But it still doesn't explain why you're now running a corner store, or what your history is with Tetsuya Suzuki and Mr Somatsu, and God knows I still have no idea why Ian and I are now on the Yakuza hit-list."

Jun doesn't look up and I fear that I have pushed too hard. But then, in measured words, he begins to fill in the missing parts. "Let me start with myself. When I left the Yamaguchi-gumi to join the new Ichiwa-kai, I had . . . certain skills . . . which gave me a very high standing in the Yakuza. I was very valuable to whichever oyabun I was serving. This is why I rose quickly within my new gang. In fact, I, like Tetsuya, enjoyed a high position. It meant great wealth and power. I was thirty-six years old, with a wife and a new baby, and I was living in a luxury apartment in Kobe. But then something happened. I could not keep fulfilling my role in the Ichiwa-kai. I did not even want to be a part of the Yakuza anymore. But you cannot just leave. As I said, the Yakuza is blindly obsessed with honour and loyalty. To leave is to lack these things. As well, I was a wanted man."

"Why?" Terri asks. "What happened? What did you do?"

"I . . . I was an assassin. I was *the* assassin. I killed Takenaka."

For a split second I actually think the whole thing is a big joke, but my aching balls and bruised throat suggest I should believe this man. "So is that why you had to leave?" I ask.

"Yes. When I sliced the throat of the most powerful man in Japan and felt his warm blood spill over my hands, I knew it was time. It was not the morality – Takenaka had killed many innocent people, something I have never done – it was the tragedy. Takenaka had been fearless in the face of death – in fact, he seemed proud to be facing an assassin's blade. It was pathetic. We were playing what Americans call cops and robbers, cowboys and Indians – except we were grown men and the weapons were as real as the lives being lost. I thought of my new child and I had an insight that there must be more to life than pride and fear. I had not smiled in ten years, Tligg. Ten years! So I resolved to leave. But as I said, this is not so easy. I did not fear for my own life, I was too much like Takenaka at that stage, but I feared greatly for my beautiful wife and my new son.

"What did you do?" asks Terri.

"We lived in hell for three months before I managed to arrange fake passports and documentation through a childhood friend in Sydney. This was not easy, there are few secrets in the Yakuza. But finally, on January the 15th, 1986, my family and I arrived on the Gold Coast to begin our new life. It will always be the happiest day of my life." Tears are forming in the corner of Jun's eyes.

"But surely they could find you," says Terri. "Your face must have been so familiar."

"True," Jun replies, "my face is well-known, but only in the highest ranks of the Yakuza. To the thousands of ordinary members, I was just another one of them. This was vital to be a successful assassin. You will notice I have no tattoos and my fingers are all intact."

"Because you wanted to remain anonymous?" asks Ian, looking at Jun's fingers.

Jun levels him with a menacing look. "Because I have never failed to complete a task."

Ian's eyes widen and his Adam's apple bulges. Jun allows himself a glimmer of a mischievous smile. "But young Terri is right," he continues, "they did find me. I spent four years discovering normal life – taking my son to the beach, riding bicycles, shopping for groceries, that sort of thing. My shop was making enough money to get by, and I had stopped looking over my shoulder every time I walked through a door. Then one day Tetsuya Suzuki . . . well, he simply turned up."

At this point Jun pauses again. The vacant, sad look in his eyes suggests he is reliving the day. He slowly shakes his head. "You know, it was just bad luck. It could just as easily have never happened." He laughs ironically. "It was a Monday morning and the shop was quiet. The rain was streaming down and it was getting close to winter. I was in the back watching Bert Newton when a customer came in, dripping all over the floor. It was just a young man looking for paperclips. As you can imagine, I do not sell that many paperclips; but I did have some, somewhere. I found them stuck up on a shelf, behind some receipt books and things. The young man paid and left, so I mopped up the floor, then attended to the shelf. I was putting the pencil sharpeners back and checking just what else I had there, when another customer entered. Without a 'hello' or an 'excuse me', the man asked gruffly in Japanese if I had any *katagiri wasabi* – it's a special wasabi sauce. This did not alarm me, a lot of Japanese people see "Jun" on the storefront and come in looking for specialty Japanese items. But when I turned around, my years of serenity came tumbling down. Our recognition was instant, there was not a single second spent trying to place one another. At first, I thought that Tetsuya had finally tracked me down, but he looked even more surprised than I did. It was a small consolation."

Jun has been turning his glass of water around and around in his old hands. Now he stops and allows himself another slight smile through the dreamy look in his recollecting eyes. When he speaks again it is more to himself than us. "To cut a long story short, he had just dropped in, thinking it was a Japanese grocery store."

"And Tetsuya Suzuki was high up in the Yamaguchi-gumi at this point?" It's Terri who dares to yank Jun from his memories.

He looks up slowly at Terri, unsure of where she is going. "Yes," he answers.

"So, excuse me for being dramatic, but why are you still standing here? You assassinated his oyabun and you said honour is everything to the Yakuza – why on earth would he walk away?"

Jun stares for a moment, as if he is pondering his words very carefully, but then Ian interrupts. "Because Jun had something over Tetsuya."

"Young Ian is very perceptive," says Jun.

We look to Jun, then back to Ian, who shrugs.

"So what information did you have over Tetsuya?" Terri asks.

Jun pauses to ponder again, but just for a second. He shakes his head slowly from side to side, a wry smile stretching the scrunched corners of his mouth. "If I had not discovered these things myself, I would never have believed them. Very few people would. Let us hope that Tetsuya never realises this. Upon entering the store and recognising me, Tetsuya turned to leave. If he had left, I would be dead. But he didn't leave, because I asked him if he had enjoyed being a butcher."

Jun stops to look at us one by one. Satisfied that we are duly intrigued and perplexed, he continues. "As an assassin, I prided myself on my research. Knowledge is three-quarters of any assignment. As such, I had endeavoured to research all the prominent Yakuza from the Yamaguchi-gumi. One of the young men was Tetsuya Suzuki.

"His real name is Masahiko Oba. He was born in a small Japanese town called Hakato where he attended a privileged school, but he achieved poorly. When he finished school, the only job he could get was as an apprentice butcher. However, even at this, he was inept. In fact, just three months into his apprenticeship he accidentally cut off the top of his little finger with a meat cleaver. His friends ridiculed him, even his parents were embarrassed by his constant failures. So as a teenager he fled to Kobe, an angry young man."

My conjured image of Tetsuya Suzuki – a six-foot-three messenger of doom – disappears in a puff of smoke.

"In Kobe," Jun continues, "Masahiko found it even harder. To escape his past he changed his name to Tetsuya Suzuki. But he was not strong. One night, he spent his remaining money on sake and got so drunk he was arrested for killing a duck that was loose in the streets. A duck! He was given two weeks in jail, and it was here that inmates saw that his little finger was missing its tip. Naturally they assumed he was Yakuza and when one inmate asked him what he was in for, Masahiko – or Tetsuya – told him, 'Killing a duck'. However the Japanese word for duck – 'ahiru' – is also Yakuza slang for a policeman.

"And this is where it all began. The prisoner told all the other prisoners that Tetsuya Suzuki was in jail for killing a policeman. Tetsuya now had credibility and respect for the first time in his life. When he was released two weeks later, his reputation grew even more. What connections he must have to get off the charge of killing a policeman! And so word quickly spread outside the prison of a mysterious young man named Tetsuya Suzuki, who was a power to be reckoned with. This is when Tetsuya Suzuki discovered his real talent: deception.

"Through an amazing effort he managed to grow his reputation. He reinvented himself as a clever, brutal Yakuza. He had a knack for claiming credit for things he was not involved in, but not so much credit so as to risk angering those who rightfully deserved it. The great irony of all this is that Tetsuya despises violence. He is weak, timid, and from what I can gather he has never been in a fight – unless you count the duck."

Jun shakes his head, but it's not with the disrespect I am expecting. Rather he is shaking his head in awe. "Tetsuya was faced with this dilemma, day in, day out. Violence, brutality, intimidation . . . yet he managed to find ways around it. I cannot imagine the pressure! I am sure that at many times he questioned what he was doing, but I believe he reached a point where he could not turn back; the only way to avoid being found out was to forge forward. All or nothing, as you say. Tetsuya made up tall stories of his past, he talked very big and got tattoos. He even had the sacred golden dragon tattooed across his back."

"That's like Mr Somatsu," I say, "he has a huge dragon tattoo across his back too."

Jun looks at me sympathetically, almost paternally, and I realise straight away. "Shit."

Jun nods.

"Stupid sodding tosser! Son of a . . . I *told* Karen Mr Somatsu was Tetsuya Suzuki. I knew it."

"Do not feel bad, Tligg, Tetsuya has deceived the best. As Akira Somatsu, he has managed to remain a mystery here on the Gold Coast for years. Many others have failed where you have."

"So that explains it," Ian says to Jun, "he wouldn't touch you because you could expose him, tell all of the Yakuza guys that he was a fraud."

Jun nods, seemingly enjoying his role of teacher. "Mind you, that would have meant giving myself up. It was a very tense time."

"What I don't understand is why didn't you give him up back in Japan, before you left the Yakuza?" says Terri.

"I never shared my information with anyone, unless I was specifically instructed to. Knowledge was power in the Yakuza. Then, when I moved to the Gold Coast, I had no interest in Tetsuya Suzuki. Until he turned up."

"So what happened after you confronted him with what you knew?" I ask, through a recently chewed-off fingernail.

"Tetsuya knew that for me, talking to the Yakuza was suicide. But it would have meant his death sentence too. We made a truce. Not only would we never betray the other's secret, but we would never even acknowledge the other's existence." Jun pauses. "It had been ten years since that day, when you walked in asking about him, so I hope you now understand if I was a little shaken."

All I can do is nod.

♣ ♣ ♣

We sit in silence for a bit, still trying to comprehend Jun's story. Then something hits me as strange. "So what's the Terry Smith bit all about?"

Jun smiles. "I sell papers, Tligger. I read them, too. And I know enough about the Yakuza to read between the lines. I have been keeping track. You see, when setting up in western country, it is a Yakuza practice to employ locals so as to avoid suspicion. It is also policy for the top man to take on the identity of one of those employees, so that if the Yakuza connections cause problems, the local can step into the head Yakuza's shoes – suddenly it is a local who is president of the holding company. This is what Tetsuya Suzuki did with the gentleman named Terry Smith."

"This is all very interesting," says Terri in her abrupt way, "but it doesn't explain why Tetsuya Suzuki, or Mr Somatsu, or whoever the hell he is, is missing. Nor does it explain why his bodyguard and chef are dead, or why Ian and Trigg were kidnapped."

We all look to Jun, but for the first time, the old man is blank. "Unfortunately, I do not have an answer to this."

"So what do we do from here?" Ian asks, his manner a little more personable than his girlfriend's.

Again, we look to Jun. "It seems to me that you must find out for yourselves why all these things have happened," he says.

"But how?" I ask. "Where do we look, where do we start?"

"If it was me, I would go back to Tetsuya's house—"

"Are you joking? For all we know, Tetsuya – Mr Somatsu – is dead."

Jun ignores my outburst. "I would go back to his house and wait. It is more than likely he is still alive."

"How can you be so sure?" asks Terri.

"What you described at the house sounds like the internal politics of the Yakuza. If they had wanted Tetsuya to be dead, he would have been on the floor with his staff. No, they must want something from Tetsuya, and for that they need him alive."

"But what good is waiting at his house going to do?"

Jun sighs. "It is better than waiting here, no?"

♣ ♣ ♣

While Jun strolls slowly back to his store, contemplating just how much his life has changed in the last hour, we are in Ian's Kingswood, driving back towards the canals. As we approach the canal-front home, all seems quiet. However, as we drive past, we can see that the gates are wide open.

"That looks familiar," I say to Terri.

It's the maroon car we saw speeding away from Karen's house the other night – an older-style sedan, with a nice collection of dents. "Any ideas?"

Terri shrugs.

There's no movement from the driveway, so we slow until we are almost stopped. The maroon car has Queensland licence plates. The thought that it belongs to Terry and Doris crosses my mind, but they have the Porsche with the personalised plates. Indeed it is a mystery. A mystery that increases a hundredfold the instant I see the two men emerge from Tetsuya's front door.

Ian sees the men too and accelerates down the road, coming to a stop about eighty yards away. He's the only one not looking back towards Tetsuya's house, but as soon as we're stationary, he rectifies that.

"Who the heck are those guys?" he asks.

We sit gawking out the rear window. I feel I should answer him, but I'm too busy trying to work it out for myself. Oh, I recognise them alright, I just can't make any sense of it.

"Maybe they're the guys who killed those men," says Terri.

"I doubt it," replies Ian, "they don't look like Japanese mafia."

"What if we've got the whole thing wrong?" says Terri. "What if it was just a burglary gone wrong or something?"

"Could be, could be. What about you, Trigg? You recognise them?"

"Yes."

Terri and Ian stop staring at the house to stare at me.

"It's Karen's brother and his mate with the itchy testicles. He may be her cousin, I'm not sure."

"*What?*" Ian and Terri say in unison.

I shrug, to indicate that it makes as much sense to me as it does to them. My speculations that Karen and her brother are somehow tied in with the Yakuza have just been confirmed, but it doesn't add up. I found Karen, she didn't find me. And I didn't even know about the Yakuza back then. The answers lie with her – the answers she promised to give me. But promises are meaningless at the moment. Eventually, though, these thoughts are overpowered by a distant shrieking. It's the sound of a siren. Several sirens, in fact.

Karen's brother and his friend (accomplice) hear them too, because not fifteen seconds later the souped-up sedan bounces out of the driveway and screeches away down the street. About twenty seconds after that the sirens come screaming along the other way. One belongs to an ambulance, the other to a police car.

A crowd quickly forms around the driveway; even in this sophisticated district, the lure of a scandal is just too much.

We get out of the Kingswood and mingle with the gawkers. Pretty soon a policeman wanders around, asking if anyone saw anything. Of course no one did. The ambulance men wheel a body from the house and deposit it into the van. Then another one. When they are driven away, the crowd thins out. We, too, are about to leave, when a long black limousine slinks around the corner beyond the house, like a snake coming out of its hole. It cruises slowly past the driveway, then guns its engine and speeds off down the street. A policeman watches it, but quickly turns back to the house. I pay it more attention, though. And when I turn to Ian he already has the car keys ready.

We have to hang back, sometimes letting the limousine get out of sight, so as not to arouse suspicion. It's a difficult task in the quiet, moneyed backstreets of the Gold Coast, but Ian does a bang-up job. I think he's actually enjoying his new role as escape-mastermind/surveillance-driver.

We drive for about twenty minutes, everyone concentrating intently on the car in front. Finally, the limousine slows down and lurches past a tall wooden gate into a driveway. My blood runs cold. Ian and I share a worried look. The gigantic timber mansion looks a lot different when you're not fleeing it. Ian slows right down and we stare. The mansion is strangely hypnotic. From what we can now see above the high wall, it's a clash of Western and Eastern architecture. And the disturbing thing is, I can't decide if I like it or loathe it. On the one hand, it's gaudy and forced and gratuitous, but on the other, it's bloody huge, and you've got to admire that.

Ian hauls the Kingswood around and we drive past the goliath once more. Just seeing it again makes me feel sick. Unfortunately a second sweep fails to shed any more light on who these people are. We park just around the corner. No one has to ask the question, because we're all thinking it. So now what?

The sun is getting dangerously low. I look at my watch. 4.37 p.m. – seven hours and twenty-three minutes until I kiss my cookies goodbye. I have the distinct feeling that a lot of answers lie in that house: who kidnapped us; why; and I'm almost certain that the crisis I have to help Tetsuya through to get my luck back is linked with his disappearance – and his disappearance is linked to that house. "I need to get inside," I say, chock-full of rare bravado. "And to do that I need Jun."

Ian looks at me as if he's about to quash my melodramatic stance, but he just nods. Yes, it's foolish and dangerous to go inside, but it's also crunch-time. I can't face coming this far only to go back to the disaster that was my luckless life. I've got nothing to lose and, at the risk of sounding theatrical, I would quite possibly rather die trying, than just throw my hands in the air and succumb. This revelation proves surprisingly invigorating. Suddenly I feel like I have nothing to fear. It spurs me on. My bravado grows. I order Terri and Ian to go back and get Jun, while I wait and keep an eye on things.

"And if he doesn't want to come?"

"Well just tell him he'd better! Tell him we can guarantee his identity will not be revealed. Tell him anything. Just get him here quickly."

Terri starts to utter some sort of objection, but when she sees my expression she falters. Like I said, I have nothing left to fear.

By the time my two friends leave, the shadows have grown long. This affords me a little cover, but not nearly enough, so I hunker down in some bushes in the parkland across from the house. The way I figure it, Terri and Ian will be at least twenty minutes, and that's assuming Jun doesn't put up a fight. I get comfortable, but it doesn't last long.

The white limousine with black, black windows slows to a stop just in front of me, leaving me to question all that "nothing to fear" toss. But no one gets out. The big wooden gates open, and the limousine rolls slowly over the grey slate driveway and disappears, just like the limousine we followed. But unlike the first limo, this one gives me a glimpse beyond the high fence. I really wish it hadn't.

At least four Japanese men in dark suits are standing just inside the gate, each carrying a small machinegun. This is very, very serious. This is the sort of thing you only ever see in bad action-movies or war-zones. I'm trying desperately to hang onto my feeling of invincible courage and empowerment, but it's like trying to catch smoke with a tea strainer.

I'm a little more wary when a burst of headlights hits the bushes some minutes later. Sure enough, it isn't Ian and Terri, but another limousine. I duck down again as it goes through the same procedure as the previous two. Very peculiar. Maybe they're having a party. Over the next fifteen minutes two more limousines cram themselves into the crowded driveway. Something big is happening. Where the hell are Ian and Terri?

The next car around the corner dribbles two insipid round beams onto the road. This is accompanied by a metallic vibrating/wheezing noise. The Kingswood stops about eighty yards down the road and I scamper back through the bushes until I'm out of sight of the house. I can make out three figures silhouetted inside the car. At first it looks like Barton in the back seat, but as I get nearer, the streetlight reveals that the dog is actually Jun. It's a strange moment. I feel relieved by Jun's presence, yet at the same time it heralds that things are about to proceed to the next level.

"What took you so long?" I pant through the driver's window.

"Yeah, sorry about that," Ian says. "I was driving to Jun's place when I remembered I had these little two-way radio thingies my surf coach used, back at my place. Thought they might come in handy."

Jun is sitting quietly in the back and I know I should address him, or greet him, or something, but I'm scared that his response will confirm just how upset he is to be in this potentially disastrous situation.

"We were just thanking Jun for coming, Trigg," says Terri. Letting him know that we understand just how difficult this is for him."

I enthusiastically nod my agreement.

Jun merely nods back. In the darkness I can't decipher much from it. "It is indeed a risk, however it is one I believe is worth taking. For you, Tligg, and for myself. Like I said earlier, I can no longer hide from my past."

I breathe a little sigh of relief.

"Ian and Terri have updated me on the situation," Jun continues. "My guess is that the men in the limousine are from a rival Yakuza gang, the one responsible for killing Tetsuya's staff. It is a shame I did not get to see any of them. Did you see the men who got out of the limousine?"

"Limousines," I reply so that the last "s" sounds like a fly buzzing.

"I beg your pardon?" says Jun.

"Well, things have changed a little since Ian and Terri left."

I quickly explain the arrival of the extra limousines and the men with the machineguns. Ian and Terri's faces grow graver and graver, whereas Jun's remains blank until I finish. Then he nods slowly, and – well, I may be mistaken, given the darkness and everything, but I'm quite certain I saw a glimmer of excitement in his eyes.

"So the big boys have come to play," he murmurs to himself. "This is very interesting. Very interesting."

If Jun is aware of the conversation vacuum he's just created, he doesn't show it. In fact it takes almost a full minute for anyone to break the silence.

"So what should we do? Who are these people?" says Terri.

The one-time assassin turns his head ever so slightly towards Terri. "To your first question, Terri, we should act quickly. Very quickly! To your second question – who are these people? – well, if my guess is correct, let me just say that if a bomb hit this house right now, Japanese newspapers would be reshuffling their 'five most powerful people' list."

"The leaders of the other Yakuza gangs?" she says.

"Precisely."

I feel my spirits drop. "What are they doing here?" I ask.

Jun turns to face me. "I think they are moving in on the Gold Coast. You see, the Yamaguchi-gumi have been using the Gold Coast to launder money and buy into legitimate business. That's just what they did in Hawaii . . . until they stepped up the operation. They waited until they had such a strong base of support that no one could touch them, then they began running prostitution, drugs, whatever they could get their hands on. I fear that this is what this meeting is about, to step up operations in Australia. Only it seems that the Yamaguchi-gumi is inviting the other gangs to participate. Yakuza Inc."

I look back through the moonless night, in the direction of the house. I can make out lights among the palm trees, blocked out occasionally by the armed men walking up and down. "So why do we have to act so quickly?"

Jun regards me as if I asked a rather obvious question. "Remember in *The Godfather* and all the other mafia movies, there is always a big meeting of the heads of all the families?"

I nod.

"And it always turns into either a police sting or a bloodbath?"

I nod again, understanding. "So these guys don't hang out together much?"

Now Jun nods.

Terri takes the silence that follows as her cue to interject. "So what should we do? We don't even know if Mr Somatsu is in there."

Without responding to Terri's question, Jun turns his fraudulently frail body around as much as he can in the back seat of the Kingswood, and squints through the darkness. We all take to looking thoughtfully back in the direction of the house. I can't speak for the others, but my apparent thoughtfulness is deceptive: my head is devoid of ideas.

The street is menacingly quiet, with only the palm fronds rippling in the breeze to reassure me that I haven't suddenly gone deaf. And the blood pulsing through my head.

"Shiro Tozoku."

I think everyone's heart skips a beat at this point.

"Shiro Tozoku," Jun repeats a little louder but a little slower.

"Huh?" I mean it to sound casual and nonplussed, but it pitches up an octave or two as it squeezes past the lump in my throat.

"Shiro Tozoku. The White Bandit . . . the white Yakuza."

"Huh?"

"That is how you are going to get inside, Tligg. The myth of the white Yakuza."

"Huh?"

Jun explains that in the years before he fled for the Gold Coast, a rumour began circulating through Japan. It revolved around the assassination of five prominent Yakuza in America. Their murders all occurred within one month. Obviously this was no coincidence, and eventually the responsibility for these deaths was placed on the shoulders of a single Yakuza: supposedly a white American, the White Bandit, ShiroTozoku.

At first this rumour was laughed off. But when no one could make any sense of the murders, the rumour began to take hold. And the Japanese have always loved a good myth. So within a year, many Yakuza, including those high up, believed in this rogue killer. As time went on, his infamy grew, to the point where he was considered the most dangerous man in the Yakuza organisation. New members were warned to kill him on sight, not that they knew what he looked like. Thousands waited for him to make his ultimate move, to finally claim the power he had killed for. But it never happened. And the longer nothing happened, the more his reputation grew. Every unclaimed act of violence was attributed to him.

"I don't know exactly what happened after I fled for the Gold Coast," Jun says, "but I do know that the Shiro Tozoku was never discovered."

"How can you be so sure?" asks Ian. "You've been out of the loop for years."

Jun sighs. "Because I invented him."

Standing near the open window of the Kingswood, in the quiet Gold Coast street, I had practically forgotten the gruesome past of the hunched figure in the back seat.

"Okay, so there's supposed to be this white Yakuza. How is this going to help me get inside?"

It's a logical enough question. Much more eloquent than "huh?" Yet everyone is looking at me as if I just asked why old Uncle Richard with the bad ticker and advanced lung cancer isn't joining us this Christmas. Oh, hang on—

"You want *me* to be the white Yakuza?"

Jun is the only one to respond. He quietly opens the back door of the car, steps out, and quietly closes it again. He looks deep into my eyes and nods. Not a sympathetic nod. Oh no. A single, curt up-and-down of the head.

"But . . . Bloody hell, I don't even speak Japanese!"

Jun silences me with an extended hand. "Tligger, I want you to listen very carefully to me." He waits until my breathing has calmed down and he has my undivided attention. "You can do this. It is about you having bigger kazungas than them."

"Oh I have quite small kazungas actually, very small. I was always being teased at school—"

"Tligger! This is all about perception." And with that the old man lunges at me.

I jump back, covering my face with my hands, but Jun doesn't touch me.

"You see that, Tligg? You are scared of me. I'm sure you did not fear me before today, and yet now you do. Why? I have not grown stronger or bigger or younger. The only thing that has changed is your perception. And that has only changed because of what I told you. How do you know I really was an assassin? I could have made the whole thing up. You see, Tligg? Perception."

"You put my testicles up around my ears with your foot and closed off my trachea with your hand. All like that." I snap my fingers.

"That is true. But you still see my point, yes?"

I have to admit I do. But trying to convince the five most powerful men in the Yakuza that I'm the meanest bastard in . . . the Yakuza . . . is not going to be easy.

I voice this observation to Jun, but he dismisses it with a wave of the hand. "All the same. All the same."

If only Karen were here, she'd know what to do. In desperation I turn to Terri. If she thinks I can go into that house and pull it off, then I bloody well will. "Terri, what do you think?"

She chews on her thumbnail. "I think it's very dangerous, probably foolhardy . . . but, given the circumstances . . . I think you should do it."

I muster all the resolve I can and nod. "Okay." Then I take a few steps and lean into the front window of the car. "Ian, what do you reckon?"

I'm desperate for an out. My steely, devil-may-care attitude of thirty minutes ago has completely dissipated. Unfortunately, the facts are clear: my curse indemnity runs out in six hours; to lift it completely I have to find Mr Somatsu; and the only people who know where he is are in that house, and they won't be there for long.

When I look at it this way, I can see that going inside is not so much a decision as a formality.

But my hands are still shaking, my heart still jumping about in my chest, and my brain still firing off synapses willy-nilly. There are so many "buts".

"How will they understand me?" I ask.

"Oh this is not a problem," answers Jun in his annoyingly reassuring way. "They can all speak very good English. Very good."

"Well, what about age? This white Yakuza would be at least forty by now. And what about names, and places and stuff? I'm going in there, saying that I'm the guy who took out five (five!) of the best Yakuza around. And they say, 'Really? Which ones?' And I say, 'Ahhhhh . . . well, there was the short one with the dark hair . . .'"

"Tligg. Tligg. You worry far too much. We have that covered. Thanks to Ian. He is a very smart man."

Ian? Ian's coming in with me? That's some solace. We're a good team. "So you know all the names and details and such?" I ask Ian, who is now out of the car too.

He doesn't look like he knows the names. Actually he looks rather confused. Then Jun taps me on the shoulder. "Ian does not know the details. I do." Jun looks at me with that expression some parents assume when they're trying to cajole their kids into going to church.

"I don't understand."

Jun's expression doesn't change, he still has that condescending, infallible smile. "Ian's two-way radio transmitters."

"His what?"

"You know, Trigg," says Ian, whose bewilderment had been replaced with comprehension, "the headset thingy that I went back to my place for, the reason we were late. Jun's going to use that."

A headset? Yes, that could work. A headset! That's even better than Ian. "How does it work?"

"It's really simple, mate. Jun can hear everything that's going on around you, and it's got an ear piece so he can talk to you, so that only you hear."

"Really? And they won't be able to tell I'm wearing it?"

Ian scrunches up his face and runs a hand through his messy hair. "They absolutely won't know that you're wearing a two-way transmitter."

"And what, I'll have ninja mask on so they won't recognise me?"

Jun nods. "Something to cover your face, yes."

"Okay. I'll do it." I surprise myself at the steadiness of my voice. "I'll do it."

"Excellent," says Jun. "But we must act now. Ian, where is the transmitter?"

Ian walks back around to the driver's side and rummages around through the window. He gives Jun a walkie-talkie type thing. Then he gives me my ensemble.

I turn it over in my hands. They are shaking again. "You . . . have got . . . to be *fucking kidding me*!"

I hold the navy-blue helmet up and turn it jerkily from side to side.

"I'm sorry, man," says Ian. "It's a surf helmet, like you wear over in Indonesia, where the reefs are really shallow. My coach had it made up so we could talk when I was out in the surf. It was the only way we could get a two-way system waterproof."

I sit down on the lush nature strip in a humph. I'm only one more defeatist thought away from breaking into hysterical sobbing. Just one more.

"Jesus Christ, Trigg, don't be such a dickhead." It's Terri – of course it's Terri. She launches herself out of the car, her sparkling blue eyes now fiery. "You're lucky you've even got it. Imagine going in there without any link to the outside world. You'd get eaten alive."

Are these people insane? Are they aware of what they are asking me to do? Walk, unannounced, into one of the biggest power meetings in the world with . . . with . . . with a bloody *surf helmet* on my head? I can just imagine it: "Well yes, hi there, I'm a deadly Yakuza assassin . . . yes, the white one, that's right . . . anyway, can I come in? What? Oh this thing? Well, you never know when a big wave might dump you on a shallow reef. Best to be prepared, hey?'

I look up at my companions. Three looming faces. I feel betrayed, cajoled into doing something I wasn't too keen on in the first place. Then asked to do it looking like some tribute to Evel Knievel. "Did you happen to bring any chicken rolls, Jun?"

"We're all taking risks here, Trigg," Terri starts up again, "Jun, Ian, me."

"Yes, but—"

"No buts! We're *all* taking risks here . . . but it's not for Jun. It's not for Ian. It's not for me. The only person we're putting ourselves out for, taking risks for, is you. You, Trigg. Don't forget that."

I play with a blade of grass. She's right. Cow. Here are all these people, standing in the darkness just eighty yards away from four friggin' machineguns. And it's for me. There's nothing in it for them. It's just to help me. And here I am behaving like a brat.

With a giant heave of my respiratory system I stand up. I nod apologetically. "You're right. I'm sorry."

Ian rests a tanned hand on my shoulder. "No worries, mate."

"Alright, love-in over," says Jun. "Let's get down to business."

Ian gives me one last supportive slap. I look at the helmet. I turn it over in my hands again. "Okay Jun, so how do I get in?"

"Perhaps we should get back in the car," says the retired assassin.

We all load back in except for Jun. For some reason he sets off in the opposite direction, away from the house, pausing to look into people's gardens. He's gone a good five minutes. Five long, quiet, contemplative minutes. Not even Ian is talking. And when Jun returns he's not alone.

It's Karen.

?

??

?????????

"I found her lurking in the bushes," says Jun. "She says she has to talk to you."

"How . . . I didn't hear a thing."

"No, I was just lucky. I was actually looking for this." Jun holds up a white flower, a rose, and passes it through the car window to me. "You'll need it later."

Jun opens the car door and lets Karen in.

"Hi," she says.

"Hi," I reply.

"Hi," Karen says to Ian.

"Hi," he replies.

"Hi," Karen says to Terri.

"Hi," she replies.

"I know, I know," says Karen to me. "You've got a lot of questions, and hey, I've got a lot of answers. But not—"

"No!" I say. "One question. Just one question: how long have you been following me for?"

"Since the day I took the money."

"Why?"

"That's two questions."

"Oh for the love of—"

"Alright, alright," says Karen. "I've been following you because I don't want you to get hurt."

"Sorry?"

"No good," says Jun interjecting. "Questions lead to more questions and we do not have time."

"Time for what?" asks Karen.

"I need to go into that house," I reply. "Mr Somatsu is Tetsuya Suzuki and he's disappeared. The people in that house are the only people who know where he is."

"You can't go in there. It's, like, the biggest Yakuza shindig, ever. It's too dangerous. Jesus, Trigg, didn't you read the note?"

"But . . . but we've got a plan."

Karen raises a dubious eyebrow.

"It's not *my* plan. It's Jun's."

Karen laughs at the surf helmet. She actually laughs. As for the rest of the plan, she merely furrows her cute little brow. "You can't go in there. You're way out of your depth."

"You don't think I know that? I'm in so bloody deep I can't see the shore anymore. But I've got no choice. If I go in, there's a chance I can get my luck back. But if I don't, well, anything that happens in there is going to be mild compared to what's going to happen if I don't. I have no choice."

"I still don't think . . ." She sighs and runs a hand through her long dark hair. Her playful mood has well and truly called it a night. "Do you really think this can work?"

"It's got a better chance if you tell me what you know about the meeting."

She shakes her head. "Believe me, if you're going inside, you're safer not knowing."

"It's got to do with your brother, hasn't it?"

"I . . . no . . ."

Jun sighs impatiently. "Are you going to give us any answers?"

"I can't," Karen replies.

"Are you going to give us any information that will help him inside that house?"

"I . . . nothing you don't already know."

"Alright, then. We move on."

I set off for the house in my shorts and T-shirt . . . and the sparkling blue surfing-helmet with the little black visor. I take a great deal of comfort in Karen's parting words. "Look," she'd said, "just pretend you ride a motorbike. These people don't know that that's a surfing helmet. You can say that you're leaving it on to protect your identity." I'm sure that in isolation this would seem like a particularly weak suggestions, but given the current context it's possibly the most sensible part of the whole plan.

"Hello, Jun, can your hear me?" I whisper into the microphone.

"*Arrgghhh! Tligg, you don't have to hold the microphone so close. It is very sensitive.*"

"Oh, sorry. Is this better?"

"*Much. Thank you.*"

"Okay, I'm walking towards the front gate now."

"*Yes, Tligg, we can see you.*"

I turn around and realise I have moved only twelve yards or so. I must be even more apprehensive than I thought. And I thought I was pretty damn apprehensive.

As I walk on, the helmet gives everything a surreal twist. Peripheral vision – you never really notice it until it's gone. I move away from the fingers of the streetlight and the darkness feels good. Comforting. Like I could just slip into the small thicket of palm trees beside me and hide until morning. But I keep going.

As I clear the palm trees, the enormous bastardised Japanese mansion looms into view again. The oriental roof on the dark wooden walls makes it look like some Pizza Hut for ostentatious millionaires. Slowly I creep along, hugging the wall. Occasionally a stray splinter snags my T-shirt, pulling it back and making me jump. The next time I turn around, I can't see the Kingswood anymore.

I slide on further, past a small grey door that looks like a service entrance. At least, I think it's grey. I remember reading somewhere that the parts of your eye used for seeing in the dark can't distinguish colour. It could be fluorescent green for all I know. It doesn't matter, I'm getting closer to the gated driveway, though it's still probably another forty yards away – it's a huge house.

My heart is beating a techno tune as I arrive within knocking distance of the little wooden door next to the main gate. Each swallow is like trying to drink hot sand. Jun must think he's somehow picked up an adults-only chat-line, the way I'm breathing. I'm dying to whisper into the microphone, which I trust is somewhere in the vicinity of my mouth, that I am about to knock on the door, but I know I can't control my voice enough to whisper. My right hand feels as if someone has slipped a lead glove onto it. In fact, my whole body is heavy. But there's no turning back now. I lift my hand and—

"Don't . . . fucking . . . move," says the barely audible voice.

I stop dead: my hand, my heart, everything – as if I were about to bungee jump and someone halted me at the very last second. My blood has a certain cold tinge to it, while my back has what feels like a gun barrel sticking into it.

"*Tligg? Are you there? Tligg . . .*"

Jun's voice booms through my head. Surely anyone within a twenty-yard radius can hear his crackly words. Bring over the plates, this goose is cooked! I try to breathe normally and arch my back away from the steel barrel. It follows me. Then, ever so softly but ever so firmly, a hand lands on my shoulder. I try to see who it belongs to, but the helmet stops me. If the gun doesn't kill me, the curiosity will.

Slowly – very slowly – the hand leads me away from the gate, away from Jun and the others. The light continues to dance on the other side of the wall as the guards move about. Or maybe it's just the palm trees twisting in the breeze. Jun's incessant attempts to get my attention continue unanswered.

The hand leads me around the corner and down the street. There are no streetlights and the only thing blacker than the night is the blanket of fear that has settled over my psyche.

"What's going—?"

"Shhh." The hand firms its grip on my shoulder.

Forty yards further on, as Jun's questioning ceases echoing inside the helmet, the outline of a car separates itself from the charcoal night. It's a maroon sedan with a person standing against it. Ten yards further on I realise it's Karen's brother.

"What's with the helmet, Trigg?" he says.

I try turning around again. This time the hand allows me and I see it belongs to Karen's neighbour, the one with the itchy testicles. He smiles, but not in a friendly way.

"What's with the helmet, Trigg?" Karen's brother asks again.

"Uhh . . . nothing," I say with schoolboy conviction. "So what's going on?"

Karen's brother smiles. "Why don't you tell us?"

"Just out for a drive."

"Yeah? So what were you doing at that house?"

"Which house?"

"Cut the bullshit, Harvey!" He breathes the words more than says them, and from somewhere in his casual wardrobe he conjures a gun. "What the fuck are you up to? What are you doing here?"

I stare down the barrel of the gun. Two of them, in fact, because the neighbour has moved around in front of me.

"Okay, okay . . . let's just settle down for a second. I'll tell you what I'm doing if you tell me what *you're* doing."

"I don't think so," says Karen's brother quietly. "Let's just stick to what you're doing."

This has the potential to go on all night, and I certainly do not have all night, so despite my pride, I cooperate. "I'm here because I need to find a man who I think is in that house."

"Who?" asks the neighbour.

"I . . . a man . . . Tetsuya Suzuki, or Mr Somatsu. They're the same person."

This does not seem to surprise them in the least.

"Why?" Karen's brother asks.

"Ahhh . . ." I attempt to scratch my head, but my fingernails find only hard blue plastic. "This might sound a little weird, but I need him so I can get my luck back."

This doesn't seem to surprise them either. "Go on," says the neighbour, still waving a gun at me.

I describe the rest of my predicament as quickly and as quietly as I can.

"So why should we believe you?" asks Karen's brother.

"I'm wearing a bloody surf-helmet into a Yakuza power meeting. What's not to believe?"

Nothing happens for an aeon. Karen's brother stares at me, but I don't look away. "You know what?" he says, smiling to the other man. "I think he's legit."

The other man smiles. This time it's friendlier. "Hnnnh, me too."

And I smile. "So does this mean you'll tell me what you have to do with . . . anything?"

"Jeez, that could take some explaining," says Karen's brother.

"I don't have much time."

"That's okay, I never said we *would* explain."

I pull out Terry's gun, catching them both off guard. "You better tell me what is going on, right now!"

"Whoa, cowboy, take it easy – don't want to wake up the neighbours, do we?" says Karen's brother, still with a gun of his own.

"Right fucking now!"

"Trigg!"

We all turn at once.

"Karen?" we say in unison.

She jogs down the street, Ian in tow. "Oh for Christ's sake, put the guns down."

"Not until I find out what the hell is going on."

"Trigg . . . put the gun down before you shoot yourself."

Ian nods his support and finally we all lower our guns.

"So?" I say.

Karen stands in between the two men and me. She takes her brother by one hand and me by the other. "Alright, the quick version. Trigg, this is my brother Luke and his partner Danny. Partner as in 'police'. They're undercover federal agents, working Vice here on the coast. And, well, I guess we all just got a bit tangled up." She tries a small laugh, but it doesn't really work.

"Federal agents?"

Luke and Danny take out their badges. I shake my head in disbelief.

"The night you walked into the store, you told me you were looking for a guy named Terry Smith," says Karen. "No big deal, I've had stranger requests. Besides, I thought you were kind of cute, in a tragic way. It's just that I knew a guy called Terry Smith was tied up with Luke and Danny's investigation. That's why I sent you to Hairy Palms, so Luke and Danny would know where you were. Then when you came in the next night and told me you'd just pilfered $50,000 in drug money from some senile coke-dealer, well, it just had to be the same Terry Smith. So I called Luke again. Right, Luke?"

"Yeah, I suppose."

"And tell him about Terry Smith."

"Well, she tells me about this old guy called Terry Smith who gave you fifty grand because of a plastic badge and a toy gun. Fine, whatever. But Terry Smith is smack bang in the middle of our investigation. You see, he's tied right up with the Yakuza and they've been dipping their fingers – those they've got left – into the vice trade here on the coast. Naturally our first thought is that you're in with this guy. I mean a plastic badge and a toy gun? Hell, maybe you're even onto us and Karen is your way of telling us to back off. Or maybe you're just a fucking loony. Either way, we had ourselves a . . . situation, which we had to contain. For starters we had to stop you from going to the local cops – I mean, Jesus, half the friggin' force should be walking around without their pinky fingers. Anyway we got Karen to stall you, you know laundering the money and all that . . ."

"But then they had to trace the money," says Karen, taking over, "to check if it really was drug-money. That's why I had to steal it, Trigg. But I didn't steal it all. I left you the clean money."

"But I hid . . . never mind." I thought I was so clever.

"Anyway," Karen continues, "they traced the money and found that it was drug money . . ."

"So we knew at least one part of your story held up – you got the money from Terry Smith" says Danny, entering the fray. "What we didn't know was whether you were telling the truth or whether you were in with him. But then one day we spot you while we're following the big fish himself, Tetsuya Suzuki."

"So, Jesus, Trigg, now you're on the Yakuza most-likely list," interrupts Luke. "Especially when you go back to his *house*. I gotta tell ya, we felt like a couple of dickheads. I mean we had to move out of our safe houses!"

"That's why you had me picked up for the paedophilia thing, isn't it?"

Danny and Luke look at each other blankly. I make a vow to keep my mouth zipped.

"We did try to pick you up at the pub," Luke continues, "but the one of the Yakuza gangs got to you first."

"So how did you know you'd find me here?"

"We didn't. We're here for Tetsuya Suzuki and you almost stuffed it up for us."

"Well you *did* stuff it up for me."

"Stuff it up? We just saved your fucking life. You have no idea what's going on behind those gates right now."

"Behind those gates, the oyabuns of the five most powerful Yakuza gangs are meeting to decide how they should split up the Australian vice market."

Luke puts his hands on his hips and shakes his head at me. "You fucking lunatic. You *knew* that and you were still about to waltz in there – you got some set of balls, man."

Karen nods, then realises the inference and blushes.

I look at my watch. "Look, I enjoy favourable comments about my testicles as much as the next man, but I've got a very tight deadline."

Luke scratches his chin. "Yeah, you mentioned that earlier." He sighs, looks at the sky and scratches his chin again. "But, you see, Trigg, Tetsuya's got a bit of a deadline of his own."

"Enough of this cryptic bullshit," says Karen. "I'm sick of playing for both sides. If you don't tell him, I will."

Luke looks at Danny. Danny looks at Luke. A couple of schoolboys trying to decide whether to confess. Luke shrugs, leaving Danny to explain. "Tetsuya is cutting a deal with the federal police. In exchange for witness protection, he's going to secure us a document from the meeting. "As you're obviously aware, these meetings don't tend to stretch on over the weekend, so he has until tonight to get the document. Or the deal is off."

It hits me like a bolt of lightning. Instant understanding. Everything. Like an unfinished, one-thousand-piece jigsaw-puzzle suddenly solving itself – SSSSSNAP! All my emotions come to the surface, like dynamite-fishing. I want to laugh, cry, love, hate . . . all at once. All the pieces finally fit; I know why Karen warned me it was too dangerous. I know why she couldn't tell me what she knew. And more importantly, I finally know exactly what I have to do to get my luck back. Roger, you're about to become history.

"I have to go in there," I say to Luke and Danny. Then I turn to Karen and Ian. "This is it. To get my luck back I have to help the owner of the other figurine with their difficult task. This is Mr Somatsu's – Tetsuya Suzuki, whatever you want to call him – this is his difficult task, turning on the Yakuza. This is why he's got the figurine. I have to get that document for him."

Ian looks at me, slightly-less laid back than usual. "Jeez, slow down, Trigg, we don't even know what happened to Mr Somatsu. Maybe he's in there getting the document right now."

"Not possible. He was abducted because they know. They know he's cut a deal with the federal police, that's why they took him. Hell, that's why they took you and me. Old Terry Smith told them I was a cop and they thought you and I were the feds that Tetsuya is doing the deal with! They thought you and I were Luke and Danny. It all makes sense! I have to get that document for him. There's no way he can get it; even if he's still alive, they'll have him under guard somewhere. I have to get it. That's the whole point, that's how I get my luck back." I turn back to Luke and Danny. "I have to go in there."

"But you can't," says Karen. "If they find out who you are, you'll blow Luke and Danny's cover. You'll all end up dead."

"Look," I plead, "Mr Somatsu is not getting that document. And while I'm sure it wouldn't bother these two here in the slightest if he was killed, I can't help but assume that they want this document pretty bad." I turn to Luke and Danny. "But you can't get it. Hell, you wouldn't even get past the machineguns on the other side of the wall . . . no offence. But I can. I've got a foolproof way of getting into the house. And I can get in on this meeting. All you have to do is tell me what this document is. I'm the best shot you've got. Those men are going to be out of there before tomorrow morning."

Luke and Danny look at each other.

"Come on, I'm the *only* shot you've got."

Luke takes a deep breath and slowly exhales. He runs his hand through his fashionably-cropped hair. "Alright," he says in a barely audible whisper. "But you've only got two hours. Then we're coming in."

Now it's my turn to breathe heavily. My all-or-nothing mission is back on. I relay through the microphone for Jun to grab Terri and join us as quickly as possible.

"Okay," says Luke once we are all assembled, "the Yakuza have been in negotiations for some time about how the Australian market will be split up. A week ago they finally came to an agreement, but they haven't all been face-to-face until tonight. The document you need to get, Trigg, is the official agreement of all five gangs regarding who gets what. But – and remember this, Trigg – it's useless to us until it's signed by all five bosses.

Jun adds more by explaining that the signing of these documents – keiyaku, as they are known in Japanese – is very ceremonial and is always the culmination of the meeting. I don't really know if this is good or bad. I guess, like a lot of the things I'm hearing, it just is.

I tighten the strap of the sparkling blue helmet and check my watch. It's 8.30 p.m. I have until 10.30.

♣ ♣

25

I move out from the shadows and back onto the white concrete footpath. There's no light dancing on the other side of the fence now. The guards must be sitting down. Or the wind has stopped blowing the palm trees. Sweat breaks out on my forehead as I get to the gate, making the helmet feel slimy. My head is unbearably hot inside the blue plastic, like my brain is about to cook. And yet my hands feel cold. So very cold. Oh well, here we go, things are about to change forever.

I curl up my fist and before I even know what's happening it has fallen against the wooden door four times.

My breath remains stuck in my throat for what seems like an eternity.

The gate moves. A gaunt Japanese face peers out from the gap and looks me up and down, eyebrows scrunching when it gets to the helmet. The man moves his hands slightly and I can tell that he has the snub-nosed machinegun just a little more ready to fire. "What fuck you want?" he demands with a heavy Japanese accent.

"I'm here for the meeting."

Either my response or the bad American accent throws the man. His eyebrows unscrunch for a second. "What fuck meeting?"

I'm relaying Jun's words as I hear them. They come as much as a surprise to me as to the guard. "*I'm here to meet with*" . . . "I'm here to meet with" . . . "*Hiroshi Takahashi*" . . . "Hiroshi Takahashi . . . Jiro Ogawa . . . Hideki Kawabata . . . Kotaro Nakamura . . . and Takeshi Sato."

This really gets the guard's attention. He stares at me for a good ten seconds, then slams the door shut in my face. On the other side of the wood I can hear excited voices speaking in Japanese. "Can you pick up any of that, Jun?"

"*Sorry, Tligg . . . too muffled.*"

Finally the gate opens again, the gap a little wider because now there are two faces (and two machineguns). "Who fuck are you?" says the new face.

"*Tell them that Takeshi will know, if not by your face, then by your reputation.*"

I relay this to the two men. The door closes again. This time there is only one voice and given the pauses in between the sentences, I'd say it's being directed into a walkie-talkie.

The door opens again. "No good. Who fuck are you?"

"*Shiro Tozoku.*"

"I am Shiro Tozoku." I say it with as much coldness as I can.

The man's eyes open about as much as I've seen a Japanese man's eyes open. Then quickly they scrunch up again. "Bullsheet!"

"*This is no good, Tligg, you have to get past these men . . . kick the door in.*"

'Are you insane?' I want to scream into the microphone, but I can't. So I just stand there.

"*Come on, Tligg, you have to act quickly . . . remember – perception. You must make them believe. Make them respect. They will, Tligg. Make your own luck. Kick the door in.*"

Arghhh! I give the door a massive kick with the sole of my sneaker and it hits the man on the other side. His body yields under the force of my kick. It's an incredibly satisfying feeling.

I push my way through the gate to confront what's on the other side. I'm expecting guns drawn, eyes glaring and fists flying, but I couldn't be more wrong. Guns are resting impotently in slack hands, eyes register only fear.

"*I am Shiro Tozoku and I am here for the meeting – the kaigo.*"

"I am Shiro Tozoku and I am here for the kaigo."

I say it with serenity, as if to imply that my previous actions were nothing – that's how I greet my parents when I visit – so don't test me. And I stare. I stare menacingly at the man from behind my tinted visor. He is lying on his back, legs akimbo, virtually shaking with fear. He pulls himself together and stands up, unable to unlock his eyes from mine. For some reason I'm surging with confidence. Jun was right – *perception*. I take a step towards the man and he rears back. Jun's assassin work must have been gruesome to warrant this sort of reaction. The man scrabbles for his walkie-talkie while the other men gape. The best part is no one's laughed at the helmet yet.

The man with the walkie-talkie begins talking frantically in Japanese. Jun is saying nothing.

"Ahgggr*jun*?" I pretend to clear my throat. "AhgggrJUN?"

"*It's okay, Tligg, you're in. Good work.*"

Sure enough, the man puts the walkie-talkie back on his belt and moves cautiously towards me. "You speak Japanese?" he asks.

"Maybe." This stumps the man. He looks at his feet for a moment, then back up at me. Using a jerk of his head he indicates that I am to follow him up a path.

The path runs alongside an ornamental Japanese garden with small hidden lights and a tiny creek. Under different circumstances it would be serene and relaxing. Maybe I'll come back here when all this is done, with Ian's deckchair and a little fishing-rod for the golden carp that are catching the light every now and then.

I'm jolted out of my plans by Jun.

"*Tligg, they are going to want proof when you get inside. Cough if you are hearing me." I cough. "Good. Now remember the rose I gave you? That is your proof. I . . . the white Yakuza left a white rose on all his victims, placed on their chest with their right hand over it. As far as I know, only the oyabuns ever learnt of this. Show them the rose and they will believe.*"

With a crippling sense of dread, I thrust my hand in my pocket. Thank God! The rose is still there and it still feels relatively intact. This single white flower buoys my confidence no end. Not that it needs much buoying. It's a strange sensation, almost an out-of-body experience; I realise that my nerves have all but disappeared, now that I am out on stage. I run my hand along the smooth stones set into the concrete wall, just to check reality.

We get to the top of the stairs and enter a vestibule. On the right is a little wooden deck covered by an ornate Japanese roof; on the left are to two huge wooden doors. Now, I'm no lumber expert, but I'd say they are two bloody expensive hunks of wood. And in front of the pricey planks stands—

I recoil slightly and my confidence wavers. I never thought I'd be saying this, but thank God for the helmet. The man guarding the door is one of the men who kidnapped Ian and me. I suck up my chest and try to make my shoulders look bigger than they are.

The man approaches, his expression not one of fear but disdain. At least he doesn't recognise me. My heart starts bouncing again and my scalp prickles with perspiration. I look around, trying to appear casual.

He keeps walking towards me.

I am aware of the eagerness emanating from the two gate-men that led me up. This is their chance to see this huge bastard cower before the white Yakuza. More disturbingly, it's obvious that the big lunk is also aware of this eagerness, and he's not about to lose face in front of two lackeys. Then he stops.

"Shiro Tozoku?" he spits, as if he's asking how this runt could possibly be the mythical white Yakuza, the most feared man in the Japanese underworld. I feel my bowel shudder.

Then, in a soft voice, Jun says, "*Have faith Tligg . . . I do.*" His words stir something deep inside me, beyond my bowel. I clench my fists by my side, straining my forearms. I take a deep controlled breath and shift my gaze into the eyes of the beast before me. Underneath the visor, my eyes drip with pure don't-fuck-with-me contempt. I bore right into his soul. And I'm pissed off. I've had enough of dragging my arse from one side of the Gold Coast to the other. I've had enough of being scared. I've had enough of throwing up, being harassed and passing out. It comes surging up from all parts of my body and concentrates in my skull before being released in intense daggers from my eyes. Pure malevolence.

And so we stand, locked in some sort of ocular arm-wrestle. I've never felt such rage before in my life. But it's controlled rage.

Controlled and concentrated on the very heart of this man before me, who right now represents every person who has ever mocked me, taken advantage of me, intimidated me or . . . or just pissed me off.

He backs down. The disdain drains from his eyes, only to be replaced with, not exactly fear, but wary respect. And then he looks away. It's only momentarily, maybe not even enough for the gatemen to notice, but he definitely looks away. He's beaten. "What you want?" he asks in a ferocious voice. But it's just for show. We both know how the cards lie.

"I have already explained, I am here for the kaigo."

He looks me up and down, as if deciding whether or not to admit me into the house. But it doesn't matter. I know I'm in.

"Take off helmet," he barks.

Remembering the plan from earlier, I refuse, claiming that I want to keep my identity secret. The man fumes and fusses, but eventually relents. Unfortunately, I had not planned on what happens next. He frisks me. I only have two things on my person, but they are two things I'd rather he didn't find. He locates the gun quickly and withdraws it from my pocket. I brace myself for the onslaught of scrutiny . . . which never comes. He merely looks it over and puts it in his own pocket, as if surrendering firearms is a courtesy, like removing one's shoes. Luckily he doesn't find the rose, although I felt him slap it with one of his oversized paws as he was patting me down.

The guard I knocked down earlier opens the dark wooden doors and I step over the threshold. I don't even twitch.

And I thought the outside of the house was over the top. Cream-coloured marble tiles flecked with gold cover the expanse of floor; there is a grand, red-carpeted staircase like something out of the movies – seven people wide, at least, with marble railings on either side. Of course, it's all lit by a bold chandelier that hovers above everything. I expect to see a footman named Jeffery appear at any second. Instead I get Toshi.

"*Toshi to mooshimasu. Kutsu o nuide itada kemasenka.*"

"*He is asking for your shoes. Just nod and take them off.*"

I follow Jun's instructions and the butler scampers off with my fraying pair of Adidas. We make our way up the impressive staircase, my former kidnapper leading the way. I'm doing my best not to look too awe-struck.

At the top of the stairs we are confronted with several closed doors, but we turn right and walk straight past them, making our way along until the mezzanine opens out onto a sea of red carpet. The down-lights in the ceiling create little vignettes on the carpet. It's all frightfully dramatic.

At the far end of the room is another set of brown wooden doors. And this is where the larger of my new friends heads.

With a gentleness of unknown origins, he raps on the wood. Seconds later, the doors open and another massive piece of humanity emerges. It's the second man from the kidnapping, the even larger one. He closes the doors behind him. What follows is an intense, staccato conversation. I edge closer so that Jun can translate:

"*Does he speak Japanese?*"

"*He seems to understand it.*"

"*Any weapons?*"

"*Just a handgun . . . Smith and Wesson, 9mm.*"

"*Well, is he?*"

"*. . . Yes.*"

"*They are not ready for him yet. We will wait.*"

They seem to say a lot more than this, but it's all that Jun reports. The new man looks me over, and a glimmer of recognition dances in his beady eyes. I turn away in apparent boredom.

"Hey!" he says in gruff English. "You look familiar."

I square the man up with as much of the previous intensity as I can muster. This stops him in his tracks. Then in a calm, icy voice I say, "I'm the last person you want to recognise." The man's head remains still but his eyes immediately dart for the carpet. Perception.

We stand for several minutes. "*Is everything okay Tligg? Cough once if it is.*" Cough. "*Okay, good. Stay calm, you are doing very well.*

Remember the rose, that's all you need. They will believe."

The newest member of our happy little gang – let's call him Menacing Thug #2 – suddenly springs to attention as the doors open and a thin, well-groomed head appears. The head speaks quietly, then closes the doors. Menacing Thug #2 then speaks to Menacing Thug #1. Menacing Thug #1 then addresses the group: "*Yoi ga dekite iru.*"

"*They are ready, Tligg. This is it,*" Jun reports.

I follow my two kidnappers towards the doors, my legs suddenly wobblier than I would like. A loud click emanates from beyond the wall, and the right-hand door slides open. I get my first glimpse of what is awaiting me. It chills my blood.

Inside sit five disarming Japanese men around a gleaming wooden table that is so dark it seems to soak up the blood-red from the carpet. Each man sits in front of a clutch of papers and folders, equidistant around the circular table: because it's so large – seven feet across at least – they each have enough room to swing the domestic animal of their choosing. They are hard men, very different in many ways – age, clothing, expressions, sunglasses, haircuts – but the one thing that binds them is their hardness. It emanates from each figure. There will be no cracking jokes tonight, no chucklesome anecdotes.

As I step into the room, I notice for the first time the men around the perimeter. About a dozen of them, all with crew-cuts, all wearing dark suits with assorted pin-striping, herring-boning and the like. These men are *trying* to be hard, but it's not something you can just slip into. Their eyes are too eager, too excitable; whereas the men in the centre aren't even looking at me. They are beyond curiosity, devoid of the ability to be impressed.

On the walls, in between the heavy red drapes hang framed Japanese watercolours. A single vase of cherry blossom has been put off to the side. But there's something disturbing about the room too. The stillness. If not for the heavy fog of cigar smoke dancing languidly around the ceiling, I would have thought I'd just walked into a still life. And not any petite Japanese watercolour, but a big, bold Rembrandt-type painting. The best my vocabulary can throw up is "intimidating", and that falls pathetically short. All the eyes of the extras are on me, but the oyabuns continue to concentrate on the centre of the table.

And then slowly, one of the oyabuns turns.

"*Konban wa.*" The words slide out of his smoke-cured throat like gravel. He's the oldest man in the room. His grey hair is swept back in a two-inch wave that constantly threatens to break over his forehead, and his eyes, although hidden by big tan-coloured prescription sunglasses, are aiming right at me.

"*He is saying good evening, repeat what he said.*"

"*Konban wa,*" I reply.

Now he just stares at me. In fact, all the oyabuns have shifted their eyes so as to take in this helmeted man who claims he is the white Yakuza. But they remain hard men.

The oldest oyabun continues in Japanese, which Jun translates.

"*My two men here tell me you are the Shiro Tozoku. What brings you here tonight?*"

"*Tell him that things became too dangerous in America, you've been hiding, waiting, and now you would like to relocate to Australia, with a slice of the action, of course. Tell him you have had your eyes on things here for a while and you were just waiting for the gangs to make their move.*"

Jun speaks quickly, but it still feels like a long time of just staring at the oyabuns before my mouth finally opens. I repeat Jun's words slowly and calmly. ". . . I've had my eye on things here for a while, and I've just been waiting for the gangs to make their move." I throw in a look that suggests that this is a fait accompli.

The oyabun snorts. He continues in surprisingly good English. "You joke with us, yes? What makes you think we will let you have any part in this agreement?"

Jun's calm voice resonates through the ear piece, although his words do nothing to calm me. Still, I repeat them: "You have two options. You can split things six ways instead of five, or it can be split just one way. There are five of you. I have killed five oyabuns before, I would prefer not to have to do it again. I mean you no disrespect, I just want what I believe I deserve."

The old man doesn't snort this time. Instead, he crosses his hands and rests them on the table. Then he motions for the bodyguards, who have all subtly shifted their hands to the insides of their jacket, not to draw their weapons. He sits like this for quite a while, a minute at least. Every muscle in my body wants to tear my eyes away from his, but I resist.

Finally he speaks again. "The negotiations were finished a week ago. We do not have time to change them."

"You are all men of honour. You will give me what you believe I deserve. I do not need to see it in writing."

The oyabun takes an eternity to reply. "Although you have completely disregarded all tradition, you have indeed proven yourself in the Yakuza. If one sixth of the operations here in Australia will make you content, and we can have your assurance that it will, then you may have it." I breathe a sigh of relief, but it's cut off midway. "Provided you can prove you are who you say you are." He finishes his oration in such a way that leaves me with little doubt that if I can't prove to these men that I am the white Yakuza, I will not be getting one sixth of the operation, or even one sixth of my life. Jun, I hope you know what you're talking about.

Every single eye in the room is poking me like a stick. Again I repeat Jun's words. "Does it not seem unusual that I happened to be wandering in the vicinity on the night of your top secret meeting? Surely my very being here, standing in front of you right now, past all your security, is validation of my identity."

The oyabun considers this. "Knowledge can be acquired. Everything has a price."

I thrust my hand in my pocket, which triggers a commotion. In an instant, all dozen extras have their weapons trained on me. With my last reserves of nerve I look at each man, one by one, until they return their guns to the insides of their jackets. With this done, I slowly withdraw the white rose. It is crumpled and several petals drift to the red carpet, but it's still instantly recognisable. The faces of the men standing around the outside of the room contort slightly with confusion. I feel an instant falling sensation, until I remember what Jun had said – only the oyabuns will know. I shift my gaze back to the men sitting around the table. They are unmoved, but they have lost a little of their hardness. Slowly, I walk towards the oldest oyabun, the one who has been doing all the talking. He twists around in his seat so that he can face me, but as I approach, I see him fold into himself, ever so slightly. Six steps later, when I reach him, I press the rose against his chest, then I take his right hand and place it over the rose, so that it's holding it in place. I step back. If that doesn't do it, I'm completely stuffed.

The old man watches me through his tan-coloured lenses. It's impossible to read his eyes, they never give anything away, but his Adam's apple rides the escalator up his throat and then back down again as he places the rose gently on the table. He nods. Just one curt, solitary movement of the head. "*Kangei suru Shiro Tozoku.*"

"*He said: 'Welcome, White Bandit'. You've done it, Tligg, you've done it.*"

I can hear chuckles of relief, not humour, from the piece of plastic stuck in my ear. I have done it. But I still have a lot more to do.

I am given a seat at the table and brusque introductions. I recognise the names as the ones I recited to the guard at the gate, but there's no chance I will remember them. Except one. Hideki Kawabata, the man I saw meeting with Terry and Doris at Hot Shots. His silver tooth catches the light as I am introduced to him. It's the same glint I saw in the back of the limo, the night Ian and I were kidnapped. I bow slowly towards him and watch his eyes closely from under my black visor. Coldness and vindictiveness stare back at me, but thankfully no recognition. Quickly, I move onto the next man.

The pleasantries end as abruptly as they began. There are no sentiments; no "Nice to meet you"s, no "Man, I dig your work"s. Even if they do believe I am the white Yakuza, it's patently obvious that they don't trust me. Hell, if someone killed five of my business associates, I guess I wouldn't give them much of a welcome, either. It leaves me feeling very vulnerable and uncomfortable, but I have to force this out of my head and focus on my task. I haven't noticed Tetsuya anywhere in the room and although the table is covered in papers, nothing looks particularly like a . . . a *keiyaku*.

I manage to relax a little as I'm given a copy of the agreement, and the conversation turns to illicit commerce. As far as I know, no one has ever ordered an execution in the middle of discussing business . . . unless, of course, execution was the business at hand. Jun calmly translates for me. As it unfolds, I begin to feel uncomfortable again. Not because I'm afraid of being discovered, but because of what I'm hearing. These five men, probably the five most powerful men in Japan, are discussing the agreement – drugs, prostitution, bribery, extortion, and even murder – with all the normality of a group of executives in a sales meeting.

Occasionally I am asked to offer an opinion, always in English, and Jun feeds me the lines to say. I repeat the words as they come to me, without thinking about them. It's like repeating lines from a language-learning tape. They're merely abstract sounds. It's the only way I can utter the things I'm uttering: supposed anecdotes from the States involving drugs, violence and murder; theories on heroin distribution and prostitution. These are very, very nasty people I'm playing with. And the nastiest thing of all is that it's so cold, so calculated. The term "organised crime" suddenly makes all the sense in the world.

The men continue reading through the agreement and the discussions drag on. And on. Cigars are smoked, tumblers of potent alcohol are swilled. The whole show is taking far too long. It's 9.45 p.m. In another three-quarters of an hour, Luke and Danny and their colleagues are coming in, probably with guns ablazin'. Why can't they just read the bloody thing without complaining? Hell, I can't read it at all – what with it being in Japanese – and you don't hear a peep from me. I can feel my heart stepping up to what is now its familiar tempo as the pins of sweat plot another escape from my scalp. I have to get things moving.

It's incredibly hard to pick an interjection point in a Japanese conversation, so I just butt in. "Excuse me. Excuse me, gentlemen. This agreement concerns the Yakuza expansion throughout Australia, using the foundations set here on the Gold Coast as a base." The five men shift the weight of their eyes towards me. "I assume Tetsuya Suzuki was consulted in the drafting of this agreement, but as the number-one man on the Gold Coast for the past three years, it seems ludicrous not to have him present at this moment."

The oyabuns look at one another. Jesus they're cold, they would all make excellent poker players. Finally, the eldest oyabun addresses my point. He's not the Yamaguchi-gumi oyabun, but I have worked out pretty quickly that age is the key in these gang relationships. "Mr Suzuki was indeed meant to be here. However, he has been detained. We have reason to believe that he was . . . in negotiations . . . with the federal police here in Australia. It seems he was planning to do a deal with them."

I was right! I knew they knew. It was the only explanation. "That is a very serious accusation. How do you know this?" I ask.

"One of our men, here on the Gold Coast, alerted us to the fact that Mr Suzuki has been keeping company with a federal agent."

I tilt my head. "In my experience, law enforcement officers can be our best friends."

"The federal agent in question is no friend of ours."

"Oh?"

The old man chooses his words carefully. "We detained the agent and his partner. He was identified as the same federal police officer who had been . . . looking . . . into our concerns without our invitation."

"And these agents admitted to dealing with Suzuki?"

"The agents managed to escape before we could obtain any information from them."

"Escape!" I can hear Jun whispering for me to stop, but I can't. It's like listening in on a phone call where you are the subject at hand.

The old man leaves his eyes planted squarely on Mr Kawabata. "It was very stupid . . . very unprofessional."

"They must be a couple of very sharp police officers. We will have to be more careful in the future."

The oyabun merely grunts.

"Needless to say, Mr Suzuki is dead," I say coldly.

"No," replies the old man through tendrils of cigar smoke.

I breathe a massive sigh of relief, mentally if not physically. "Why not?"

"We need to know just how deep his negotiations with the Australian Federal Police go. He is being quite uncooperative."

"So where is Mr Suzuki?"

"That is irrelevant."

"I beg to differ." I curl one fist inside the other and squeeze until there is a cracking sound. "If you would like this information I can obtain it for you." Corny, but these are the people who made Godzilla such a hit.

The oyabun's thin lips turn up at the corners. Not quite what I'd call a smile, more a sadistic hint of a grin. "I understand. You will visit with Mr Suzuki when our meeting has adjourned."

Bugger! I need to see him now. Tetsuya is the only one who can give me specific details of the keiyaku. I can't very well look at my watch but I'm sure it must be about 10 p.m. "That will not do," I say. "I am not about to enter into an agreement as important as this one when there are federal police running around with, what? A little bit of information? Or an in-depth understanding of the whole Yakuza operation here on the Gold Coast? Surely you can see my point."

"Indeed we can, but we simply do not have the time. We cannot afford to spend an hour as sitting ducks while you attempt to get the information we have so far failed to obtain ourselves."

"Five minutes," I reply in a menacing whisper. "Just five minutes."

The oyabuns look at each other. One subtle nod dominoes the other four. "Alright, Shiro Tozoku, you may have five minutes with Mr Suzuki. Hurry."

The old man nods to one of the extras. The gangly young man seems very pleased to be a part of the evening. He tries hard to look serious and menacing, but it's all he can do to stop himself from beaming with pride.

I follow the skinny trainee-thug not to the pool-house where Ian and I were held, but into the bowels of the mansion, where carpet gives way to dusty tiles and natural light is a memory. We encounter two young guards, both Japanese and both carrying machineguns. Well, they're not really carrying them, the weapons are sitting on the table where they are playing cards. I briefly wonder if they're playing the game that gave rise to the Yakuza name. It's funny the things that run through your head when you're tense.

My reputation must have preceded me, because the two men jump immediately to attention. Their guns clatter to the floor. They can't take their eyes off me. It would be unnerving, except that I am actually getting into my role. At this point in the evening, I am more white Yakuza than not.

The man who led me down garbles something to the two guards in hurried Japanese. Jun translates for me. The men nod as if their chins are operated by pieces of string. One steps forward and unlocks a door, the other steps aside.

Tetsuya Suzuki, aka Akira Somatsu, aka Terry Smith, looks like he's had seven shades of shit thumped out of him. His once voluminous hair is plastered down over his forehead with sweat and grime and blood. His eyes are puffy and black; there is no sign of the mirrored sunglasses. His forehead is grazed and he's running his tongue over a raw looking split in his bottom lip. And his suit – his once wonderful Don-Johnsonesque suit – is filthy, the right lapel torn; his peach-coloured shirt is stained with blood. He looks up at the guard and me completely without expression. He is tapping his gold ring.

"Leave me with him." The gangly extra complies. I wait until he has left the room, then I shut the door. I turn around, still wearing the helmet.

"Hello, Trigg," says Mr Somatsu.

My mouth drops. "How . . .?"

"How did I know it was you? Unimportant right now. You do

not have much time. You need to get the keiyaku. It will be a single sheet of rice paper. Do you know what rice paper looks like? It is a browny-cream colour, with a rough texture. It will be signed with a special quill dipped in ink. This is important, because they will be signing the copies of the agreement, too, but they are irrelevant. The keiyaku is the key. It will be the last thing signed, at the end of the ceremony, and it will only be signed after each oyabun has drunk sake. Do you understand?"

I nod. Rice paper, special pen, sake.

"Once you have it, you must get it to the federal agents."

I nod again. Federal agents.

"Okay, you must go now."

I have my hand on the doorknob before I realise that I can't leave just yet. "I have to tell you something. The police, the ones you were dealing with, will be coming in here in" – I look at my watch: 10.05 p.m. – "twenty-five minutes. I'm going to tell them where to find you, so hang on until then and don't get caught up in any crossfire, if there is any. And I need to tell the oyabuns something about your deal with the federal agents. Something that will make them trust me."

Mr Somatsu rolls his ring around his grubby finger. "Tell them . . . tell them that the federal agents know only of the legitimate businesses and the money laundering, they know nothing of the expansion. Tell them I was doing this deal not to thwart or betray the Yakuza, but merely to delay things a few years. I do not think the Gold Coast can handle the expansion yet."

I scrunch up my eyes, as if this will help me discern whether this is true or just a diversion. I can't tell, and right now it doesn't really matter. "Okay," I say and turn for the door.

"Trigg," says Mr Somatsu with a raspy voice. I turn back, waiting for him to wish me luck – the thing that has brought us together from opposite sides of the world. "What is the story of the helmet?"

I smile in spite of myself. "I'll tell you later."

When I get back upstairs it's 10.10 p.m. I have twenty minutes to get the keiyaku – signed. The oyabuns look expectantly at me through the carcinogenic smog as I sit back down at the table. I look at them in return, one by one, before I speak. "Tetsuya Suzuki says he did not tell the federal police about this meeting. They do not know about the expansion. All they are aware of is the structure of the legitimate businesses here on the Gold Coast and the way they are being used to launder money."

My words hang in the air like the cigar smoke, until one of the younger oyabuns interjects, his finely-trimmed eyebrows moving slightly with his mouth. Hiroshi, I think his name is. "Was he telling the truth?"

"Yes," I reply, in a manner that suggests no further questions are necessary. Hiroshi nods once. The others follow suit. I have sixteen minutes to get the document. Enough time.

The eldest oyabun snaps his fingers. The extras stir. One brings over two clay cups, another delivers a clay bottle, Menacing Thug #2 produces the quill. All the items are placed in the centre of the table. The old man then speaks. Jun translates.

"*Gentlemen, we must finish reading the agreement and sign it. We have all read drafts previously, but this is the final copy. If you wish to question any item, then you must do so now. Only when we have all signed our copies will we sign the keiyaku.*"

My blood zings at the mention of the keiyaku. Just having it spoken of, its existence confirmed, makes my whole mission seem that much more tangible. It's now within my grasp. Figuratively.

The five oyabuns concentrate harder as they slowly read through the final pages, grunting, snorting and nodding. I check my wrist again. 10.17 p.m. Thirteen minutes. Christ, this is getting too close for comfort.

I pretend to read the final pages of my copy of the document. "Well, it all looks good to me," I say, in an attempt to get things moving. I grab one of the pens from the middle of the table and scribble an illegible signature on the blank line on the last page. My only hope is that there are no rebuttals of the document that require negotiation.

All the while, I can hear Jun talking in my ear. "*Time, Tligg, you're running out of time. The detectives are getting ready to come in. All the reinforcements are here . . . there must be over forty police officers."*

Time is indeed running out. I have to push this thing through quickly, like a parliamentary pay-rise in the House of Commons.

"Well, what do you all think?"

The men look at me, not quite in annoyance, more puzzlement. Perhaps I'm excused because I'm thought to be American. Then, slowly, they return their attention to the pages.

I tap my foot under the table, my bare toes sinking into the plush red carpet. The prickles of perspiration have bloomed into little trickles that run over my scalp and pool at the edge of the helmet. The oldest oyabun, the one who has been running the show, regards me with an icy gaze. When he peels his eyes off mine he picks up one of the pens. With his most flamboyant gesture so far, he signs the paper.

This seems to start a bit of a chain-reaction. The youngest oyabun signs his copy, then the one with the salt-and-pepper flat top. I sneak yet another look at my watch. 10.24 p.m. Jun is giving me a blow-by-blow report of what's going on outside. The police are ready. And waiting. Waiting for the minute hand to hit the six. Then they're coming in. The oyabun with the pitiful excuse for a little finger and the raw-looking scar across his cheek picks up a pen. He hesitates. Then he signs. Four down. One to go.

10.25 p.m. Five minutes left. 300 seconds. Enough time to get one last signature, then all six onto the keiyaku itself. The last man, my sparkly old chum Mr Kawabata, continues to flip back and forth through the pages. Not to worry . . . plenty of time . . . hell, enough time for Dwayne Chambers to run the hundred metres twenty-eight times . . . twenty-seven times . . . twenty-six times . . . JUST SIGN IT, FOR FUCK'S SAKE!

I'm losing it. I can barely sit still in my chair. It's like my muscles have been replaced with hundreds of anxious mice.

10.26 p.m. My fingers are slimy with sweat as they wriggle over each other, my mouth couldn't be drier.

"*Tligg, they are about to go in. Tligg? Have you got the signatures? Cough once if you have them, twice if you haven't.*"

I can't control my coughing, two turns into a fit. The oyabuns look at me, including the one whose signature is missing. Shit.

Finally Kawabata looks up from his papers. "*Watakushi wa . . .*" I listen with disbelief to Jun's translation: "*I cannot accept this . . . the Itchiwa-kai must have more control over the distribution of cocaine.*"

"Have mine," I splutter. "I don't really need it . . . I'm sure I'll have plenty. It's yours, just sign the paper, we can nut out the details later—"

"*Shizuka ni!*" barks the old man. "*Silence!*" I stop my blabbering. The old man continues, Jun translates: "*The Itchiwa-kai is very fairly represented. You have already agreed to this in principle. You have control over the whole West Coast distribution of all amphetamines. Do not be greedy.*" This last piece of advice is more of an accusation, jabbed at the man like a switchblade, than a suggestion. The other oyabuns weigh in with their own menacing looks, so I follow suit. Anything to get this man to sign.

The reluctant oyabun looks at us. He closes his eyes and wipes his brow. An involuntary sneer allows the light to bounce of his impressive dentistry. 10.28 p.m. He opens his eyes and with a hastiness born of surrender, picks up a pen and scribbles his signature on his copy.

This is going to work. Two minutes. Yes! We can get six signatures in two minutes. I look expectantly at the old man, raise my eyebrows as if to say, "No point just sitting around, let's get cracking".

He ignores me and instead addresses the gathering. I can hear the edge in Jun's voice as he translates. "*Excellent. This agreement has been many months in the making. And that is what this is, an agreement. Not a directive. Because the only way we will continue to expand and profit is if we work together and bury the grudges of the past. And now we will sign the keiyaku, finalising an agreement that will serve us all very well. Let us commence the ceremony."*

"Ceremony?" I don't mean to blurt it out, it just happens. There's no time for a bloody ceremony. Oh, but that's exactly what Mr Somatsu told you, you daft tosser! Remember, the sake, the quill? Sweet Jesus! Even if it takes the police five minutes to find the front gate there won't be enough time for a . . . a ceremony! Suddenly I realise that every face in the room is zoned in on me. And they aren't happy.

"Do you have a problem . . . Shiro Tozoku?" asks the old man.

"*Tligg! They are moving in, Tligg. Can you hear me? They are moving in!*"

I'm so close.

So fucking close.

Then I relax. I'm not about to give this up. Not now. "We have to get out of here," I say calmly.

The anger in the oyabuns' faces skips to suspicion. The old man regards me with tried patience. "Come now, you are being extremely—"

"NOW!" I scream. "We have to get out of here now! This whole place is about to be raided!"

"*Tligg? What are you doing? Be quiet, you must . . .*"

I block out Jun as much as I can. There is a general panic around the outside of the room, even the oyabuns look perturbed.

"How do you know this?" asks the oyabun with the scar.

"Look, you're just going to have to trust me. There are over forty armed men at your front door right now and they're not selling bloody cosmetics. We've got to get out of here."

The old man snaps his fingers and Menacing Thug #2 lumbers out of the room.

There is absolute silence in his absence.

Then he reappears. He nods.

And all hell breaks loose.

♣ ♣
26

The extras around the outside of the room draw their guns and begin babbling in jerky Japanese. They rush about, but essentially they are lost. The oyabuns are on their feet too, the imminent threat like a blowtorch to their ice-like facades.

"*They are almost at the gate, Tligg . . . you have to get to the back right-hand corner of whichever room you are in and stay low . . . can you hear me, Tligg? Tligg?*"

I'm not about to huddle in any corner, not without my keiyaku, my ticket to curse-freedom. "Out the back," I yell above the cacophony of voices. "They're coming in from the front, we have to get out the back."

"*Yamero! Yamero!*" It's the old man. I have no idea what he's saying and Jun is too busy giving me updates on the action outside the house to translate. Whatever the strange utterance is, it settles things down instantly. The writhing mass comes to an instant halt. "Continue," he says to me.

Somewhere in the back of my mind, in between Jun's voice and the million other thoughts that are surfing through my cerebrum, I know this is a significant moment. I am being trusted. Possibly because there is nothing to lose. I don't have time to sift through the motives now, though. "The raid is coming from the front," I say. "We have to go out the back. They may have men there, but the main thrust is definitely from the front. Does anybody know where the back entrance is?" A young man wearing a suit far too big for his skinny frame raises his hand. "Well, let's go. Lead the way."

With the table's entire contents hurriedly thrown in a tote bag, the oyabuns – and myself by default – are positioned in the middle of the throng of guards. As a single unit we shuffle-shuffle-shuffle out the doors and across the red carpet. It's hard to tell what's going on outside of our little group hug, but I can hear urgent voices squealing high-pitched Japanese at one another from various parts of the house. And then I hear it. We all hear it. A gunshot!

As we jog alongside the marble railing, all heads turn to the left, to the direction of the staccato firing. "*Tligg?*" Jun's voice continues with a certain impassive quality to it, as if the gunfire has caused him to revert to his former self. "*Okay, Tligg . . . there is a gunfight at the front gate. One policeman is down already. But they seem to be making progress, the guards are retreating. I say they will be inside in less than two minutes. You have to stay put, Tligg, get back to the room and get down . . .*"

I drown Jun out again.

We turn the corner at the stairs, a big, bustling, anybody-in-the-way-gets-knocked-over troop. *Ackackackackackack!* The gunfire is getting closer, you can feel it as much as hear it. Jun is still filling my head with reasons to go back into the room, but I am busy trying to figure out what we are going to do when we get to the back door. If we get to the back door. These men are not about to give themselves up.

We shuffle down the steps and back underneath the majestic staircase. The sound of gunfire seems to recede as we make our collective way through various corridors and hallways at the rear of the house, but this is just an acoustic trick. Finally we stutter to a halt. The back door.

There's no way of knowing what's on the other side, and a sense of indecision settles on the group. I am unnerved to find that they are all looking to me. Talk about pressure. And then it comes to me. The canals! "A boat? Does this place have a boat?"

Several heads nod. That's good enough for me. "We have to get to the boat."

The wave of indecision washes away. The door is opened very, very slowly . . .

And then the group spills out to a deafening cacophony of gunfire. The extras form a lethal defensive circle around the five oyabuns and myself, every gun firing repeatedly in a 360°-spray of bullets. With my head down and all my peripheral vision swallowed by the helmet, I have absolutely no idea what's going on. All I know is that my feet keep inching along, like I'm caught in the middle of a gun-toting rugby-maul. Jun is talking away but I can't hear him over the clatter of gunfire.

Suddenly I'm on the ground; our group-hug has collapsed. The weight that pins me to the grass quickly lifts, except the load on my legs. I squirm and squirm and then watch in horror as the load – the little man in the big suit – rolls off my legs. It's deadweight. *He's* deadweight. Half of his head is missing. My guts contort and I retch, the chinstrap of the helmet digging painfully into my throat. I undo it quickly and retch again. This isn't happening. Surely this can't be happening.

I'm barrelled over again by a stray set of panicked legs. This shakes me back into action. I lift my face off the grass to see a dark-suited Japanese man rolling across the lawn, while out of the corner of my eye I see another three Japanese men running my way. The corner of my eye? Fuck! The helmet has been knocked clean off.

The men charge over me. It's pandemonium. I scour the ground in search of the helmet, now unaware of the gunshots or the hysterical screeching. What I am aware of, though, is a single clover, sprigging up out of the carpet of green, as if in defiance. I pick the clover, pulling its little roots up from the soil. It has four leaves. What place does a four-leaf clover have on this immaculate Gold Coast lawn? THHHHUT! The grass explodes a few feet in front of me as a bullet tears into the ground.

I pick up the helmet and begin lurching towards the water, towards the steel jetty. Bullets sizzle through the air around me, some sailing past, some digging up the turf. I know they're not being aimed, they're being fired sporadically. Randomly.

The steel surface of the jetty bites my bare soles. Twenty yards ahead a large speedboat is being untethered. I can see some of the oyabuns huddled in its furthest corner, while younger men stand on the near side and rain bullets back towards the house. Between them and the police it's a miracle I've made it this far.

My feet make dull thudding noises as I bounce down the gangway. The metal pontoon bobs up and down. I launch myself towards a gap in the blazing men and just squeeze through, landing half on a seat and half on Mr Kawabata. We share a bizarre moment. "Sorry," I say.

He grunts. Then I realise he's looking at my face with concern. Oh shit! The helmet, it's in my hand!

"You are the federal agent," he says, surprisingly calmly. "You are the one we kidnapped. You are doing the deal with Tetsuya."

Oh Christ, this is just what I need. Think quick, Trigg. "It's a long story," I yell above the gunfire. "I am most certainly not a federal agent. Would they be trying to shoot me if I was? Would I have warned you about the raid if I was? I swear I'm not an agent. I'll explain it all to you when we get a chance."

He nods curtly. There are more important things at hand.

I put the helmet back on and hunker in silence, praying to hear Jun's voice, some contact with the good guys. As it is, I feel like I really have switched teams, like I'm one of the bad guys. Unfortunately, all I get inside the helmet is static, interrupted by the occasional scratchy word or two. It's no good. Whether it was busted by the knock or is just out of range, I can't tell.

Suddenly the speedboat's engines gurgle to life and the last ropes are thrown clear. Before I give up on the two-way, I speak into the microphone. Very slowly, very clearly. "The Marriott. The Marriott Hotel, Jun. Ask for Shawn." I can only hope he gets the message.

The huge engines brag with a steady guttural roar as the boat begins to move. Bullets are still ripping through the air. The boat then tips back at an alarming angle as the engines chunder their full power. The sound of the gunfire recedes quickly into the blackness as we speed away: five oyabuns, seven minions and one white Yakuza wannabe.

I bury my helmeted head in my hands. This whole situation has gotten totally out of hand. My God, people have been shot. *Killed*. What if police officers are dead? Because of me? Stop it, you sad toss, get a grip! I push my fists hard into my eye sockets. I have to get this group to the Marriott, back on my turf. I have to get the keiyaku. It's no good if the police get it without me. To lift the curse and get my luck back, *I* have to help Tetsuya, *I* have to get the document – with signatures.

We are drifting. The engines must have been cut for some time, but it doesn't dawn on me until now. I remove my bunched-up hands from my eyes. Everything is black. That's pretty much how it stays. All lights on the boat have been killed and the only sound is the small wavelets slapping against the hollow fibreglass hull. Have we run out of petrol? Are we at the Marriott? Hang on, I haven't even told them about the Marriott. What's going—?

They are looking at me again. All of them. Dark, menacing faces, hidden in shadows, swaying gently with the current – all levelled accusingly at me. The hairs on my arms rise to attention and it's got nothing to do with the gust of chilled wind that finds its way down to where I'm sitting.

"*Herumetto o nuginasai*," says the oldest oyabun slowly, speaking to me in Japanese for the first time.

Without Jun, I can't understand him. The faces keep looking at me and it's not for guidance this time. "Take off helmet," the old man barks in English.

"I . . . I can't . . . I . . . my identity . . . it's . . ."

The old man reaches over and takes a pistol off one of the minions. He takes two sea-swaying steps towards where I sit on the hard floor. Bending down, he places the barrel of the pistol on my forehead, where the visor would be if it hadn't broken off. The cold steel circle sends a shivering surge through my body. "Take . . . off . . . helmet."

I realise I'm holding my breath. I let it out in a hurried gasp before sucking more air in and holding it there. I reach up and slide the helmet off my head. My ears are the first to receive the chill that moves over the water like a spirit, then my whole scalp responds to the coolness. I let out my breath and suck another one in. Slap, slap, slap go the wavelets.

"You are the federal agent. You are doing the deal with Tetsuya."

I realise just how easy it would be for the old man to pull the trigger. Blow my brains out and throw my body over the side. I would float for a little while. Then I would sink. I would wash around the bottom of the canals and then the gasses in my rotting stomach would raise me to the surface. What was left of me.

"Explain," the old man spits.

"I . . . I am not a federal agent." I slowly lean my head backwards, but the barrel follows.

"Bullsheet," says Menacing Thug #1. "Bullsheet. I know you. We lock you up." He mutters something in Japanese to his friends. It raises a few nervous chuckles. "Now we gonna fark you up."

Come on, Trigg, don't quit, you're so bloody close. Think. Jun's words from earlier wash through my head. Perception. Perception. They will believe. It has come down to this. Now or never, make or break, cliché one or cliché two. I look up at my former kidnapper. "Yes, you fucking locked me up! You dim-witted moron!" I rise to my feet, suck up my chest and all of my almost six feet. "You almost ruined everything!" My voice echoes loudly over the black water towards the house lights that illuminate both sides of the wide canal. The assembled mobsters look alarmed, including the old man. The gun is still stuck to my forehead, but I figure if he hasn't shot me now . . . I whip my hand up and grab the pistol by the cold steel barrel. I snatch it away from the old man's grip. No one raises a finger. I'm weaving my spell. Shiro Tozoku's spell. Jun's spell.

I walk briskly over to my mountainous former kidnapper and stick the barrel in the middle of his chest. I thrust it with all my force. He doesn't even budge. No matter. This isn't about strength, this is about threat.

"Federal fucking agent? Are you people insane? I killed five oyabuns. I'm the most wanted man in the Yakuza. For years no one has touched me." With each emphasised word I jab the barrel into the man's chest, but I'm addressing the whole boat. "Five years you looked, and you found nothing. Nothing! I finally decide to come out of the woodwork, here, tonight. Do you think I'm just going to turn up? No precautions? Nothing? Well? Of course not. That would be stupid. And I am not stupid! I outsmarted all of you for over five years. The Gold Coast is my retirement plan. I . . . TOOK . . . PRECAUTIONS! I wanted to know where the weak link was. There's always one, you know. Somewhere. So I tested the infrastructure here on the Gold Coast. I made myself into a federal agent and I leaned on people. Only I didn't have to lean very hard. Suzuki folded, like that," with the gun still in one hand, I make the Superman-bends-a-steel-rod action. "You should all be very fucking grateful to me. I found the weak link, before it had a chance to snap in front of the real police. At least I thought I did. Our Mr Suzuki must have been hedging his bets. Playing me for a fool. He'd been dealing with the police long before I even showed up . . . spineless piece of shit!"

With this last word, I shove the big man. He still doesn't budge. I lower the gun and skulk away in disgust. "Call your contacts in the police. Ask them."

I think it was a pretty convincing performance, but it's always hard to tell. I turn my back to them, just to show I'm not afraid, and stare out towards the canal-front homes while I shake my head contemptuously.

"But you knew about the raid?" It's Mr Kawabata. I don't have to see his face to identify the voice.

"Of course I knew about the fucking raid!" I yell without turning around. I wait until the pause is in its third trimester, then I wheel around and look at them with the wild-eyed bewilderment of a man addressing complete ignorance. "Are you listening to me? I TOOK PRECAUTIONS! In that helmet is a radio transmitter." I pick it up and pull out the wiring. "I had seven men, armed to the goddamned teeth, parked up the road in case things went awry. They're good men, very alert – forty federal police officers armed with automatic weapons did not escape their attention! They kept me informed. Which is why we are here, alive, and not back there, dead."

I feel I overdid act two. I don't know much about the Japanese, but I'm pretty sure they don't like being talked down to. It would be just my luck to actually convince them of my story, but in doing so, insult them so much that they kill me anyway. I look slowly about the boat. It's difficult to read their faces at the best of times, let alone when the only light is from the moon. "I apologise," I say. "I pride myself on not losing my temper. I just find it particularly insulting when I am accused of something I am the very antithesis of. Please, we must get to safety and continue this meeting. These waterways will be swarming with police any minute."

The gangsters regard me coolly, but there's nothing more I can do to convince them. I'm spent. Now it all rests in the hands of one man, the eldest oyabun. His amber glasses are trained on me. His expression is surprisingly calm, except for a slight furrowing between his eyebrows. We bob for an eternity on the inky water, then he speaks. "What would you suggest we do?"

I reply slowly, so as not to appear overeager – you know, take it or leave it. "I have a room at the Marriott Hotel. It is under a false name and I have an understanding with the concierge. He can be very discreet. I am sure we can get up to the room using a service lift. And we can reach the hotel by boat."

I look over my right shoulder, towards the neon explosion of Surfers Paradise. The good thing about the Gold Coast is that they have artificial stars for you to navigate by. "It's just over there," I say, pointing to the large building set back a little from the main nucleus.

A siren breaks the silence. It is distant – hell, it may not even be for us – but it is enough to remind everyone of just how dire the situation is. These men just want to get the hell out of the Gold Coast. However, they have to sign the keiyaku first.

The silence continues, but the siren grows louder.

"*Yoroshii* . . . okay," says the old man, keeping his eyes on mine. I get the message loud and clear: "We're trusting you, so don't betray us". Somewhere in the back of my mind, I realise that this is exactly what I intend to do. I nod sincerely to the old man.

The boat's engines garble again and the vessel moves off, a lot more smoothly than last time.

The Marriott is not hard to find. I have no idea what's going to happen when we get there, though. It seems I've gotten into this rather uncomfortable habit of acting on impulse – James Bond style. It does not sit well with my personality. Will there be a pontoon? Will Shawn be working? Did the dodgy radio-transmitter deliver my message to Jun? More questions than a three-year-old watching an X-rated movie.

Fortunately, the Marriott does have a pontoon. Unfortunately, it's brightly lit. I assume shoot-outs don't go unnoticed on the Gold Coast, so chances are a multitude of police are already out looking for a boatload of Japanese. Given these assumptions, and the bright light, I suggest that the men do something with their guns – people tend to notice things like that – and that one or two of them take the boat and deposit it somewhere far away. The old man considers this, but not as lengthily as his previous decisions. I believe I'm growing on him. He nods and his orders are quickly followed.

It's not until we are walking along the pontoon to the gangway that the next problem raises its head. The procession stops dead. We have company. Perched at the top of the ramp is a little guardhouse, resplendent with its own vicious-looking steel gate. In hindsight, it was foolish to think the most exclusive hotel on the Gold Coast would leave its jetty unattended.

My first instinct is to panic – it's an instinct I have honed over the last few weeks. I'm in good company, too. Several of the faces with me also register fear. But then the old man places a hand on my shoulder. "We are just tourists," he says, with the coolness of someone who is accustomed to tricky situations. It makes sense. Surely word hasn't travelled this far this quickly. So I lead the group of barefoot Japanese up the gangway to the little guardhouse. A moon-faced head with slicked-back black hair peers out. "G'day," it says to me in a jolly voice. "*Konnichi wa,*" it says to the men behind me. The greeting sounds terribly Australian, but the head seems quite pleased with its efforts.

"Hi there," I reply. "I've got a boatload fresh from Japan. Heh, heh, heh!"

"Sure thing," replies the head. "What's your room number?"

"Twenty-one-oh-three," I answer, giving my old room number.

The head looks down below the level of its little window. Then its brow furrows with confusion. Thumpa-thumpa-thumpa, my heart picks up tempo again. "Ms Johnston? Sue Johnston?"

"Not the last time I checked! It's Mr Harvey, actually. There must be some mix-up. I've been in that room for four, five, days now . . . mind you, the concierge, little fella, sandy blond hair—"

"Shawn?"

"That's the one – Shawn. He said something about upgrading me to a better room. You might wanna check with the young 'un."

The head nods, it thinks this is a good idea. Let's just hope "the young 'un" is working tonight.

"Hello, Shawn, this is Bill down in the boat house . . . yeah, good thanks, mate, how's yourself? . . . That's great, great. Listen, Shawn, I've got a man here with a Japanese group, a Mr Harvey. Apparently he was in room 2103, but I've got a Ms Sue Johnston on my list here . . . hello? Shawn? . . . Boy that's a nasty cough you've got there. Anyway, Mr Harvey said that you'd said something about a room upgrade . . . aha . . . aha . . . yep . . . that's right . . . okay, not a problem, thanks, mate."

He puts the receiver down and disappears. "Not a worry, Mr Harvey. Shawn just said to see him when you get in there." The head smiles.

A chill sweeps through me as the large glass doors shut behind us. I turn to check we haven't lost anyone – always the vigilant tour-guide. The men look at me expectantly.

Up ahead, the massive ceiling-fans slowly stir the air. I don't remember this part of the hotel, but I assume we must be near reception. I begin walking and the men follow. I stop and they stop. So this is how a mother duck feels.

A little further on, we pass an empty lounge and I suggest that the men stay there while I arrange an alternative way up to my room. "The fewer people that see us all together, the better," I say. The old man agrees.

When the Yakuza are settled amidst the mahogany coffee tables, I jog towards reception. I can't believe they're letting me go alone, and for a brief second the thought of running out the front door is awfully tempting. But I'm here for a reason. A keiyaku. So instead, I seek out the concierge desk.

"It's been a while," I say as I round the wooden counter of Shawn's concierge desk.

"Trigg!" Shawn splutters. "What the hell's going on?"

The "where do I start?" combination sigh-and-head-shake doesn't satisfy him. "I don't have time to go into in now, Shawn, but trust me, I'll explain it all to you later."

He frowns. "Yeah . . . I've heard that before."

"Listen, I need a room, just for a few hours. I'll pay whatever it's worth. But it has to be *the* room. You know, the presidential suite or the prime minister suite or whatever the hell it's called here. And I need it, well, right now."

Shawn makes a noise like a plumber inspecting a badly blocked drain. "Jeez, Trigg. That's a big ask . . . I don't even think it's available right now."

"Okay, do you have a 'leader of the opposition' suite or something. Your next best room, I'll take it. Whatever it costs."

Shawn regards me very seriously. "How long do you reckon you'll need it?"

"Hopefully only about an hour."

"Hmmm. Hang on a minute."

I rap my fingers impatiently on the dark wood of Shawn's desk as he clips his way across the polished Marriott foyer towards the check-in desk. He confers with a rather toff-looking guy for a minute or two. The other man looks flustered and he gesticulates wildly, then he appears to capitulate. It appears to me that he has a bit of a crush on our young sandy-haired concierge.

Shawn returns with a hint of a smile. "Okay, I've got you an executive suite on the twenty-seventh floor. It's not our best room, but it's pretty damn good."

"Thank you, you're the best, Shawn."

"Oh gee, ta. Now here's the key, don't wreck the room."

"Absolutely not."

"And Trigg?"

"Yes."

"What else is there?"

"What do you mean?"

"There's always something else. What is it this time?"

"Oh. Ahhh, well I do need to get the men I'm with up into the room without anyone seeing them, like a service lift or something."

"Hmmm. What else?"

"There may be a bunch of people who come looking for me. I told them to come and see you. . . an oldish Japanese guy, two girls and a surfy-looking guy . . . Ian Berrisford – you know him?"

Shawn's sun-yellowed eyebrows lift, giving his a face a dubious look.

"I'm serious, Ian Berrisford. Anyway, if they come you've got to get them up to the twenty-seventh floor, but don't let them come into the room, just have them standing by."

"And?"

"And . . . you might be required to tackle a few Japanese men, it shouldn't be too hard, they don't play much rugby over there."

Shawn groans.

"Oh come on – the police should be here by then anyway."

The loitering Yakuza cause a crease to form on Shawn's recently acne-cleared forehead. I don't think he was expecting quite so many people.

"Everyone, this is Shawn, he's going to look after us."

"Who are these guys, Trigg?" Shawn asks out of the corner of his mouth.

"Yakuza," I say out of the corner of mine.

"Fucking hell!" A few of the men glare at him nervously.

"Okay everyone, let's go," I say.

The oyabuns look at each other, then at me, but they don't move. Something has changed. Perhaps going to the reception alone wasn't such a good thing.

"We will wait here," says the old man. "Three of the men will go up with you, if everything is as you say it is, they will come back and get us. If not . . ." He trails off as Menacing Thug #2 and two others step forward, their hands inside their jackets.

They don't trust me. Gone for just a second and all that goodwill goes out the window. Or maybe it was never there in the first place. Coming to the Marriott was not really a big deal, given the options, but being cornered in a hotel room on the twenty-seventh floor, now that's another thing. I have to regain their trust, quickly.

"As you are aware, I am a big fan of precautions. All I would suggest is that you remain inconspicuous until your men return; you never know who you'll find lurking around the foyer of a hotel like this." Shit. Does that sound like a threat?

The three Japanese men and I set off behind Shawn towards the service lift. When we emerge on the twenty-seventh floor, it strikes me how different the layout is to my old floor. The carpet seems plusher, the chandeliers are chandelierier and the paintings on the walls are real, not prints.

The ostentatious decorations guide us around several corners before Shawn comes to a stop at one of the doors. He gives me a sort of telepathic nudge and I produce the card-key he gave me downstairs, which I slide into the slot by the door handle.

With a whining clunk, the lock releases its grip and I push the door open. Oh my. . . this is the business! The level of luxury is similar to the room at the casino, but where that was all introspective and moody, this room is bright and spacious. Beautiful yet simple.

My three associates push their way in and begin nosing around.

I guess they're used to this sort of thing. I, on the other hand, stand and take it all in. It's one of those rooms you see in movies. Actually, it's more than a room, it's a suite. A suite with flowing white carpet, soft white couches that must be a bugger to keep clean, and a huge wooden cabinet that houses the plasma-screen, stereo and DVD-player.

"How's this?" Shawn asks quietly.

"Perfect. I bet this room has seen some characters."

"Absolutely."

I walk further into the suite, taking in the kitchen and the opulent bathroom. Yes, this is nice. Very nice. I walk out onto the balcony and drink in the vertigo. The thicket of high-rise rooms is impenetrable, even from up here. They rise out of the darkness like a still-life of fireworks. Hundreds, thousands of rooms. Some burning brightly, others suggestively hidden by curtains, and yet more in complete voided black. They all have their stories to tell, too, maybe not as glamorous as those of my suite, but just as vivid, just as bizarre, just as sweaty.

I walk lightly back inside, where the three Japanese men have assembled themselves near the entrance. "Well, is everything okay?" I ask them, slipping back into character.

"Where are your belongings?" asks the big one.

"Ahh . . ." I look to Shawn.

"Mr Harvey's belongings are in storage down in reception. Would you like me to bring them up now, Mr Harvey?"

"No . . . no thank you. I'll call you."

"Certainly."

Shawn stands awkwardly, not quite sure what to do. We're waiting for the Japanese men to make a decision, or an announcement, or whatever the hell they're up here for. But they just stare. An awkward silence works its way into the room. It begins scratching at my eyes, harder and harder. The sort of silence that would drive Terri insane. I want to break it, but something tells me to stick it out. Aloof, Trigg, like you've got nothing to hide and nowhere to be.

And so we stand. I keep my sights on the men, and they watch me menacingly. Tick-tock, tick-tock. My face is a study in relaxation, but my body is aching to move. WHAT ARE YOU WAITING FOR??? Say something. Say something. Say something, you techno-junkie, wacky-TV-show-inventing tossers, say something before I—

"We shall summon the rest of our party," says Menacing Thug #2.

Pah. Amateurs.

Shawn holds the door open as the Yakuza from downstairs file past. The men stop just on the other side, forming a bottleneck. And they stare. What is it with these Japanese and staring? The old man stands at the front of the group, looking about the suite, as if he doesn't quite trust the investigative skills of his own men. When he's finished, I indicate the glass-topped dining table beyond the couches. The old man walks briskly over, followed by the other oyabuns, while the extras fill the gaps around the outside of the room. Shawn stands uneasily at the door.

Luckily there are six seats at the dining table, otherwise it would have been musical chairs, and someone always ends up in tears. The oyabuns sit, leaving the seat directly opposite the old man vacant. I wonder if this is significant in Japanese culture? I take the seat, fully aware that, unlike our previous meeting, I am the host. "Would anyone like a drink?" I ask.

"Cognac," replies the old man.

"Cognac," says the man with the scar.

"Cognac," replies ol' glinty-face.

"Cognac," say the two other oyabuns.

"Shawn," I say, "do we have any cognac up here?"

Shawn cringes. "No, Mr Harvey, there's no cognac up here. I can go down to the bar and get you a bottle if you'd like."

"What do you fellas think, a bottle of cognac?"

More silence.

"Better get two bottles."

♣ ♣ ♣

The old man waits until Shawn has left before addressing the table in a mixture of Japanese and English. He speaks slowly. "This has been a most disturbing evening. Indeed, we are lucky to be here right now, and we have Shiro Tozoku to thank for that. Arigato." The old man bows at me, the others follow suit, so I bow back. I'm sure that's what Jun would have told me to do. The old man continues, "However, I am sure that we are all in a hurry to finish our business and depart for our respective destinations. After all, it is getting late . . ."

I don't hear the rest of his speech. I'm too busy trying to deal with my anxiety-prone bowel, which is threatening to lose all tension. My watch reads 11.37 p.m. My deadline with Luke and Danny is long gone, but now I have an even more pressing deadline to meet. In twenty-three minutes, Roger's back. In twenty-three minutes, I'm . . . Rogered!

I shuffle the thought as far back in my head as it will go and try to concentrate on what's at hand. The old man is still talking. "Agreement in good faith" . . . blah, blah, blah . . . "Must uphold the agreement" . . . yada, yada, yada . . . "Profit and prosperity for all" . . . yes, yes, yes – come on, let's get this show on the road.

". . . and since we have all signed our copies of the agreement, we may begin the ceremony."

Thank God!

The objects are produced from the tote bag and placed with various clinks and clanks on the glass-topped table. Two small clay cups, one large clay bottle and a big feather. Then, there it is – the keiyaku. The big, neckless bodyguard handles it softly, resting the rice-paper parchment in the fingertips of his two massive hands. With the nervous care of a new father changing a nappy, he places it precisely in the centre of the table. From where I sit I can make out lots of small but elegant Japanese kanji characters adorning the page. Menacing Thug #2 bows. We all bow.

The old man addresses the table again. "The keiyaku will be passed around. It symbolises the strength of the agreement we have made. It speaks of what this arrangement can achieve, not in a monetary sense, but as regards power and unity for the Yakuza as a whole. I know time is not on our side, but I suggest we each read it." Not this again. 11.40 p.m.

The old man picks up the keiyaku and passes it to the oyabun on his right, my friend with the silver tooth. His brow creases as he begins reading. Come on, pick up the pace!

Meanwhile, another man has entered the fray. His job, it seems, is to pour out the contents of the clay bottle into one of the clay cups. He pours it slowly and with great precision. He places the cup in front of the old man, nods and withdraws.

It's 11.48 p.m. when I finally get my hands on the keiyaku. Twelve minutes to go. There are three columns of exquisite characters. Each stroke starts out fat and gets thinner as the ink is swallowed up by the thirsty parchment, each horizontal line is rendered at precisely the same angle . . .

I pretend to read it then quickly pass the piece of paper to the youngest oyabun, who is sitting to my right. He crinkles a lone eyebrow, as if questioning the thoroughness of my reading.

"It's all good stuff," I say.

The phone comes as a welcome distraction, albeit a disconcerting one. I stand abruptly and walk quickly to the kitchen bench where it is jangling away.

"Trigg, it's Shawn. Can you talk?"

"Ahhh, not really, what's up?"

"I came down to get the cognac and your friends were here. They want to know what's going on."

"Uhuh."

"So I told them about all the Japanese men and the room.

"Uhuh."

"They want to know if you've got the . . . *kei-ya-ku* yet."

"Negative."

"Uhh, okay. What should I tell them?"

"That cognac sounds fine, just bring it straight up, thanks." I have to suppress a desire to sing as I hang up the phone. My friends are here! My friends are here! I check my watch. 11.52. The musical monologue stops.

♣ ♣ ♣

I retake my seat at the table as the document is passed to the penultimate man. The minutes drag by as he considers every character. Suddenly all eyes dart to the door. Someone is knocking.

"It's okay, it's just the cognac," I reassure as I jog to the door.

I pull it open, not one hundred percent sure of just how many people I will find on the other side. It's only Shawn, brandishing two large bottles. "Thank you, Shawn. Just the two bottles? Did you bring any *others* up with you?"

Shawn shakes his head. "No, you only asked for two."

"Yes, but on the phone earlier you said you had one *Japanese* and three *Australian* bottles down there. I thought you might have brought up a selection."

"Ahh . . . oh right, yeah. Umm, no, I left them downstairs, would you like them brought up?"

"Yes, please."

"Okay, I'll go and get them now."

Shawn hands me the bottles and starts to leave. I grab his shoulder. "Don't I have to sign for these?"

"Ahh . . . do you want to sign for them?"

"Yes."

"Okay." Shawn produces a pen from his light brown concierge jacket and a pad from the back pocket of his trousers.

I snatch the implements and in flamboyant handwriting I scrawl: "DISTRACTION – 10 MINS." I have a plan.

I give Shawn the pen and pad back with a curt nod. He winks and retreats down the hallway.

With the outside world shut off again, I return to the world of organised crime, handing the bottles to one of the meeker guards. By the time I sit down, the old man has the keiyaku in front of him. It's 11.55 p.m.

At 11.56 p.m. and thirteen seconds, the old man looks up. "I believe it is time."

Five heads nod, one a little more enthusiastically than is warranted.

"Excellent." He locates his bodyguard and gestures with a curt nod.

Menacing Thug #2 ambles over and arranges the pottery and quill so that they sit before the old man. Then we all do the bowing thing again.

We watch the old man with as much anticipation as we dare show. He doesn't let us down. He sweeps up the clay cup in his wizened hands and holds it to his mouth. Then he tips his head back, the cup with it, and slurps loudly. After putting the cup back down, he picks up the quill, dips it delicately into the other clay cup, and scratches an indelible, aggressive mark at the bottom of the keiyaku. One down.

Menacing Thug #2 returns and moves all the bits and pieces over to Mr Kawabata. The wary, evil-looking man goes through the same procedure. 11.58 p.m. Two down.

I can feel my heart rattling my rib cage as it bangs relentlessly against the slim bones. I'm going to run out of time!

The assembly is passed to the third oyabun. My saliva glands are pumping. I can actually feel them bulging and relaxing, but nothing is coming out. The well is dry. For the first time in a fortnight, the curse is more than just an abstract concept. My mind is being bombarded with an asteroid shower of vivid memories of misfortune.

Finally, it's my turn. My kidnapper-cum-waiter places everything in front of me. Not a single eye in the suite is focussed on anything but me. And I'm losing it. My face is twitching with anxiety, my shoulders are piano-wire taut, ready to bare the brunt of the impending doom. I am definitely going to run out of time.

I steel myself. It takes the cooperation of every last nervous neurone to rise above the fear of what now seems a certainty. It's all about perception. I have to keep their perception of me intact. Because when that clock ticks over to midnight, I'm going to need it more than ever.

I hold the cup to my lips. Perception. Perception. Perception. I take a mouthful of the sweet rice wine. Perception. Perception. Perception. I put the cup down and pick up the quill. I dab it into the inkbottle. I scribble an illegible signature on the rice paper. Perception. I put the quill back and the paraphernalia is passed along to my right. All eyes follow its movement . . . and I begin shaking uncontrollably. 11.59 p.m.

The keiyaku, the sake, and all the accessories are in the hands of the last oyabun when Thursday night rolls over to Friday morning. I am a rock climber hanging grimly to a slippery precipice and I've just watched my safety-rope spin past my head. I officially have no luck. My nine-day curse-indemnity has just expired.

I sit perfectly still, my hands in my lap, my chest the only thing moving. Carefully I suck air in and slowly let it back out. The last signature. I don't even move my head to watch the oyabun deliver it, just my eyes. Otherwise I'll probably crick my neck and lose the use of my arms. Or something similarly unfortunate.

The last oyabun dips the quill into the ink, dabs the end of it on the edge of the clay pot, and scratches his signature onto the rice paper. The keiyaku is my ticket to freedom and it's just been validated. The only problem is, now I have to get my hands on it. And then get it out of the room.

The keiyaku is gingerly moved around so that it sits in front of the old man, back where it started. He looks at it and nods slowly. "*Yushu na*," he says. He stands and grins at us. "*Shukuji*."

I have no idea what he's saying, so I watch the other oyabuns for a lead. They all stand, too, but I'm so tense, I spring up like a cat, my thighs catching on the glass-topped dining table and giving it one hell of a shunt.

The sake tips over, as does the inkbottle, but luckily the youngest oyabun has the reflexes to snatch up the keiyaku before it can be damaged. The rest are looking at me with utter contempt. Don't apologise, Trigg, remember – perception.

I try standing again, more slowly this time, taking care to move my chair out first. I make it to my feet. The oyabuns continue to stare disapprovingly at me, so I glower back, daring them to voice their annoyance. It doesn't happen. Despite their individual power, as long as they are involved in the ceremony, they all defer to the old man. And as for the old man, well, he looks a little pissed-off, but then he always looks like that. I think he's just glad to finally have the signatures.

Not as glad as I am.

The oldest oyabun continues speaking, thankfully now in English. "Congratulations, gentlemen. I have no doubt that this agreement will see a very profitable and, if we honour it, sustainable future for all of us and all of our men. I thank you for coming all this way for this one evening. It has heralded a new era of cooperation among our many members, so I am sure you will agree it was worth it, despite the . . . problems. I am also sure that you all want to be on your way. As tradition dictates, I will keep the keiyaku, but remember, it belongs to all of us. To all these men," he waves his hand towards the extras, "and to every single Yakuza on this earth. There has been much blood spilled in recent years. Too much. I sincerely hope that this is the beginning of the end of such a dark history."

The old man bows deeply and the four other oyabuns and myself follow suit. The evening is over. I check my watch again. It's 12.03 a.m. Where's my distraction?

"Excuse me, Shiro Tozoku," says the old man. "We have no transport from this place, but we must leave the building quickly, in secrecy. We'll need separate cars to travel to Brisbane, to the airport. You will call the concierge and organise this immediately?"

"Ahhh, I can. But what's your hurry? Stick around for a while, have a drink." I race over to the kitchen bench. "I have all this cognac."

"No. We must leave immediately."

I rummage around in a drawer beside the sink. "Look, playing cards. We can play blackjack . . . you people like blackjack, don't you?" I take the cards out and begin shuffling. In keeping with my recently reacquired curse they spray all over the kitchen. I drop to my knees, scampering to pick them up. "Fifty-two pickup?"

Not a sound disturbs the room. I look up at the various faces and not one of them registers fear. My facade is cracking. "How many cars will you need?" I get to my feet and wipe my hands on my shorts.

"Five limousines."

I nod and pick up the telephone. "Hello, Shawn, this is Mr Harvey . . . Fine, thank you . . . Listen, I need five cars – limousines, to go to Brisbane . . . Pardon? . . . Right now . . . Yes, that's right . . . What? . . . No, I need them immediately . . . I don't care . . . I don't care . . . Are you listening to me, you fool, I said I don't care . . . I don't give a flying fuck, just get the cars . . . Ten minutes? . . . Alright, I guess that will have to do."

I place the phone back on its cradle. Right now there is a very frightened laundry-woman running around trying to organise five limousines.

"Ten minutes," I say to the room.

The old man looks to his cohorts. He's not impressed, but he understands there is little else that can be done. He nods brusquely. "We will have a drink then."

I shovel around in the various drawers until I find a corkscrew. Given that I am now without luck, and this is a pointy object, I take extra special care inserting it into the cork of the cognac. Careful . . . easy does it . . . there. The pointy bit is in, and my arteries are still intact. The men begin to huddle into little groups, firing lines of Japanese at each other. So no one really notices when I uncork the bottle with a pop – and whack myself in the face.

I grab a pile of serviettes and shove them up my nose to stem the bleeding. Then I drop the crystal goblets and they tumble to the tiles, shattering into thousands of pieces. I wipe some blood from under my nose. Through my tears I can see it's 12.06 a.m. Where the bloody hell is my distraction?

One of the extras takes over bartending duties while I carefully retire to the couch to remove the glass from my bare feet. Surely nothing bad can happen to me on the couch. Not in a few minutes.

The old man also sits down, clutching the keiyaku possessively to his chest. Gradually the four other oyabuns remove themselves from their huddles to rejoin the elite.

We sit. They watch. It's unbearable.

I pick up the television remote control and offer it up for any objections, but none are forthcoming. The television springs to life with an electric snap. *Are You Being Served*? re-runs. Ahh, late night television . . . when all this is over, I'll have to reacquaint myself with it.

Suddenly the picture is cut with a newsflash. As a morbid teenager, these interruptions had titillated my dark side with the promise of disaster, now it just makes me feel uneasy. A handsome female newsreader flashes up on screen, looking professionally concerned. Behind her is a picture of a handgun, a chalk outline of a body, and the words "Gold Coast shoot-out". This gets everyone's attention.

"The Gold Coast was rocked with gunfire tonight as the police raided an alleged Japanese mafia gang-meeting in the exclusive suburb of Berowa Waters," the woman reads. "We have unconfirmed reports of several people suffering gunshot wounds and at least one fatality. Sources close to the operation say that the leaders of the various gangs involved managed to escape and are still at large."

I'm not sure how this makes me feel. On the one hand, it may put the group at ease to know that they are still at large; on the other, some police would be very welcome right now. The newsreader continues, "Police hold grave fears for one man, who is believed to still be with the group." Suddenly one of my old school photos is taking up the whole screen. It was taken back when mullet haircuts were fashionable and pimples were unavoidable. Hairstyles and dermatology, though, are the least of my problems. "Although we can't confirm it, police sources indicate that Mr Trigger Harvey was involved in an undercover operation that went horribly wrong . . ."

I switch off the television, probably the worst thing I could have done. It leaves me as the only focal point. Perception, Trigg, perception.

"Ha, worked like a charm. I told my men that if anything went down to say they were part of a top secret undercover sting and that I was the point-man. You know, precautions."

The room is far from convinced.

"Hey, would I have warned you about the raid if I was part of the sting?"

The old man glares at me as he lets a curl of cigar smoke escape his thin lips. He holds up the Keiyaku."Perhaps you did not have what you needed when the police raid came."

Oh boy, I'm fucked. Stupid curse.

"Now hold on just a goddamn second." I inflate my American accent and jump to my feet, which draws the attention of the extras. "Let's not jump to conclusions . . . you wouldn't want to wake up with a white rose on your chest."

"Ahh yes, the infamous ShiroTozoku," says the old man. "Tell me, what were the names of the five men you assassinated?"

It's getting harder and harder to remain in character. "Ahh . . . well let me see – it was quite a while ago now – there was, ummm . . . Barry . . ."

There's a knock at the door. The old man swears in Japanese. He snaps his fingers at Menacing Thug #2, then rolls up the keiyaku and places his hand inside his jacket, where he swaps the document for a handgun. He jams the gun into my ribs. Meanwhile, Menacing Thug #2 ambles over to the door, his hand inside his own jacket.

Everyone stands up, including myself and the old man. The bodyguard opens the door a crack and leans his massive head into the gap. I hold my breath.

Menacing Thug #2 recoils, but not with fear. It's surprise more than anything. He is then pushed effortlessly aside as the two girls enter the room. Terri and Karen, dressed in blue, figure-hugging kimonos, undone to reveal the edge of their lacy bras. They look absolutely, well, tarty – but in a good way. A *very* good way. They each have thick makeup on, paint-brushed mascara and bright, bright red lips. They sashay their way towards us, all wavy hair and embellished cleavage. Everyone is gobsmacked. Especially me. This is my distraction, and oh boy, what a distraction.

The old man is the first to regain his wits. "Who are you?" he demands.

The girls jump. Whether they are actually startled, or just acting, I can't tell. Either way, their reaction gives them a big stamp of innocence. "We . . . Shawn . . . the concierge thought you gentlemen might like some . . . company," Karen says with wide-eyed innocence.

The old man stays firm. "No! You leave now."

Terri looks disappointed. "But sugar, we came all the way out here to put on a show." She runs her hands up her body, over the smooth silk of the dress, until they are forcing her boobs out of her bra. "It would be such a shame to just . . . turn around and leave."

Karen nods in agreement. She edges towards Terri and shifts the soon-to-be-lawyer's blond hair from over her right eye. It's such a simple gesture, but it just oozes sweaty sex.

There is a smacking sound as every man in the room swallows in unison.

Terri arches her neck luxuriously as Karen runs her hand down her back. I feel the pressure of the pistol against my ribs retreat just a little.

Terri then moves behind Karen and begins to help her undo the rest of the kimono. Jesus Christ, hang on a minute, that's my sort-of girlfriend! I look around with horror as eight lascivious men eat Karen up with their eyes. She begins to writhe a little as Terri slowly reveals more flesh. The men are totally and utterly transfixed. Terri gets down to the point where Karen's matching lacy knickers become visible. Both girls let out little moans. No one has blinked yet.

She's just a schoolgirl, you perverts!

The good news is that the pressure on my ribs is now negligible. I have to act. Right now.

As subtly as I can, I move my hand so that it's poised over the old man's handgun. Karen has now turned her attention to Terri's dress and the men are as captivated as ever. I have forgotten about the girls, I have forgotten about Roger. I have only one thing on my mind. Quickly, I snatch at the handgun and stick it into the ribs of the old man. His eyes widen beneath his tan coloured glasses. I continue to stare blankly at the girls. No one has noticed a thing.

Karen is now stroking Terri's breasts through the thin material of the kimono. While this is happening, I reach inside the old man's jacket and withdraw the keiyaku from an inside pocket. He stares pure hatred and revenge right at me, so I give the pistol a twist. His body twitches and he grimaces, but he makes no sound. Slowly, I edge him away from the couch towards the door. Still no one has noticed. Then, quickly and quietly, I move the gun from his ribs to his head. Time to go for broke.

"Ahem."

No one responds.

"Ahem!" A little more loudly this time.

It's only when the girls stop their act and look at me with horror, that the significance of the situation finally hits the group. I wait until I have everyone's full attention, then I speak. Firstly to the girls: "Get out of here! Now!" I give Karen the smallest possible nod, to let her know that I think I know what I'm doing.

The girls scamper out the door, playing like a couple of hookers in the wrong place at the wrong time. Now I turn my attention to the men, still in my Shiro Tozoku drawl. "Gentlemen, I don't wish to kill anybody, but I will if I have to. All I want is safe passage out of this hotel. Then you can do what you want. So don't try and stop me. Many, many Yakuza have tried to stop me in the past. . . to no avail."

I begin leading the old man further towards the door. Luckily there are no dogs in the apartment; they would have sensed my fear. All hands are inside jackets, but no one dares to draw their gun, even the thugs can only stand by impotently. The other oyabuns look on coldly. Jesus, what does it take to get a rise out of these guys?

I make it to the door with the keiyaku and the old man. "I'm going to leave now. Follow me and I *will* kill you."

I edge slowly out the door, the pistol still stuck to the old man's skull. Then I close the door. And the group is gone. They are no further away, but a physical barrier can be so comforting.

The old man sighs. "You are making a terrible mistake. You will die, you realise this?"

I ignore him. We march slowly down one hallway, then another, past the paintings, under the chandeliers.

"Have you stayed in this hotel before?" I ask the old man.

"Yes."

"Umm. Do you know where the lifts are?"

The old man takes this opportunity to swing around, breaking the contact between steel and skin. I point the gun in his face, but he doesn't flinch. He just regards me with an aggressive grin. "Shiro Tozoku. Ha! You are not him. If you were, you would have killed every man in that room, and the two hookers. You are just a policeman. Dickhead."

He walks steadily towards me. I retreat just as steadily. I have a gun in the man's face, but I can't pull the trigger. Suddenly we are both distracted by a commotion. It's the sound of frenzied Japanese voices coming from the direction of the room. At that moment, the old man lunges. I jump away, aim the gun down and pull the trigger. The explosion echoes down the otherwise silent hallway, advertising my presence to the whole floor.

On the carpet, the old man clutches at his leg. But he isn't doubled over in pain, he's still staring at me with that bloody malevolent grin. I bolt.

The plush carpet springs me along as I sprint down the unfamiliar hallway, more lost than ever. I find a stairwell, but it's locked, so I keep running. Around one corner, then another. All the hallways look the same. Then, as I tear around yet another anonymous corner, I slam into something. Someone?

I'm on my back and my ribs are on fire, but by some ancient survival instinct, I force myself up onto my elbows to find the gun.

Ian?

I ran into Ian! Good old Ian. Oh bless. He'll help me . . . only he's unconscious.

"Ian? . . . Ian?" Despite the raking pain in my chest, I shake him as hard as I can.

Groggily he comes to. "Trigg. Shit, what happened?" He's holding his head.

"We've got to get out of here, where are the lifts?"

There are four lifts: three are down at ground level and the other is travelling up slowly from the third floor. Hurry up, come on! Fucking curse! I'd punch the wall if my ribs weren't on fire. Suddenly I don't have to. The wall to my left explodes as a bullet smashes into it. A hail of Japanese shouts follow. Ian and I look at each other and take off. In opposite directions.

I need to find a stairwell, it's my only chance, but the doors I pass belong to hotel rooms or utilities rooms. I toy with the idea of hiding, but the thought of being cornered appeals to me even less than being on the run. Another corner disappears behind me, just in time to hear – and feel – two bullets thump into the wall.

My ribs send a new surge of pain screaming through my neurones, enough to cause me to crumple the keiyaku as I pick up the pace. God, I hope Ian is fairing better than this.

The maze of luxury has swallowed me now. I pass doors which I'm not altogether sure I haven't passed before. All I find are more corners and more hallways. Unfortunately, my pursuers keep finding the same ones. How big can this floor be? After an indeterminate amount of time, I find myself at the lifts again. The useless bloody lifts. Only now one of them is here on the twenty-seventh floor. I stop and listen for my pursuers. Footsteps. But distant enough. Just maybe. I push the down button and the lift doors slide open.

The gun falls from my hand and suddenly the pain in my chest seems a little more remote. Inside the lift stand the old man and his massive bodyguard, Menacing Thug #2. In the race to regain our wits, I lose badly. Menacing Thug #2 reaches out and grabs me by the shirt, yanks me into the lift. The old man's lips curl with satisfaction. "A very pleasant surprise," he says as he presses the close button and the doors slide shut behind me.

We start to descend and the pain in my chest begins a new verse as the bodyguard shoves me hard against the doors. The old man limps towards me. I notice the blood on his hands and look down to his leg. I can see where his dark trousers are even darker. Like he's wet himself. I hope it hurts.

"I will take the keiyaku, thank you," he says. But I hold it tight to my chest. The old man shakes his head pitifully, then looks up at his bodyguard. The human dinosaur lets go of my shirt, but only to backhand me with one of his huge mitts. With my spare hand I reach up and clutch at my cheekbone. I can feel the warm ooze on the palm of my hand. More blood to join the flow from my nose. The thug hits me again, in the same place. This time it's more of a stinging sensation. Come on, Trigg, hold on, just hold on. I'm facing the back of the lift, but I can see the luminous numbers in the mirror. We're going past the eighth floor. If I can just hold on, we'll be at the ground floor, then there'll be cops everywhere.

"The keiyaku," demands the old man again.

Eighth floor . . . seventh floor . . . The human brick wall hits me again, this time in the chest. The blow forces my own hand to twist my already mangled ribs, which makes the pain explode like a bright light through my synapses. I holler involuntarily, which hurts my ribs even more. Clutching at my chest with both hands now, smearing the piece of rice paper with blood, I try to hang on. Sixth floor . . . Fifth floor . . . just a little bit longer.

The bodyguard backhands me again and I feel the small cut on my cheek split open. I can feel blood openly flowing down my face. My eyes water. I can't see. Then I feel the lift stop. Salvation.

The doors open and I brace for the commotion, the barrage of voices. But there is nothing. I look up through the tears. Fourth floor? The old man turns to see what I'm looking at. "Surely you do not think we are stupid enough to go to the lobby." He steps out of the lift, Menacing Thug #2 forces me to follow. It's all over.

I trudge along between the two men, down a hallway and into a stairwell. We walk down the stairs and emerge on the third floor. My ribs scream and my face throbs, yet these are the least of my worries. I am completely petrified. Who's going to look for me on the third floor? Oh, I'm sure they'll get around to it eventually – maybe after I've been beaten to a pulp, stabbed, and had all my fingernails removed. Jesus, even if I give the old man the keiyaku, he's not just going to let me go. I shot him, for God's sake, the most senior oyabun! And what's my excuse? A curse! I'm not too worried about dying, I mean, I'm terrified, but if I can't deliver the document and get my luck back, then I might as well be dead. What really worries me is the interrogation, the revenge, the torture. I am not a brave man.

The oyabun knocks on the door of the first room we come to. There's no response, but then it is 12.30 in the morning.

He knocks again. This time there is movement, a shuffle from the other side. The door opens about halfway and a meaty man with a flushed face, tired eyes and a bad comb-over stands at the door in his white towelling robe. "Yeah?" he mumbles.

The old man looks past me to his bodyguard. The unfortunate victim leans out further to see what's going on. He doesn't get very far. The bodyguard smashes open the door with both hands, knocking the guest flat.

The gargantuan bastard then bustles me into the hotel room. We step over the poor guy whose comb-over has come unstuck and is splayed out on the carpet like a cockatoo's crest. I'm forced to sit on the couch (not as nice as the one in the executive suite) while Menacing Thug #2 takes care of the room's original occupant. He ties him to the toilet with the towelling belts from the bathrobes. Humane; if they take a few hours to find him, at least he won't be busting.

My erratic little thoughts are cut short when the bathroom door shuts. The attention turns back to me. The one positive is that

I have no intention of pretending to be brave. I'm planning to sing like a canary.

The old man takes a seat opposite me. He lights a cigar, sucking on it with great heaves. He holds it by his face while the smoke twists out of the corner of his mouth and drifts towards the ceiling like a Balinese dancer. "What is your name?" he asks with disarming calm.

"Trigger Francis Harvey," I say in the Queen's best English.

"What are you doing here?"

"I'm here to obtain the keiyaku so that I can get my luck back from Tetsuya Suzuki."

The old man shakes his head. He drags on his cigar, leans forward and unloads a throatful of smoke in my face. "Bullshit." He hits me, more of slap really.

"Look, I don't want to get hit any more. I've got nothing to hide. I know it sounds ridiculous, but it's the truth. There was this witchdoctor – Philip Matango – somewhere near Fiji, and he put a curse on me that took my luck and gave it to Tetsuya Suzuki, because of my girlfriend, see, I shagged her best friend. It was nothing too serious, I mean a bit of a drunken romp, but still, you've got to know Kelly, she's a—"

The old man raises his hand impatiently. "How did you know about Shiro Tozoku?"

I hadn't considered this. I was ready to tell these guys anything – but betray Jun? After all he's done to help me? After his ten years of blissful anonymity? "I read it. . . on the internet."

The old man is not amused. He folds up his calm demeanour and puts it back in his pocket. Menacing Thug #2 drags his knuckles over to where I'm sitting. "How did you know about Shiro Tozoku?" asks the old man again.

"The . . . internet?"

The old man nods at his massive minder.

WHACK!

I feel my lip split open and blood spray out. It actually sprays; I can feel it on my arm, warm and unwelcome on the wrong side of my skin. I can't see it though. I'm paralysed with fear. Absolute mortal fear. All I can see is Menacing Thug #2, staring at me with pure hate, just aching for the chance to thump me again. I made him look like a fool by escaping. I had him scraping the ground before me thinking I was the white Yakuza, and I managed to shoot the one man he's supposed to be guarding. He is possibly the only person in the world who could hate me more than Kelly . . . or Terry and Doris.

He hits me again.

I hear my nose crackle, pain explodes through my sinuses to the rest of my head and the world swims. I pray to pass out this time, willing unconsciousness to take me away from this hellish situation. But with my luck, or lack thereof, the one time I actually want to faint . . . the world stops swimming. It's replaced with incredibly vivid pain as the rusty blood dribbles off my chin.

The old man blows more smoke in my face. It may be a psychological thing, but it makes my open wounds sting more than ever. He shakes his head contemptuously. "Why make this difficult?" He waits until this sentiment has set in. "No one is going to look for you here. No one is coming to save you. We could be here for hours. Do you have any idea what I can do to you in just thirty minutes?"

I have a few ideas, but thankfully my imagination isn't working too well.

The old man gets to his feet. He grimaces and looks down at his leg like he's wondering why it hurts. He wipes his hand over the dark area on his trousers. "Do you know the difference between you and me?" He holds his hand up to my face, the blood is dark and congealed. "This does not scare me."

He then puts two fingers against my cheek and holds them up for me to see. My blood is redder, fresher. "Whereas this scares you. This is why I will find out what I wish to find out. One way or another. Sooner or later." He snatches up the keiyaku from my grasp. Slowly he uncrumples it. It is creased and torn and stained with blood. "Why did you want this? Are you an undercover officer?"

"No, I swear."

Nod.

SMACK!

The pain is like fire this time as the minder hits me on my already swollen left eye. It doesn't subside, just keeps burning, through my screams, through my clutching hands. I start crying. Enough to make my head shake and my hands fill with salty tears. "Oh, Jun . . . I'm sorry. I'm so sorry."

"Jun?" barks the old man picking up on the Japanese name. "Who is this Jun?"

"Come, Takeshi, my name may have changed, but surely you remember me."

The old man spins around. His jaw heads south as his brain makes the appropriate connections. Through the blood and the tears, I watch his face register a month of expressions: recognition, astonishment, bewilderment, incredulity, but above all, one I had not seen before – fear. There is Jun, standing just inside the doorway and he looks bloody fantastic.

"How fuck did you get in here?" asks the obviously unaware bodyguard. He rises to his almost seven feet and takes a step towards Jun.

"No," warns the old man.

But he's too late. With speed that is too fast to follow and precision that is too perfect to comprehend, Jun lays out the giant, leaving him unconscious on the ground. Then, as calm as you like, he steps over the lifeless hulk and sits down. "Hello, Tligger, lucky I still know how to pick a lock, yes?"

I sniffle up a line of bloody snot that's running across my upper lip, and nod.

"You okay?"

I nod again.

"H . . . H . . . Hirato," the old man stutters. "What . . . how?"

"Oh look what you've done," says Jun with mock annoyance, "you used my real name in front of the boy. Now I'm going to have to kill him."

My eyebrows leap off my forehead and my heart lurches. "What? No . . . no . . . I didn't hear . . ."

"Tligg, Tligg . . . joke – yes?"

It's an incredible scene. This small shopkeeper cracking jokes, while four feet away, the most powerful man in Japan sits in terror – a gun in his hands that he's too afraid to use. In fact, all the old man can do is stare and shake his head in disbelief, as if he were looking at Satan himself – or whatever the Shinto equivalent is.

"Tligg, I believe you came for something," says Jun, indicating the keiyaku in the old man's now unsteady hand.

Hesitantly, I reach over and snatch back the document. The old man doesn't even blink. He hasn't blinked since he laid eyes on Jun.

"Now get out of here, Tligg, go down to the lobby. Luke is there, he will look after you."

"But—"

"It's okay, the others have been rounded up. I just want to have a word with Takeshi here."

I don't move. I can't believe this whole ordeal is over. "Go on, Tligg," insists Jun.

I walk unsteadily towards the door, but I stop halfway. I look back at the old man. He's still staring wide-eyed at Jun. "I was telling the truth," I say to him. "I'm not police."

The old man turns slowly, the disbelief and fear unmoved from his face.

"I was telling the truth." Then I walk out of the room. Something I sense the old man will not be doing.

I stand by the lifts on the third floor for quite a while, clutching the keiyaku bloodily to my chest. I can't face anyone just yet – not Karen, not Ian, no one. I cry like a nursery-schooler, my emotions once again flooding to the surface. The closest I can come to describing it is the feeling a marathon runner must experience just before finishing the Olympic race. All that training, all the pain, all the ups and downs, the loneliness, the shared times, a life devoted to this one moment – and here it is, the culmination. I'd understand if every marathon runner paused just before crossing that line. That's how I feel, standing by the lift, crying my eyes out.

I sit down against the wall and think about everything that has happened over the past few weeks – the people I have met, the things I have come to realise. My whole world has changed, it can never be the same again. I laugh through the tears and the snot. It's the luckiest thing that's ever happened to me.

27

I am back on Ian's deck. The sun is stabbing its dangerous little fingers at the 15+-coated skin of the hundreds of people shuffling around on the beach. The wind has turned onshore. It was better this morning, when Ian went for a surf. I wanted to go, too, but it's a little difficult with broken ribs and a stitched-up face. Oh well, there are other things to do, like getting to know my new friends under less trying circumstances.

Long days and longer nights, that's what the last few days have involved. Mostly talking, with a glass of wine usually within reach. When prodded about my past, it felt like I was recounting the anecdotes of another person. A boring, floating-through-life, five-a-side and drinks-after-work person. It's been a strange few days – for everyone – since I stepped out of that lift.

When the doors opened, there must have been thirty gun barrels aimed right at my head. I'll be happy now if I never see another gun in my life.

Karen managed to break through the police line. She threw her arms around me and squeezed any lingering doubt out of my aching body. It was perfect. Life is all about adventure – it's the journey, not the destination. Actually, there is no destination, just places where you change trains. It's about getting off the couch of apathy.

So if I choose to start seeing a girl who's just started her final year of high school, that's okay. You can't spend your life worrying about what other people think. As a girl wise beyond her years once said to me, "there is no right and wrong, only debates about right and wrong". Besides, Karen revealed that she turns seventeen at the end of April.

It was a long night, Thursday, February the 18th. Luke quickly secreted me away from the hotel in his sedan. I wouldn't find out about Danny until later.

I saw the dawn in sitting at a green laminate table in the kitchen of Luke and Karen's new safe-house, in front of my sixth cup of Nescafé. We'd been over everything – absolutely everything – from the moment Kelly and I split up, to the point where I stepped out of the lift. And then we went over it again.

When I'd handed over the keiyaku to Luke, I was expecting it to be a significant moment in my life – that was my blood it was smeared with, after all. But instead it just felt very matter of course. Don't get me wrong, it was a very pleasant sensation; I guess I'd just had my epiphany earlier. Anyway, just like Philip Matango promised, it seems to be doing the trick. My luck is now back in my control . . . well, as much as it ever can be.

Speaking of luck, it really went my way on that fateful night. Four Yakuza were killed, but no police. Ian managed to find a Marriott stairwell in time, and Luke found Tetsuya locked in the downstairs room where he'd been abandoned by his guards. He was taken to hospital with a broken jaw and a few other niggles, but generally he was okay. Danny didn't even go into the house.

Obviously Jun got my message about the Marriott, and he, Karen, Terri and Ian managed to slip away from the house during the shootout. They found Shawn and he told them all he could, which wasn't much really, but it was his idea to send the girls in as prostitutes. I guess he's dealt with enough Japanese gangsters to know what stirs their sake. The blue kimonos were actually Marriott uniforms, which get used when important Japanese guests are in residence.

The other stroke of luck was not really luck at all, and I guess that's half the point of my little odyssey. It was Jun. Jun the assassin. The police had shut off all but one lift, and when they saw it stop on the fourth floor, they all went barrelling up. But Jun was smarter than that. He quietly snuck up to level three, figuring the fourth floor would be a decoy and any escapees would rather be closer to the ground than the roof. Then he silently picked the lock of every hotel room door until he got to the one I was in.

Unfortunately, after Jun sent me back to the lobby, there was a "struggle" in the room and he was forced to defend himself against the only two men who could identify him. Two Yakuza died as a result. Not that the courts or the newspapers will ever know about this. Actually, there's a hell of a lot they'll never know about. Thanks to Danny.

Basically, Danny took the heat. He was kept out of sight for just this reason. Officially it was Danny who went into the mansion with a blue surf-helmet on. It was Danny who directed the boat back to the Marriott. And it was Danny who shot the old man and his minder dead in the third floor room . . . in self defence. I was merely an unfortunate hotel guest in the wrong place at the wrong time, and when I stepped in to try to help the young gentleman with the red hair, I was beaten to a pulp. As for Jun, well, when Danny entered the third-floor room, he was gone. Like he had never been there.

There were seven Japanese men who refused to confirm that it was Danny they had spent the evening with – but who's going to believe the Japanese mafia? Unless, of course, they're rolling over on a couple of elderly drug dealers. The police raided Terry and Doris's house and found two kilos of cocaine in a hollowed-out section behind the washing machine. It seems they knew exactly where to look.

Of course, it's early days yet, and who knows what will come up in the future. But for now it seems things have worked out quite well. Luke and Danny got their document, Jun has kept his anonymity, and I may or may not still be the white Yakuza. As for Mr Somatsu, he's going to get his witness protection.

"You ready to go, Trigg?" Karen asks. It takes me a while to register the question. I squint through the glare and I can see her tapping her watch.

At the hospital, there are forms to sign, and watches must be removed. Karen waits in the hallway, fiddling with a somewhat limp, somewhat battered four-leaf clover I'd found in my pocket when the ordeal was over. I'd told her I wouldn't be needing it. I walk past the police officers and push open the white door. I feel my heart speed up considerably. It's the first time my system has seen any sizeable quantity of adrenaline since Thursday night, three days ago.

Mr Somatsu is lying on one of those steel hospital beds, propped up by a few pillows. He has a remote control in his hand, his eyes glued to a little black TV. "What are you watching?" I ask.

Mr Somatsu looks up from the screen. "Trigg," he mumbles, through some sort of contraption on his broken jaw. He waves the remote control at a plastic chair by his bed. I sit down and we watch the end of a *Some Mothers Do Have 'Em* rerun in companionable silence.

"He is the funniest man on earth, that Frank Spencer," says Mr Somatsu as the credits roll.

I smile. "How's your jaw?"

He makes the so-so gesture with the remote control. "Your ribs?" he mumbles.

"They're getting better. I won't be able to surf for a month or two, though."

"That's a shame."

"Not really, I'm terrible."

"Oh."

"When do you get out of here?"

Mr Somatsu looks thoughtful, probably dreaming of whatever mystery place he'll end up, with his new identity and his new life. "They said I can leave in one week." He tries to smile, but it obviously hurts too much. Instead he raises his eyebrows a few times.

He's a different man. I look at him for a while, lying there with his big hair and without his dark glasses. I can't work out whether he has actually changed, or whether my *perception* of him has changed. Either way, he's not a gangster. He's just a harmless Japanese man with an unhealthy fixation with an awkward decade that's too recent to be retro, and too distant to be cool. One day the eighties will come back again, and Akira Somatsu, or whatever his name is by then, will shine.

We don't say anything for a while. We don't have to. We both know what the other has been through, so we can appreciate the pleasure of just sitting and not worrying. But as with all silences, they must be broken.

"Mr Somatsu?"

The Japanese man looks at me. I don't really know what to call him, but Mr Somatsu feels more correct than any of his other aliases. "The other night, when I found you in that house . . . how did you know it was me? You knew I was coming, didn't you?"

Mr Somatsu starts to smile, but catches himself in time. He nods.

"How?"

"Because a little Fijian friend of ours told me you would."

"But how? You bought your figurine first."

"Not you specifically, Trigg. He told me that someone would show up to help me overcome my predicament."

"When did you know I was the one?"

"The night you walked into my casino. I knew straight away."

"It was the suit, wasn't it? It's not mine, you know, I—"

Mr Somatsu shakes his head. "It was not the suit. I just knew. I felt some sort of connection with you, maybe it was just mutual desperation."

"So why the hell didn't you tell me? You told me the figurine was your boss's. You put me through hell."

"I could not tell you, Trigg, those were the rules. Besides, you had an important job to do . . . I had to test your steel."

"Mettle."

"Medal?"

"Never mind."

I sit back in my plastic chair and consider the macabre little rules set by a macabre little witchdoctor.

Mr Somatsu doesn't ask me how I managed to get the keiyaku.

He doesn't need to. He'd had this sort of frightening confidence all along that it would all work out, just because we owned similar-looking wooden figurines. It takes me a while to realise that if I'd shared his confidence, nothing would have worked out. I needed the drive of uncertainty, the desperation . . . and he needed the strength of confidence. He needed me, more than he needed my luck. In that instant, I wonder if Philip Matango really is magical, or just a clever little man who knows a thing or two about the human psyche.

A repeat of *21 Jump Street* has caught Mr Somatsu's attention, so it's as good a time to leave as any.

"What are you going to do now?" he asks as I stand at the door.

It's a question that used to bother me. Not now, though. Now it's a good question. It makes me smile. And I still have no answer. "I'm not altogether sure," I reply. "I think I might stay here for a while. I've got a bit of money and there's a small flat at Greenmount I've got my eye on."

"Well if you want to buy a golf course or something, let me know. I know of some that are going quite cheap."

"Thanks, I'll keep it in mind. For now, though, I think I'll just see what happens. Jun offered me a job. Not quite as exciting as mixing it with the Yakuza, but a lot better than working in an office."

Mr Somatsu nods, although I'm certain he has no idea what I'm talking about. "Jun is a good man. You will learn a lot from him."

I smile and turn to the door.

"Trigg."

I turn around.

"Good luck."